Published by Darlington Press Australia

ISBN: 978-0-9873305-5-0

Praise for The Gisborne Trilogy has manifested in gold medals and honourable mentions from the Book Readers' Appreciation Group Awards and Readers' Favorite Book Awards in the USA in 2014, and from the RONE and Golden Claddagh Awards from 2012 and 2013. The three books continue to rank unbroken in Amazon's e-book Top 100 for Biographical Fiction in the UK.

BOOK OF PAWNS

'This is a true page-turner, a real rollercoaster of emotions and one that leaves you wanting for more when the last page is reached… A very entertaining and recommendable read.' (Amazon)

'Everything is here: sweeping narrative, vivid description and fresh, living characters, ranging from the minor roles of a nun or a sea captain to villains who are only the more chilling for their originality and utter plausibility…' (Amazon)

'Batten's understanding of this world is profound, and she wears her learning lightly enough to make every potentially jarring historical fact seem natural. The flow of the narrative glides around and over the details of daily life, and illuminates the characters rather than distracting from their story…' (Amazon)

BOOK OF KNIGHTS

'This story is fast paced and thrilling. Batten keeps us gripped until the very last page – and delivers a shocking twist which I certainly could not have anticipated.' (Amazon)

'A previous reviewer described it like reading silk, and this couldn't be more true. So many times it seemed to me that the writing kept me very much in the moment, and Batten knows how to control the pace of the story … I truly felt history driving these people without being bombarded with information.' (Amazon)

'The plot is intriguing and exciting, with nice touches of romance. The characters fascinating, and the twists unexpected. There are clearly a few untied threads in this part of the saga – but a few hooks to ensure readers read on to book three is not a bad thing.' (Helen Hollick - Historical Novel Society Independent Review Managing Editor)

BOOK OF KINGS

'That is one of the author's strengths, the ability to draw you into a character so completely that you feel what they feel; the anguish, the fears, and yes the joys. Indeed the rich variety of characters makes this book(and the other two) such a joy to read…' (Amazon)

'As always with Batten's work, Gisborne III is a joy to read, smooth and eloquent, with a well-constructed plot woven around well-imagined characters and, despite the grace and charm of her writing, no punches are pulled with the scenes of violence and destruction that are a necessity of a thriller, especially one set in such an era.' (Amazon)

'A satisfying conclusion to a rip roaring saga.' (Amazon)

OTHER BOOKS BY PRUE BATTEN

The Chronicles of Eirie

THE STUMPWORK ROBE
THE LAST STITCH
A THOUSAND GLASS FLOWERS
THE SHIFU CLOTH

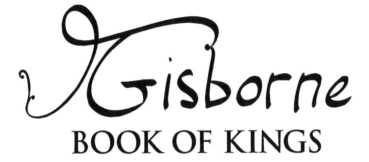

BOOK OF KINGS

BOOK III OF THE GISBORNE SAGA

AUSTRALIA

*Remember, O most gracious Virgin Mary, that never was
it known that anyone who fled thy protection, implored thy help,
or sought thy intercession was left unaided. Inspired with this confidence,
I fly to thee, O Virgin of virgins, my Mother to thee I do come, before thee
I stand, sinful and sorrowful. O Mother of the Word Incarnate,
despise not my petitions, but in thy mercy hear and answer me.
Amen.*

The Memore – Bernard of Clairvaux

CHARACTERS

Ysabel, Lady Gisborne

Sir Guy of Gisborne – *Ysabel's husband and knight of the realm*

William, Master Gisborne – *Ysabel and Guy's son*

Peter the blacksmith – *a Moncrieff man and Ysabel's servant*

Gwen – *Peter's wife and Ysabel's maidservant*

Bridget – *Gwen's mother and Ysabel's maidservant, cook and housekeeper*

Tobias Celho – *minstrel, dwarf and one of Gisborne's skilled spies*

Tommaso Celho – *Tobias's twin brother, minstrel, dwarf and spy*

Cecilia, Lady Upton – *Ysabel's godmother*

Brother John – *priest at Moncrieff*

Beatrice of Locksley – *Abbess of Locksley*

Richard Lionheart, King of England

Saul Ben Simon – *Jewish moneylender and silk merchant*

Ariella – *Saul's daughter*

Tanti – *Ariella's dog*

Guillaume of Anjou – *archer and guard*

Adam of London – *guard*

Johannes of Lübeck – *guard*

Walter of Moncrieff – *guard*

Young John – *guard and former crewman of the Marolingian*

Baron Benedict de Courcey – *deceased husband of Ysabel*

Sir Simon de Courcey – *brother of Benedict, knight of the realm and supporter of Prince John*

Sir Robert Halsham – *Gisborne's cousin and Templar knight*

Arnaud de Vermond – *Templar knight*

CHAPTER ONE

1191

The body balanced on the rail, wrapped in a worn and stained canvas sail – nothing grand for someone I considered nobler than any nobleman I knew.

Except one.

Eli and Davey held it firm whilst a small prayer was spoken by Sir Guy of Gisborne. I could read nothing in his face, his eyes inscrutable. But his hands? They clenched bone-white as he nodded to the ship's master. The body fell feet first, the attached rocks breaking the water with a hard splash that served to hide my one and only wracking sob. The man I had considered family, my friend, Ulric of Camden, sank below the surface of the sea, leagues north of Cyprus and I watched him disappear forever. The speed with which he vanished was too frightening because now I had nothing left but memories and the most recent so violent and pointless.

'Ysabel,' Gisborne's voice was hoarse, cracked with disappointment and guilt as he reached to touch me. We had left behind a blood-soaked house and an enemy that had been vanquished, but the price had been too high because we had lost a friend as well and hated the manner in which it was done.

Gisborne had lost someone he called his brother and who had been the most trusted man in his life but he had also misplaced his faith in himself. Always able to judge a man, he had completely misread the direction of Ulric's emotions and it disturbed his equilibrium to think he could have been so blind. For myself – my selfishness, my need to lean so heavily on Ulric – it had fanned an affection within him that flamed into blind love, a love far greater than I was at liberty to return. And the awful thing was I didn't even see it happening. Now, my little son had only to say 'Oowic'th gone, Mama. I mith him,' and guilt would choke me, deathly fingers that squeezed my throat.

Mehmet counselled in his wise physician's way as he re-splinted and bound my arm after the incident. 'It is no one's fault. Ulric was his own man. He made decisions built on false assumptions. He paid the price.'

He did. I killed him.

'And Ysabel,' he continued, clucking at the fact that I would be in a splint for so much longer, 'if you hadn't done what you did, William would not have his father nor you the man you love. Instead, Gisborne would be pinned by the length of a sword to a fig tree. What price your affection for your friend Ulric then?'

But despite the simple truths, both Gisborne and I could barely touch – our love and guilt were so entwined it was as if Death sat at our shoulders warning us away from each other. *Look what you did, it said. You are killers, both. Ah, my children...* It seemed to throttle any thought of a simple future together and I found I could not even care at that point.

'Time,' said Mehmet kindly as he tied off the bandage. 'You need time. And you need to forgive yourselves and each other.'

The *Marolingian* shifted its course toward Rhodes and points along the Adriatic and Ionian Seas, always heading toward Venezia, the voyage gradually giving Guy and I that time, peeling back the insulated layers of emotion until we could stand next to each other calmly. Earlier, if we found our hands brushed together, or we bumped in the close quarters of the ship, we would flinch and look away. What had been tempestuous had turned mouldy in an instant.

Our passage was uneventful, the seas gentle and the winds behind us, surely an unbelievable occurrence when one considered the storm-driven turmoil of our previous lives. The only moment of unease came at the end of August, when we heard that my cousin the King had slaughtered more than two thousand Saracens at Acre in front of Christians and Muslims alike. Bile sat in my belly like a trebuchet's stone, but the terrible incident was far away and I chose not to think this act was carried out on the orders of the god-cousin who had seemed to care so much for me in Cyprus. I preferred to think it was another man altogether as I tried very hard to bleach the bloodstains of the past from the fabric of my life.

'What do you think, my lord?' I heard Mehmet say.

'I am sorry for those of your brothers who suffered at the hands of my King, Mehmet. I cannot justify what he has done and even his own God would not justify it. Kings and war make sick bedfellows.'

They moved out of earshot and I continued to comb William's hair, thinking on more pleasant things as Davey chose a meandering course with deliberate intent. We anchored in coves where the clarity of the sea made us feel as if we floated on nothing but air, and where the ocean floor was white and the rocks warm. William became brown and healthy, wandering along the shore naked, splashing in the water, and I took a moment to teach him to swim the way Brother John had taught me. He took to it naturally, as naturally as floating in his mother's womb, and the crew, some of whom couldn't swim, were in awe of my little two year old who splashed like a flapping fish.

We met villagers and fishermen on the coasts of Corfu and Zakynthos, of Albania, Serbia, and the coast of Italy. We ate simply – peasant fare that we purchased with gold and silver coin. Gisborne and I mellowed – days of shipboard monotony in which to indulge ourselves and work our way to acceptance of awful truths. And somehow, our continued proximity to each other provided the mutual strength we needed – the first time in over two years that it was so. The pain and guilt dropped away like unwanted pieces of armour; plate after plate fell until we stood unencumbered with distrust and dismay. I felt as free as a butterfly that finally shrugs itself out of its cocoon. My 'garden' was enclosed by the length and beam of the *Marolingian* and whenever Gisborne stood close, my face would turn to him like a flower to the sun.

One day as we sat on deck watching Tobias and William playing tablemen by what we ruefully called 'William's Rules', Gisborne said quietly, 'You will be my wife, won't you, Ysabel?'

My head flicked round so quickly I ricked my neck and as I rubbed it, I studied his face, looking for a reason to say no. The eyes were as painfully blue as ever, the fans of crinkles at the corners even more marked. He had clipped his beard, the silken strands of grey evident only to me who looked closely. I reached out a finger and stroked his lips and he smiled, cocking his head to the side, giving me the glance that I loved more than any other. A quirk, quizzical, sometimes loaded with sarcasm. Anyone watching would say I just dashed a crumb from his beard perhaps, but Mary Mother, the feel of the mouth that kissed mine with such intensity sent resounding vibrations through me. He waited patiently, silently – the epitome of the Gisborne who had escorted me from Aquitaine to England, the journey where I had met a man who had thrown my life into the most God-awful ripples. Would a future life with him be any different? It was easy to think it would be filled with calm after this sea-journey because it was now so untroubled. But when we took to land, what then? The shadow of fear cast itself across my mind and I must have frowned.

'Ysabel? You doubt me?'

'No, I do not. Of course I will be your wife.'

He took my hand and kissed the palm and then rolled the palm closed over the kiss. Leaning back against the mast, he was like a man who has had his own way.

And so it was.

We dropped anchor in Zadar, and whilst the crew and Davey were busy reprovisioning, we found a small church. In the name of all that was holy, we persuaded the priest that William must have parents who were married in the eyes of God if he was to continue a blameless and blessed life. That and the coins that clinked into priestly hands seemed to ease us quite smoothly onto the path of connubial bliss. We told our companions only after we had set sail again, avoiding celebrations and merely eyeing the horizon as we moved ever closer to our new home, Venice – the place they called Venezia in the local patois.

If ever we could call Venezia a homecoming, it was surely underlined when we saw who waited at the docks as oars were shipped and lines were cast out. Gwen shrieked so loudly that William's lips trembled and I had to sweep him into my arms.

'No, look, look William. Whom do you see?'

He surveyed the people lining the edge of the wharf and his little body tensed and I heard his breath suck in.

'Peter, Peter!' he waved his hands madly. 'Mama, it'th Peter and Biddy too!'

Gwen was crying and laughing and like an overexcited pup William scrabbled to be put down, then danced around her chortling and calling 'Peter, Biddy, Peter, Biddy!' so that it sounded like the chorus of a harvest song. Such joy and excitement was the mark of our landing in Venezia and I felt it coloured almost every God-given day from then on.

Biddy hugged her daughter, crushed William to her ample bosom and then eyed me off.

'My lady, if I could I would put you over my lap and thrash you for what you did and what we all went through.'

'Just what I say too, Biddy.' Gisborne hoisted himself off the boat and stood next to me. 'But all's well and all manner of things will be well so you must forgive her as I have done. So much so, I asked her to be my lady wife and she accepted.'

'You never did!' said Biddy. 'Well it's not before time. Dear God but it's good to be together again. My little William, look at you, so big, so brown.'

'I thwimmed in the thea, Biddy. Like a fith.'

She tousled his hair. 'I'm sure you did. Now, have you greeted Peter yet?'

William ran then, yelling at the top of his voice and my giant blacksmith scooped him up and swung him round, Gwenny laughing as tears poured down her face.

Such pain my friends had suffered. The sheer happiness currently writ large was evidence and it stirred the embers of guilt deep inside me. I stood apart and watched Peter with Gwenny hanging off one arm and William the other. Biddy walked alongside, a smile of satisfaction on her cheeks. She had lost weight and Peter too, but they seemed in good health. There was a story there and I would find out.

'You feel some pain I think.' Gisborne ran his hand under my veil, letting his fingers rest on my nape, drawing me from the spectacle. 'As *I* do.'

'When does the guilt go, Guy?' I asked, turning back to my family as the ruckus from William rose above the dockside crowd. 'Will it always be like this? Responsible for everyone and when being so and making wrong decisions, having wrath come down upon one like the heavy hand of the Devil?'

'Yes. As long as you are a woman of noble rank with familiars for whom you must think and act, so it shall be.'

I frowned.

'Ysabel, they forgive you because they love you and are loyal, but a word of advice – you must think twice before acting. You have William and many others under your care…'

I thought back to Brother John who had once written a letter that said *'Daughter … I must ask you to think twice, pray and ask for God's guidance and then act once with assurance for there is none but God and your own resources to help you make decisions of great bearing.'*

It was something to live by.

1192

Shadows and light.

It was how I might always remember this place.

The family lay at anchor within a quiet villa on a calm waterway off the main thoroughfares of the burgeoning town. We spent time sinking into the fabric of the place, just living. For sure, my husband continued his intelligence gathering and I knew he sent frequent word to King Richard, news gathered across Europe of how besmirched my god-cousin's name had become at the hands of Phillip of France and Leopold of Austria. Accused of all manner of things, his bastard act of beheading so many Saracen prisoners at Acre was the most damning to my sensibilities. We heard too, of French envoys who informed Pope Celestine that Richard intrigued with Saladin and the Saracens – a crusading sin that could never be forgiven by Christian Europe. Phillip of France further gulled the west by convincing Henry VI, the Holy Roman Emperor, that Richard was false and unchivalrous. Men! It seemed to me they could never be trusted to rule the world. So much ego, so many tantrums – and all in the name of God.

Ha!

We heard about Arsuf, about Ascalon, about snakes and huge spiders, about noise and fierce fevers, starvation and Saracen horsemen who pricked the crusaders full of arrows like we women fill a cushion with needles. They worried at the men from the west like loathsome horseflies. This went on until I lost interest. Sick of the thought of men being killed, hating that our beloved Tommaso might succumb as he paced between Richard's command and coastal exits, passing news to and fro. All this information was enough for me to hate Richard forever and I already knew well that I could hate with the best of them.

Instead I became a chatelaine, loving my husband, my son, my family of servants and my strange crumbling villa by the water. It was a blessing that each day I could smell the lagoon, feel a watered-down breeze and be happy. I would stand on the edge of the strip of water that separated our islet from others, protected from the sun by the foliage of trees growing along the banks. Light glared from the water – silver vied with pewter on the rippled surface as a boat or two floated by, poled easily by men standing in the stern. Some drifted from island to island, cadging work by ferrying people or cargo to and fro. But many travellers and merchants rode horses and mules, the sound of hooves an oft-heard tattoo on the flat bridges and walkways that connected isle upon isle.

I thought of Moncrieff – its lake and the rivulets that fed the land – and was amused to find that this place too had its own magical shadows and watery charm. Perhaps it was the lap-lap of the water close to the door, or even the damp soil smell, even the God-given pearlescent light. It seemed to me that all my life I had been holding my breath – just because – and now I could let it go. My mouth drew up in a secret smile. It happened more readily now, as if it too had been tied to the feeling of breath-holding. Perhaps, with the Virgin's hand directing our lives, such lack of air was to be no more.

I heard William's shriek of laughter from within the house on this day at the end of November and I turned to examine the place. Like our Genoese dwelling, it was built of stone. Solid foundations pierced the mud and coped with the ups and downs of tides and floods. There were marks on the walls where floodwater had reached and to be frank I wondered how it remained standing till Gisborne told me it had an old Roman core which seemed to explain everything. Suffice to say the main living quarters were all on the first and second floors, the ground level nothing but storage – a cavernous place where we stabled the horses and where William would go and just yell, listening to his voice as it bounced round the aged interior. The horses were so used to him doing it, they barely twitched an ear and one could hear resigned snorts and the odd scraping of a hoof in response – nothing dramatic.

Walls surrounded the house and contained a space as big as a small bailey and it was littered with purposeful trees – olives, lemons, a pomegranate, a peach tree and a massive fig. In the beginning I hated the fig with its reminders of Cyprus but eventually its shade became a thing of pleasure. For William, its lower branches beckoned, for boys are apt to climb and I could hardly scold when it eventually happened. After all, Cousin Richard – duke, count and king – had told me once that I too was a fig tree climber.

The house basked in the late autumnal sun and comparing it with Genoa, that city they call Genova, I wondered if Gisborne had his men source places as similar to a master plan as he could manage. I loved its Roman heart, its soul. Part of the kitchen floor showed a mosaic of fishermen, boats and fish and William would lie on the cool tiles tracing the design with his fingers and making up stories; sometimes Jonah but most often sea tales told to him by Dante.

The sea-captain's boat, the *Occitàn,* was in dry dock in the Arsenale, the newly created dockyard of the town. Davey and the *Marolingian* had departed long since to prowl back and forth between England, France and the Baltic. It would have been nice to think he and Eli, Young John and the rest of the crew were respectable seamen, but I suspect they played at piracy more often than not.

Guy often left me.

Perhaps for a mere sennight but unease would sit at my shoulder when he was gone. There was still the ghost of times past that rattled its chain every now and then and fear of loss can leave a mark. Bridget filled hours with story after story of her enforced time with the nuns in Toulon but Peter was less forthcoming, as if he carried scars. Once as a pair of Templar knights walked past us, I glanced at him and saw his face had paled to the colour of chalk but in the time we had been together as a family, he had said nothing of his experience, as if by saying nothing, he could pretend it had never happened and that he was at peace within Gisborne's walls.

I would occasionally give thought to the faceless men of Gisborne's web. That they existed at all one would wonder, because we never saw them. Messages were delivered to us by one of our household who would go wherever he must to meet and retrieve that message. Likewise, when Gisborne sent a message, it would be taken far from the villa and transferred to shadowed hands and I asked Gisborne once why this was so.

'I prefer for our home to be that, Ysabel – a home. I would not have strangers forever at our gates. These are insecure times and whilst I trust most, one never knows.'

'But surely Guy,' my vitals curled as I spoke. 'Anyone can find out where we are.'

'Of course, but why make it so easy?' was his reply. 'Toby, the guards and myself are more than able to despatch and retrieve things outside of the villa. It suits me to handle it in such a manner.' He had turned his back then, continuing to saddle the huge dark grey he had recently acquired. A long-legged animal, it looked as if it could run for leagues and never tire. Gisborne's shoulders stretched as he reached under the belly to cinch up the girths and I thought that life had weighed heavily on him and for overlong. His core had been shaken so deeply by Ulric's awful defection that trust was as much of an issue as it had ever been.

In between times, Tobias was the light of our existence – he and William. The troubadour talked with me as an equal as Ulric had often done. His twin brother, Tommaso, had taken over the role of the Spanish minstrel Di Dia, to live amongst the knight crusaders and succinctly gather that aforementioned intelligence. He did it well, I knew – Gisborne thought highly of the twins. And in the meantime Toby and I bickered, discussed, disputed and then laughed uproariously. He knew exactly when to prick the bladder of my self-importance and when to be riotously disrespectful of self-indulgence. He also knew when to be civil and whilst I loved him, my son adored him, shadowing his every move, singing songs with him, learning snippets of the languages from the world of spies.

Once I asked Gisborne what he himself did when he left us. I knew it was secret, but who for? Popes, emperors, *routier* captains? Or maybe…'King's business'? I posed.

'In a manner of speaking. A king must protect his kingship wherever he is. Richard's barons lost interest in me when the ship went down off Tyre, and it suits him to have me so dismissed as it makes secrets even more so. I have a way of sending messages to Tommaso who feeds them via conduits to the King. So yes, King's business.'

'Guy, what does the King think has happened to me? He gave instructions that I should leave for Aquitaine when I was well and de Turnham and de Camville must surely have wondered at my absence from a house filled with blood and bodies.' I hated saying the words, the images too fresh in my mind despite the drifting past of a year, but some things had the capacity to rise again before being re-buried.

Guy lifted his head. He had been writing and I watched him lay down the quill with care before he answered me.

'The King knows you are safe, that you have not been abducted to the eastern slave markets by corsairs.'

'It's as well that Ceci and Brother John know I have not.'

He picked up the quill and began to scratch across the parchment. He secreted my notes to my godmother and priest with his couriers, and I felt heartened that we were able to correspond, albeit sparely.

I had been stitching at the start of my conversation with Guy and had let the frame fall to the floor. As I reached for it, I said, 'But what about the King?'

'What about him?' By the way he spoke, I could tell he answered me more from habit than true engagement.

'Does he know I am here?' It was the first time I had asked about the King as I had never really cared before. It was enough for me to sink myself into our daily life, learning to be Lady Gisborne and being William's mother.

'Yes.' Busy writing again, still not listening – not really.

'Is he angry?'

The quill lifted, a small sigh emerging from the holder. 'I think he has more important things to worry him just now, Ysabel. Suffice to say Richard and your godmother, Queen Eleanor, are more than content you are safe. It is all that matters. Now, dear sweet annoying wife, may I please finish this?'

Wife.

How smoothly those words flowed off his tongue. Almost as smoothly as the oil with which Halsham had greased every word he ever spoke to me. But of course there was a qualitative difference. When the word 'wife' was uttered so deftly by Gisborne, it was not oiled at all, but couched with respect and love – two things that had somehow survived the barbaric dénouement in Cyprus.

I stood, placing the frame on my stool, flicking back my sleeves and walking over to Gisborne's chair. I stood behind him, marvelling at the closeness.

I do love you, Gisborne. So much that my heart hurts. Is it the same for you?

I laid my arms over his shoulders and rested my chin on the top of his head. His hair was not quite as silken as William's but it was smooth and the smell of lemons pervaded. Surreptitiously I noted more grey strands, and again the expression lines that fanned from his eyes when he smiled.

Ah, Gisborne, Time takes us all prisoner eventually.

'Ysabel,' he growled. 'Look what you have made me do…' But there was little substance in his complaint and he kissed the fleshy inside of my bare forearms as he spread sand on the inkblot. Giving up, he moved quill and pot away before turning round to face me.

'I dare you to love me, Gisborne,' I said, toying with the side-laces on my gown.

'You play at *whoring* now? My God, Ysabel, what *have* you become?'

'I *became* your wife, my lord. The only difference is that my whoring, as you call it, is blessed by God.'

'And I would have you now, this very moment, and revel in it if I could.' His kiss was a reminder of velvet nights and delicate touches. 'But I must hurry the message to the courier who leaves for Trieste today.'

'Then, my lord, I shall wait till tonight and in between times, shall go to the market to buy silk. I am perturbed that my husband dresses like a peasant.'

He looked down at his stained and ripped chemise and grabbed his old gambeson to cover the worst. 'No one shall see. It is of no account. I am no one here.' He threw another kiss upon me and I could not help comparing times past with now. Was it because we were husband and wife or that we had been through Hell and Damnation on the path to Paradise?

'But take one of the men with you, Ysabel. Please do not go alone.'

'If you say, but I am surely quite safe.'

'Probably. But it is a chance not worth testing.' He rolled the parchment and applied warm wax and his arrowed seal.

A secret missive…

'And besides, it isn't at all seemly for a knight's lady to be unaccompanied.'

I slipped my arm guilelessly through his as he walked to the door. 'But as you say, we are nothing here, no one knows that we are a knight and his lady. And besides, when have I ever been seemly?'

'Quite,' he said with resounding irony as he parted from me, he walking one way and I walking the other.

The final autumn days had remained mild, chasing the breezes off the water in winter's face. We had been little troubled by rain although there had been the odd wind-driven tide to our door and which William thought was wonderful, saying that we must bring out the old punt that lay in the stables. As I stood on the strip of ground that separated us from the water, I could see behind the villa to fields and trees. Closer to the heart of the town, such areas had been swallowed by larger structures, an enormous square built, and churches, the strips of dirt between walls and water becoming narrower and paved. But we were removed from the mercantile creep of the town even though we were only a short journey away. To walk on a fine day over walkways and along the edges of the canals from islet to islet was a pleasant enough thing. My silk merchant lived close to the heart of Venezia and as I turned from gazing at the tired villa, I gave thanks to the Virgin that she had given us happiness and protection along with steadiness and regularity. My fears had lessened just as Mehmet had reiterated as he finally removed the splint, bandaging my arm gently with a soft linen support.

'Time, my lady,' he said. 'It is a great healer.'

I flexed my arm as I stood by the water, noting that the bones and muscles were becoming less stiff, but I rubbed at the point of the break. I had been left with a fearsome ache in the bone; it must surely be my cross to bear and I would not tell Mehmet. When I nocked the arrow into the war-bow back in Cyprus and drew back the string, I knew the bones would shift. I knew this was the price I would have to pay, because my abiding affection for Ulric aside, I would have drawn that bow again and again to protect the lives of any of those I loved more than life itself – those who lived within the villa.

I could hear Biddy as she prepared food for Gwen's and Peter's marriage feast in two days. We would dress in our simple finery and promenade to a little chapel to observe the two pledge to each other before God.

Simple finery.

I pulled myself back to reality. Unless I bought my silk this morning for Gisborne's chemise, he would *have* no finery to wear and as I stepped away, a shrill voice called from the door.

'Mama, Biddy sayth *I* can come.'

So you say, William.

He ran from the gates, the run changing to a hoppity canter as he waved something in the air. 'Thee,' he skidded to a halt and chopped downward with a small sword. 'I can cut bad men like Papa.'

'William, do not speak so.' I bent to pull down his rucked tunic as he tucked the sword into his belt.

'I can come too? Pleathe?'

I gave a pretend growl and held out my hand. 'Come then,' and we stepped off together toward the wooden bridge that would take us in the direction of the silk seller.

Venezia was a town with an eye to commerce and power. Perfectly placed as a gateway to the Empire in the north, to the exotic lands to the east of the Adriatic and to territories even further east, it laid claim to strength from the sea. Everyone who lived around us was as comfortable on water as land and such familiarity had slipped into the blood of the Venetians hundreds of years before.

Thus as William and I walked closer to the square in the centre of the town, I could see what Gisborne meant when he commented one day as he leaned out through the shutters watching cargo drift by, that this town would become a city-state, a force to be reckoned with. He said it idly but as with everything he uttered, there was hard calculation behind the words.

'Guy, do you think to settle here?'

Finally. Roots.

He turned to me and there was a measured look in his eyes, as if he had indeed given this much thought. 'One could do worse, Ysabel. You must remember I no longer have Gisborne for William, only the small manor of Locksley and *that* by the King's decree. It could all be taken away tomorrow. I see much enterprise here, scope for investment…'

He returned his gaze to the window – ah, so much more relaxed these days.

Had I wrought any of that change? I would like to think so.

I admired his height, amplified by the long garnet-coloured tunic he wore.

'And spying, no doubt,' I uttered wryly.

He merely threw a half smile in my direction and then returned to his perusal of life beyond the shutter.

'Mama, look!' William tugged at my hand, jerking me back to the present. In a corner of the square a young jongleur sat plucking at a Byzantine *lyra,* the bow lying on his lap. He sang a rather lovely melody partnered with Greek lyrics and at his feet a small black dog lay with its head cocked to the side.

'A dog!' William leaned wistfully against me. 'Can I have one?'

'Not yet. Not till Papa says we are staying here forever. Why don't you pat the dog? I am sure the jongleur won't mind.'

I raised my eyebrows and the singer nodded as he sang on.

William walked up cautiously to the little animal and let it sniff him before squatting with his bottom almost on the cobbles, reaching out his hand to touch. The jongleur finished with a flourish of the retrieved bow and I threw a handful of coins into his leather cup. He looked up in surprise.

'Thank you, Madam, you are generous.' The young man's voice had a honeyed tone and his hair was pulled back under a floppy cap, his clothes tired but clean.

I didn't think I was overly generous really, a silver *denarius* would have been more so, but I noticed he had very little else in the cup. 'I pay for the song and for the dog's friendship to my son. You sing well.'

'I am at peace when I sing,' he replied. 'Tanti likes the little boy.'

'So it seems,' I smiled. 'He is a sweet dog.' The animal was as black as my Sorcia at Moncrieff and all at once I could see Cecilia of Upton, Lady Fineux, walking to the village with my giant hound on one side and the funereally garbed Brother John on the other. My eyes stung.

'Madam?'

'I'm sorry?' I focused on the singer as he stood and hooked the *lyra* over his shoulder.

'Your son says he sings too.'

I pulled myself together. 'He does. A gift from his father, to be sure. For such a young one, he can hold a note in tune. But it does not serve to praise him too highly as moments of peace are to be treasured with a youngster. Sir, we must away. Adieu. I thank you again for your music.'

He bowed, picked up the dog and settled it in his arms before walking ahead of us across the square where he was rapidly lost in the ambulatory flow. I took William's warm palm in mine and we headed toward the far end of the square to where a compressed space between a row of buildings would lead me to the silk merchant. The sun drifted behind clouds and unfriendly shadows deepened.

'Mama,' said William, puffing a little by my side. 'Pleathe can I have a dog.'

'No, William, not yet. When Papa says…'

We passed three or four conjoined dwellings with new doors and walls and I could hear the sound of people behind, of poultry and cats and the untimely bark of a dog.

'*They* have dogth,' William dragged on my hand with uncommon sullenness.

'Then they are very lucky. Listen,' I squatted down and looked into the mirror image of Guy's face. 'I allowed you to come with me because I think you are a good boy, not an argumentative one.'

A heavily worn gate of studded iron bars and wood that looked as if it were a hundred years old stood before us. I glanced round at the people passing – mostly men with their faces hidden by shade or caplet. There was nothing to indicate wealth in this neighbourhood and I always supposed the silk merchant wished it to appear so. For one brief moment, I wished I'd taken a guard from our villa because my back felt curiously exposed as I lifted my hand to rattle the clawed doorknocker.

The silk merchant had a booth in the market place but I had learned early on that he welcomed clients to his house. He dealt in many commodities, not the least of which was money and I felt comfortable with him because he reminded me of our precious Aaron of Antioch, the man who had died defending our household in Genoa. This merchant, Saul Ben Simon, had a tall upright gait, shoulder length grey hair and when he moved, the elongated folds of his robes rippled like water. He watched Venezia begin its transformation, planning for his family to be at the forefront of the age of expansion quietly and with subtlety. He travelled to the east to trade and I doubted that I was wrong when I assumed he was one of Gisborne's secret couriers. He would tell me of silks that would confound me, silks of outrageously fine quality that one could hold to the eye and see through but yet which trapped light and brilliance and sparkled like precious stones.

As the vibrations of the rapper bounced through the thick wood, I knew Saul would be disappointed in a small sale of white silk when his storeroom held a king's woven treasure. He answered our summons himself, pushing aside a grille and looking out, for he was after all a Jew and caution was their byword.

'Ah!' There was a rattling and sliding of bolts and the gate peeled open. 'Lady Ysabel. How good it is to see you. And you, little Master Gisborne…' He looked beyond my back. 'No guard?' He tsk-ed and drew us in, slamming the gate behind.

William swung annoyingly off my fingers but I would not let him go, not

15

yet. Not till he had tempered his mood a little.

'See there, William. Saul has a pond and if you look you might see frogs.'

'Really?' And thus he was diverted, kneeling and looking around the edges of the pond, under the fronds of water plants to see what he could find, for the garden we had entered must surely be the Garden of Paradise. Not one for formality, it was as if Saul had thrown seeds of any and every plant into the air and let them fall where they may so that one could barely see his house and only a small path led between thicket and shrub. Most of the plants were unknown to me, many springing from seeds sourced on his travels or from rooted remnants carried damply in his saddlebags. Some of course had died but many survived and it was a thing of joy to see unique roses climbing rampantly through pillar and post, smelling the sweet fragrance of their blossom.

'No frogs, Master Gisborne? Then come and we shall see if the cook has some marzipan or pastries, yes?'

Petals lay across our path and Saul reached a long-fingered hand for a lone and fully blown flowerhead to catch it to his nose. He passed the loosened petals to William to sniff. 'See, young master, no need to smell your mother's pots now. God grows such fragrances in a garden.'

But William's attention had already drifted to a butterfly and he followed it from shrub to shrub, trying to catch it. We had reached the loggia and Saul bade me sit, pouring a goblet of juice from his summer peach harvest. I found the nectar thick and cloying but coolly pleasant. He was well known for playing with produce from his garden – some with less success than others.

'So. You want silk. And you did not go to my booth? Phillipus is there today.' He reached for a falling lock of his hair and tucked it behind his ear.

Bees buzzed around us and William froze to a statue-rigid pose, hand stretched out, the butterfly perched on his dimpled knuckles.

'I could have but I thought to see you if you are not too busy, and to immerse myself in your garden of a thousand delights.' The exotic garden always charmed me, the more so because it was a haven in the labyrinth of watery islets that made up Venezia and Saul was one of the few people I had truly made friends with since settling into this place, he being one of the only people who knew that we were noble folk with a chequered history.

A door slammed further along the loggia and there was the sound of scampering claws upon paving stones before a little black bundle hurtled into our space. Behind it ran a woman of Gwen's age calling, 'Tanti, Tanti!'

William had spun round, butterfly and nature forgotten as the pup danced up to him. He giggled as it ran through his legs to then turn, a pink tongue licking his hand ferociously.

'Master Gisborne is not afraid of dogs,' noted Saul, 'which is just as well because Tanti seems overflowing with canine largesse today. Does he not, Ariella?'

The young woman stood watching, her arms folded, dark chestnut hair plaited and knotted at her nape. Her seagreen woollen gown had long tight sleeves and was covered by a fine loose-sleeved *qaba,* the hood lying back, clever silk embroideries down the opening. A product of one of Saul's journeys to the east, I was sure.

'Lady Ysabel, I don't believe you have met my daughter, Ariella. She has been missing today, instead of at her chores.'

I had not. Whilst I was not a frequent visitor to Saul's house, each of the times I had been, this lady had never been present. Interesting – perhaps the perfect chatelaine, ever present and yet not.

The woman eyed me as she said, 'My lady,' dipping her head politely. In that swift glance, she dared me to tell her father she had been singing in the square dressed as a man.

'Ariella,' I said. There was never any doubt I would betray her. I lived in a world of secrets, why would I? 'Tanti and my son seem to have bonded.' William and Tanti were running in and out of the shrubs with the loud abandon that only dogs and boys can manifest. 'It's as well, because it gives me time to choose my silk.'

'Ariella, we are selecting the best chemise silk for Lady Ysabel. Perhaps you would like to join us.'

Saul's invitation was hardly that though. It was more of a silk-covered order to his daughter. Her face crinkled almost petulantly and her father caught the expression. 'Ariella prefers the world out there to the constraints of counting off ells of fabric for the next day's market. When her mother named her Ariella, Lioness of God, I don't think she realised how independently spirited her daughter would be.' He took the sting from his words by pulling her to him and kissing the top of her forehead and her hand reached to his and squeezed.

17

'Father, I do not find the work so bad; it is just that I want to do much more.' Her voice reminded me of velvets, of furs and the warmth of fire on a cold night. But her eyes as they drifted to the wall, said *'Out there.'*

William had found a bench and he sat with Tanti, relating some tale or other from his imagination.

'They will be safe,' said Saul. 'The gate is bolted. Come.'

The coolness of the cavernous storeroom recalled early autumn mornings and goosebumps rattled up my arms.

'You are cold, my lady? My father's house is built of stone slabs so the warmth does not penetrate. But it makes for a chilling winter in here – one needs furs as we cannot light braziers or the fabric would smell of smoke. Here…'

Ariella held out a blue cloak and my fingers grazed the surface. Only rarely had velvet made its way to Aquitaine from the markets of Persia, let alone to the far-flung shores of temperate England but when it did it produced sighs of awe from men and women alike.

'It's beautiful and I crave it but I am not so cold that I need to wrap in a cloak, thank you. I do not mind the cool. I was born in England after all.'

Saul smiled as he heaved bolts around. 'It is easy to forget. You have the look and sound of one who has lived afar, Lady Ysabel.'

'Not as far as you perhaps, Saul, but far enough of late.'

'You are lucky then, my lady,' Ariella spoke quietly and Saul sighed. That there was an issue between father and daughter was obvious to a blind beggar and I endeavoured to lighten the moment.

'Mary Mother!' In front of me was a length of the most translucent silk. Tinted the colour of the waters of the Adriatic and Middle Seas, it was shot with gold strands like spiderwebs – a finely formed pattern along it's selvedge.

'It is from far away. Brought to Byzantium by camel train. You may still smell some fragrance in it.' He sniffed. 'Ah, yes. *Olibanum.* We burn it in our Jewish rituals, did you know?'

I took up a fold and held it to my nose. The odour was exotic, a reminiscence of those places now being trodden by the Crusaders. In its way it was a sad fragrance, a reminder that its source had a history of displacement and fierce struggle behind it, of sand and obscure towns built of daub and that shimmered in the basting sun. Heavens knows what working with such things did for an adventurous spirit like Ariella's.

'I have never seen anything quite so beautiful.' My fingers caressed the goldwork as from outside we heard the excited shouts of a boy and the uninhibited yapping of a young dog.

'You would like a length? I can sell it for a good price.' Saul was quick to pinpoint a woman's desires.

I thought of my practical life – of that messy, loud child, of an old house, and of caring for our family. I thought too of my husband.

'Sadly it does not fit the way I live – once perhaps, but not now. And if I presented Sir Guy with a chit for the expense, I doubt he would be pleased. No. I have come for other silk and must be content with that.'

Saul shrugged. 'Beauty is for every day, Lady Ysabel. If we ignore it, it is a sin against all that God has created and continues to create in this world.'

I heard a tiny harrumph from the direction of Ariella and thought how Saul fought a losing battle with his daughter. I also thought that with church views on personal indulgences, I would be frowned upon for a purchase of such superb silk so all I said was, 'I need a clear white silk. You know my lord's colouring, Saul. I'm of the opinion an ice white would become him…'

But the merchant had already pulled out a chemise silk that shone like a snowstorm and was cutting, the sound of his shears like the mournful cry of some odd Venetian heron or water fowl. He folded it into the smallest bundle and wrapped it in a dour piece of rough linen, tying it with a fine hemp cord and handing it to me.

'There. And I expect to see Sir Guy wearing my most perfect silk in due course, my lady.'

I laughed. 'Then I shall have to hope that my embroidery skills meet the quality of your silk, sir.'

He took my arm and led me to the door, Ariella giving me a slightly removed smile as we left her stitching beneath the mellow light of the one long window.

As we trod the length of the loggia, Saul sighed. 'You must forgive my daughter. She wishes to attend me on my travels far and wide but I am of the view she is best here where it is safe. She does of course think I am overly worried about nothing and holds me to blame for what she considers a narrow life. But I do what I must. It is very hard making the right decisions alone when I crave her mother's opinion.'

Saul's wife had been one of the many Jews to die during that dreadful time in York at the beginning of Richard's reign, and I felt empathy with Ariella and Saul because I had often craved my own mother's counsel during the length of my most recent twisted past.

'I am sure she knows you wish only the best for her,' I said. 'And in the end, Saul, that is all any of us can do. Be the best parents we can and trust to God for the rest. Speaking of which, my errant and loud son seems to have grown very quiet. Perhaps Tanti has succeeded where I as a parent have failed. William … William!'

But there remained the most perfect silence, broken only by the sound of doves.

'Odd,' said Saul and placing tongue against teeth whistled loudly. 'Tanti. Tanti!'

But still nothing and we went around the garden of secrets lifting branches, looking behind tubs and shrubs in case one little boy and a dog were hiding. Even, God forbid, checking the pond. Nothing. My heartbeat picked up tempo.

'The kitchen? Do you think he might be in the kitchen?'

But he wasn't. We hurried back along the winding path toward the boundaries of the garden.

'No…' I gasped.

The gate stood ajar – just wide enough to allow a small child and a dog to squeeze through to see what life offered on the other side.

'No. Please no. William!' I ran through the gate, Saul following, his hand reaching for my arm.

'William! I called, pulling from Saul, turning in a frantic circle. 'He's gone! Saul, help me,' I begged. 'William's gone!'

CHAPTER TWO

I spun away from the silk merchant's gate, Saul and now Ariella shouting, but I heard no words.

This town had nothing of the size of London or Paris or Bologna and yet in that moment of fear it was the largest town in my world – unknown and yet I thought it had been so familiar – small alleys, dark shadows, buildings pressing in and at every turn the glimpse of water like some repeating vision of Hell.

I shouted as I ran, 'William, William!' But he didn't answer and so I started to shout at bystanders as I fled past, trying to examine newly darkened paths and half-opened gateways.

'Please, have you seen a little boy with a dog?'

People turned half-hooded faces to me, shielding expressionless eyes and saying nothing. If this was a nightmare created by the Devil, he must surely have been roaring with maleficent laughter at my crazed distress.

Oh Virgin mine, help me. In the name of Your Son, let me find mine.

'Hey, I seed 'im wiv two men, that way…' A scabrous finger pointed and I grabbed my folds, fleet of foot, flying over excreta, mud, refuse, along a twisting alley between buildings – smelling the dank, rotting mildew of the watery ways that made up Venezia.

Don't let him drown, dear God. Protect him…

Because for all that William could swim like a newly-hatched duck, he was a mere baby, and if he were scared…

'William!' I screamed. 'William!'

Were there tears on my face? There was no time to feel.

Listen!

I pulled to a breathless halt.

'Mama, ma…' The cry stopped mid-word but a dog barked in a frenzy.

There!

A narrow path – shadowed and obscure, leading to a yard filled with the weak light that is permitted by encroaching half wood, half stone slab warehouses. In an instant I saw wooden beams, planks, rope coils and pails and smelled the acrid aroma of pitch.

It was a yard at the back of the Arsenale and in the middle of it William, kicking and trying to scream, and Tanti barking like a rabid mongrel, snapping at ankles, leaving bloody holes. The dog flew in, biting and dashing away before he could be brutally kicked and beaten. As I ran closer, I ripped out the *misericorde* that had hung from my girdle every day since I had met Gisborne.

The men looked up and William began a fresh bout of frantic squirming as he saw me.

'Put him down,' I hissed in common French, evil and as mad as a cornered snake. One of the men, hooded and unrecognisable in muddy browns said, 'Oh aye, missus. Oh sorry – *my lady.*' He gave a pathetic attempt at a bow and he and another giggled.

'I said put him down! Now!' I coiled my anger deep inside, ready to strike. Tanti ran to my side, lips curled back over his fangs, a rolling growl far bigger than the dog itself filling the yard.

The man holding William laughed and my little son squirmed like the child of the snake-mother he was, his heels flicking back and forth like a reptile's tongue to punch a fleshy scrotum. The kidnapper dropped him, hands reaching to cup his groin as he moaned.

'Run William!'

He took a step as I pitched my dagger into the chest of his captor. The man fell, one hand between his legs, the other clutching his chest from where blood was spreading. But as my son tried to step further, a tall man in a dusty cloak grabbed him and threw him over his shoulder as the child screamed.

'Shut up, yer little bastard or I'll slice yer mam inter strips and boil 'er in oil.'

A child from a house of many languages, William knew what was spat at him and lapsed into a cruel silence.

'Please don't hurt him,' I begged. 'He is but a baby.'

'A boy's what he is an' Christian boys fetch a right price at the slave markets.' William's captor spoke rustic French, the edges of his speech vanishing into the dark recesses of his hood from where lank ringlets of hair dangled.

'No,' I gasped. 'No, you mustn't. Take me, please…'

'Maybe…' the other smaller man said as he kicked at their knifed partner. 'Maybe we'll take the both o…' He sucked in his breath loudly as an arrow thunked into bone and sinew, probably into his heart as his eyes rolled back and he fell instantly dead.

I spun round. A stranger stood with an eastern bow of a style familiar to me, casually nocking a further arrow.

'Put the child down,' he called unambiguously across the yard, 'and I will not feel the need to skewer your skull from front to back.'

'Yer think?' the felon holding William said, trying to draw a dagger at the same time. 'I don't think so.'

'Well,' said the archer as William slipped, forcing the kidnapper to use two hands to hold him. 'You're an easy target. I shot your friend right through the heart. One shot on the mark and he was gone. Think on it, have a look…'

The felon's eyes went to the arrow poking from the dead man's chest, blood oozing from a gaping mouth whilst eyes stared into a forever nothingness.

'But I got the boy,' he said. 'I'll use 'im to shield me.'

'You think that'll stop me? I can nock and loose faster than you can lift that child from one shoulder to the other…'

'Please,' I called to the archer. 'You might hit my son…'

He ignored me, loosing a shot that seared across the felon's head so that he had to duck. 'Put him down gently,' his voice was almost melodic. 'That's it … little boy, go to your mother…'

But William froze, staring at the two bodies at his feet, then turning a streaked and mottled face toward me as tears rolled down his cheeks. I picked up my folds and ran to him, with Tanti barking at my heels. And as the felon whipped the dagger from his belt, an arrow whistled a death tune past my cheek.

It hit the man's forehead with a subtle whack. His eyes widened, dagger dropping, his fingers plucking at something immoveable in the centre of his head. He fell almost at my feet and I grabbed William and crushed him to my skirts to block the terrible sights around him. Behind me, I could hear

Saul shouting, Ariella too.

And another voice.

Guy…

I turned and he caught me up in the safety of his glance as it swept over the felons, over William, to settle on the archer. I began to walk William away from the blood, but a hand clutched at my hem and in a moment I saw filthy fingers move to a knife – the man I had apparently not killed, only wounded, thinking on rough justice.

Ariella saw him as well.

From her girdle, she flipped a pair of shears, pitching them perfectly and with great force so that they embedded deep in the man's chest, finishing the job that I should have done. The air groaned out of him like a stuck pig's bladder and I felt no remorse as I grasped William even tighter.

God rot them all.

Tanti was barking, jumping up against Ariella until she bent to pick him up.

'Be quiet, my Tanti, good boy!'

'He bit nathty men in the legth,' William whispered.

'Did he now,' Ariella said with a matter-of-fact tone to her voice. 'What a supreme guard dog! Then shall you and I take him from here?'

William held tight to my hand, his own trembling and gritty with sweat. 'I want Mama…'

But Gisborne spoke to his son, rubbing the top of his head. His expression was neutral if you did not know him, but I knew that when grim lines traced from nose to mouth and when his eyes were depthless, that he had been stretched almost to his limits. He knelt down and pulled William close and held him there, eyes closed momentarily but then bending a little further to engage with his son. 'Go with Mama, William. She needs a strong man to escort her. Can you do that?'

'Yeth,' William answered eventually, nodding his head.

'Good boy.' Gisborne stood then, not bothering to brush the dirt from his tunic. 'Saul, will you attend them? I would speak with our archer friend.'

Saul took my arm and we walked with his daughter, my son and the dog along the path that had darkened even more as the sun shifted. Even so, as we headed away I heard Gisborne speak to our redeemer.

'Thank you, sir, I owe you my son's life.'

'You owe me nothing. Anyone would have done the same.' Clear French tones answered Guy back, the voice almost as deep as my husband's. I turned to see the archer stood as tall as Gisborne, his hair only lighter by a few shades and cut shorter than Guy's. His clothes were serviceable, unremarkable even, and he shrugged on a tired gambeson that he lifted from the warehouse steps. He reminded me of a piece of yew, bending like a bow to the string as he leaned down to pull at his boots. *Those* were expensive and like his bow, I suspected they were cherished possessions.

'Perhaps,' replied Guy. 'But it was a master shot.'

The fellow nodded as he slung the bow over his shoulder. 'The bastard moved, I countered. It went better than I expected.'

So cold...

'May I know the name of the man to whom I owe much, sir?'

The archer shifted uncomfortably. 'Guillaume... Just Guillaume. Lately of Anjou.'

Richard's lands. Richard, Count of Anjou and King of England.

Gisborne held out of his hand – and Guillaume of Anjou looked at it, finally accepting the clasp to the elbow.

'My lady?' Saul's voice broke my concentration.

'I'm sorry, Saul. So much...' I indicated the bloody ground behind us.

'Indeed,' he said. 'Ariella, are you... Do you...'

'I am perfectly fine, Father.' She smoothed Tanti's head. 'I did what had to be done.'

'Had to be done?' I said in wonder. 'Mary Mother, Ariella, you pitch as if you know a blade intimately.'

'I pitch as I have been taught,' she replied quietly, all of us trying to discuss things without drawing William's attention. If he heard us he said nothing, just held my hand tightly. Ariella placed Tanti on the ground and at last William's expression unknotted as the dog put its front paws on the child's belly, licking his face.

'It tickleth,' he said, letting go my hand and walking along with Tanti.

'Who taught you?' I asked of Ariella.

'Father.'

Of course. Why wouldn't he?

'We are Jews, Lady Ysabel,' she explained plainly. 'It would be foolish to be under-prepared.'

Of course. York, at the time of Richard's accession – that bloody time in York when my former husband and his men had gone Jew-baiting. All at once I wanted to repay her for her courage.

'Then Saul, if I may say, you need to take this competent woman with you on your journeys. You want her to learn about your business – what better way than by your side?'

Ariella fixed me with a calculating gaze. Then she smiled – the first truly warm smile since I had met her, as though steel had been rendered to velvet, iron to soft linen.

What a beautiful woman…

'In many ways,' Saul said, measuring his words like so many ells of silk, 'you are right. Today proved it and be assured, my lady, I shall heed your words.'

Ariella slipped her arm through Saul's. 'I thank you, Father, for considering the matter. Now we, all of us, little William as well, need wine and refreshment after this cruel adventure. Before Sir Guy and Lady Ysabel leave for their home, I suggest we take a moment – if nothing else,' she cast her eye over William who was standing, one hand on Tanti's head, the other sucking a thumb, 'it will act as a buffer for Master Gisborne. And you, Guillaume of Anjou, you will join us?'

Saul opened his gate, his garden lit gold by the late afternoon sun and we filed into his bee and butterfly-filled paradise, his doves chastising us, stamping back and forth along the eaves of the house, dipping their heads up and down in disgust. None of us was clean and Ariella ordered bowls and towels and soon we were dipping our hands in scented water.

I wiped William's face; he predictably pushed me away, for what child of any age wants a mother washing his face? But I managed to reveal shining pink beneath the tear-streaked grime. I took his plump hands, one after the other, Ariella's towels a stained mess and as I rubbed between his fingers, he whispered,

'Mama.'

I knelt down to his level, my gown folds shifting the many fallen petals in the loggia. 'Yes…'

He looked up at me with vexed Gisborne eyes, 'Ith the gate locked?'

'Yes, William.'

'No bad menth coming?'

'Not at all,' I replied. 'Never.'

His father stood at my shoulder, I could feel the heat from his thigh, and then he squatted down beside me, taking William's fleshy palms in his own. His hands were such a contradiction in terms – finely boned with long fingers but just enough width to put him on the side of knight rather than minstrel.

'Besides,' he said. 'We have a champion archer here, so they would not dare!'

William looked up at the slim streak from Anjou. 'Can you thoot them?'

'Of course,' Guillaume's face broke from its remove, a somewhat gentle smile that changed his countenance and surprised me. 'But they will not come because they are scared of this.' He held out his bow and William gave it serious thought. Finally,

'Good!' he said and turning, became a happy child again, calling Tanti and the two racing from shrub to shrub.

'I think they both run off their fears,' I said to no one in particular, but I heard Gisborne say behind me,

'You see, Guillaume of Anjou, Master Gisborne has decided you are his security.'

And you, Gisborne, what do you think?

'I am happy to be of service at this moment, my lord,' Guillaume replied.

'Then let us repay you for your courage,' Saul appeared with cups and wine and poured one each as Ariella laid down a platter of cheese and bread. 'To you, Guillaume of Anjou,' Saul said.

We all raised our cups and I drank mine dry in a moment, waiting impatiently for the looseness to sweep through my muscles. I glanced at my husband as my legs turned to blessed honey.

Guy was calculating something – assessing risk versus value. It was a look he had given me a hundred times as he escorted me in times past – a vestige of an expression, like a ghost and then gone, his face unnervingly blank. Anyone who didn't know him would think he was assessing nothing, but I knew better. I wondered if he would be able to get beneath Guillaime of Anjou's skin and whether by reverse, Guillaume might get beneath the master player, my husband's.

The sun had decided its job was almost done as we began our homeward journey, Saul's gate shutting firmly, the bolts sliding into place. My legs now ached with a ferocity that reminded me of long journeys on wide horsebacks and I wished Guy would summon a cart. But instead he picked up an exhausted William, turning to Guillaume as he settled the child in his arms.

'Sir,' he said, including me in his words. 'It would suit Lady Ysabel and myself very well if you accepted an offer of hospitality. It is the very least we can do to repay you.'

The archer straightened imperceptibly. 'Thank you, my lord, but…'

Gisborne began to move off and we trailed in his wake as if he were some powerful magnate and not an almost dispossessed noble. 'Oh come now, you say you are new to Venezia so you must need to lay your head somewhere.'

'Yes…'

'Then surely it is settled.' Gisborne stopped mid-stride and I almost ran into him. William by this time lay asleep on his shoulder and was oblivious to his father's machinations. Because that's what they were, I had no doubt.

'You know nothing about me.'

Yes, Guy, it is true. We know nothing about him.

My eyes flicked from Guillaume to my husband.

'I know you are from Anjou, that you handle a bow with masterful intent and that you saved the lives of those who are dearest to me. For the rest, I am merely offering you food and a bed for the night. What you do on the morrow is your affair.'

Is it, Gisborne?

Guillaume's glance shifted from Gisborne to myself and I offered as genuine a smile as I could manage. 'You are more than welcome, sir.'

'Then I thank you both and will accept.' He shifted the bow on his shoulder and Gisborne nodded.

'Good. We must make haste before my lady wife's legs fold and before my housekeeper calls out our guards. If you have possessions to collect, I can arrange for one of my men…'

'No, there is nothing,' Guillaume said.

Odd.

Biddy was standing at the gates, clenched fists on hips, the expression of an officer of the watch emanating in angry waves from her fierce little body.

'And about time too,' she grumped, reaching for William and settling him in her arms. 'Jesu but you've had us worried.' She cast a look at Guillaume and then continued, 'Get inside and clean yourselves before we eat and I shall do what must be done with the young master.' She turned away, mood changing as she crooned to William who had begun to stir.

I bade our guest excuse me, leaving Gisborne to do what he must with the stranger in our midst. Guillaume bowed, his eyes not meeting mine as he dipped his head, and I cared little. I heard the word *Acre* mentioned as I walked away but had no interest in pursuing his history. My son had almost disappeared from my life this day and there was so much of it that seemed more than coincidence. The kidnappers had called me 'my lady' for one. It may have been mockery but I thought not, in which case how did they know I was noble-born? My clothing was passing ordinary and I wore no gold nor silver.

I needed Toby. I should have liked to throw out a few lines to see what we could catch. He had a way of dealing with me when I was like this – by either playing the fool or offering a logical reply to an illogical question. Peter walked through the hall with an armload of wood and I called to him.

'Peter, have you seen Toby?'

He placed the wood at the side of the large fireplace with a clunk, the logs emitting a resinous tang. Clapping his hands together to remove the dust, he replied, 'To the docks, my lady. Seems there's a ship with a message for Sir Guy.'

Of course, when isn't there?

I palmed my parcelled silk. 'And Mehmet?' If Toby were unavailable, my physician would offer his thoughts on the matter of the day.

'With Toby.' Peter began to set kindling in the fireplace. If the evening became damply chill it would be lit. Otherwise we would cope until winter's cool breath really began to bite. 'He thought there may be new shipments of them sticks and leaves he uses in medics.'

He's as much a trader in secrets as herbal tinctures, Peter…

I nodded, turning with tired resignation to the stair. We had been in the house such a short time and already it was as familiar and cosseting as Moncrieff had been once in my life. I trailed my fingers along the chiselled stone as I climbed. Cross-hatched with a stonemason's blow, it told a story of survival and protection and I felt heartened. The stone had been rinsed with a pale tint long ago and someone with much time on their hands had painted golden stars all the way to the very roof beams. I liked the largesse of it even though they had faded and begun to peel away from the roughness of the stone. But William had learned many tunes of stars and moons from Toby under their watch.

I could picture the two now – innocence and worldly experience, sitting together on the stair as Toby strummed his *vielle,* William banging time on one of Biddy's pots as if he played the tabor.

Innocence – innocence that had been shattered as he was confronted threefold with the blood and brutality of man today.

I would need time to prove to myself he survived with no ill effects.

'My lady,' I turned as Gwenny puffed up beside me. 'I just heard…'

I shook my head, pressing my lips together. 'William?' I asked.

'Yes. He tells it like one of Dante's stories, but…'

'But?'

'His hand shook as he lifted his pie…'

My lips pressed harder.

'It's a God-rotten world we live in, my lady, when an innocent babe is at risk. I saw a cutpurse today by the fish-seller's booth at the market. The mongrel thief just snipped the purse as lightly as if it were a feather in the wind and the owner remained unawares. I longed to shout out but remembered what Sir Guy said about not drawing unwanted notice. Anyways…' she stopped for a quick breath, 'Wills is eating quite well and Peter made two balls today from old leather and will play a game with him.'

A reminder that William's care was in everyone's loving hands, and that today's ill effects would be ameliorated every moment until he was old enough to manage without such support. What a lucky child and what a fortunate mother.

'Do you need me just now, Madame?' Gwen pulled some of Saul's petals from my hair.

'Shortly perhaps, but I would that you stayed with William until Biddy puts him in his bed.'

'Aye, he might need us all for a little,' she said, turning back down the stair, her soft leather boots barely making a sound.

I continued on to my chamber and pulled off the dirty gown, letting my hair fall around me. Beyond the shutters, dusking had settled so that all was now shadow and the world stretched darkly away to the centre of Venezia. A silky cloud folded itself across the sky, shielding any likelihood of moon and stars – it had the feel of rain. I washed again, removing the taint of the day and quickly plaited my hair, flinging it behind my back.

The chests holding my clothes yielded nothing suited to entertaining a guest until I spotted the lone coffer that sat beneath the window and which was usually covered in cushions. Now they lay scattered across the floor, courtesy of an earlier visit from William. I hadn't ever looked inside the chest because there had never been any need and neither Biddy nor Gwen had ever indicated it contained anything of value. Someone had lit the fire in the room and smoky tendrils floated up the chimney. I took a candle and held it to the dancing flame, placing the light within a horn lamp and standing it close by the coffer. The lid opened with a faint sigh and the smell of dried lavender drifted out, a momentary vision of Cazenay flashing by. Inside lay a world of memories and I sat back on my heels, stunned that neither of my servants had mentioned the contents to me at any time.

On top of the flattened pile was a small square of pale linen edged in fine silk thread. I held it to my nose, expecting my mother's fragrance to emanate but there was nothing but a faint odour of lavender. The seductive sound of chainlink rattled as I pushed deeper into the chest, unearthing a fine girdle of interlinked gold loops in the shape of leaves, one that was familiar and which lay alongside a small palm-sized prayer book, beautifully scribed with rich pigment and delicately wrought Latin.

My mother's … everything I wished to have of hers…

How came these to be here? Why hadn't I been told? Had the rhythm of our Venetian life taken over so quickly? I reached into the treasure-trove and pulled out a cloth I remembered well, letting it roll down my lap to release its valuable contents on the floor. Suddenly I realised from where this coffer had come. Somewhere deep in the hold of the *Marolingian,* it had sat filled with my small inheritance from Moncrieff, an inheritance scrounged and secreted by devious means, perhaps the hands of my godmother, Lady Cecilia, when de Courcey had been my brutal husband. Somehow, it had been transported to Davey's ship between our flight to Wales and then our secret journey to meet him on the south coast of England. I saw any number of friends arranging this – Cecilia, Brother John, perhaps Guy. Even – and my heart skipped a beat – Ulric. Davey would have added the Saracen book to the contents after I had left the ship in Cyprus and then quietly deposited the chest here.

The little book glistened shyly. If I weren't hardened by circumstance, I would say it held messages of intent. Good messages. I ran my fingers over the gems and then wrapped the book back into the cloth, rolling it tightly and placing it back in the bottom of the coffer, it was William's inheritance. And then I pulled the last folds of fabric out – the finest woollen gown dropped away from my fingers – gold as the girdle but with a deep tawny pattern laced through the weave.

At once a wave of nostalgia swept over me, drowning me in thoughts of the watery surrounds of my old home, of my mother's Lady Chamber, the solar from where she ran the demesnes. Oh yes, she had been the chatelaine, the very model of the lady of the manor. She had been the definitive power behind my poet Papa, and he a lovely, lost man with no real care for the management of the estate. My mother ordered the domain and he would dance to her gentle tune, comfortable in the knowledge she ran it to all our benefits.

I layered the clothes over my head – chemise, then gown, and reached for the side lacings as the door thrust open and Gisborne's voice filled our intimate space.

'So!'

I turned to him, puzzled. His tone chilled me after the glance we had shared at the Arsenale.

'I ordered you to take a guard to Saul's, Ysabel.'

'I know...'

'And because you went your own sweet way, my son could have been...'

'Do not!' I sat down hard on a stool.

'I will!' Guy's anger increased as he spoke, the atmosphere thunderous with disapprobation. 'Because what I say is true.' He began to walk around the chamber, stripping garments – muscle and sinew rippling as he did so. The scar on his side, silvered now, reminded me of his abhorrent cousin Halsham, whose reach had been long. 'Ysabel, I ask you to do these things so that you and William are protected at all times. So that you can be at ease.'

'Mary Mother, Guy,' I held tight to a fold of my mother's gown. 'I can't see how being in a permanent state of alert and with an armed guard can contribute to a sense of ease...'

'And yet,' he took up the damp cloth, dipped it into the bowl and rubbed at his neck with ferocious strokes. 'When you ignore such a thing look what happens.'

He had his back to me and I noticed he had gained the weight lost after Ulric's demise. 'I am sorry,' I said.

He swung round to scrutinise me. '*Are* you?'

'Of course! William is *my* son too…'

'Indeed,' his voice became muffled as he flung a clean chemise over his head followed by a long, dark grey tunic. He pulled on short boots and buckled his sword around his hips. The effect was no less thunderous. Running his fingers through his hair, he continued, 'If you respect me at all, respect my judgement.'

With a dull thump of moulded leather as his scabbard hit the doorframe, he left the chamber, leaving me feeling as if a windstorm had just swept through. They say that silence can shout and it is true. I sat there chastised and hating that I must entertain a guest to whom I didn't warm. I put my elbows on my knees and leaned forward to hold my head in my hands. It ached ferociously and in truth, after the day's excesses I wanted to cry to ease the lump that sat in my chest like the stone that sealed Christ's burial chamber.

The door eased open and I took a breath and muttered from the depths of my hands. 'Gwenny, I am glad you are come. My head aches and I need your help to tie my side lacing.'

'I am sorry.'

I spun round. Gisborne stood at the door, looking as contrite as it was possible for him to be. He walked to me, pulled me up and lifted my arms to shoulder height, beginning the process of lacing the sides of the gown neatly and with precision.

'When I heard you and William had disappeared and the guard not attending you, I swear Ysabel, my heart stopped beating and didn't start again until I saw you both alive at the Arsenale.'

'Ah, Gisborne,' I said as he finished the task and I smoothed the folds. 'You have no idea how I longed for the guard when I realised William had gone, that the gate was open, that my…' my voice broke and Guy wrapped his arms around me. 'That my son had vanished. I swear I was blinded with fear. Suddenly a place one thinks one knows well changes beyond belief. It becomes a massive expanse of dead ends and horror.'

He rubbed my back, his chin on my head. The circular motions drew me back from the memory. 'You did well,' he said. 'You stood your ground. You and Ariella.' His voice rumbled through his chest. 'But I thank the Lord especially for Guillaume of Anjou.'

I pulled away and sat again to place a veil over tidied hair. 'Do you seek to employ him, Guy?'

I watched my husband's face reflected in the small hand-mirror I picked up. A bitter expression etched lines where there had been few. It was something he might try to hide from me because he hated to be caught with weakened defences. But I knew he was remembering Ulric – recalling his failure of judgement, how he had such affection for a man who had grown to hate him.

The expression wiped clear in an instant, almost as if he knew I had spied. 'I could do worse. But I know nothing of him and would be cautious until I discovered more.' He straightened the veil, laying out the folds over my shoulders. 'No, today I repay the debt in the only way I can. Beyond that, he is his own man.'

Cautious, Gisborne. More than ever.

'But I have been gone long and must be courteous to him.' He turned to go, his hand sliding from my shoulder to rest on the hilt of his sword.

'Guy, one thing…'

He cocked his eyebrow, inviting the question.

'Do you think William was kidnapped with forethought?'

Deny it. Please deny it.

He chewed at his cheek, his answer well-considered. 'Anything is possible…'

My face must have paled to marble whiteness because he reached for my hands, bending to engage with me. 'We can never forget that the intelligence service I run for the King has the potential to arouse much ire. Many are aware the network flourishes, even goes to a greater strength. Amongst spies, Ysabel, no one is safe – least of all my family. I have enemies – you know this. This is why I have guards.'

I broke in then, my hand kneading my own scar, rubbing at my forehead, almost as if I needed to remind him of insecure times past. 'Then we shall never be safe…'

'Do not be so naïve. You surprise me, you of all people, who has seen so much over the last two years. We live in a violent unsteady world where men take advantage of a moment to make money. We could live in the far north or even in the east beyond Outremer and it would be the same. There will always be enemies. But at the moment the King's enemies are our enemies.'

'The King's enemies?'

'Yes.'

'So my son might be held to ransom for the King?'

'Ysabel, you are being alarmist. Do calm, please. We are all safe at the moment.' He gently brushed my cheek and then bent to place his lips on mine. My husband rarely touched me with anything other than gentleness and finesse; as if he knew that the slightest roughness, the merest hint of rapaciousness would send me spiralling back to that moment when de Courcey had raped me. And so his lips grazed, their softness pressing against my own, as slowly our mouths opened and I could taste his nutmeg-scented breath.

Apples, Biddy's poached apples.

A smile crept between us and he asked, 'You laugh? Now?' He straightened himself, tidying where it mattered.

'Your breath smells of Biddy's apples, Gisborne. 'Tis tasty.'

Gisborne gave a hollow growl. 'Tasty? Christ, I could throw you on the bed and ravish you for that, my lady.'

'But you will not,' I murmured. 'Will you, Guy?' I lifted my head to meet his gaze. 'You know that in this chamber the lion and the lamb always lie together in peace.'

It was his turn to laugh. 'Ysabel, I missed out sorely on repartee before you and I became acquainted. Every moment of every day since, you have been a surprise to me.' He ran his hand down the side of my neck and over my chest and I didn't shrink away. For a long time, I had distrusted him, loving and hating him in equal measure and every day since Ulric died and my husband lived, I reminded myself of time wasted. Gisborne and I talked of this often when on our own. I would say how his introversion, his lack of openness had turned me into someone distrustful and he would say my behaviour had caused him to lack trust; a wicked Devil-made circle. And then we would make love and thank God, The Virgin and the Holy Son that we had found sense before our lives shortened any further.

'As you are to me, my lord. But go – your new friend will be waiting.'

If he detected any scathing note on my part he did not say and with a final kiss, he left as swiftly, if less angrily, as before. I followed in his wake thinking on what he had said. In the world of spies, no one is safe. My spine chilled and not just with the faint breeze that tickled the gold-starred walls of the passage.

I stepped into William's little chamber where a light burned in a horn lamp alongside Biddy's cot and taking it up, the ring at the top squeaking faintly, I held it over William who lay sleeping, arms outspread above his head, mouth agape.

A sleeping child is a God-given thing to behold. Even though they may have grown from infancy, it's as though time rolls backward just for those hours of the night. Silky lashes fan out across rounded cheeks, little lips purse like ripe cherries, the skin feels like Saul's velvet and a gentle flush spreads with the warmth of the cot. My son's chest rose and fell and in consequence, his breath huffed in and out. I reached my fingers to his mouth, caught the air in my hand and held it to my own lips, thanking the Virgin that he could give his mother such a gift.

Juices seethed in my mouth and belly with the aromas emanating from the kitchen and dining hall. I had eaten nothing except Ariella's bread and cheese since breaking my fast and as my footsteps quickened, the sound of steps further to the end of the passage dragged at my attention. Two figures hurried into view.

'Toby,' I said, aghast at the sight of him, Mehmet by his side.

My small friend grinned. 'Ah, but you should see the other fellow!'

Our minstrel had a bruised eye that was turning all shades of a storm sky as I watched. Above his eyebrow a deep cut oozed blood and was closed with expert stitching.

'God in heaven,' I whispered.

'They just didn't seem to like people like me.' He said it lightly but I knew he despised discrimination.

'How many?'

'Two. That was enough.' Mehmet's calm tones served to dampen the fear that had begun to assert itself once more, throwing up suffocating tendrils from some shadowy place deep inside my soul. I thought how blessed we were to have such a physician attached to our house – one that could quell all manner of pain, even of the mind. But he too was injured. A gash on his cheek leaked blood in sympathy with Toby's.

'My God, Mehmet, that's a knife slash…'

'So it seems.'

'Were they thieves?'

'Ah…' We had reached the door to our hall and he continued, 'I think we should not discuss this any further until we can talk with Sir Guy privately. I understand we have a guest…'

The thought of the dour Guillaume was salt to my own wounds of the day.

'You do not like him, Madame.' Toby whispered. It was not a question.

You read me like a book, Toby…

'I do not know him, Tobias, but these days I am cautious of coincidence.'

'Ah, you worry too much.' He shrugged off the day's events just like that. How I wished *I* could.

We entered all three, Mehmet as my escort, and introductions were made. Gisborne took in the bruised pair. 'You gave your attackers their due?'

'Indeed,' Mehmet replied with a quiet smile.

No other mention was made and we all took our places along the table with Guy at one end and myself at the other. If Guillaume of Anjou seemed surprised by the way our household sat at the table like family, he gave no indication.

To me it was perfectly normal that they should be seated thus. Only Biddy and Peter jumped up every now and then to replace one platter with another. But the hunger that had gurgled moments earlier had disappeared to be replaced by a whetstone that sharpened my concerns with ever-increasing rapidity.

Mehmet and Toby play-acted, as if being attacked was an acceptable occurrence in Venezia. And I suppose it was. In any city, town or village across our world, beatings and worse happened with such frequency that it seemed normal to expect it. Thus it was that conversation ebbed and flowed around the table. I would occasionally glance at Guillaume to find a face devoid of animation, almost as if he could not hear what was being said and yet I *knew* he listened intently. When he was spoken to, he would answer politely and expeditiously in a manner that invited no deeper engagement until Gisborne said to the table at large:

'Guillaume must be lauded as a saviour tonight. His willingness to defend an innocent child, and his accuracy, will never be forgotten.' He raised his goblet.

'As I said, my lord, it was a matter of being in the right place at the right time.'

'Too right it was,' said Biddy. 'And we owe you for our little one's life, Master Guillaume, for being in that place.'

The others around the table agreed and threw off a gulp of wine to toast him.

'But why there?' asked Toby, wincing as his fingers worried at his stitches. 'It's the back end of the Arsenale. An odd place to be, surely.'

Ah, Toby. My little 'advocatus diaboli'.

Guillaume, smooth as can be, did not demur.

'If you know Venezia, M'sieur Celho, I agree. The back end of a shipyard offers nothing. But I am not fortunate enough to know this town and was hopelessly lost. Sailing here from Outremer, I had heard there might be work for able-bodied men at the boatyards. When I disembarked, I just kept asking "Arsenale?" Finally, someone pointed down the lane.' His glance took Gisborne and I back there. 'The rest you know.'

Peter walked in then, with a platter of seafood and all the men fell to it. But Toby was circumspect and as the others picked meat from crab claws, he surreptitiously studied Guillaume and I longed to ask why.

When the meal was done, when juices and gravies had been sopped with bread and our sweet fancies had been satisfied with harvested figs and late peaches, Gisborne took advantage of a momentary lull to drop a stone upon our calming moods and which then proceeded to set up ripples that fascinated and discommoded me equally.

'Guillaume fought at Acre with King Richard.'

Mehmet's head turned quickly toward our guest and Gwenny piped up, 'Master Guillaume, you're very brave...'

'Indeed you are,' said Toby and I could decipher nothing in his tone. 'Acre was a test for all who fought there.'

'Both Christian *and* Saracen,' Mehmet said quietly.

Guillaume played with the stem of his goblet, his fingers rolling it back and forth. He had elongated bony hands, so that when they moved, it looked as if the bones were dancing. 'You are right, sir,' he said to Mehmet. 'Both Saracen *and* Christian. And if I may say, lives lost perilously, courageously and pointlessly.'

The bones stilled and his skin showed white between them, stretched tense and tight where the desert sun had missed its chance to burn.

Mehmet lifted a goblet and filled it with wine, the trickle cutting into the loaded silence. 'War is always pointless, Guillaume of Anjou. It is the product of egos and sadly, innocent men die because of it.'

'You have attended the battlefields?' Guillaume asked.

The oddest sensation filled the room. It was as if these two men had ceased to recognise they had company. Gisborne's scrutiny of both men was total; he would be weighing every word that came from Guillaume's mouth, I was sure of it. Gwen excused herself, knocking Peter on the shoulder to follow her to the kitchens where Biddy clattered and bashed.

Mehmet's face was carved with lines of sadness, his beard silver in the flickering candlelight. 'I have. I have seen too much and worked extremely hard but made little difference. Sometimes, no matter what treatment God directed, men died. Our rulers would say men had to die.'

The bones started dancing again. 'One wonders if God just turned his back on us all.' Guillaume's fingers described a cross over his chest and I wondered at the profound thing he had just uttered. Perhaps this was a man who *had* seen too much. Had he seen those two thousand or more heads rolling across the sands outside Acre?

I glanced again toward my husband and saw pity and *that* concerned me. For as much as I suspected Guillaume of Anjou *had* seen terrible things that haunted him, I was disturbed by his manner. He was so very still – like the waters of Scylla and Charybdis in Sicily – quiet above but a twisted maelstrom below.

Toby spoke, breaking the heavy atmosphere.

'Did you see King Richard in your time there?' It was such an innocent question, if you didn't know Toby.

Guillaume shook his head. 'In the distance for I was a mere archer. I walked on my own feet whilst he and his knights rode horses, Master Celho.'

'Why did you go to Outremer?' Toby pushed further.

Guillaume shifted, perhaps uncomfortable with the inquisition. 'I served my liege lord. *He* served his own, who happened to be the Count of Anjou – the King of England. I had no choice.'

'Would you have gone otherwise?'

'Toby!' Gisborne broke in, exasperated and a little terse. 'You sound like an inquisitor. My apologies, Guillaume, it is not our purpose to make you uneasy. Toby has always found anyone new intriguing. It gives him words for his redoubtable songs. Please forgive him.'

One side of Guillaume's mouth hooked up in what passed for a smile.

'Toby,' said Gisborne. 'You must give us a tune or two else Guillaume shall be sorry he entered this house. We have a debt to repay…'

Gisborne's glance flew along the table to me and I knew he remembered that time when I had saved *his* life not long after I had met him. An arrow nocked into a Saracen bow and a felon killed. I knew too that he would never forget the arrow that had taken Ulric's life thus sparing his own.

Toby jumped up to fetch his *vielle* where it habitually rested by the door. Toby was used to singing for his supper and there was always a willing audience within the household. We all relaxed as he tuned the instrument – the palpable tension disappearing like fog before the sun.

'I must beg your forgiveness, Guillaume of Anjou, but my lord is quite correct,' Toby said between sweeps of chords. 'I am a curious sod.'

Gisborne and I laughed, Mehmet smiled and Guillaume graciously murmured, 'It is nothing.' One could almost think he meant it as Tobias began to sing softly.

'Of every kinnë tre,
Of every kinnë tre,
The hawthorn blowëth sweetest,
Of every kinnë tre.
My lemman she shall be,
My lemman she shall be,
The fairest of every kinnë,
My lemman she shall be…'

How I loved Toby's voice – mellow, quite deep and as fluid as warmed honey. It occurred to me that I would love to hear him partnered with Ariella whose voice was as creamy. Along with the chords from the *vielle,* Tobias transported us immediately to the sweet paths and hedgerows of England.

'At night by the rosë, rosë,
At night by the rosë I lay.

Dorst ich nought the rosë stele,
And yet I bar the flour away.'

Despite the fact that we entered the cold months he determined to remind us of all that was blossom and spring and sang:

'Lenten ys come with love to toune,
with blosomës and with biddës roune,
that all this blissë bringëth...'

A long song and we all sat back in our chairs allowing the music and wine to induce a fair conviviality and to smooth over the scars of war and crime. Eventually the notes from the *vielle* were all that lingered that night, Toby's voice having stilled, my eyes closing and me longing to go to my chamber to sleep.

I stood, the rest of the table hastily following, furniture scraping the floor, an empty goblet falling and rolling back and forth on the table. Walking to Guillaume, I held out my hand. 'Guillaume of Anjou, I thank you...' For the first time I really looked into his eyes – deep brown and filled with something I couldn't place. 'It has given me such pleasure to welcome you to our table so that we can endeavour to repay some of what we owe you. My son is well-loved and thus you are valued for what you did to protect him. Please have a comfortable night and I hope I shall see you before you leave us on the morrow.'

I smiled. My words were well meant as I could never deny what I owed him.

He merely bowed over my hand.

CHAPTER THREE

Leave us on the morrow?

Was that churlish after what I had seen in his eyes? I wondered if I merely heaped my own fears upon him – he was a likely candidate, an unknown and appearing on this day of coincidences. I chided myself for my uncharitable thoughts and as I walked to my chamber, wondered what Brother John would have thought. Not just of my lack of empathy but also of Guillaume of Anjou. But Brother John was far away and I must draw my own conclusions.

I began to turn the corner away from the passage, Toby's and Mehmet's voices drifting after me as they made their way to a chamber on the other side of the kitchens. The kitchens had lapsed into quiet whereby I assumed Gwen and Biddy had gone to their own cots in William's room and Peter had descended to the stables, to a small room Gisborne had ordered built for the new husband and his wife. It was a puzzle of a house but it suited our mixed nature.

The hall door groaned open again and I heard Gisborne speak in low tones. 'Guillaume, I would give you this…' the clink of coin echoed seductively in the night quiet. 'I can see no other way of thanking you.'

'My lord,' the coins rattled again and I peeked round the corner of the passage to watch as Guillaume handed the bag back to Gisborne under the dipping light of a cresset. 'I would never accept money for what happened today. It is in my nature to save those who need saving.'

'Jesu, you sound like a Templar!'

'No, if I was a Templar, I might have taken your money and invested it wisely. Look...' he leaned against the wall and Gisborne stood easily, balling the bag of coins and rolling them from hand to hand, the clinking noise counterpoint to Guillaume's words. 'Let me put it this way. No one can measure the value of a child's life, that's a God-given fact. That your son is alive and may grow another day was within the power of God to grant. Sir Guy, sometimes hands are guided for a reason. Mine were guided to protect your son. It is enough for me at this time.'

'By the Saints,' Gisborne growled, a slightly incredulous note to his voice. 'You are a hard man to deal with.' He shook his head and I shared my husband's incredulity because he could charm salt from the sea if he so wished but he hadn't managed it in this instance. 'Then let me show you your quarters for this night. You will sleep with Peter – it is a modest but comfortable space.'

They walked off together – two men height for height, dark hair, one inordinately thin, one might say starved, and one robust and vital. I turned into my chamber to undress and climb into the bed, not even caring that my husband might find more than half the bed taken up with my outflung, exhausted limbs.

As I lay waiting for sleep to claim me, I wondered at Guillaume's odd nature. It seemed he was a man with nothing and yet he refused monies that could give him a security of sorts. But more than anything, I remembered a small statement he made. *Sometimes hands are guided for a reason. Mine were guided to protect your son.* It stuck in my mind like a barbed arrow.

Ah yes, and God be thanked, but what is the reason you mention?

I puzzled over it as my overtired body throbbed and hummed. I wished I had asked Mehmet for some valerian, so badly did I want to sleep and forget about today. My mind jumped from one wretched thought to another. Was Guillaume the King's enemy and therefore ours? And why would I think that?

Coincidences, Ysabel, coincidences.

How would we ever know what he was in this complex world we inhabited? Gisborne could no doubt try but such things took time. Perhaps Guillaume *was* merely a disabused soldier, tired of war, bereft of home and coin and merely trying to find a way forward. William was a welcome step out of the mire of an archer's misbegotten memories. I curled my toes into the wool-stuffed mattress, glad of the fine linen pillow sheet upon which I could lay my aching head. I pulled the covers a little higher as a night breeze snickered around my neck, wishing we had drapery to pull around the bed, but what we had was basic and I was grateful to have it at all after what seemed a lifetime of travelling. My eyelids, already heavy, shuttered down and I knew nothing until the coverings were lifted and cold penetrated. My groans stopped when the mattress dipped and dived and Gisborne curled his naked body around mine.

I slept again.

But such luxury was short-lived as the mattress moved and Gisborne rolled onto his back. The blankets shifted a little, by which I assumed he lay with his hands behind his head and there followed a sigh.

'Guy,' my voice was husky with sleep as I hunkered closer to him, my head reaching his armpit. Placing an arm across his chest, I asked, 'What ails you? Is it the archer?'

One hand descended to the top of my head, stroking as if I were a tame breeding bitch. 'Guillaume? No. At least... No.'

Not definite enough, husband.

'The message that Toby and Mehmet collected – it was valuable enough for them to have been attacked to prevent it from reaching me.'

'You say?' He stopped rubbing and I sat up, dragging a cover around my bare shoulders. The cool night offered a foretaste of winter to come.

'Your cousin the King has received the intelligence we sent that France and Italy were barred to his entry. He is being hunted like a hind, Ysabel – turned and turned again until he, like the hind, collapses with exhaustion. He cannot get to any port without problems. On the water he is subject to attack from any who know of him. He has sailed into Crete, Corfu, Zakynthos and around every bay in Cyprus to deter his enemies. I find it incredible that a man who sought to wage war on the Saracen probably has less to fear from *them* than his fellow Christians. The most recent information is that he has divided his men between two newly chartered ships. He's sent most of his men to sail northwesterly and is himself sailing northeasterly to a landfall with a small handpicked force. De Turnham is one.'

I remembered de Turnham and de Camville in Cyprus. Two noblemen who had sought to comfort me as my memory slowly returned. I would hate anything to happen to either of them and prayed Richard would not do something untoward.

'It seems that he thinks to travel overland to England, avoiding the Holy Roman Empire and France by trekking through Hungary in disguise. In fact, he could be heading our way for a landfall. 'Tis a pity he allowed his ego and temper to get in the way of politic behaviour.'

'He's a Plantagenet,' I muttered, hoping he wasn't sailing *anywhere* near us.

'Quite,' said Gisborne, almost consigning his liege lord to the dusty corners of history. He flung the covers back and grabbed a cloak to warm his naked form, lighting a candle from the smouldering remains of the fire. The ugly smell of tallow filled the room, reminding me I must renew the supply of good wax candles. He unrolled a map and the flickering flame cast dark shadows over his face – he could have been some frightening character from beyond the Styx, an almost unfamiliar face. I shivered and pulled the covers up further.

'He is in danger then, our stalwart Richard?'

'Yes. Always.'

'And you seek to protect him?'

I hoped with all my heart he wouldn't see it as his obligation to go charging off to fight at Richard's back. There would be little thanks if my husband expired in the pursuit of chivalric duty.

'I can do little that his knights don't already do. My duty is to keep him abreast of intelligence that could affect his existence. To be frank, his freedom is already forfeit. A blind man can see that. He has no option but to play cat and mouse across Europe.'

Somehow I didn't think such a thing would worry someone like Richard Plantagenet. In the desperate journey back to England to reclaim his throne and begin battle with Phillip of France to retain his beloved dukedoms, he would consider such a thing child's play.

'You do not like him, do you?' I said, remembering the sunset gold presence that had swept into my chamber in Cyprus, a king who thought to piece together my broken memory with his own.

Guy sighed. 'As a commander, a strategist, as a man amongst men, he is exceptional. But he has a cruel reputation in respect of women after the uprising in Aquitaine, and his support of the Jews at his coronation was less than kingly. In truth, he suffers from ego, from blinkered vision and from the most appallingly quick temper. But if I hate anything, it is that the whole of England has been held to ransom one way or another for his obsessions and in my heart, Ysabel, I think he may be paying the price.'

'Do you mean that he may be killed?'

Another king, another England. When does it end?

My husband shrugged. 'It is highly likely given the life he chooses to lead. I think bloodlust and battle fever are to Richard what bread and water might be to a starving man. Truth? I am more concerned with how many others will die as he pursues his ambitions. That's what matters.' His quill scratched away on a piece of parchment and vaguely I wondered if he wrote to King Richard and whether he was brave enough to counsel him.

'To whom do you send a message, husband?'

'Tommaso. He will tell the King that Leopold will be watching every inch of the Hungarian border and that the Italian coast rumbles about manoeuvring to exclude him as well. Dante has heard word around the Arsenale from Pisan mercenaries and Genoese ships.'

My lids grew heavy again as I banished my regal cousin from my mind but jerked open when I remembered Guillaume, my voice ushering from deep against the pillowsheet.

'And what of the man from Anjou, Guy. You seemed circumspect when I asked you if there was a problem. For myself, I think he is a damaged man.'

Gisborne laid down his quill, the shushing sound of sand being sprinkled and blown touching the edges of the room, whereupon he then rolled the parchment. I smelled molten wax as he applied his seal to the message, twisting a thin strip of leather round the roll. He came back to the bed, threw off his cloak and slid in beside me, skin against skin, and his expression settled into lines of thought.

'Does he frighten you?' he asked.

'No,' I demurred, although perhaps he did and I was too afraid to admit it outright. 'How would one know? It is hard to see beneath the surface of the man.'

'It is. But then he is injured, he has seen too much.'

'Oh come now, Guy, we've all seen death.'

'Yes, but he has waded through rivers of blood, brains and body parts daily. It plays with a man's mind.'

'Then I feel compassion for him and would light candles for his soul.'

'Would you indeed?' my husband commented wryly. He leaned over me, his body hungrier than I would have thought under the circumstances.

I pushed at him. 'I was shattered into many pieces when Wilf and Harry were murdered, Guy, and with what happened in Cyprus. It threatens one's sanity and I would not wish that on the man who saved our son.'

Gisborne rolled me to face away from him, curling around me again. 'He needs support,' he said cautiously.

I flung myself over so that I could see his face but it was so predictably unreadable. 'And you plan to give it to him?' My voice screeched unbelievingly.

Silence.

'Guy!' I was incredulous. After Ulric, a man he thought he knew, he now thought to draw a man he did *not* know into our fold.

'He shows inordinate skill with a bow, he plays the anonymous dice with immense skill…'

'Then does that anonymity not worry you? He could be anyone!'

'Ysabel, I will make enquiries as far as it is possible to do, but he says he has nothing and no one in his life and you know well enough that is the kind of man I would employ if I could find out enough to warrant my trust in them.'

'To replace Ulric?'

Even in the warmth of our nest, I felt him stiffen with anger.

'Never.' His voice reminded me of a frozen stream and incautious footsteps trying to move from one bank to the other. 'You know there are very few men in this world that I trust.' The silence following this crackled like the ice breaking. 'Ulric shall never be replaced.'

I had been put in *my* place, it seemed and I accepted it because we both hurt…

Peter, Tobias, Tommaso, Mehmet, Davey, Dante, Brother John, Saul – Guy's trusted cadre.

Softly, softly, Ysabel.

'Then why?' I continued less sharply. 'If Guillaume is as damaged as you say, might he not be a liability?'

'Indeed he may prove to be. In between times, I need to augment our guards. He could suit.'

'Have you asked him?'

'No…'

'He may refuse you.'

'Given his manner till now, I would say that is highly likely. Wife, I am perishingly tired and would sleep,' he yawned and flipped me back on my side again, curling close so that we resembled two crescent moons. 'Have I your permission?'

And thus our frosty moment passed and was gone, if not forgotten.

The next morning, the cool of approaching winter entered the house and would not leave. Biddy huffed and puffed about aching knees and hands and hurried to the markets to seek *melissa* and *femigrek* for soothing concoctions. I had yet to see Mehmet and Toby, and Gisborne had been gone when I woke, a situation as normal as breathing. But Peter had been in the kitchen and was unusually quiet, even as William hung off his knee. His eyes were bruised as if he hadn't slept well and he barely acknowledged William's persistent questions. For the first time, I noticed lines from his mouth to his nose.

I left to find Gwen, directing William to Toby's chamber. Gwen and I must stitch like the Devil possessed to sew Gisborne's chemise for the wedding and as we sat, needles shushing back and forth through Saul's fine silk, I asked, 'Is aught amiss with Peter?'

She lifted the thread to her teeth to break it and sequestered her needle through the woollen weave of her *bliaut*. 'You noticed?' She laughed. 'He's a bit awry today, my lady. It happens. Don't they say a man gets more nervous than the bride before the wedding?'

'Are you at all afraid?'

'Never. We've loved each other since we were babes and have almost lived as husband and wife since we left Moncrieff. Besides, we've been hand-fasted for too long as it is. This gives us the Church's blessing and perhaps we can have a child.' She smiled at some far away image in her mind. 'Begging your pardon, my lady, but if we had a son, he could be a friend to William.'

'Mary Mother, Gwenny, I should hope so! You are more like my sister or my very best friend than my maidservant. Which reminds me, I have this for you…' I walked to yesterday's chest and dug deep, saying nothing of its contents. Gently I lifted my mother's diaphanous veil and placed it in Gwen's hands. 'For your church business,' I grinned as her her mouth stood open wide enough to catch a fly.

I left her to her wedding fancies and hurried down the stable stair where I knew I would find Peter. Guy was with Guillaume of Anjou in our yard, leaning against the guardhouse wall in what passed for sun on this brisk day, deep in conversation. Our guards, all four, sat honing swords, halberds and daggers, the pale sun sheening on the metal blades. In front of them on the ground, saddlery had been undone and cleaned and they were far enough away not to intrude on their lord's discussion. William ran in and out of the trees, shouting at Toby who stood in a corner with his eyes shielded and counting. I smiled at William's raucous idea of hiding so as not to be found and was more than grateful to Toby for making sure a little child remembered happiness not horror.

For a moment as William ran past the guards, I examined the men. Aware that not once had I bothered to find out their names or their history. I thought of Wilf and Harry and that these men were no different – as vulnerable in their care of us as Wilf and Harry had been. It did not show the former Moncrieff men any respect to ignore those who came in their place. It seemed I was finally waking to my wider duties, not just as Lady Gisborne but as a Christian.

And not before time as Gisborne's laugh rang out around the yard and Guillaume grinned in response.

Salt charmed from the sea.

My stomach curled. Whilst I admit that over past years my intuition had proved unerringly wrong more often than not, this potential for Guillaume of Anjou to join the ranks of the Gisborne family did not sit easily upon me.

Peter was grooming Guy's horse with long strokes. As the beast heard me approach it shifted, its hooves scraping the stony floor and Peter clicking his tongue at it, looking up. 'My lady…'

'Don't stop, Peter. I want to talk to you and you can just as easily keep grooming.' He nodded, not meeting my eyes, and began the sweeping rhythm again.

'Peter, are you happy?'

A glance.

'Of course, my lady…'

'Are you looking forward to your wedding?'

For one brief moment his face relaxed. 'Aye. My little Gwenny has waited long enough.' He ran the brush in an arc across the rounded hindquarters of the horse.

'But that's Gwen. What about you?'

'Me? I would do anything for my Gwen…'

'Even accompanying her to fearsome unknown places.'

The brushing ceased for a couple of breaths and then, 'Aye.'

'Ah, Peter. My family have always held your own in such high regard for your loyalty and respect and nothing has changed. You have been William's protector from his birth and we honour that. In those early days, I could never have survived without you, Gwen or Biddy – you were … you *are*, my backbone.'

''Tis nothing,' he mumbled, a flush sweeping his cheeks.

''Tis *everything*,' I said. 'Loyalty is a commodity more valued than gold, Peter. And because you are so important to me, it is why I want you to be happy.'

He moved to the farthest side from me and I couldn't see his face as he bent to his task. He began to lift the foreleg, holding the bent knee against his own, and using a nail to grind out pebbles and manure from the hoof. One hoof done. No comment.

'You seem not quite yourself, Peter. You seem … different.'

'I'm alright, my lady.'

Two hooves done.

'But Peter – since we became a family again – after Cyprus – it is as though something sits upon your shoulder.'

Three hooves.

'You weren't hurt in Toulon, were you?'

The fourth hoof was dropped with a loud scrape and the horse's head arced up.

'No…'

'Did they treat you badly?'

He picked up a wisp and began dragging it over the horse's hide, polishing it. Guy's mount, Aelf, was a dark brown rouncey – nothing flashy, just competent and like all our horses, a mannered temperament.

'Peter?'

'I was treated like any prisoner, my lady. I was fed, housed and made to work.'

Jesu, how is that any different from here? Do you consider this *a prison?*

'And that is all?'

'Aye…' The answer came so swiftly I knew he must have been lying. He continued, 'I was left on my own a lot. I was in a cell on my own, I was set to work on my own…'

'No chains, no beatings?'

'No beatings, no.'

Chains?

He finished Guy's horse, led it to its stall and led my own mount out. The mare was nothing grand – brown, serviceable and thick of leg, but with a smooth stride and a sweet manner and I called her Thea. Like everything in our lives, nothing stood out to attract attention, least of all our horses and this horse could hardly compare with my beloved Khazia, but she was gentle like Sister Thea of Saint Eadgyth's and there are worse names. Peter began brushing her thickening winter coat. Truly, as I spoke to him, it was like getting blood from a stone and I wished I had my husband's salt-charming skills.

'So you were kept prisoner and not punished or damaged in any way?'

Surely if they took you prisoner because you tried to defend the family, they believed you had done something to offend them or their beliefs. Either that or they had a plan…

He shrugged. 'The worst thing of all was being apart from Gwenny and the young master. My lady, I can see you're uneasy. They was Templars who kept me under lock and key. If they did anything bad at all, it was not to believe me when I said I was a good-living, innocent man. Seems they thought otherwise and decided my soul needed saving.'

Incarceration creates its own wounds and Peter was not immune. I tried to get deep beneath his skin.

'They took you prisoner because you thwarted them in Genoa, fighting them. Even so, they captured you all and sent Gwenny and William to Cyprus to use them as leverage with me. Using them, Peter! Using you. They proceeded to put pressure on Gwen that if she let me know anything at all about my past life as I tried to regain my memory, her mother and yourself would be killed. She was meant to turn my mind in a certain way. It was beyond cruel…'

'Aye. If you look at it like that.'

'Did you realise that those knights in Cyprus were from the same cadre as the knights in Toulon, and headed by Sir Robert Halsham?'

He flushed again. 'Aye. It were obvious...'

'You see, Peter, I find it hard to believe they just left you alone without a purpose.'

'But they did, my lady,' he stopped brushing. 'They left me for days and nights at a time. Alone...'

Solitary. Excluded from contact.

'Peter, you are so loved by us all. As we owe Guillaume of Anjou for saving William's life, so do we owe you and for many years longer.'

'I thank you, my lady,' he said, beginning to lift hooves. In its own way, it was a dismissal.

I could say nothing to draw him out further and I could not upset a man who had been my stalwart protector.

'You must excuse me. I worry, 'tis all. I shall leave you to get on. Thank you, Peter, from the very bottom of my heart for being who and what you are.'

As I left I thought I heard him speak. I thought he muttered *'Guillaume of Anjou!'* followed by a spit, but I kept walking.

Et tu, Peter. Et tu.

Peter hadn't answered my concerns about his time in Toulon at all. Why had they held him prisoner anyway? He was a mere blacksmith, as like to be valuable to them as crumbs on a table. He had said they tried to save his soul and I imagine such a rescue if it happened, would not come cheaply. They would have threatened him first and then withdrawn to let him suffer in his loneliness and when he began to fold, would have bribed him. And in a weakened man, what is the difference between threat and bribe and when does such a man begin to trust and believe his gaoler? Peter was such a simple, steady man. The threat would surely be that they might kill Gwen or William, maybe all of us if he didn't succumb to their wishes.

But what wishes?

This went far deeper than the saving of souls. It was Halsham's men who had held him and they would not tax him lightly. Guy's men had scoured Aquitaine for news of the old woman and massively built young man from Cazenay who had disappeared. Much prying, coins changing hands and eventually Dante had been sent to Toulon with his men. When Peter had been rescued, the Commanderie had been empty and Peter left alone, locked in a cell. An odd thing, although Dante believed the Templars had gone into hiding not long since. Biddy was retrieved from the nunnery's *frater* in the centre of Toulon where she cooked, her life bearable if insular and she told us much about her time there, making us laugh with how often she broke the House's rule. There was none of the introverted torment for her that I saw in my blacksmith's eyes. I needed to talk with my husband, if I could ease him from Guillaume's side, as the man from Anjou had aroused something in Peter that disturbed him and so close to his marriage to my maidservant, it seemed wrong.

Reaching the top of the stair, I glanced out to the yard. Gisborne had gone, leaving Guillaume sitting in the weak sunshine, his head against the wall, eyes closed and hands clasped across his thin body. He reminded me of a volcano – like *Mongibello* in Sicily that smoked with incipient threat. Further away, the guards still worked, weapons now in a gleaming line, saddlery being buckled together. I hurried to the kitchen where Biddy, returned from market, was cutting vegetables with the dull clunk of blade against wood.

'Biddy, is there something sweet to be had?'

Her brows creased, a deep line at the bridge of the nose. I could imagine her wanting to ask why.

'*Gaylede?*' She held out the bowl in knotty fingers.

I loved the almond-filled dried figs, had been known to sneak a few in the purse at my waist – a sin I couldn't be bothered confessing. I took the pottery bowl and hurried out the door, back down the stair and into the yard, my purpose to right wrongs.

Guillaume had disappeared and Toby and William could be heard singing inside the house. Somehow I suspected our minstrel was longing for William's rest time, the shrillness of the child's voice suggesting it was not long away. From the guards' quarters on the far side of the yard, the sound of metal being honed had almost stilled and in amongst the trees that provided us with fruit, I could see bridles hanging in various stages of being re-buckled.

Biddy had dug and planted vegetables and herbs under the fruit trees and such a garden kept the quarters separate from us, so that I rarely saw the guards. Whenever I needed a guard, a situation quite rare because Peter most often escorted me, the same fellow had come on Guy's or Mehmet's orders.

A tall man with curling red hair that flopped wantonly on his forehead, he had a rigid white scar down his cheek and a strong square chin, freckles all over his face. When we rode into the markets, he wore a leather gambeson or a chainlink vest, and his boots were strong leather with a heavy sword hung at his waist. As for the other guards – they were mere shapes across the yard, two brown-headed fellows with hair to their shoulders and one who was lanky with Saxon-fair hair.

The redhead and one of the darker men saw me approaching and hastily stood, surprise ringing in the air as loud as the sword that Red knocked from the trestle table at which they had been working. He bent hastily, picking it up and saying, 'My lady...'

'Please sit, I don't wish to disturb you for long.' I lay down the bowl of *gaylede*. 'I brought some sweets from the kitchens...' I took a breath, '...as an apology. I have never made the effort to acquaint myself with you since you have been with us. It is not the kind of thing of which I am proud. Please tell me your names and from where you are come.'

From inside the guardhouse, I could smell some sort of herb-loaded stew and smoke issued from the side-hung chimney.

They eat away from us, sleep away from us ... live away from us.

I did not mean to use this as an excuse for not meeting them but they had been grey shadows in the distance and I had been engaged in domestic affairs.

That is no excuse!

Red's face had creased – a perplexed frown pulling at the scar on his cheek. 'I'm Adam, my lady. From outside London.'

'Adam, I am pleased you are with us and offer you thanks for escorting me as you have done.' My gaze shifted to his companion who was strong and broad-shouldered and I suspected that he had been an archer at some time. He had a beard that he had clipped into brutal submission and his grey eyes invited no fools to sit with him.

Noted.

'Johannes,' he dropped his head politely. 'From Lübeck.' His accent was strongly Germanic but he spoke clearly.

'Johannes, I have heard that Lübeck is a pretty place. Perhaps you can tell me about it when you have time.'

'An honour, my lady,' and the head dipped again, a scar along his temple shining proud and a damaged ear tip showing as his hair parted.

'The others, Adam, are they at their duties?'

He put fingers to mouth and whistled an ear-piercing sound that sliced the air like the sharpest dagger. 'Beggin' your pardon, my lady,' he said.

I could hear stools scraping and the guardhouse door flew open, two men running out with swords at the ready.

I jumped back in shock. Not because of the advancing men, but because of the sight before me.

'John!'

I could barely believe it. In front of me with his most perfect face was Pretty Boy, or Young John as I preferred to know him – carefree deft sailor, occasional nun and a partner of my headstrong, headlong voyage across the Middle Sea to Paradise and Hell.

'My lady,' he said, bowing, his hair fairer than ever, his face tanned and stubbled where once there had been baby-smooth skin.

'Well you know John,' said Adam drily. 'And this other chap is Walter. Tell my lady where you're from…'

He too bowed and as his long hair fell round his nape, he reached to grab it with a hand missing a little finger. A purple scar laced from his wrist beneath the sleeve of his tunic and I needed no more proof that these men were veterans of many a skirmish.

'I'm from Moncrieff, madam.'

'No … surely…' I studied his face, but what would *I* remember? I had been in the midst of a tempest on my return to Moncrieff and the only guards I ever saw were de Courcey's handpicked men – more often I was surrounded by my handmaids, my godmother, my priest and Ulric. Once again the guards had been chainlink grey shadows on a wall.

'Do you hear news from Moncrieff?' I asked.

But how could he? *I* would know more from the sporadic missives from Ceci and Brother John and besides he could probably not read. As if to underline it, he shook his head and I resolved to ask Brother John about his family.

I gestured to the *gaylede*. 'I come with a peace offering…' Honesty was needed if I was to bind these men to my side. I had learned a lesson at the Arsenale – one that had taught me how important it was to have a loyal force behind us wherever we were. 'I have ignored you…'

'My lady,' Adam broke in. He seemed to be the spokesman, perhaps the captain of the guard. 'You must not fret. Begging your pardon, but our pretty-faced John here has told us what you've been through and in truth, we knew there was nought to worry about. He says you aren't a deliberate person.'

John coloured and I said, 'Then I am glad to have the advantage now of names and faces and I look forward to you meeting Sir Guy's young son more properly…'

'Beggin' your pardon, my lady,' interrupted John, 'but Master Gisborne knows us well. He calls Adam Rufus after the Latin – well Rufuth really. Toby told him…' The colour that flooded John's face after this pronouncement was so red he could have been named Rufus himself!

I burst out laughing. 'I stand admonished, John. Even by my own son who has been more hospitable.' I clicked my tongue and sank into a pretty curtsey. 'Again, I ask your forgiveness for being wayward.'

The men were silent, I suspect not knowing what to say to this odd noble lady, until Adam said gruffly, 'Done, my lady,' clapping his hand down hard on the trestle. 'Now, do you need any of us immediately?'

I shook my head.

'Then we shall store our stuff,' he said, gathering a couple of *gayledes* which he threw into his mouth.

The smell of stew drifted on the damp breeze as I turned and I said, 'One or all of you are good cooks. The stew smells enticing.'

'Ah,' Adam replied. 'That the saints should smile so. No, 'tis Biddy who sends down a pan of whatever the house is eating. We just heat it over the fire.'

'You don't think to eat in the house?' I asked. 'We are but a small group, Adam.'

Adam buckled the cheek strap of his bridle and shook it out. 'We can not my lady. We are most often two on, two off. Better to be here as we are needed and getting our victuals as when. Kind of you to say, though.'

'Then I am glad you are content. John, will you attend me back to the house?'

He cast a look at Adam who nodded and we walked together, through the fruit trees whose leaves had coloured and almost shed over the past month and past the beds containing hopeful winter vegetables and greens. The day's shadows had crept across the yard as the pallid sun had moved behind grey vapours, promising rain in the evening. Somewhere, I heard a cockerel but in our own yard there were meadow pipits, wagtails and doves and above it all, the call of terns and gulls and the many herons and ducks who fed on the fish and grubs of the reedy waterways.

'Land, John, not the sea?'

He jumped in. 'Oh aye, madam. It seemed the right thing for now and Davey says he'll take me back when Sir Guy's done with me.'

'This was your decision?'

'Aye. I've a lot of respect for Sir Guy, yourself and Master Gisborne.'

'Then I have to tell you how glad I am to have you amongst us. Do you like the other men?'

'Surely, madam. They're good sorts. We laugh as much as I did on the *nef*.'

'Do you think Davey's being honest and observing the laws of the sea?'

He glanced at me from the corner of his eye and tapped the side of his nose. Silence… and then we laughed together.

'Ah, my sailing friend, 'tis so good to have you here.'

'My lady, I thank you.'

'One thing,' I added. 'Have you met your new fellow guard?'

'The man from Anjou? Aye.'

'And?'

'Early days, my lady, but he seems a decent enough man. My lord Gisborne says he's pretty sharp with a bow.'

I stepped onto the stair and turned to John. 'He is that, John. Very. I hope he fits in with you all. Now thank you for answering my questions and I shall see you anon.'

He took a step back, grinned from his divinely sculpted face, turned about and hurried back to his fellows.

I trod on up the stair, happy to have met the men and to have found John. But concerned that Guillaume was so easily inveigling his way into our household and there was still the antipathy between he and Peter that must be resolved. I proceeded to our chamber in a house that dozed. There was no ringing mayhem from William, nor kitchen sounds. I had a chemise to finish stitching and a husband to whom I must speak.

Pushing open the door, I found Guy standing at the table, leaning over a spread-out map. He looked up.

'I have just met our guards…'

He crossed his arms and sat on the corner of the table, the map springing back on itself with a crusty crackle. 'Yes…' The word was drawn out, rumbling forth, a sound I remembered well from the past – as if he waited resignedly for me to admit to wrongdoing.

'Why did you not inform me of who they were?'

'You didn't seem to care about that detail of our life here, Ysabel.'

True. So many times sallying forth alone – but I would not admit to it.

'But Young John. He and I on Davey's ship. We shared so much together.'

'Methinks it's hardly an issue and that you are casting about for *entrée* into something more important. Say and be done.'

You know me too well.

I sighed. 'Guillaume…'

'Ysabel,' he uttered, his brows drawing in.

'And Peter,' I said hurriedly because Guy's expression had begun to harden, impatience pulling the edges tighter. I continued, 'Guillaume has upset Peter in some manner.'

'I doubt it…' He picked up the map and dangled it between his hands.

'Gisborne, Peter is very unsettled today. Uncharacteristically so…'

'He is nervous…' He rolled the map and tied a strip of leather round it, placing it in a chest with others.

'He is not nervous about his marriage. That's something steady and dreamed of in his life. This is something else. When I tried to draw him out about Toulon, he was reticent and then when I left him, he muttered Guillaume's name under his breath and then cursed and spat.'

'You tried to draw him out about Toulon? Why would you do such a thing? He will not talk about his time there at all.' Guy sat on a stool, crossing an ankle over the other knee and holding it, looking up at me. I was surprised that he took me seriously enough this time to sit and listen and heartened, I continued.

'You will know that more often than not, if I took anyone to the markets with me, I would take Peter. Several times we have seen Templars and Peter would shrink, his face whitening.'

'And what prompted this, do you think?'

'I tried to find out today. But he denies they ill-treated him. Guy, they confined him solitarily for a long time and I think in their way, they may have broken him and I wonder what price he will be forced to pay…'

Guy frowned. 'He is paying a daily price, I think, if you say the sight of Templars so upsets him.'

'Halsham's Templar brothers were the ones who held him prisoner, Guy. You know this. It is hard to imagine they will not demand their piece of flesh.'

'And what would that be?'

Round and round in circles.

'I don't know.' I sat, my legs thrust out in frustration, the leather-slung stool squeaking in protest.

'And where does Guillaume fit into this?'

'Again, I don't know, but I believe he does. Why would Peter utter his name with such disgust? That has never been the kind of man Peter is.'

Gisborne stood, gave me a considering look, walked to the casement and leaned out through the shutters, into the ordinary day. He was quiet and I knew he was thinking. Finally he turned back. I had thought he would dismiss me out of hand, but it seemed not.

'You are more than observant, Ysabel, and I don't take this lightly. However, I think it may require someone more delicate and removed than you or I to investigate more fully. Mehmet perhaps. Has Gwen said anything?'

'She is blissfully naïve.'

'Could she perhaps dig deeper?'

'Gisborne,' I said somewhat scathingly. 'She is his love. She will be his wife. Her duty is to cosset him, care for him, do what he asks of her and not stir the dust. The answer is no.'

'Then why is it, *wife*, that you are so different from what a wife should be?'

'Oh hush. You mock. I would say because my husband has unlocked *most* of his secrets and volunteers information readily.'

'But I needed you to turn the key,' he came to me and tilted my chin. 'Perhaps Gwen needs to turn Peter's. This is actually of import, Ysabel. You have stumbled across something. Halsham, even in death could be feared and if there is the slightest chance brother Templars of his ilk still stalk my family, I must get to the root of the danger and dig it out.'

My heart began to pick up pace.

'So you *do* think William was threatened with forethought.'

Silence.

'Gisborne! Answer me!' I grabbed his hand.

'Calm yourself and I will answer.' His hand began to rub my own gently. 'Yes. I do,' he continued. 'Which is why I am expanding our guard.'

'Jesu, Guy! And you trust Guillaume?'

No response. He moved to the bed, picked up his sword and strapped it on, the jingling of buckles the only sound in a room that had reverberated a moment before with the worst thing I could hear.

'Gisborne! Don't withdraw from me!'

He turned, his face sharper than I wished. 'I have no intention of withdrawing from you, Ysabel. You are very astute, I realised that long ago.'

'Huh,' I muttered, fiddling with my slipper.

He gave a short laugh. 'Listen – in respect of Guillaume, he has done nothing yet which would give me cause to distrust him but I will be alert to everything, you can be sure. And now I must find Toby. We are to meet a courier before dark falls.'

He left me with a sense of reassurance and unease dancing together in a bizarre *carole*. I also remembered words I was sure he had uttered long ago: *'Your friends you keep close by your heart. Your enemies you keep close by your hand.'*

Gwen had left the chemise laid on our bed. It was all but finished, the hems to sew and some braid to attach at the neck and wrists. A pedlar had confronted me with ribbons and braids one day at the markets and my eye settled on a white length with silver phoenixes woven into its threads. When he handed it to me with grimy fingers and dirt under the broken nails, he had grinned slyly. There was barely a tooth left in his mouth and he asked for a ducat but I beat him down, all the while wondering how such an ill-made pauper could have come across such a piece. Even so, I thought I had paid too much for it until I washed it on returning home, only to find the little roll was almost two ells in length – more than enough to trim my lord's chemise. Thus I set to diligently, determined to finish the garment by Biddy's call to dinner.

William pushed open the door not long after I had finished the first sortie round the neck, his eyes heavy with sleep, Ounthee and Githborne clasped firmly in his hands. 'Where'th Toby, Mama?'

'Gone to the docks with Papa.' I stitched swiftly, small neat stitches – the kind expected from a noblewoman's hand. It was no penance; I loved the feel of fabric and thread.

'I'm hungry,' whined William.

'Then have some fruit from the platter.'

'I don't want…'

'William! Mama must finish this…' I held up the shirt, '… for your father to wear tomorrow. Don't you want him to look like a knight?'

'Yeth…'

'Then while I stitch I shall tell you a story, one that your father told me when we first met. Do you know the one about Fionn and Sadhbh?'

'The magic deer lady that wath chathed by the big dogth?'

'Yes, that's the one…'

'Toby tellth it better.'

'Then,' I frowned at his mood. I had just the other wrist to do and I was done. 'Why don't you see what you can find in that box?' In fact the box held scraps of parchment and slivers of charcoal, not something I wanted anywhere near the silk chemise, but he needed to be occupied. 'Will you draw me something?'

He gave a world-weary sigh and sank to the floor after putting the carved horses on the table and telling them to be *good hortheys.*'

He picked up a sliver of charcoal and began to draw in a naïve fashion – a man and a bow and a figure as big as dog but which I hoped was a horse as there was something menacing in the thought that the image provoked. The last stitch slipped into place, I oversewed twice and bit the thread. 'That is excellent, William. Do we have a knight? Perhaps Arthur the King?'

'No, thilly, itth Guillaume! Thee hith bow? And thatth Tanti. He wath brave too, biting the menth.'

The needle pricked my finger, drawing blood.

A valiant man in the eyes of a child…

I could not alter his view because the one thing standing between a young boy's wild adventure and unmitigated terror was that man.

'Do you like Guillaume, William?'

Your names are the same – did you know?

'Yeth!' he nodded vigorously and then jumped up, all sleepiness and moodiness forgotten, standing tall with an imaginary bow, nocking an illusory arrow and releasing it, then shouting when it hit its bloody mark.

From the kitchens, Biddy crashed a ladle against a pan like a call to arms.

'I'm hungry!' William yelled and ran out the door before I could stop him. I listened to the silence of the room – childish echoes lessening and then gone. Laying the chemise on the bed, I smoothed the silk and then smoothed it again, folding it and laying it in Gisborne's chest atop the dark tunic he would wear on the morrow. Leaving the door wide, I left to join the others at table.

Mehmet was there and I sat next to him, unsurprised at the absence of Gisborne and Toby. So often we were without one or more of our number at the table that we took it in our stride. And our newly made 'friend' of yesterday was now eating with the guards. Biddy chatted non-stop about the market and Mehmet and I let her gossip run over us until she piped up.

'And they say Richard the King is in Ragusa or Lambi.'

I sat up.

So close, too close.

My fear of Richard needing Gisborne by his side increased with every league closer to us that my cousin covered.

'Where did you hear that?'

'At the markets, my lady. Seems the Pisans know quite a lot!'

She rattled on and Gwen played games with William to encourage him to eat more of the sardines we all loved. Peter went to the kitchens to fetch a platter of fruit and *gaylede* and I took the moment to speak quietly to Mehmet.

'If the Pisans shout such things from the rooftops, I can't see the point of coded messages by ship to Gisborne.'

'True, but what messages Sir Guy receives and imparts are not necessarily what the Pisans are saying.' He clicked his tongue. 'King Richard has certainly backed himself into a blind space...'

For the hundredth time I wondered why Mehmet stayed within a Christian house, not returning to the Holy Land to serve the might of Saladin. I had said as much in the past and he replied, 'I tired of the Holy Wars, my lady, and old age grabs at my *thawb* each day. If I can choose to lead a life in a gentle house, it is a heaven-sent existence.'

'Gentle!' I had laughed with no little irony.

'Yes, well ... with people I am fond of, then. And you forget, there are many like me, citizens without borders who work for Sir Guy.' He gave me a knowing look, his eyes filled with wisdom. 'Perhaps in reality we all work to break down distinctions between believers of faiths, rather than to build such barriers.'

And I had said to him, 'How I wish that were true,' recalling the news that Richard and Saladin had great respect for one another, swapping gifts and paying compliments. But Pope Celestine and almost all of Europe was convinced by Phillip of France and Holy Roman Henry that Richard had *consorted* with Saladin, threatening Christian Europe's right to possess Jerusalem. From that moment on, Richard's problems resembled the story of the plague of locusts – insidious and multiplying until his life was a misery. I could only begin to imagine Eleanor's anger at her son being treated so.

I played with my knife, turning it over and over on the table. 'Richard, as everyone knows, is his own worst enemy, Mehmet. It's just a shame he drags so many others into his tawdry life.'

'Indeed. But if it wasn't Richard that Sir Guy must support, then it would be someone else. Better someone you know well than not, surely?'

'I suppose. But Richard has so many enemies, and as Sir Guy informed me, those enemies by their nature become *our* enemies.'

Mehmet laid his hand over mine and withdrew the knife, which I hadn't realised I had begun to jab into the table. I followed his gaze as he looked up, noticing that Biddy had gone to the kitchens, no doubt to chivvy Peter, and that Gwen had taken William outside. 'You are thinking of yesterday's incident, aren't you?' he said.

'Yes. I had thought Venezia would be safe but we have had a bare year here and already trouble stalks us again.'

'You do not think yesterday was just a coincidence?'

'No and neither do you. Honesty is best, dear Mehmet. And in fact neither does Sir Guy. We are under threat and I wonder if it will ever end.'

At that moment, Biddy walked in. 'Well I really don' know what's got inter that great lump of a blacksmith. He's just disappeared, and right in the middle of dinner too.'

See. Something is so very wrong with Peter.

'Biddy, do you not think he is as nervous about tomorrow as any other prospective husband?' Mehmet was laughing. 'I think we should all give him leeway and maybe put a big jug of wine by his bed this night.'

At least Guillaume would be sleeping in the guardhouse, leaving Peter to pull himself together, but wine would do nothing to ease whatever had begun to grow inside him. In the yard, William's voice had risen to laughs and shouts and Toby's voice answered back. Toby flew in ahead of my maelstrom son, saying, 'I have to eat first, William. I need my dinner!' Guy followed on their heels, his hand at the purse at his waist.

'Sit you down and I shall fetch you some food,' said Biddy, reappearing in moments with baked fish, fried sardines, warmed bread and a large plate of steaming field roots and leaves. The men set to and ate as if they starved, William walking round the table singing nonsense and me sitting thinking how much I loved *this* type of chaos to yesterday's.

I caught Gisborne's eye, lifting my eyebrow questioningly. He frowned slightly, shaking his head and my spirits so lately raised by the sight of my family being normal at our table, took another dive to my boots.

Bad intelligence lay in Gisborne's purse and I kicked my toe against the table leg.

Chapter Four

The dusk had crept in surreptitiously whilst we were at table, the birds loathe to sing, a mist curling from the waterways through open doors and shutters. Biddy demanded everything be shut and a fire lit in the great fireplace against the wall.

Gwen had found Peter in the stables tending to Toby and Sir Guy's horses and it seemed a good enough reason for him not to have returned from the kitchens with our fruit. I bade Gwen make sure he was as warm as the horses, that he must light his own fire. The hall, kitchen, our own room and William's had fireplaces, chimneys side-hung to the house, additions made long past the original Roman construction. I was glad as I hated smoke filling chambers so that hair and clothes smelled, eyes stung and bouts of coughing hacked and spluttered round the house. I would rather stack a bed with furs and blankets than reek of a peasant hovel all day. We had yet to experience a cruel winter in Venezia, our previous one leading from a state of moderate cool to a gentle spring, comfortable summer and autumn. I thought winter in Venezia must surely be no worse than England where we sank knee-deep into snow the minute we opened our doors.

William lay in Biddy's lap sucking his thumb, a vestige of infancy, as she spindle-spun wool over the top of him, his eyelids heavy as he watched the mesmeric gyration of the spindle. Toby and Mehmet played chess, speaking quietly in Latin, the light hovering over their cuts and bruises. Gwen had not returned from the stables again and the lack of propriety did not concern me – they had spent more time together over the last two years than a married couple and under great strain, and if it smoothed Peter's ripples, who was I to demur?

How different this household was to houses of my past. All of us existed on an almost equal footing it seemed, because shared trials and tribulations are great levellers. There was of course, still deference to Guy or myself but the same equality most often touched us all. If we ever returned to the shores of England, I wondered what would become of status then. Would forelock tugging be resumed?

It was not a comfortable thought.

Outside, two or three of our guards would be patrolling whilst the rest ate Biddy's food or perhaps played at dice in front of their own fire. I sat working at a tapestry, a small piece, the woollen thread growling through the fabric whilst Gisborne slouched, legs stretched out, staring deep into the fire's flames. I watched him surreptitiously, trying to imagine what he must be thinking. I decided there could be two veins – one led to Richard the King, the other to Guillaume of Anjou and neither set my mind at ease. His elbows rested on the carved arms of his chair, his hands forming a steeple, the tips touching almost pursed lips. His breathing was deep and steady so I guessed he plotted and planned with the skill for which he was known and I wondered if he would impart the results of such scheming to me.

Biddy left, carrying William who was asleep and Gisborne stirred, drawing in his legs.

'*Eschec*!' uttered Mehmet, clicking his queen down on the board, the winning call concluding the game.

'*Scaccomatto*? Holy hymns and harmonies, Mehmet! I'll beat you tomorrow, I swear it!'

Gisborne and I exchanged a glance because for all our time in Venezia, Mehmet had not lost a game and I admired Toby's persistence without doubt. Mehmet packed away the pieces in a drawstring pouch and placed the board under his arm, nodding to us and wishing us a good night. Toby saluted and hurried along beside the taller chess champion.

The fire crackled and spat as it died down and I took the opportunity to broach my ongoing concerns with my husband. 'I presume you spoke to Mehmet about Peter?'

'Yes. He will talk to him when the right occasion presents itself. With that, you must be content and so must I. Mehmet can judge a man's state of mind and how to treat it.'

'But time is surely of the essence if it connects to Guillaume or Halsham…'

Or both.

'I would agree but I have to trust Mehmet. I would not push Peter to his limits. We owe him more than that. And it would perhaps make us no better than the Templars who may have broken him in the first place.'

'You think he *has* been broken?'

'I don't know. I have not seen him as you have, but if what you say is true then he is not the Peter we know. But enough for now.' He stood and stretched. 'Shall we to bed, wife? A busy day awaits.'

He referred of course to the wedding. We both owed Gwen and Peter so much – more than could be paid for by the cost of a marriage and its parts. Peter had deflected attention from Gwen, William and Biddy, had guided them, fed them, sheltered them until they were safely within the confines of Linn. And nothing had changed. The big, quiet man had been the rock upon whom we all leaned so often, particularly William who treated Peter as a most favoured uncle, especially since the death of Ulric. And Bridget and Gwen? I could face the wrath of God with them at my back. As for caring for William? They were more surrogate mothers than aunts in my son's mind.

I had offered them their freedom in Cazenay, saying they could leave at any time and they said almost as one, 'No, this is our home.' But of course things had changed drastically since Cazenay and I had not repeated my offer. Perhaps I was afraid they may leave, and that would have broken William's and my hearts.

So the best we could do was pay for clothing for the wedding day, grease the palm of the priest, pay for wines and a cook to prepare the feast as Biddy must surely be free to be the bride's mother. Gisborne had purchased a bed, a plain wooden one with a good mattress and blankets and I had bought linens. I had secured two fine horn lamps with good beeswax candles and a coffer big enough to store their clothes. After the marital chamber had been finished, I gave Peter a carved cross that a relic seller had palmed off, saying it had a sliver of the True Cross inserted in the joins. I doubted it but Peter hung it above the bed. It irked me to think Guillaume of Anjou had lain in that special bed before the wedding and I was thankful the linens had not yet been bestowed.

In our own bed, Gisborne took my hand, pulling me to him and holding me quite firm.

'The news is ill, Ysabel. King Richard's boat, the one my men believe was his, appears to have been swamped and sunk somewhere close near Ragusa…'

I struggled. 'Tommaso. What about Toma? Oh, poor Toby! He behaved as if nothing was awry…'

'He is philosophical. Says it is part of the job of a spy, but more so he says he is a twin, the closest brotherhood, and he would know if his brother was dead and he says not.'

'He has spoken of the connection before. Jesu but I hope he is right.'

'Indeed. But that aside, I have to be objective. There are no signs of bodies, nor much wreckage and I would say that God still protects the King. I have to go… No, ssh, ssh. If Richard and his men are ashore, I must find them or find word of them.'

I pulled away from him, climbing from the bed and pulling a fur around me. 'God forsaken King! Because of him Toma might be dead. And what of de Turnham? Gisborne, *why* do you need to go? For England you think? I doubt the country cares any more than I do unless Eleanor has pleaded his cause and ceased John's excesses. Or perhaps you think it is for any of those who inhabit his dukedoms? I would think they would be as happy with Phillip of France as their liegelord as Richard of England who emptied *tresories* in the pursuit of wargames.'

'You are harsh. Ysabel, the King is my liegelord,' said Gisborne. 'I am the King's man, his *espie*…'

'Gisborne, our son was kidnapped yesterday and three men were killed. We are under siege. You must excuse me if I think that our needs are greater than my god-cousin King's.' My fingers worried through my hair as I spoke.

'I have no option, Ysabel,' Gisborne stepped out of bed, his voice rising. 'Do you think I want to go? Christ, don't be ridiculous! But if I wish to see my son with any sort of legacy I must protect the King and by so doing, secure an inheritance for William. I am loyal to the throne of England, even though it sticks in my throat to think I must waste time searching for a man who brought this upon himself but I *have* to go.'

I faced him, crossing my arms and hugging the fur close. 'Who do you take with you?'

'Toby and Adam.'

'You leave *Guillaume* here?' My voice sharpened more than I wanted it too, it would only anger him further. 'Knowing my antipathy?'

'Then you shall have to show maturity, won't you?' His tone had a honed edge to it. 'You will accept what I say. Guillaume's excellent weapon-skill makes him more suited than anyone to protect you. Besides, Adam knows the marshlands around Aquileia from his mercenary days and I need him with me because I suspect that is where we may pick up Richard's scent.'

I remained unconvinced and silent and Guy softened.

'I am leaving you John as well. You know him and trust him. And there will be Johannes who is an archer and swordsman of great skill. Ysabel, I leave a superior force for you. In addition you will have Mehmet to make critical decisions, and, Peter's inner problems aside, with his height and bulk, the man will provide tremendous physical strength should it be needed. You must not complain.' He came to me, drawing my arms around him so that the fur fell away. 'All will be well.'

But I had heard that before in my life and was little comforted as we climbed back into our bed. Sleep was haphazard and at cockcrow I stirred, aware of a heavy feeling on my shoulders. In the past year I had been used to Gisborne's absences – never happy, never that, but I managed, believing he was merely sourcing information, not courting danger. This time, I felt as if a malfeasant sat by my side, grinning at me, waiting, biding his time to attack either my husband or my family.

Trust, Ysabel. Trust the men he has given you.

The bell for Sext was chiming from the little stone church as we made our way to its panelled, closed door. Unlike the clangour of cathedral bells, this one rang like a high-pitched alarum and I had to remind myself it was for a marriage.

Gisborne had promised a substantial payment to the priest because we were asking for a marriage to be performed during Advent, a proscribed period. The church lay far on the outskirts of Venezia, away from the disapproving eyes of church hierarchy. It suited us too, to be removed from the public. A marriage ceremony is obvious to all and we would draw a small crowd regardless but none in this corner would know us and it was deemed as safe as it was possible to be.

Gwen wore her new gown – our gift – a field green symbolising love. She could hardly wear blue for purity, having shared many a night with Peter. But she wore my mother's diaphanous veil with her hair flowing down her back for the last time, as was the tradition. On her head was a small circlet of *rosmarinus officinalis* and she had not stopped smiling since we began our promenade across the islets and bridges of Venezia.

Peter wore a fine linen chemise, more gifts from his liegelord, a dark green tunic and brown hose, new leather boots and a fine studded belt. His hair, kept short since Toulon, had been freshly trimmed and he had shaved his face, leaving a small cut on his chin. His gaze remained on Gwen, and Bridget presided over them like a mother hen, her chin straining from her wimple and wobbling like a hen's wattles.

We stood at the steps of the church, the priest in questionably clean cassock, William swinging around off my grasping fingers, Johannes and John at our backs. Guillaume, Walter and Adam waited at our home with Mehmet who had also stayed behind. He believed, rightly so, that at a Christian church, a Saracen in his robes would stand out like an enemy banner, drawing even more unwanted attention to our group.

The priest began, *'Venistísne huc sine coactióne, sed líbero et pleno corde ad Matrimónium contrahéndum?'* William swung more, stretching and straining my fingers until Gisborne grabbed him as he whirled around, hissing at him to stop. There was a moment of rebellion until Gisborne swung him up onto his shoulders like any other commoner might do with their child. My husband wore a faded black tunic, his leather gambeson over the top – leather that was scratched and slashed from a hundred vengeful encounters. As his lowborn wife, I wore a pale crimson *bliaut*, plaiting and knotting my hair underneath a wimple and veil in the manner of a matron, which should have made me laugh…

Instead, something dark and savage stared at my neck – pinpointed at the base of my skull. Like the whisper of an arrow as it speeds to kill. My fingers reached to rub underneath my veil and I would swear that they might have touched icy drips beginning to trickle down my spine.

Don't turn round. Don't…

But who would not?

As the priest intoned endlessly, I edged round, sweeping the small paved area on which we stood, sure that I would see someone staring back.

There! Over there!

My heart stopped.

Nothing.

'Mama, Gwenny'th got a ring!' William's voice pierced my nerves and I turned back to the church steps as Peter slid a beaten gold slip of a ring onto the third finger of Gwen's right hand. Man and wife then waited whilst the priest pushed at the squeaking doors to lead us all to Mass before the altar. We filed into a dank, small space ready to have our souls saved and I breathed a sigh of relief that we were safe thus far.

Safe!

Some peasants from the outlying area had joined us in the church, a chance to be absolved of any sin, the smell of bad breath, body odour and incense drifting amongst the wooden benches that served as pews. William sat quietly, looking around and grinning at people he didn't know, his heels occasionally drumming against the wood of our seats. Candles burned and smoked and we lifted our voices in the responses, a small breeze blowing from the door down the nave to the altar. The flames of the candles dipped and dived, two fading entirely and I confessed to God that I was cold and weary after the previous night, and for Him to forgive me for wishing the priest would hurry and conclude. And then, swiftly, God be thanked, it was over and there was no reason to dally.

The priest approached Gisborne who had a small bag ready and then we were on our way back to the villa. To anyone watching we were a disparate group of very ordinary people – five men, three women and a child. Peter and Gwen held hands like young lovers and Biddy beamed, her happiness palpable.

'I'm content,' she said to me. 'I am content.' To me those words implied that her own family had been solidified and no matter what eventuated she and her daughter were safe under the care and consideration of Peter. That they all depended on Gisborne was a given of course, but in Biddy's eyes the familial circle had been closed as the ring was slipped onto Gwen's finger. It was a wonder I had not heard Biddy sigh with relief when it was done.

Guillaume opened the gates for us but I was too busy chastising an overexcited child to notice what Peter's reaction may have been and presently we were climbing the stair to the dining hall, the smell of roast pig and poultry, of cooked onions and spices, of bread fresh baked all filling the air. Mehmet stood at the door, reaching to clap Peter on the shoulder and bowing over Gwen's hand whereupon she blushed as if she had dipped her face in a dye pot. It made me laugh.

'Fair you well, Peter?' our physician asked and winked, and I would bet a ducat that the wink was to soften any concerns Peter might have of being pressured. I suspected too, that in his own way, Mehmet was manoeuvring gently under Peter's skin.

'Oh aye, Master Mehmet, sir. T'was meant to be between Gwen and I and it's only happenstance that we didn't wed long since. Now we can get on with our own lives.'

My ears pricked up like a horse's when it senses a sound far off. *'Happenstance'* effectively meant everything my precipitate life had done to drag him away from his former ordered existence. But that aside, I had never thought that since we came to Venezia, his life was any less his own than mine was my own. He must surely remember that he had been offered his freedom. I began to feel a weight settling deep inside – that I had taken Peter too much for granted. I think if he and Gwenny hadn't been so devoted to William, nor caring deeply for Bridget, they may well have left long since. It perhaps wasn't loyalty to Moncrieff or Gisborne, it was loyalty to a little boy that tied them here.

Think on this later, Ysabel. Talk with Mehmet.

I shook my head, determining that at this moment I mustn't pick at straws, fixing instead on Gwen and Peter's smiles and with increasing noise from our group, we filed in to eat, drink and be merry. My spirits lifted as I saw Saul and Ariella waiting for us and William's shriek as he spotted Tanti could have lifted the tiles from the roof.

Our festivities began with raised voices, happiness, a dog barking and much wine and food disappearing. Biddy, her cheeks rose-red, eyes glazed, gave the visiting cook her seal of approval, her hand waving as if she bestowed a royal honour. A wave of laughter flowed down the table as she sat like our family matriarch or some grand potentate. Even Peter grinned, any troubles vanishing in the joy of the moment.

Gisborne stood and as in the best houses, the noise dwindled and all eyes settled on the lord of the manor. None more so than my own as he complimented the new wife, wished the husband many years of connubial bliss at which the dye pot seemed to be shared by both Gwen and Peter, and then gave them his blessing for a God-protected future.

To my surprise Peter stood as Guy sat, begging his lord's pardon and offering stammering thanks to everyone for this day. 'And for…' he stopped as if he had forgotten what he wanted to impart, his swinging gaze halting for a moment on William but then continuing to Gwen who sat nodding her head encouragingly. Heartened, he finished quickly, 'For everything, Sir Guy.' He sat with a thump, throwing back a vast mouthful of wine.

More laughter and slapping of hands on table, Tanti barking with William cheering in his childish way as he stuffed bits of candied fruits into his mouth.

'A song, a song,' called Biddy. 'Come, Toby – sing for us!'

Tobias leaped up with alacrity, always happy to be the minstrel. A forgivably vain man, he'd cast aside his dull peasant's wear on returning to our house, in favour of black velvets and silks as becomes a troubadour of note. To whistles from the men, Mehmet making a strange ululating sound with his tongue and we women clapping, he began with a gentle little ditty of love and devotion. Then with a quick strum of chords he changed to a dance tune and our feet tapped, William cantering round the table until Ariella swept him up into her arms to dance with him. We all joined in – Peter with Gwen, Biddy and Mehmet, Saul and Tanti.

And myself and Gisborne.

For me there was no one else in the room. His eyes met mine and melded, our bodies joined and parted, his hands light, always touching – such sensation in the fingertips that my heart beat like a tabor. I twisted around him, curling beneath his arm, the steps of the *carole* rhythmic, echoing the chords of the *vielle*.

Toby took the rhythm and melody away from us then, straight into a witty little song, and I felt as if a rope had been cut and me marooned in a current that I couldn't swim against. Gisborne must have seen the insecurity on my face and bent to kiss my forehead and I loved him all over again.

We laughed at Toby's choice of words for a song we all knew well and which pinpointed our bride and groom. When he had finished, his fingers kept moving over the strings and he drew breath to begin the next piece. Into that momentary break, a *lyra* plucked in time with his *vielle,* and he looked up in surprise at Ariella, her red hair a brilliant foil for the blue of her gown, no attempt made to conceal that russet glory. Almost as if they could read each other's minds, the music changed tempo, voices synchronous as they plucked, played and sang chords that plaited themselves into a superb harmony. Honey and cream I had called the likely result of their duet if ever it should happen, but this was even better – like golden wine from Candia, the Middle Sea's best – mellow and fluid, intoxicating and spicy.

William had climbed into Biddy's lap, Tanti lying curled asleep at Ariella's feet and my hand crept under the table to weave itself into Gisborne's. The long song told of great beauty and unrequited love with a simple refrain.

Blow northerne wind,
Send thou my swetyng.
Blow northerne wind. Blow ... blow ... blow.

Toby and Ariella alternated the singing of the verses and combined in the chorus until the final verse which they sang together.

For hirë love in slep I slake.
For hirë love al nicht I wake,
For hirë love mournyng I make more than any other man.

The thought of Gisborne leaving me for an undefined period, looking for a man who may have been dead, filled me with pain and I knew I would not sleep well, grieving and fretting. But I had to swallow my sadness and be Lady Gisborne, a noblewoman in hiding, but one of calibre nevertheless – mother to Master William of Gisborne and lady to a whole household.

Blow northerne wind,
Send thou my swetyng.
Blow northerne wind,
Blow ... blow ... blow.

The vielle and the lyra concluded in a gentle flourish and we showed our pleasure, throwing words of praise towards the musicians. Casting only a flick of an eye at William, Toby began a lewd ditty which served to pull we women to our feet, dragging Gwen by the arm, laughing, down to her new home where the bed had been made with the handsome linens and the horn lamps flickered kindly. We stripped her of her clothing, pulling her hair round her shoulders and urging her under the bedding as the men, William in Mehmet's arms, escorted Peter to the door. His face was ruddy and soft with liquor and it did my heart good to see him so. We should have stayed close to make sure of consummation but it was a custom I despised and the two had spent many a night together previously, so I chivvied us back to the hall to survey the wreckage of our entertainment.

Gisborne and I were adamant that Saul, Ariella and Tanti take advantage of hospitality rather than making their way through the newly arrived winter's night amongst the ruffians of the town, because the Arsenale sat heavily upon us all. Under Biddy's haphazard, wine-infused guidance we arranged for father and daughter to share a small chamber.

William had begun to grizzle, Biddy overcome with tiredness, and so I took him from her, leaving the hall behind with its table of crumbs, crusts and cores. The fire could be fed with all those remains and I thought I would see to it on my return. The household and our guests sat exchanging views and laughter but as my child stirred tiredly on my shoulder I realised that whether they told stories, danced, gamed or even moved to sleep was of no account as I had my son to undress and place in his cot, perhaps singing to him until he slept.

But it was done with speed, William falling asleep immediately, eyes closing, body loose and easy. As I watched this creature of my loins, I realised that if we were ever to return to England or even Aquitaine, he would only be mine but a few years more, then sent away to another noble family to grow and learn about chivalry and war-games.

But far from those *places, Ysabel, he will not.*

Exactly so, I thought. If we never return, if we stay in the Middle Sea, our money invested in commerce, my son can learn a far better trade than war-games. And he can grow legitimately alongside the best teacher of all, his own father – not some baron recommended to us by Richard's courtiers and designed to further a noble ascendancy. We must…

'He is the sweetest child.'

Honeyed was the voice…

'Oh,' I jumped, whispering back, 'Ariella, I didn't hear you.'

'I apologise. I thought to say goodnight to him and let him know Tanti will still be here on the morrow and that I shall bring him back again.'

'Ah well, he sleeps, as you can see. But you will him see him in the morning because I assure you, he is an early riser. Sometimes better than a cockcrow or the bells for Matins.'

'You love your son deeply.'

'When does a mother not,' I replied as we walked from the room, Biddy meeting us in the passage.

'My lady, I'm done in. Will you excuse me if I take to my cot?' Her voice slurred and I forgave her because she deserved to celebrate her daughter's marriage.

'Of course, Biddy, and you must stay abed in the morning. Send William to me as soon as he wakes.'

'But food for the house…'

'We will manage. Come down when you are ready.'

She kissed my cheeks, sloppy kisses smelling of garlic and wine.

'You're a good girl, Ysabel Moncrieff. Lady Alaïs would be proud…'

She trailed away into the chamber, the door shutting behind, and we moved on.

'A unique treasure,' murmured Ariella.

'Indeed. Like William,' I agreed.

All at once I wanted to tell Ariella what I thought, to get another woman's opinion. I told her of William's likely future if we should ever return to England or Aquitaine and how I would prefer to put down roots where we could avoid the strictures of noble society by being unknown and ignored. 'Not Venezia though. It seems we may be known here…'

She did not disabuse me of my thoughts, merely said, 'My father and I thought the same after the Arsenale. But you must talk with your husband. You say he shows interest in Venetian commerce and there is much to be had in the Adriatico and even Constantinople. It may be that he could settle in those places where you are unknown…'

I sighed. 'I have done nothing but run from so many things for so long, Ariella. Even my king has banished me to Aquitaine for…'

'Yes, I know of de Courcey.' She lifted the folds of her gown as we descended the stair. 'Gisborne apprised my father.'

I could hear Toby playing in the hall and someone accompanying him on a flute.

'Ha! Father indulges himself. He plays well, does he not? Tell me, if King Richard originally banished you to Aquitaine to keep his barons content after your attack on one of their own, one must assume that on resuming the kingship of England and his many domains that he may request you return immediately to Aquitaine to serve your time there. Would you allow yourself to be so ordered?'

We rounded the corner of the passage and stopped by a window embrasure, the shutters closed against the cold, a breeze disturbing a cobweb stretched across the corner. Its torn filaments fluttered like a moth's wings.

'I tell you honestly Ariella, I care little for what he says and does, except when it affects my family. So in answer to you – no, I would not go. I would run far with William to prevent him being taken from me. So far that no one could ever find me.'

'Not even Sir Guy?'

I was about to answer when I thought I heard footsteps and I turned, expecting Biddy to tap me on the shoulder, but there was no one. Would I run and leave Guy behind? Of course not. But I would never return to Aquitaine with our son, and I hoped I could talk rationally with my husband about it.

'I would never leave Gisborne, Ariella. Never.'

She said nothing more and we entered the dining hall to see the men lounging round the fire, haunting melodies between *vielle* and flute drifting on the air like the torn cobweb. I reached for Ariella's arm, holding her back. 'I can never repay you for what you did for us in the Arsenale.'

She smiled, her tawny eyes dancing, the cressets catching the lustre of her hair. 'But you and I are equal now, Lady Ysabel. There *is* no debt at all. Did you forget you kept my male minstrel identity secret? Or that you persuaded my father to take me with him to the foreign markets? So you see?' She reached forward and kissed me on the cheek. 'No debt.'

I knew then that in whatever capacity I wished to engage, Ariella would be a trusted friend and ally and I was heartened.

The horses snorted in the weak drizzle that drifted down. Beyond the walls there was nothing but a mist twisting about and smelling of the odours of life by the water – muddy shingle, brackish water and what rolled in and out in the tides because today, Venezia shared its most unlikeable and rank qualities along its waterways. All that was malodorous hung in the air, determined to make this day of departures despicable. How I wished for a stiff breeze from the sea to clear the air and my mind.

Toby was sitting on the steps telling William an heroic tale no doubt designed to lessen the impact of his and Gisborne's leaving. But, I thought, he could tell me the story of Odysseus or even the story of Arthur the King from Galfridus Arturus, and such heroism would never ease my heart.

Adam tightened girths, Gisborne speaking with Johannes and Mehmet; that he gave them last minute instructions for our ongoing safety I had no doubt. He called to Guillaume and the tall archer loped from the gates, meeting Gisborne halfway. Gisborne put his arm across the man's shoulder and the two walked away, Gisborne speaking earnestly and Guillaume nodding.

So familiar, Guy. Why do you treat him so?

Biddy stood by my side as I juggled three filled costrels. She had fleshy pouches beneath her eyes, looking her age and more. Despite being dressed, she was possessed of a crumpled veil and a wimple that needed care. A few grey hairs escaped at her temples.

'Biddy! I said to stay abed.'

'And miss farewelling young Tobias and Sir Guy? Never.'

'Tis very kind and will be remembered,' I said, laying the costrels by my feet and hugging her close.

Guy had finished his conversation with Guillaume and had walked back to the horses, nodding at Saul and Ariella as if to say *'Thank you. I know I can rely on you.'* He opened his saddlebags, checked and then buckled them closed again, rubbing the horse between the ears before climbing the steps as the bells rang for Terce.

Please do not go yet. A whole empty day with you gone and more to come...

'Tis time, Ysabel.'

'Yes...' I handed him his costrel.

Biddy, for once tactful, moved away to stand with Peter, Gwen and William who was filled with woe. To lose his adored father was a pain he could not understand, but to say adieu to his partner in play, Tobias, was more than he could bear and there would be tears in moments, I was sure.

Gisborne held out his arms and I slipped into the warm circle, pressed against his thick shadowy cloak. Beneath was the gambeson but I wished it had been chainlink and threw a prayer to God to bless it. I could think of nothing to say that hadn't already been said and which would hold him back. I hadn't the opportunity to discuss our future, that we must never return to anywhere dominated by the English throne. That a legacy for William in England would mean little to me or to my son and that a legacy in the Middle Sea was so much more, *so* much more. I hadn't wanted to create tension in my last hours with my husband; wanted him to leave content with me, not heartsore as so often in the past. None of us knew where he would find the King or even *if* he would find him, nor how long it would take. His lips pressed on the top of my head and I lifted my face to meet him, soaking up the sensation like a sponge in water. It was by necessity a chaste kiss in front of the household and he stepped back as William pulled at his cloak.

'Papa.' The blessed child tried so hard not to cry, his bottom lip trembling. 'Pleathe take me with you.'

Gisborne knelt down. 'Next time, William. Whilst Toby and I are gone, I want you to practice your sword and bow. Guillaume will help you...' He looked up at me, the blue eyes darkening. *Don't defy me, Ysabel,'* he was saying. 'And John and Johannes will help you with your riding. By the time I return, you will *be* a young knight, won't you?'

William's eyes glittered with unshed tears. 'Yeth,' he said softly.

'*Then* you shall be my right-hand man because there is no one else. Can you do that?' He held out his hand and William looked at it and then placed his own small one within his father's grasp.

'Yeth...'

Gisborne whispered so that only William and I could hear. 'You are my life, my son. Stay safe and you must do what your mother asks of you. Promise me?'

William sucked in a jagged breath. 'I promith,' he said and bowed stiffly.

Oh William, do not. We are beyond such harsh formality here.

Gisborne pulled him into his arms, holding him tight, two heads touching. It was enough and a tear rolled down my own cheek.

I took William's hand, hoisting him to my hip and kissing his cheek. He buried his face in my neck as Gisborne mounted with a creak of leather and a shifting of the horse's hooves on cobbles. Peter gave Tobias a leg up onto his chestnut rouncey and Adam swung up as if his mount was bareback – a smooth motion intrinsic to the born horseman. I passed Toby his costrel from the steps and he grinned.

'Cheer up, William. I'll be back before you can count to one hundred and we shall have such fun when I do. But listen, *amic*...'

William lifted his head.

'Don't you grow taller than me, huh? That's not allowed.'

William perked up at that; he rather liked that he grew a little taller every day.

Toby clicked his horse on, letting the reins sag as he pushed the costrel into his saddlebag, humming *'Somer is y comin'*, William singing the occasional word.

Bless you, Tobias Celho. An angel you are, a divine angel.

Adam rode up behind and I passed him the last costrel. 'Adam, don't let them take unnecessary risks. The King is not worth their lives nor yours.'

'Aye, my lady. I agree and you can be sure I'll be watching out for them. That said, my lads'll be watching out for you so trust in them and use them. Ain't no good having excellent guards if they're not used. And my lady, if I may say, that goes for the Anjou archer too. He's a handy fellow to have at your back.' He tapped his horse's flanks and the three men rode abreast through the gates, Guillaume pulling both sides open. All of us called our farewells and the yard rang with blessings, arms waving back. William and I ran to the gates and watched them as they filed along the shore, turning onto one of the bridges, the hooves echoing like a blacksmith's hammer.

The grey mist enfolded each one of them and Adam, Toby and Guy disappeared from view as if they had been magicked by Ambrose Merlin. When Gisborne had left in the past, I had leaned against the gates and watched till he crossed the furthest bridge from sight, but this was denied to me today – as though a drawbridge had opened to Hades and then shut swiftly, cutting short my last desperate pleasure and creating a feeling that I might never see him again.

Behind me, Tanti barked and William tugged away from me, his sadness easing at the sight of the dog. Saul and Ariella insisted it was time they returned to their home.

'Phillipus is attentive, but to leave him alone too long invites business problems so you must excuse us,' Saul explained.

'But I have a suggestion before we leave,' said Ariella. 'William, can you come, *libling?*' she called.

He and Tanti came immediately and Ariella knelt, pushing at the dog which jumped and licked.

'*Libling*, if your mama agrees, would you like to have Tanti to stay here for a day perhaps? Maybe two? You would have to look after him as if he were your best friend.'

William's face lit up like a sunrise – all vestige of gloom dissolved by Ariella's offer. He begged me but there was little need – anything to assuage the recent loss and perhaps even more, to ease the blood-soaked events of the Arsenale.

Guillaume opened the gates again and Saul and Ariella departed. Tanti, at a loss, whined momentarily but was chivvied to the kitchens to pilfer food. I lingered in the yard. A sense of emptiness settled on me, as if I doubted I could function without Gisborne. In the past, the knowledge that Gisborne was near was all the spark my tinder needed. But what is tinder to do if there is no spark? The fire remains as dormant as death…

In my heart I knew this absence was like none other. He searched for the King who could be dead, killed by his enemies or if he lived, imprisoned by those enemies. And by their very nature, they would be our enemies. Killing games would ensue and I knew that as with Halsham's obsession with Gisborne, no quarter would be given. The frightening thought was that it wouldn't be expected either.

'My lady?'

I jumped, spinning round to face Guillaume of Anjou, my hand grabbing at the *misericorde* hanging from my girdle.

He glanced at my tense fingers. 'I did not mean to startle you. I have this for you,' he held out a parchment roll tied with leather. 'My lord gave it to me to pass on as he left.'

I recognised the seal – Cecilia Fineux of Upton – and took the letter from him, barely glancing at him as I turned away, a careless thank you thrown over my shoulder.

Cecilia's seal shamed me. The woman herself would be shaking her head and saying, *'Really Ysabel! Methinks Alaïs, your mother, would have raised you to be so much more than that.'*

'Guillaume,' I called in reparation. 'Thank you…'

He nodded, somewhat blank. Perhaps he wondered what I *really* felt.

'I would thank you also, for agreeing to join our household. We are the better for it.'

He grunted. I suspected that he had got my measure and doubted my utterances. 'Your servant, my lady,' he replied, holding his hand to his heart and bowing. 'Do you need me further?'

And thus *he* dismissed *me* with consummate skill and I could hear Cecilia laughing and saying, *'Oh well-played, Guillaume!'* I almost threw the roll in the trough but for the need to hear from my loved godmother – the woman who had supported me through the darkest time.

The corner of the yard under the bare giant fig was quiet. Biddy's garden sat winter pregnant and the birds that had made our home theirs chirruped a cheerful sound in the pewter gloom. William chattered within the villa and Tanti answered. In the stables, Gwenny could be heard, Peter rumbling a reply. Johannes had taken gate duty and John and Guillaume walked back and forth at alternate ends of the furthest reaches of the grounds.

All is well…

I untwisted the strip of leather, cracking open the bee-imprinted wax, watching the flakes flutter as I had done many times before. The parchment unrolled easily and Ceci's writing revealed itself. I held the letter to my nose to catch a fragrance of my godmother or even Moncrieff but there was nothing but the smell of good parchment – a faint animal scent and the odour of pumice or starchgrain. I wondered if Cecilia had sat in my mother's Lady Chamber as she wrote and if Brother John had occupied another chair, idly stroking black Sorcia's ears. By now my hound would be at full height and would sit easily at his elbow.

As if to underline thoughts on canines, William and Tanti dashed past, missing me sitting under the shelter of the fig, and I was not perturbed that they had.

My dearest God Daughter,

I am returned to Upton, windswept, barren but loved place of mine. Your God-Cousin, redoubtable John, despised Prince of the Realm, has assumed right to Moncrieff. *"For the Crown"*, *his sheriff says. I however, should like to know what Eleanor thinks.*

Do not be concerned for the villagers. Brother John is their keeper and he has friends in the strangest places. Neither must you be sad for the loss of your birthright. It must surely be a temporary thing until Richard's return…'

Ah, if only Ceci knew how *little* I cared. I wished I could tell her how it meant nothing, that William's future rested far from England's shores.

And as for Gisborne's Locksley, it has suffered the same fate but I am sure you know this. Gisborne's men would have sent news long since…

Would they? He had said nothing more than that he must protect the inheritance of Locksley for his son, so if he was indeed apprised of this knowledge, he did not share it with me. But again, I really had no care. Locksley could be damned and I would care even less because I was convinced our safest and most prosperous future lay along the eastern reaches of the Adriatic…

There are foul rumours in respect of our King. Of sedition, intrigue, crimes against God. It is time he returned to make matters right – England is unsettled and I do not like it. Thus, my dearest child, I am of a mind to take a retreat…

I sucked in a breath. Ceci in a retreat?

I am a widow of means, I have the time and have already paid my dues at Canterbury. I thought to ask Beatrice of Locksley, as you know my friend of longstanding, if she would allow me to enter her House for a time. I told Brother John I would be an intercessor for anyone who needs it. He says I am ambiguous but knows better than to let the Church stand in my way. In truth, I am lonely and tired, my dear, but enough said.

Lonely and tired. My poor Cecilia. Of course she was lonely – her husband Hugh had died when I was young; my mother, her dearest friend, had died not long since. I was gone from England. She had no children and only Brother John for company. But she was also well loved by villein and noble alike so I suspected something else at play. Would that Mehmet could talk with her.

If I survive the retreat, and I have no reason to think I will not…

If God did not see her safe and sound, I knew she would have a word to say to Him!

…I may make a pilgrinage to Rome one day. And a pilgrimage to you. The very thought of seeing you gives me strength.

I am your loving Godmother.

It was unsigned.

I sat back. Dear Ceci. How I longed to hold her and to sit and talk. The note was dated a month since, so she and England had no knowledge of Richard's most recent shipboard catastrophe. A month since and she could well be in Locksley with the abbess, Beatrice, overseeing her spiritual and temporal care. And for a long moment, I recalled and revelled in the bliss of St. Eadgyth's – of the cloistered calm, the swish of nuns' robes as the women made their way to prayer, of the orderliness and simplicity of life. William's shout disturbed me and quickly rolling the note and slipping it into my purse, I jumped up to see what excited him.

He stood at the far end of the yard with a small bow raised – fitting an arrow, aiming, Guillaume squatting by his side, his arm holding my son steady, a hand pushing the small elbow up. The arrow flew to the straw target, embedding firmly. Another shout, Guillaume smiling broadly, patting William on the back, passing him another arrow. I watched till ten arrows had been loosed, every one finding its way to the mark. William turned to Guillaume, his face alight as he no doubt imagined the moment of joining his father as a proven archer.

He slipped his hand into Guillaume's, looking up at him, devotion writ large. Guillaume called Tanti and the three set off to the target to retrieve the spent arrows.

My stomach lurched as I remembered another such devotion – a man called 'Oowic' who in the end could not be trusted.

CHAPTER FIVE

'Mehmet,' I called as I ran into the house, up the stair and along the passage toward his chamber. 'Mehmet!' I burst in as he stood, a concerned hand reaching for his *janbiyah*.

'My lady, what ails you?'

'Oh. Oh, nothing really,' I said breathlessly as I dragged the letter from my purse. 'Except I have had a note from Cecilia. She enters an abbey for a retreat. She seeks comfort and succour. Mehmet, I had a thought. If we went to an abbey, to a nunnery, we would be out of harm's way. If John and Johannes could take us north, I know we would find sanctuary…'

He reached for my arm. 'Sit down,' he urged, drawing me to a seat. He knew of Cecilia and how important a part of my early life she had been. 'You say "we". Who do you mean?'

'William, me. Perhaps Biddy. We can remove William from danger.' Not once as I spoke did I realise that an old pattern was asserting itself – the desire to run…

'Lady Ysabel, under normal circumstances I am sure Sir Guy would say it was appropriate for you to retreat behind church walls for a time, should you so wish. But we are not in normal circumstances, you must see that.' He bent and took my hand. 'I must counsel you. You are safer here, far safer. Besides, winter begins and the roads will be slow, potentially impassable if you travel north to the mountains. I am sorry, my dear, but it must not be.'

'But Mehmet, think on the Arsenale. And on the change in Peter since Guillaume arrived within the villa. Danger is here, I am constantly alert, as if I feel someone watches us.'

He examined me closely. 'You say? Beyond the walls?'

'No – within. Our walls have surely been breached.' I pulled my hand away as respectfully as I could.

'My dear,' he sat next to me, his white robes pooling around him, his red *keffiyeh* creasing over his shoulders. 'Do you refer to Guillaume?'

I dipped my head, embarrassed that personal dislike should take such a turn.

'Ah. I see you do. All I can say is that I am treating him for wartime maladies and that you must rest easy.'

'And you do not think that Peter's manner, Guillaume and the Arsenale are oddly connected? Because I have thought on it deeply and something about it all scares me.'

'I agree. The incident at the Arsenale raises many worryinging issues. One would be foolish to ignore that. But I tend to think Guillaume was an innocent bystander till he saw young William threatened so heinously. Sadly, on his entry into this house, something about his soldierly experience has upset Peter. Perhaps his very presence reminds Peter of being captured by the Templars. The mind is a labyrinth, Lady Ysabel, and one can only be gentle and understanding.'

I wanted to say to Mehmet that I preferred a calm house where everyone was at ease, but I went to the window and looked out. William laughed as he and Guillaume practised at the butts. I could hear Biddy singing in the kitchens and Gwen calling for her to desist before she frightened the birds away. Johannes and John were patrolling with intent but calmly and it seemed the house was indeed happy, except for two people – Peter and myself – and I had no idea how to remedy the situation.

Mehmet had spoken plainly. The pilgrims' ways afforded us little safety from those who might want to hurt us. Perversely, I also believed the insides of our walls provided no safety but could see no way of convincing the man my husband had left in control of our wellbeing.

''Tis as you say then, Mehmet, we stay. But are we completely immured here? I tell you, it will become as much a prison as Toulon was for Peter. And such constraint *again* for William. It was exactly like that for us in Genoa and I grew heartsick because of it.'

He took up a book from the table and shelved it amongst other wooden-covered volumes. 'It is against my judgement to allow you to venture forth, Lady Ysabel. At least until we have permission from my lord Gisborne to do so.'

'You see? Always a prisoner. Wherever I go with my son, I am always a prisoner. I might as *well* be in a nunnery with William.' God curse it, tears came to my eyes. 'I thought Venezia might be different, Mehmet. I thought we would be safe and could build a life here…'

He scrutinised me closely, brows drawing together and a troubled sigh emerging. 'Perhaps once or twice with guards then, although it goes against my judgement. And if in the meantime we hear from Sir Guy that on no account are you to leave these walls, then so be it.'

A caveat. Always a caveat.

'But you cannot suit yourself, Lady Ysabel,' he continued. 'The sortie must be planned. You *do* see that, do you not?'

I didn't want to agree with him but I knew he was right. I would not lose William to my ill-thought actions. Perhaps at last, I was beginning to grow and so I nodded and thanked him from the bottom of my heart.

'Mehmet,' I said. 'Who do you believe attacked William?'

My question caught him off-guard and he took time to answer it, shifting dried herbs and pots around on the table.

'Please Mehmet…'

He sighed. 'I believe it was Sir Robert's ill-made Templars who instigated it, my lady. There is still a poisonous taint, even since his death, and we must be wary.'

'Jesu, but I hate him. He has done nothing but wound and hurt since the day he crossed my path.' I paced back and forth, the folds of my gown slapping the table legs.

'To continue to hate can blind you to rational thinking, my lady. Because we are dealing with a shadow threat here and we must think clearly and be alert. You have seen what they can do.'

'But why do they threaten us now? I don't understand. Halsham is dead and thus they are without leadership. The Templars proper have disowned them, the Pope has declared them enemies of the Church and they are excommunicated. They stand to gain noth… Holy Christ!' I swung round, realisation illuminating like a candle in the dark. 'Revenge! This is revenge for a leader, all of it. My son was abducted in revenge for Gisborne killing Halsham. Do you think I am wrong?' I stopped pacing, standing in front of him, willing him to tell me my deductions were the stuff of an overwrought woman's mind.

'I believe you may be perfectly right. And it will not stop until *they* are stopped, I think.'

'But how can we accomplish that? We are five men, three women and a child. How many are they?'

Mehmet took me by the elbow, urging me to sit. 'How can we know? We have been told the Toulon Commanderie housed ten Templar knights and perhaps twenty or more men in lesser positions, some villeins, but when Dante released Peter, the place was as empty as a graveyard. All vanished. Except for Peter. Odd.'

I shook my head in despair.

'My dear, I did not wish to scare you but it is far better to be cognisant.'

Yes, it is!

I wished so much that my own husband had thought to tell me such things. He had let me lapse into a somnolent and relaxed state of mind on settling in Venezia. Perhaps he saw it as a kindness but there was a tiny part of me that believed he had slipped back into his secretive habits, forgetting that his wife had the capacity to stand and be counted.

'When did you become aware that Halsham's ghost had risen?' In my mind was an image of some deadly spirit from Hell rising from below and pulling other deadly spirits with it. Hair stood up on my arms.

'We knew about Toulon, of course. And until three days ago, we truly thought we may have been wrong, that we worried too much. But after you left the Arsenale, and while you lingered at Saul's, men were sent to check the bodies. There was one, a tall man. He wore the cloak of a Sergeant-Brother...'

I remembered him. The one Guillaume had killed with a master shot through the forehead. 'He spoke French. He called me *"my lady"*.'

'Yes.'

I closed my eyes, the sneering faces of the felons as clear as if they stood before me now. 'How much longer must our lives continue like this? I remember asking my God once what I had ever done to deserve such treatment.' The laugh that emerged from my mouth was as sharp as a war-sword edge. 'Strangely He did not reply. Mary Mother, it seems my enemies, *our* enemies, are winning. Already we are prisoners, already we are besieged.'

'In some ways, yes. And because of that, it is best that we take one day at a time and live as normally as possible. We will not let them have the advantage.'

One day at a time and my knightly husband on a ridiculous search that could take months.

It was like salt in raw wounds.

In essence we pulled the drawbridge up to restore our breath. Mehmet and the guards knew why, of course. But for the remainder of the household, they seemed perfectly happy in their cloistered existence. And even though I watched Peter carefully, I did not catch him observing Guillaume again. As the new wife, Gwen kept him occupied and when William was not at the butts or riding lessons, he and Peter worked together in the gardens or with the horses. One day, we opened the gates wide with Johannes and John on watch, and Peter and William walked to the water to fish. It felt blessedly normal – as if life could almost be as it was before the Arsenale, and I thanked God.

A short and essentially pointless message arrived from Gisborne from Aquileia, saying nothing of note and urging me to keep safe.

Where to beyond Aquileia, Guy? I need to know…

I crushed the parchment in my hands, growling as I threw it on the fire, watching the flame grab for it, then leap with excitement as it consumed it in a ball of red and yellow.

I wondered whether I should have been glad that he did not report the King's death and decided if Richard was dead, I could perhaps have had my husband returned to me. But then I felt guilt for such a thought and begged God's forgiveness.

Ariella came to retrieve Tanti. He was so happy to see her, I felt sorry for William and vowed to buy him a dog of his own as soon as I could. In the meantime, Ariella said that I must take him at least once a sennight to play with Tanti in Saul's garden.

More normality. Thank the Lord. If I am permitted to go.

For me, it meant a day of talking with my new friend, of being a woman and talking of woman's matters, of admitting my fears to a woman who would understand. Laughing at my weakness. Breathing beyond the cloister. Forgetting the heavy responsibilities that yoked me to Gisborne's life.

Thus it was arranged that I visit and soonest.

Mehmet organised for John and Peter to be my guards, no doubt aware of my feelings toward Guillaume. Johannes, Walter and the archer would patrol the house, keeping it safe whilst we were gone. And of course Mehmet would remain behind, but he knew how to handle a knife…

William frothed with childish excitement. 'Mama, will Tanti remember me? Can 'Ella let him come home with uth, again?'

He could not say Ariella and I smiled as I pulled on his tunic and buckled the childish leather belt around. 'We shall see.' I pulled on his boots and smoothed his hair. 'You must be a true Gisborne today, William, so that Papa will be proud.'

I had asked Mehmet to send a courier with a note to Gisborne wherever he was and I sat and wrote thoughtfully the night before, telling my husband of Cecilia and also expressing my views in other ways:

'… You need have no fear that we are not well guarded because Mehmet has drawn the circle tight around us. Indeed, one might say he has been a strategist in his time, protecting city walls. I go to Ariella tomorrow and he has timed everything to a heartbeat, drilled John and Peter and has even arranged for Saul's own guard to meet us in the square. And yet he tells me no one will be aware of our circumstance, that we will blend into the crowd like honey into yellow anbar.

But you have oft commented on my intuition, so I must tell you I am concerned again for our safety and I say, husband, something is awry. I cannot identify what is in the air, but our walls feel as if they are breached although each day goes through its unremarkable cycle and I hope I am, by God's Good Graces, proved wrong.

And yet I crawl into our bed at night with the misericorde *under my pillow, William's cot on one side of the bed and Biddy's at the foot.*

I would that you returned from searching for Rex Derelinquere. *He abandoned his country on a fool's errand, and you have long known what I think of kingly crusades so I think you should abandon* him *now, and find those who threaten us. I am aware of the remaining Templars and their vengeful energies. We are in the middle of a secret war here, Gisborne, and a castle always needs reinforcements when it is besieged…'*

Mehmet had taken the missive and despatched it with one of Gisborne's couriers even before William and I were organised enough to depart for Ariella's.

The day glistened with pewter winter light, a light that softened Venezia's changing, growing shape. As we stepped onto the first bridge outside our gate, there was the notion of moving into a world without end after our constrained existence. It was enlivening and enervating all in one. John led the way with Peter behind, compressing William and I into a tiny space between them. William began to giggle as John's boots squeaked, saying breathlessly, 'John thoundth like horthes' fartth, Mama.' And then pealing into childish giggles. I raised my eyebrows at his lack of etiquette but John turned round and grinned so it was a battle of manners I would have lost anyway.

But William was as quickly diverted by life as we approached the bigger waterways, vessels poling past loaded with fish and poultry, sacks of grain and baskets of vegetables. If we were lost, all we needed to do was to follow them to the market but we knew the way and walked apace. Prickly fear and lack of confidence began to melt in the bright winter sunshine. No breeze tickled the water and sounds rang with unobscured clarity. Bells were ringing for Sext, there was the clopping sound of horses' hooves, dogs barking, men and children shouting, women shrieking to each other, the tramp of feet and the overarching sounds of seabirds.

The square seethed with folk hurrying about their business — to the church, to vendors, to the offices of the Great Council and the Doge. And over it all, the sound of adze, hammer and chisel as more and more buildings grew with elegant effort to surround the place. In the sennight since I had last been to the town centre, the stonemasons and carpenters had been busy.

John halted. 'My lady, this is where we are to meet your friend.'

Peter and he casually stood at our backs and I subsided onto a block of stone, looking around, making sure William held my hand tightly. Silks and linens and matted woollens passed by. Olive skins, white skins, black skins. Pale hair, brown hair, ebony and russet. And eyes — brown, blue, obsidian, hazel — gazes which caused me to wonder if they wished us ill. Wrinkled faces and smooth, bearded and not, clean and dirty — after our quiet, it almost overwhelmed.

A monk stopped next to me, looking back as a wooden clapper sounded behind us. A leper approached, pushed on by the city guard. I smelled piss

93

and sweat on the servant of our Christ, his sandalled feet grimy and the toenails horny and broken underneath his religious garb and he made no effort to bless the poor leper, turning aside as if he truly did believe the scabs and sores the leper might bear were a curse from God. The poor man was covered neck to ankle in tunic, cloak and hood and on his head a broad-brimmed hat – the uniform of an outcast. His face was in shadow and people shrank from his path and all I could think of was the ostracism of Gisborne's father in Jerusalem, and he a Soldier of Christ. What price love of our fellow man?

William, habitually twirling off my fingers, suddenly yelled, 'Tanti!' as the monk moved away. His small hand struggled to break free as Tanti emerged from the folds of Ariella's tawny cloak, another's *brunete* cloak halting him in his path momentarily. Images of Genoa and similar cloaks flashed into my mind and I jumped up, dragging at my *misericorde,* about to cry out as two enormous shapes leaped from behind the *brunete* pleats, rolling Tanti over, trying to grab him as he jumped up and ran yelping in a circle.

Two large hounds, one brindle and one brown, growled with horrendous ferocity, massive teeth gnashing, their coats rippling with boar-killing muscle. Tanti fought for his life as William screamed and I grabbed him hard against my skirts with one hand, holding him with the tenacity of a wild animal holding her baby away from its killers. With my other, the *misericorde* sprang to attention and I scanned the crowd around me. Ariella thrust herself into the brawl, grabbing the hounds' collars and pulling them with all her might. Tanti moved fast, trying valiantly to run around behind his mistress. I called to John and Peter to help and on turning, could see neither and my heart pounded as I struggled to contain an hysterical William. Ariella's dagger lifted and stabbed, one of her guards forcing his way amongst the thrashing canines. Ariella roared – an unearthly cry of hatred and fury and she lifted her knife again, thrusting it into the animal closest to her as it jumped at her, her free arm held up as a shield and grabbed in dragon's teeth. She twisted the blade so that the animal impaled itself the more it moved, teeth finally releasing their hold on my friend's arm. Her guard wielded his own blade, slitting the other dog's throat, one fast deep slash filled with ire – an intake of breath from the eager crowd as the dog fell in its own blood, light sliding from its rabid eyes.

My friend bent and picked up her pet, wrapping him in the folds of her cloak. 'He lives, he lives,' she wept. 'I can yet save him. Quickly, quickly, Phillipus, come. I must get him home.' She spoke to us without seeing and we ran, all four, heedless of the loss of John and Peter, caring only that Tanti should live. We breasted Saul's street, sliding into the garden, Ariella calling for warm water and bandages before the gate had even been bolted.

In the kitchens, she laid Tanti on the table, his body and head flopping, his chest barely moving. Grabbing vinegar, she dripped it onto a pad, beginning to swab his wounds. I could barely say a word as the innocence and happiness of the animal bled before us. I held William with tender, sad hands.

'No broken bones,' muttered Ariella. 'No wounds in his belly. Only around his neck and head. Infection is the thing. I must clean…'

She kept swabbing, cooing and kissing Tanti and he lifted his head as she touched a deeper bite. His eyes followed her every move. Once, she stopped and just let her fingers slide across his face, his tongue licking the passing caress. She placed a folded pad with powdered yarrow round his neck where the worst punctures were, binding with a linen strip as the dog began to shake.

'Warm,' she said. 'He must be warm.'

She barely registered our presence and grabbed a woollen shawl, holding it to the fire to heat, William whispering, 'Tanti, I love you. You mutht get better.' His hands were desperate to pat the dog but I could see he was too afraid of hurting his companion.

Ariella returned, wrapping the animal, cocooning it in comfort, laying it on a large pillow in front of the fire. When her gaze finally met mine, her handsome face was as pale as ivory, her hair twisted and unkempt, her gown stained with blood. The sleeve was ripped, the skin beneath red with gore.

'Ariella, look to your arm. You are bitten…'

She glanced down at the spatters and to where the wounds dripped on the floor and as she called for the cook to bring her more warm water, Saul rushed in.

'I heard – the square is alive with the gossip of a woman and a dog and two rabid hunting animals attacking her. One of our clients saw you and Phillipus, and ran to the booth. *Harah!* Your arm…'

He ripped her sleeve open, taking a clean pad and dowsing it in vinegar, swabbing and cleaning. 'Ariella, it needs to be stitched together here…' He pointed to a spot on her lower arm where the hound had dragged at her, puncturing above and below. He ran a needle through a candle flame until it glowed red and then used vinegar to clean away the charring, threading with linen as he said quietly, 'This will hurt.'

William's eyes widened and I took a step to remove him.

'No,' Ariella said. 'It is good for him to see that pain can be managed. Only the Prophets know if he will need such fortitude. But you can hide him away from today, or you can allow him to confront it. One is perhaps kind and the other a chance to build skills...'

She sucked in her breath and bit her lip as the needle passed in and out five times, her pallor whitening even more. 'You see, William,' she said, her voice tight. 'I am almost as brave as Tanti. Now, I need you to sit with him and talk softly of your adventures together and I will have cook get you some almond cake and milk. Go now.'

William needed no urging, sinking quickly by the fire and beginning to murmur childish words to Tanti. Saul knotted off his embroidery, Ariella's arm still dripping, and she grabbed her gown folds to sop the excess.

'Ariella!' Saul admonished.

'Tis no matter,' she replied. 'It is beyond redemption. What of Phillipus?'

'Not a mark,' her father said, 'which is in itself astonishing given the size of the dogs. Boar hounds, I believe.'

I thought of my father's alaunts and lymers and shuddered. The lymers had always scared me with their skill at scenting the prey. Nothing was safe.

Neither are you, Ysabel. You are prey; they have their lymers.

The alaunts though – their jaws could have ripped my throat out, huge hounds with no fear for their own lives. The prey was all.

Familiar, Ysabel?

Saul busied himself with removing the detritus of his work. And for the moment I sat with my thoughts, Ariella wiping her hands and hissing at the mess.

'It was deliberate.'

'Your pardon?' I said. In fact I was not at all sure I wanted to hear her reply.

'Ysabel,' said Ariella and I noticed my title had been dispensed with. 'There was a man...'

'In the *brunete* of a Templar seargeant-brother? I saw him...'

'He whistled as he brushed past and I think someone let loose the dogs at that moment. Father is right, they were boar hounds. Phillipus, Tanti and I are lucky to have escaped with our lives.'

'Ariella, I am so very sorry. If we hadn't arranged to visit…'

This is what I hated about my very existence, that everyone who touched me, who was part of my life, was vulnerable.

'It would have happened somewhere else, and they will keep…'

'Trying and trying. Indeed, you are right.' My heart bolted, it's rhythm everywhere as the lymers closed in.

Saul had listened to his daughter, his mouth drawn tight – a furious line. 'Lady Ysabel, you shall stay here for the moment whilst I send word to Mehmet. Where are your guards?'

My guards? What guards?

I shook my head. 'I don't know. They were there and then gone.'

Saul took up a roll of bandage and began winding it round his daughter's arm. 'This will happen again and again and we need to be prepared.'

Again and again…

I thought to myself that I had no option but to run because my husband had left me so vulnerable. And all in the name of the King!

'…shall send immediate word to Sir Guy.'

'Saul, there is little point. He is so far distant now that the damage would be done before he returned. No, whatever action needs to be taken, it shall be my decision and none other. It is my son and I who…'

A ruckus sounded beyond the house and in a moment the door flew open and John pushed in, breathless, hair on the side of his head clotted with blood. William looked up from his vigil by Tanti's side, a momentary glance at the guard, but Tanti whimpered and my son returned quickly to his responsibilities.

'John!'

'My lady,' he sank to his knee. 'I beg you to forgive me…' He reached for the table corner and held on.

'John, you're hurt.'

'My head's a bit sore…'

Saul grabbed him and thrust him onto a stool and once again began doctoring, clucking like an anxious hen. 'Nothing that needs stitching. A lump…'

'Ow!' John lurched away from Saul's probing fingers.

''Tis not so bad,' Saul said.

'They came at me as the dogfight began, my lady, pushed me round and knocked me down before I could get to my blade. All I could see were cobbles and feet and then someone hit me there...' he gestured to his head. 'And I passed out.' He clasped his hands together. 'By all that's holy, Madam, I beg you to forgive me.'

'Tis no matter, John. It was all beyond our control. But Peter ... where is he?'

'I don't know, my lady. And there's a thing. They pushed us apart. All I remember is being hit and waking on the edge of the water in a dark alley. Not a sign of Peter anywhere.'

Saul finished washing the blood from John's head. 'No one intended to kill you, I think. Merely delay you. Perhaps if you had fought back things may have been different. Sit for a moment and I will get cook to fetch food and drink.' He hurried away to find the cook who had tactfully left us when we took over the kitchens.

I sat opposite John, my fingers clasped tightly.

'John?' I said, not remotely sure of what I was asking him.

'My lady, this was deliberate – the attack on Peter and me, the release of the dogs. Their next step would have been to grab Master William while the ruckus occurred. I can't think what stopped them.'

I thought back to the square, of Ariella and Phillipus jumping into the fray, of me pulling William so tightly against me, the crowd closing around us.

'Luck stopped them,' I replied. 'Nothing but luck and their misfortune. They'll not fail next time.'

Damn you to Hell, Gisborne. You should be here!

Saul returned with a brimming tray and I swallowed the wine in desperation.

We stayed at Saul's whilst he sent men to comb the alleys for Peter but they returned with no sign. I fretted for our quiet, troubled smith, seeing him lying bloodied somewhere. Or worse, dead.

Tanti slept and William lay by his side, his head on a cushion close to the dog – boy and pup, victims of circumstance. And Peter as well, innocent bystander, damaged by his involvement with me.

Surely not dead. Not that.

How could I tell Gwen?

Ariella uncovered her dog and checked his breathing and the wounds, and William whispered, 'Ith he alright, Ella?'

She nodded and kissed the dog and boy and after scrutinising them for a moment longer, she rejoined John, Saul and I, closing the circle.

'My Lord Gisborne needs to leave his negligent King to his own devices, methinks.' Saul toyed with his mug.

'As I have asked him to do, Saul, with little success it seems. Assuming he has received my request. But tell me, what of Peter? He is dear to us all and more importantly he is Gwen's beloved. How do I tell her that once again, he is hurt because of me and mine. It is the stuff from which hate might spring.'

'If these felons do not want him found,' Saul said, 'then he may remain lost to us. Our only hope is that the Watch might find him turned up somewhere. You know Venezia, my lady. A hundred different islets, a thousand building sites filled with rubble and any number of watery ways.'

The simplistic but devastating picture Saul painted dashed hopes and cares to the ground but John butted in.

'Please give him a chance, sir. He is at home with any kind of weapon and he is big and strong. Don't commit him to God just yet. If you pardon me for saying so.'

Bless you, John.

'Indeed, you are right, young man. And I will not dismiss him, as you say. But we must perhaps put our faith in God's help in this instance as well as Peter's own instinct to survive. And we must convey William and yourself home, Lady Ysabel. I can raise six guards quite easily. With myself and this energetic fellow here, I think we can return you safely to the villa.'

Ariella shifted, her leather-slung seat creaking. The fire popped as it settled into a comforting glow. 'I doubt your assailants will try again so soon,' she said. 'I think they will allow your house to slip into a more relaxed state…'

'I agree with you, Ariella,' said Saul. 'And when I see Mehmet we shall send urgent couriers to Sir Guy. There will be no laxity nor relaxation in the way in which the house is guarded.'

'Could we not augment Ysabel's guard with some of ours, Father? At least until Sir Guy returns?'

If he returns. And why did he leave us so visibly underprepared for these events?

I was aghast that my husband hadn't foreseen we would be under such constant threat. If he knew Halsham's men were bent on revenge, why did he not leave us with a full garrison? I couldn't understand his lack in this instance. I was boiling with fury and fear all in one and I knew such an attitude coloured my ability to think clearly.

But my friend Ariella talked on such things as if born to a life of caution and of course that was the truth. Jews straddled a miserable Christian world – recognized as excellent traders in goods and money, despised and relied on for the same, they had hundreds of years of practice at security and protecting their homes.

They lived with the ingrained distrust of their Christian neighbours in a society where envy and jealousy balanced along the cutting edge of a sword. It was no wonder that Ariella could read men's minds and speak so, and I valued her friendship even more as she said:

'We have enough for just the two of us.'

Saul did not disagree, the ferocious expression of earlier softening as he looked at his daughter with admiration and pride. 'Of course. I was about to suggest exactly that. Give in gracefully, my lady. You have no argument.'

Dusk settled over Venezia as we left Saul's on horseback. One might think that we left with a fully armed company of men. In fact, William and I left with Saul and John – myself behind John and William in front of Saul. As to the other six guards, all mounted, there was no obvious sign as they mixed with other street-goers who were mounted or on foot.

At times like this, when my nerves were stretched, I disliked twilight. Tracts of deepest shadow drew my eyes, then there would be a last patch of grey light and my attention would jump to it, convinced it had moved, then back to the shadow – porticos, cloisters, overhanging corners, walls from which cats and men could leap. It seemed to me that dusk had long darkened fingers that could grasp a horse's reins.

When we reached the open spaces of Venezia outside the city centre, I took a breath, relaxing my hold on John's sides.

'My lady, you feel easier?' he asked.

'Yes,' I replied.

The horses plodded on in a line of folk returning to their islets over the bridges.

Which were the guards?

I knew not. It was just reassuring to know they protected us. As we approached the final bridge, they filed in a line behind, just like any other journeymen returning to their hearths. But whilst the dark might be too solid for us to be seen, the tattoo of hooves across the bridge sounded like the approach of an army and Gisborne's edict of not being noticed floated into my mind.

Night had indeed settled, a clear moon rising in the sky and our staunch gateway lit with flaring torches. Never had the villa seemed more welcome as we rode in, Johannes and Guillaume holding the gates apart and bolting them as the last pair of riders slipped through. Guillaume looked up at me as I rode in, his face solemn, mouth tight.

Biddy predictably was waiting. Mehmet unusually, was not.

'Oh Madame, give me my little boy, bless him. Please, I'll take him to his bed. There's things you must see to.'

Saul passed a sleeping William down. Like Tanti, he whimpered, but then his head lolled on Biddy's shoulder, her face pale as she tut-tutted in the moonlight, the flames emphasising pools of shadow beneath her eyes.

'Biddy!' I called after her as she hurried away with her bundle, but with the sound of horses shifting around, of men speaking and harnesses creaking and jingling she must not have heard and continued on up the stair.

'Lady Ysabel, I will speak briefly to Mehmet and return to Ariella. There are only Phillipus and two guards in our house…' Saul said.

'Of course and I thank you…'

'But I am leaving four of my guards here. Together with your own, I feel you are adequately protected.'

He quickly dismounted as I slid from behind John, the two of us hurrying up the stair to find Mehmet. But Biddy emerged shadow-eyed, from our chamber, intercepting us.

'Mehmet is in the stables, my lady. He…' she bit her lip.

'Yes?' I tried to rub the throbbing tightness from my old scar.

'Oh, my lady…' she dissolved into uncharacteristic tears, turned on her heel and fled back to William, her veils flying in her distress.

'Biddy!' I called out, meaning to follow her.

'Come, my lady, there is something awry here.' Saul took my elbow and we retraced our steps with speed, heading to the stables where light flickered.

The smell of hay and oats, of fresh straw and horse should have comforted us but instead in the living quarters set aside for Gwen and her husband, I heard my maidservant crying and Mehmet's low voice.

I rushed in, preparing for the worst.

She knelt by the bed and Mehmet bent over a supine shape, applying a bandage to a bloody upper leg.

'Peter!' I cried. 'Dear God, thank heaven! We thought…'

Gwen looked up. Our eyes met and something I did not wish to countenance passed between us. It reminded me of Cyprus when she rounded on me for my behaviour and it pulled me up sharply.

'Mehmet, what happened?' I asked.

He finished bandaging Peter's leg and already blood stained the pad. 'He turned up at the gates an hour ago, confused, wounded in the leg and with a clout to the head. He makes little sense, seems to have forgotten about you and Master Gisborne and keeps talking about a dogfight.'

'That much at least is the truth,' Saul said. 'Or part of it. His leg?'

'A stab wound which fortuitously missed a vital blood vein. But I have stitched it and he will live. His head is not broken and will ache and he may suffer some confusion for a day or two, but with rest he will be the Peter we know.'

'Oh my poor Peter,' I said, reaching to touch his hand. His eyes were closed and his colour as pale as Biddy's.

'*Your* Peter?' Gwen hissed. 'If he'd never been Moncrieff's Peter, none of this would have happened.'

I stepped back with the force of her words, dragging my hand away quickly.

The stuff of hate.

'Gwen! Enough!' Mehmet ordered. 'Show a little respect for your mistress. Come, Saul, my lady. We will leave Peter to rest and Gwen to comfort him. Gwen, you must call me if things worsen.'

She said nothing, turning her back on us and reaching to remove her veil and wimple.

'My lady?'

Mehmet pulled at my arm and I allowed myself to be taken back to the yard, vaguely aware of Saul informing Mehmet of this afternoon's events. 'You received my message?' he asked the physician.

'I did. Along with others of sorts. It has been a day of surprises in so many ways.'

'I can tell you nothing more, then. Mehmet, I leave you four of our guards and we will talk in a day, yes?'

'*Insh'allah,*' Mehmet replied, a grim expression parting his lips.

Saul nodded in return, turned and with a swirl of his long crimson tunic, his sword and dagger rattling, he gave me a passing smile and left.

'Saul, I am grateful…' I called after him.

'Tis nothing,' he replied and hurried to his horse, mounting and ordering the remaining guards to follow.

The gates were opened and as quickly shut and Mehmet was ordering space for the extra horses and men. As we climbed the stair to his chamber, even the faded gold stars glistening in the light of the cressets failed to lift my mood.

'Gwen, Bridget, Peter – they are hurt again and again through their association with me.'

'And yet you have offered them their freedom and knowing the risks, they stay.' Mehmet stood aside to allow me to pass through the door.

But the expression on Gwen's face was not one filled with respect or devotion.

As I stepped across the threshold, there was movement from the shadows of the room.

'Well, my lady, I took a bet with John that you would attract trouble while we were gone…'

'Toby!' I managed a bitter laugh. 'And of course you bet on my spontaneity, yes?'

He grinned and held up a bag of coins, shaking it.

'Won by default, Tobias. *I* did not go seeking trouble. *It* found me.'

'Money is money, my lady. Winning it by default is immaterial. But enough levity – in the name of Saint Baudolino, it is a blessing that you and the little one are safe.'

He crossed himself as I asked, 'Toby, is Gisborne to return? Is he with you? Did he receive my message?'

'In answer, yes, he is to return…'

Thank God!

'Is he on his way?' the minstrel continued. 'Very soon. Did he receive a message from you? I am unaware as I have been on the road, picking up some of our men on the way…'

Mehmet broke in, 'We have a surfeit of guards, my lady, but the Gisborne men have been travelling for some days and I sent them to makeshift cots to rest, which is why I am happy to have use of Saul's men tonight. They will return to his house tomorrow morning.'

I threw myself in a chair, leaning back, my hands at my forehead.

'How have we gone from a household at ease to a place under siege so quickly? I try to understand why these men of Halsham's are so hell bent on avenging his name and I find I cannot. Who leads them? If we knew that, we would be able to discover flaws, a weakness to be exploited.'

Hollow words, Ysabel. Do you not think Gisborne has thought of that already?

But I knew not. If he had been so aware, I doubt he would have left us so underprepared.

Toby sat on a stool, pushing his feet toward the fire, Mehmet pouring some wine and passing it around as I thought of something of great import.

'Jesu! What about Tommaso? Have you found him? How does he?'

'Ah, did you think we Celhos could be killed off so easily?' Irony chimed in the room. 'We found him in Aquileia. Tired, not very well with a bad chest, and abed in a monastery. He fared badly in the shipwreck and it seems Richard and his men thought it a kindness to place him in such care than for him to try and ride with them, and for once the King made a compassionate choice. My brother has some mending to do before he travels, but my lord has paid for his care and will have him conveyed to Venezia in a sennight or so, when he is stronger. He was able to confirm to Sir Guy that the King makes for the Hungarian border and the protection of King Bela, possibly through Udene. We of course followed swiftly and Gisborne suspected we were only a day's ride away when two things happened. One directly affected my lord's response to the other.'

I waited. Tobias looked well, if a little tired and he walked like a man who had been in the saddle for some days. His boots, mud-caked, had left a trail of clods on the floor as he had moved to the stool and his hose had a hole at the knee. His hands were grubby, nails rimmed in black and he noticed my scrutiny. Always a proud man and engagingly vain, his appearance would have been a blow to his self-esteem.

'My lady, I apologise for appearing so ill-made before you, but I needed to talk with you and with Mehmet…'

'Toby, it does not signify. I am so heartened to hear such good news – that Tommaso is alive and will be with us soon, that you are well and with us now and that my lord Gisborne will be here in a moment. I feel hopeful again.'

'I have ordered a bath to be filled in our chamber, Tobias,' Mehmet added. 'Your saddlebags are being taken there as we speak.'

'I think Biddy shall be somewhat taken aback when I leave a ring of Aquileian soil on the tub linen,' he said ruefully.

'Biddy has other things to worry about now, Toby. Peter…'

'I know. Sad…'

'But,' said Mehmet. 'You must continue with your news. You said two things…'

'Yes,' Toby took a quick swallow of wine. 'We were about to depart Aquileia and a message arrived for my lord from Queen Eleanor…'

'Eleanor!' The power behind the throne, I thought, the loins that launched a bevy of strong personalities upon our unsuspecting world. My most royal godmother…

'Of course she knew of Richard's plan to return to England,' continued Toby, 'to reclaim his throne and to avoid the tenacious tentacles of holy Henry Hohenstaufen, and lovely Leopold, aware of the slander of her son's name through Europe. Like any mother, she worried for his safety, and respecting Sir Guy's skills, she said, *"Sir, if you can unearth vital secrets for King Richard, then you must surely be able to find Him and keep Him safe for Us. We would that you pressed forward to do so as His many lands need Him returned swiftly. We charge you with that duty. We write in haste, sir, believing that you must now depart in haste".* She signed it with a looping swoop of her name, *Eleanor By the grace of God, Queen of England.* Although she's not, is she? Queen of England I mean. Ha! Mother of the King to be sure but rather a big ego I think. Nice signature too.'

Toby loved embellishing a story…

'So he is not coming home immediately, is he?'

'Now, now, don't be so precipitate. I said two things – remember?' Toby settled on the stool, one leg crossed over his knee, his ankle held by his hand. 'We headed off immediately on the Queen's orders, moving swiftly, Udene in our sights, knowing that the mountains that ringed the place would be where Richard was headed. If he could get over those before the heavy snows fell, then he would conceivably be safe from those who wanted to capture and ransom him.'

Our minstrel took a swallow of wine and ate a *gaylede* and I waited impatiently.

'Toby…'

He held up his fingers, begging silence and continued, 'We believed the King pressed forward in disguise, but were not sure whether he pursued the Templar guise…'

Templars! Damn them…

'…or as a pilgrim newly returned from Jerusalem. He had only to mix with the last of the travellers hustling to make camp behind friendly walls before the snows and he would be concealed. We galloped on behind him, hoping to overtake him before he reached Udene, and as we emerged from a twisting road and looked back, we saw a movement of what seemed to be a group of riders in the far distance, making haste. It was hard to tell as the land is quite flat, but they were approaching with speed and Gisborne thought it politic to hide in the small forest that surrounded us. We thought they might be men in pursuit of Richard as all Christendom knew a substantial reward was offered for his capture. Gisborne made a decision…'

'We cannot assume they are benign. They ride with intent and I am concerned.' He jumped from his horse and threw the reins to Adam.

'Take the horses, Adam, and you and Toby go far back into the woods, keep the mounts quiet and I shall watch here. Keep a dagger close at hand both of you. Go!'

Gisborne's and Adam's horses danced a little but followed when the guard withdrew old crusts from his purse. By now, the sound of the approaching horses rumbled, and birds flew up with a piping alarm as the convoy drew ever closer.

Toby had jumped from his horse as it began to dance, sweat beginning to darken its shoulder and neck.

'Toby! Go! For Christ's sake!' Gisborne hissed, taking a position behind a wide-girthed tree just off the rutted and time-damaged road.

'Whoa, easy, easy!' The minstrel sang softly but the horse refused to listen, arching back, threatening to pull its reins straight from his hands. Gisborne looked on in despair, conscious that much more movement would draw the riders' attention and all would be lost. He sucked in a breath, his hands clammy.

Toby tightened the reins and jerked twice, the bit bouncing cruelly in the horse's mouth. The animal froze, looking at Toby, its ears flat back; but then it dropped its head and began to follow as Toby whispered, 'Come up', leading it further into the verdure. Adam had found a small copse of winter grass and the other animals pulled hungrily at food, chewing and snatching more, although their ears twitched mightily and their tails flicked from side to side.

Gisborne sighed with relief, unable to see his men as he looked into the woods. The sound of the hooves was tumultuous now – he guessed six horses, heavy with men, and he sank his back against the rough bark of the fir, barely noting the resinous tang. Someone yelled and there was an answering cry from further away down the road, the troupe halting in a skirl of pebbles, dirt and oaths.

'Bleedin' balls, what now?' a common hoarse voice asked in French.

'I need a piss. A big one.'

'Christ, Teo, yer bloody bastard! I can see movement far ahead. If it's those we've been following, we have to head 'em off before the gates of Udene.'

'Then let me bloody piss and be done.'

Footsteps approached the trees, closer and closer to where Gisborne stood. He held his breath, sweat forming in his armpits.

'By the saints,' another voice said, 'This bloody excuse for a road! The damned horse is lame!'

'God rot the souls of the lot o' yer,' the common Frenchman spat. 'Then you can bleedin' well stay be'ind and make yer way back to Aquileia on foot. Get goin' and don't speak to no one!'

By Gisborne's foot the acrid smell of piss drifted up, a strongly yellow pool filtering under the sole of his boot. Carefully, he lifted his toe out of the mess. Finally the man turned, his sword scabbard hitting the tree, a fart drifting behind.

'Are we done then?' ordered the Frenchman. 'Right, now let's go! An' remember. Catch 'em alive. He wants Gisborne alive, although you can rough 'im up. And as for the woman and child, truss 'em, but don't touch 'em!'

'Pity. The woman sounds like a nice piece…'

'Shut yer face, Leo. Sir Simon'd shove a sword up yer arse and pull it out yer mouth if yer so much as breathed on 'er.'

'So much fer a knight's bleedin' chivalry,' muttered the man who had thought to have the woman they chased. 'He's no more knightly n' me!'

Gisborne heard it, his own guts curling. The rough-cut Frenchman did not, as the horses began to move out leaving one behind. The man watched them gallop away, his horse hanging its head and propping away from the sore sole. The fellow turned, lifted his hand and swiped it hard across the horse's head.

Gisborne stepped out from the trees. 'Hey there, what goes?'

The man flung round, drawing a dagger, suspicion rife in the air. 'My horse is lame.'

'Bad luck then. Where do you go?'

The man thought about this, sheathing his knife again as he looked along the road to where his companions were a fast-moving speck. 'Should have been Udene but now it's Aquileia.'

'As I said, bad luck,' Gisborne said, whistling a sharp note.

Adam appeared with the three horses and Gisborne moved easily to stand by him. 'We'd offer you a ride but maybe you'd best walk back to Aquileia. We'll follow your friends and see what they're up to.'

The man studied Gisborne for a moment, shocking realisation opening his face wide as he said, 'But we followed you, three of you, one small as a child...'

'That'd be me,' Toby said and the fellow spun round, his dagger lifted from its sheath again.

Gisborne launched in behind him, his own knife across the man's throat, pressing it, drawing just enough blood to frighten, the fellow's weapon dropping to the rutted road with a metallic clatter.

'Who are you?'

'Gaston...' The word flooded from the fellow's mouth in an instant.

'Where from, Gaston?'

'I'll not say...'

'Then shall I draw a pretty pattern?' Gisborne's dagger pressed harder and blood trickled more heavily into the neck of a filthy chemise.

'Pity me, sir. I was doing what I was told.'

'Then do some more of the same,' Gisborne's very breadth and height smothering the man he held.

'Toulon! I'm from Toulon...'

Gisborne and Adam exchanged a glance.

'A routier?'

The man said nothing and Gisborne etched the blade further into neck skin, the fellow struggling against the pressure.

'Yes, for pity's sake, yes!'

'Tell me, who is your commander?'

'Please sir…'

'Tell me!'

'Sir…' Suddenly the man lurched, hammering back hard with his heel on Gisborne's foot, his hand whipping a needle-thin dagger from his belt, spinning round as Gisborne's hand loosed, swiping it toward Gisborne's waist. A weapon whistled through the air, lodging with a dull thunk and the man fell forward into Gisborne's arms, a knife stuck obscenely in his back.

Gisborne held him, pulled the knife out and rolled the fellow over, kneeling by his side. The routier's eyes fluttered and he panted in shallow breaths.

'God forgive me…'

'He will,' Gisborne pulled a small cross from his purse and thrust it into the felon's hands. 'If you tell me who is your commander.'

'Sir…' he looked beyond Gisborne, far beyond. 'Sir…'

'Yes?'

'Sir…' The word rushed from his mouth with a trickle of blood, his lips pale and eyes glazed, the little cross slipping from his hand into the broken down surface of the road. 'Simon.'

'Jesu, Adam!' Gisborne growled. 'We were so close!'

'Begging your pardon, my lord, but if I had not, he would have pierced your innards and it'd be you lying there.'

Gisborne paced around the dead man. 'I know, I know. But to be so close and now no nearer…'

'Sir,' Toby interrupted. 'I think you are wrong. We now know your family is being hunted by men from Toulon. We know they are led by a man called Sir Simon. For us, for your web of men, the rest shall be easy. Your most important decision, I would venture to say, is do we follow the others?' Toby tipped his head in the direction of Udene. 'Or do we search for the King, or perhaps we return to Venezia where I think…' the minstrel halted in full flood, blushing.

'Oh don't stop now, Tobias,' Gisborne's irony rolled round them like low thunder. 'Give me the benefit of your wisdom.'

'No, my lord, I beg your forgiveness. It is you who must decide what we shall do.'

'I thank you,' Gisborne bowed, his action reeking of derision. 'I do believe it is.'

His anger was palpable, the shoulders more rigid than a pike handle. And yet, as he swiped hair from his forehead in that most familiar gesture, both Adam and Toby took no umbrage, knowing the man lived and breathed with threat and fear for his family.

Adam legged Toby up and threw himself astride his own horse as they waited for their leader's decision. Gisborne untacked the lame horse, giving it a smack on its rump, and it limped in the direction from which it had come. He picked up his cross from near the body of the dead man and mounted, sorting his reins – playing for time, Toby might have said.

Then, 'Adam, you and I will follow them as far as Udene and see what we can discover. Tobias, go back to Aquileia and seek out Berto. He'll be at the wrestling or at dice. You know where to go. Tell him I want he and three of his best men to attend you back to Venezia where you will all wait under Mehmet's orders until we return. I suspect we will only be a day behind, two days at most. Be more alert than you have ever been. And Toby, tell Lady Ysabel I…' He looked down at his bare hands and reached into his saddlebags to retrieve leather gauntlets. Then he said quietly, 'Just tell her.'

Toby nodded. He was not a singer of romance ballads for nothing. 'But my lord, what of the King? Your orders from Queen Eleanor?'

'My family is more valuable to me, Tobias, than a king who builds empires on the graves of honest men.' His horse pranced sideways and he sat easily, smoothing its neck. 'I find that being a traitor to my king comes more easily than I thought.' There was no grin to accompany the words as he gathered his reins. 'I will return forthwith. Be safe, my friend.'

Toby held his horse in check as Adam and Gisborne cantered away. Glancing at the dead man and asking for God's forgiveness this once, he also begged God to protect Gisborne and Adam, hoping against hope they could return from the sortie with information that would allow the household to fight the fair fight.

'…and so here I am, my lady and,' Toby nodded his head toward Mehmet, 'my honoured chess partner. You now know everything and I have arrived with Berto and his fellow giants. I swear if they so much as breathed on me, so big are they I might have been blown to Sicily!'

'But how long?' Oh how plaintive I sounded as I asked when my husband would return.

'Not long – perhaps two days, as I said. Be patient and everything can be as it was.'

'No, Toby,' I said, 'It can never be as it was. This is a *war* that we begin and until we or they are decimated, the war will continue.'

Mehmet patted my shoulder. 'Unfortunately I think you have the truth of it, Lady Ysabel. But we will be given a day or so's reprieve to collect ourselves, become comfortable and make mistakes. That is what they will be waiting for. We *must* be vigilant. I want men posted at every corner and at the gates all day and night and no one comes or goes without clearance from me. I have told Johannes to take command of the whole guard in Adam's absence.'

'Indeed,' said Toby. 'And now please can you both excuse me?' He stood and stretched, as easy with the house becoming a fortress of war as if it were a common thing. 'Horses are not built for my comfort and I would soak my weary muscles…'

'Yes, of course, you must go. And sleep, Toby. I will see you on the morrow.'

He bowed in a manner most courtly and I thanked the Virgin for her care of us and for returning Toby to our fold, and Tommaso, Adam and my lord husband soon after.

CHAPTER SIX

Mehmet stood at his table as the door closed, selecting flowerheads from a pile of dried lavender. He placed a small handful in a bowl and began crushing them and the aroma filled the room, soothing and calming.

But I had run dry of words after Tobias's revelations, watching the physician and trying so hard to accept the idea that we were indeed entering a form of warfare.

My poor William…

'You are surprised that my lord Gisborne chooses to deny the King in your favour?'

My mouth twisted. 'He denies Richard *and* Eleanor, Mehmet. There will be Hell to pay. Traitors are put to death.'

'If they are caught,' said Mehmet. 'My dear, Sir Guy has, over the years, become remarkably adept at disappearing. This will be no different, I am sure. The question is can you accept that this will be the case?' He tipped up the bowl and allowed the lavender powder to trickle through a parchment funnel he had rolled, filling a small glass jar. Taking a cork he stoppered it. 'Because, Lady Ysabel, make no mistake – when he returns it is as you say, there will be a war and you will need to fight and perhaps run. Are you willing?'

'I would have run the moment this disaster began, Mehmet. But I was afraid of arousing my husband's anger and losing his faith.'

He smiled. 'Methinks you have grown since I met you.' He patted my hand. 'Find some food and retire for the night. We have a big household with a multitude of needs to deal with tomorrow.'

He walked me to the door, the fragrance of lavender and a more exotic aroma of sandalwood drifting from him. As I left, wishing him a good night, I thought that he could almost have been my grandfather, so diligent was his care.

I hurried down to the kitchens, found some bread and dipped it in olive oil, sprinkling a little salt across it and chewing as I returned to my chamber. The cressets flickered and one by one were dying out and when I entered my room, I noticed one horn lamp had been left alight and placed by William's cot. Biddy's outline marked the end of my own bed and I resolved not to wake her. William slept on, peacefully breathing, unaware of the turmoil unleashing about us and blithely insensible to his mother's twisting heart.

A faint light marked the shutter edges – the first thing I noticed as my eyes flew open. The second was a shape moving toward the door. In the distance, the bells for Prime tolled and a rooster crowed then squawked as if a stone had been thrown.

'Biddy,' I whispered.

'Go back to your pillow, my lady. I only seek the *privé*.' She spoke in a breathless murmur. ''Tis not yet dawn.'

'Biddy,' I grabbed her hand as she passed. 'Hark to me please. When Peter is able, I would that you, Gwen and he go. Leave here, return to England, to Moncrieff and the village where you will be safe.'

She huffed and then said, 'Now's not the time to talk of such things. Now's the time to sleep. I shall not be long.' She disengaged her hand and hurried out. In the dim light of the fading horn lamp, I could see her pale grey, almost silver plait swinging down her back as she turned through the door with a slight stoop.

When did I wreak age upon you, Bridget?

I threw myself on my side, knowing full well that I would never return to sleep, that Biddy had in fact gone to see how her family fared and that in this house we currently had nine able-bodied men of our own and four of Saul's to keep us safe. Even though there were apparently only ten former Templars lined against us, I imagined they could order another ten men and another ten beyond that to fight with them and for them. The Pope had excommunicated them to be sure, but someone unknown held me and mine to ransom. We could annihilate one cadre and I believed he would swiftly organise another to take its place. It was the very nature of evil and I knew not one way of stopping it.

William prattled in his sleep. It sounded as if he talked to Tanti and I realised the imperative of securing a dog of his own and soonest – something to assuage the strange tensions within the house.

The cock crowed again and this time I pushed back the bedding, went to the bowl and splashed my face and opened a shutter quietly. The sky bled with the roseate glow of dawn and an array of birds sang – such a curiously choral harmony. The air was chilly and my breath puffed out in a small cloud to mix with the strands of river mist weaving through the grounds and rising to the tiles of the roof. A solitary punt poled past, its paddler warmly clad in a hooded cloak. I shivered as the thought of danger arose but the paddler moved on, swallowed by the moist vapour. Leaning out, I could see the corner of our wall, observing a shape on the parapet watching the paddler, making sure he floated away.

The smell of winter had twined itself deeply into the morning mist, redolent of dead things, hiatus, rain, maybe even snow and ice and I closed the shutter and turned away to see William watching me.

'Good morning, little one. Did you sleep well?'

William always woke seriously, as if he divined the future of his world. So much of that demeanour reminded me of his father and besides, perhaps there was not a lot to be joyous about right now.

'Mama, ith Tanti going to die?'

'Oh William, we must hope not. Perhaps we should go to Mass today and light a candle. What say you?'

'Yeth. God needth dogth like Tanti to be here. They are like angelth.'

'Indeed, my little boy. Avenging angels. Then we shall get dressed, break our fast and go to church.'

If we are able.

But I thought Mehmet may have a contrary idea and rightly so.

We sat round the table, William and I. He eating bread and some remnants of hare pie, me picking with desultory fingers at the crusts he left behind. He made an exhibition of feeding Githborne and Ounthee who stood four square on the table, a cup of water placed like a trough before them.

I heard Toby coming down the stair, singing *'Somer is y-comen in'* and William's chatter stopped, his hand freezing in mid-air, his face a picture of unbelief. The deep blue eyes were wide, the mouth a perfect O and then his chair toppled as he yelled 'Toby', jumping down, running out the door, not even noticing his toys had fallen over and his trough had splashed water across the table.

'William!' Toby yelled back and I had to smile because one could not be blamed for believing there were two children within the house. He entered the kitchen with William on his back and immediately his face sobered.

'My lady, good day to you. Where is Mehmet? It seems he was gone from our chamber long before I woke.'

'I suspect to doctor Peter, Toby. I wanted to ask if William and I could go to Mass and light a candle for Tanti…'

'I think he would naysay you.' He persuaded William to slide off his back, stretched out the cricks and sat at our long table, picking up morsels, inspecting them and then putting them down again. He took his knife from his belt and cut a slice of wastel.

'I dare say you are right,' I said. 'In any case, now William has his best friend returned he may prefer to play than pray.'

'It happens with three year old children, my lady,' he remarked wryly. 'In fact it happens with fully grown men. Praying is so … boringly godly. Besides, we can make our own little chapel and light a candle for Tanti here.'

'Oh Toby, I could light candles for so many today. Everything sits heavily upon me and will do so till Gisborne returns.'

'Lady Ysabel, things do tend to have a way of sorting themselves, although such a lot requires faith.'

'In God or in Fate?'

'A question for a priest most assuredly, or perhaps a philosopher and I am neither.' He pulled his tunic down, readjusting his belt. 'Any pie left? I'm as hungry as a foot soldier who hasn't had a decent swive in a sennight…' he stopped, stared at me, mock horror, hand clamped over mouth. Then he winked and I laughed.

Bless you, Master Celho.

'What did Toby thay, Mama?'

Toby and I sat for a moment and then roared with laughter.

'I'm pleased to see you happier than yesternight, my lady.' Mehmet swept in, dressed in a storm-grey robe and white *keffiyeh*.

'Tobias has a knack, Mehmet. The troubles are there but he is like Merlin Ambrosius, diminishing them for the moment. It helps.'

'Indeed. He is a master at the art of illusion.'

'How does our friend?' asked Toby through a mouthful of the cold hare pie. William lay on his stomach on the *tesserae* of the mosaic telling the wooden horses a story of fish that could swallow men, of seabirds and sunsets and a little knight's adventures.

'His wound is perfectly adequate with no infection. What I would hope for. But his mind is a little addled which is what I predicted from a hit to the head. Gwen and Bridget are like mothers around a babe.'

'May William and I visit him?' Toby wiped his mouth with a fastidious linen square and sipped at watered wine.

'Of course. It will help him along, I dare say.'

William jumped up and grabbed his toys in one hand as Toby reached for his other.

'Tobias,' Mehmet warned. 'He tires easily…'

Toby nodded and Mehmet and I heard the two of them chattering as they descended into the yard and through the entrance to the stables.

'He is the breath of life, is he not?' Mehmet said idly as he cleaned his medicinal instruments with a vinegar-soaked cloth.

It did not require an answer and the sound of voices outside drew me to the shutters where I could look down on the yard. Guillaume and Johannes talked, Johannes pointing to the rear of our villa and Guillaume nodding. Johannes clapped him on the upper arm and walked away and Guillaume's head turned. What made him look up to the kitchen, I wondered? He never smiled and this was no different, but he placed his hand on his heart as our eyes met, and gave a small bow. For some reason it shocked me and I nodded and moved to the side of the shutters, my cheeks aflame.

Jesu, he discommoded me and I wanted to understand why. Sometimes I wondered if time and circumstance had turned me into a suspicious and cynical person and my attitude toward my son's saviour was the result. I wished for my *prie-dieu*, where I could kneel and talk to the Virgin Mother about my concerns, begging her to intercede, promising to be a good daughter if She would only help me. But this house was my church, my chamber or the fig tree my *prie-dieu* and I vowed to spend time in prayer and soul-searching when I could get a moment alone. Looking out the aperture again, I could see Guillaume striding away, his bow over his shoulder, arrows slotted into his belt. The yard through which he walked was lit with a grey ambience this day, as though all that was good had been sucked from the world. Beyond flowed the waterways that had so calmed me in the past and around which the shadow of winter stretched cold, unfeeling arms.

'Mehmet, do they surround our walls?'

He knew I meant our enemies and answered readily. 'Ah, my lady, who is to know? This is not a castle siege. We cannot stand at the top of the walls and see an army waiting, a trebuchet creaking toward us, or a catapult, a battering ram or some such and we cannot parley with someone we cannot see.'

'But we know the leader is a Frenchman, do we not? A former Templar…'

He frowned, moving to the fire to remove a pan of steaming water. 'No, we do not. We know he *may* have been a Templar and we know he has a connection to Toulon. We know his men are mostly French, but we cannot assume *he* is French.' He placed the pan on the table and proceeded to drop the tools into the slowing seethe.

'I see. Then can you explain why, after the Grand Master denounced them, he did not close Toulon, lock it up, pronounce it cursed?'

'It is a valuable estate worth money to the Templars. No Grand Master in his right mind would allow that to happen. The Templars *make* money, my lady. They do not lose money. I think you will find the Grand Master has required that Toulon be sold at a handsome profit. If we can find out to whom, I think we will have the man we seek. Madame,' he said carrying the pan back to the fire and watching it for a moment. 'May I give you a word of advice? This is a house under threat and there is a great deal of expectation in the air. You must shelve your own fears and lead the household. These people need to follow and until Sir Guy returns, you are their banner and their figurehead.'

Mehmet's words stayed with me long after he had scalded the tools, removed them, packed them away and departed for the yard. For so long I had lead a life of indulgence, responsible to no one but myself – a factor that contributed so obviously to further self-indulgent behaviour in later years and with disastrous results. Life had now caught up with me and I could be forgiven for thinking that God was asking for a change in me, in my manner. Looking around the kitchen I realised that without Biddy, the place was in a state of total disorganisation. Always outspoken, our housekeeper was as tart as a piece of lemon and yet never complained about her work, always making sure we had everything for our continued and comfortable existence. I had often chatted about a new flour, or dates or the possibility of fresh sardines from the fish stall, even about meals for this or that day. But she had been in control, not me. I doubt my own mother ever let things slip to the point where the cook or the bailiff became responsible. That was later, after she died and my father became lost in his grief and Guy of Gisborne became his steward.

Perhaps you are more like your inept father than you think, Ysabel.

In a fit of repudiation, I hastily checked our little buttery and granary to ascertain what could feed us and for how long. The overhaul of our supplies revealed serious weaknesses and I ran after Mehmet to explain the problem. Gwen and Bridget could patently not attend the markets and similarly it was too dangerous for myself, so he sent word to our Jewish friend with the guards who were just leaving.

The gates slammed shut, the bars scraping across and I returned to the kitchen, rolling up the sleeves of my gown to begin to scrub and tidy, glad beyond belief that nowhere in this house were floors strewn with rushes. My mother hated rush floors, believing they were prone to create illness and the attitude had been passed to her daughter. Cazenay had stone floors and I had led a sophisticated youth treading them. These thoughts danced through my head as I filled pail after pail from the well in the yard.

We needed meat and I worried what to send to the guardhouse until the supplies had been augmented. Bread and olives would hardly suffice, so with much less skill than my housekeeper, I filled an enormous pan with water and placed it over the fire, heating it whilst I chopped garlic and onions, carrots, cabbages, turnips and some sorrel. Biddy had bunches of dried herbs hanging around the kitchens and rosemary and mint were thrust into the pottage. We had never eaten a meal that wasn't handsomely flavoured with whatever she could grow or find by the wayside and I tried to follow by example.

But what of bread? How did one make it? Often enough as a child, I had woven in and out of the cook's legs at Moncrieff, smelling, watching, but never baking. At Cazenay, I was educated in finer pursuits – language and poetry, music, needlework – ostensibly sophistication. And other skills less admired by my potential suitors because it placed me on an equal footing with them. That I could win at dice and shoot an arrow was of far greater matter to me than the baking of bread.

I threw flour into a bowl and added honey, water and ale-barm. I had no idea of measurements and some faint recall had suggested the use of a sweetener and a rising agent. The bread must rise, surely, because food mattered to men. My hands slipped into the soft silkiness of the flour – perfectly fine flour with no husks and much suited to making the loaves that Biddy's hands contrived for us.

Her hands…

They were scarred with many nicks from blade and tine or from the odd infection from a lodged thorn and they were becoming spotted and bent with age and effort. Her nails were short and square; nothing elegant about her hands at all. But they were soft. Bridget had been my mother's herbalist, the village midwife and healer and much respected. She could create an unguent from wild plants that would mend and soften and could oft be seen hooking the knotted fingers into a pot, removing a creamy potion and smoothing it over her skin.

Ah, Alaïs' Bridget. My Biddy to whom I had caused such dislocation – Linn in Wales, Cazenay in Aquitaine, Genoa, Toulon, Venezia, trial by sea, capture and imprisonment by the false Templars – hardly treatment from a loving and caring mistress. The woman could be safe in her *cote* in the village of Moncrieff, caring for her friends and for Brother John.

Yes, Ysabel. Look at the lines on her face and mark the journey she has made across the map of your life.

And what of Gwen? A pert Saxon lass whom I had been drawn to the minute she sidled into my chamber during those fraught days as the wife of Baron de Courcey; feisty, loyal Gwen who gave up life in a place with which she was familiar to follow my whims and my child in to the world of the unknown. From her mouth in Cyprus, had come these words:

'Why, my lady? Why do you behave like this? Is it not enough that they hold Peter and my mother … that they hold my family, that William could have been killed? Sometimes madame, I just want to walk away from you.'

120

And more recently, she had hissed, *'Your Peter? If he'd never been Moncrieff's Peter, none of this would have happened.'*

The expression upon her face had flattened me. Gwen had been my sister-friend and one from whom I drew strength but it seemed I had not been reciprocal enough. She had been the hand that had held mine when I was delivered of William. Her fingers those that had held a damp cloth to my brow in Cyprus when headaches threatened to dismember my mind.

But now, Ysabel. What about now?

A moment of intense realisation. That whilst one could think one was a friend to a villein, one was really only acting the role whereas in truth one lived and breathed the role of master with servant. Unconsciously. It was as natural a part of one's life as breathing air. And wrong. Wrong when one relied on these people for one's very existence. I had thought that our house had been an equal house but I was fooling myself.

And then there was Peter. Staunch, quiet Peter who had suffered so much. More than any Christian soul could ask of him. For him, if no one else, I found myself bought to trial and found guilty. And how did I recompense him? By dragging him to the marketplace because I couldn't abide Guillaume and now he lay on his bed with injuries that had come from me.

Gwenny thought so. He mattered to her so much and I wondered what mattered to me?

As I mixed the bread, I thought that my son mattered – he whose little hand fitted into mine like a key into a lock. My husband, of course – he of the stern face, the sarcastic line of speech and who could love better than any hero about whom a troubadour might sing.

But was there aught else that could cause hearts to sing, like Gwenny's did for Peter? My floury hand flew to my chest as I realised there *was* nothing, because for almost four years I had been running with no time to allow my heart to hum, let alone sing like it should. Brother John had said to me when I was the Moncrieff child, that it was not a politic thing to rely on people for one's happiness because they could be removed in a moment, leaving nothing but memories. Apart from God, about whom one's heart should lift every day, Brother John claimed there should be something that raised you beyond the realms of drear days.

I pummelled the dough as I recalled Bridget doing, and shaped the bread into six loaves, placing them in a pan near the fire to warm and rise and as I stood back, I knew that nothing would ever change for me. I could become Christendom's most accomplished trobairitz or a talented needlewoman, I could spend my life being saintly and interceding for all in need. I could become a healer, a gardener, a renowned philosopher studying life, God and the stars and still *nothing* could induce a joyous song from my heart like my son or my husband.

In short, I thought I would give my life for them both and sing loud in the doing.

Something about working in that humble space and creating something as fundamental as our bread had given me backbone and direction – more than any urging from Mehmet or even Tobias. In truth, I had no time for vacillation. The house would be led to be sure, and by the wife of its lord.

Later, while the pottage simmered and the bread baked, and after I had carted jugs of ale and wine to the table and heaped the last of our olives and cheese on platters, I walked to the guardhouse to call the men to the house to eat. Johannes, surprised that I should include them rather than sending food to the guardhouse, said they would come in shifts and I was indeed relieved to know the house would still be under watch as food was consumed.

I had heard Toby and William outside while I worked, a riding lesson proceeding with much noise. When next I listened, John and Johannes were eating and noticed my attention at the shutters.

'Master William is at the butts with Guillaume, my lady. He has a good eye and good aim.'

'Guillaume does not stand at his post?' I asked. Immediately I felt guilty for suspecting him of dereliction of duty but I had to heap something on him to give my intuition veracity.

'Tis not his turn, my lady. By rights he should be sleeping as he was on the wall all night. But he sees his time with Master William as part of his duty so Johannes cannot gainsay him, can you, Jo?'

Johannes shook his head as he chewed on my bread.

'You don't think he might fall asleep on his next post?' I asked.

'He says he rarely sleeps more than an hour or two in grabs. Claims it's a result of Acre…'

Oh yes. Acre. Outremer. How could I forget?

There was another man who had been as dour as Guillaume of Anjou. His name was Arnaud de Vermond – a false Templar. He had called me a bitch, a Devil's whore, and had tried to kill Gisborne until Ulric opened his neck with a knife. De Vermond had been tall and almost monkish in his manner. When his eyes surveyed me, they had the strength of a wolf fixing upon a hind. And then when I chose to stand and fight back, if he could, if it had fitted with his Templar code, he would have spitted me for love of Gisborne's cousin, the rotten and redoubtable Robert Halsham.

So it is a memory that discommodes you, Ysabel?

But I did not know. Mary mother, I did not.

Then if it is a memory, can you not see that memories of Outremer might affect Guillaume in a similar manner?

Jesu, but I hated my conscience.

Listening to my son chattering guilelessly and then laughing and hearing a rumble from Guillaume by return, was it possible I was wrong? I asked myself this question a dozen times a day, because surely Gisborne could not be wrong about *two* men in our lives…

'My lady!'

I swung round. Biddy stood at the kitchen entrance.

'Where did the bread and pottage come from?'

'I made them,' I said diffidently.

She slipped a ladle into the vat of thickened pottage, drawing some up and tasting. 'Huh,' she muttered, not caring if Johannes or John heard. If they noticed my reddened cheeks, they were tactfully avoiding my eyes and Biddy's, gathering themselves to leave.

'Walter and Berto shall come next, my lady,' Johannes said, bowing his head. 'My thanks for the meal.'

He left swiftly and in the ensuing quiet, Biddy finished chewing the wastel. 'It needs salt. So does the pottage.'

'Biddy, I never professed to be a cook but the men needed to be fed and we had little of anything left in the store and I would not worry you. I took note of what we needed and sent word back to Saul with his guards.'

'Jesu, but you *have* been busy!' A cracked bell could ring no better off key.

'Biddy!'

She subsided at the table like a pricked pig's bladder. 'Oh I'm sorry.

You must excuse me, my lady. It has been so worrisome.'

I sat by her, taking her hands, rubbing at one of her scars as if to smooth it away. 'Biddy, I owe *you* an apology. I owe Gwen. But I especially owe Peter. And in respect of this kitchen, I was merely trying to help. I wanted you to stay with your daughter, with Peter. I would not have you worry about us at this time. It was easy enough to see what was missing and to make arrangements for a delivery. The trouble is, we have more men…'

'Indeed. More mouths,' she sighed.

'Biddy, we can work together you and I, and if you need to be with Gwen and Peter then so be it. Gwen already holds me to account. I would not cause her more distress.'

'You must forgive her, Lady Ysabel, she don't mean to be like she is. She's just not herself. She's tired and…'

I thought of Gwen's moods of late. 'Biddy, is she with child?'

Her head flew up. 'How…'

I grinned. 'I didn't. It was a wild guess and I am thrilled. This must surely make she and Peter happy.'

Another sigh. 'Peter does not know and Gwen will not tell him just yet. She is afraid…' She stopped and looked out the kitchen entrance into the passage.

'Biddy?'

Her hands tightened in mine. 'She's afraid to bear a child here. She does not want her babe to share the kind of danger that Master William experiences.'

I knew what must be done. 'Then she must go back to England as soon as Peter can move about freely. They must go together, I will tell them…'

'No, you must not!' A shrill tone edged Biddy's words and her hands slipped from mine and knotted together. 'Not yet. Not till she's told Peter he's going to be a father. Not till then.'

I could not understand at all. I would grant Gwen and Peter anything to help them be delivered safely of their own child and surely time was of the essence. They *must* travel before winter closed the roads completely, before the boats from Calais ceased sailing, if they had not already done so. Oh my God, how I would miss her. How William would miss them both.

'But what of you, Biddy? Would you go with them?'

Her eyes filled with tears. ''Tis my own grandchild, Lady Ysabel…'

A chasm opened up and swallowed me. I would be alone…

Stupid woman. You have a son and a husband…

But no, I would have no one left, no one who knew my own family intimately. No one who could remember my mother or who could read me like a Book of Hours. I was shaken to the core. It was at that moment that I realised offering Peter, Gwen and Biddy their freedom in the past had been a mere token, that I never ever expected them to leave me.

So blind was my ego.

'Then, Biddy, you must leave as well. I tried to tell you this when we woke this morning.'

She looked around her domain hopelessly. I truly believed the word 'domain' summed up everything. Here in this household, within the house of Gisborne, she was queen. Everyone deferred to her over household matters far more than they deferred to the lady of the manor. She lived in a moneyed house, had quality clothes, ate well, wanted for nothing. And she had the love and adoration of a little boy and his family.

If she returned to Moncrieff, she would live in a dirt-floored hovel, scratching a living from herbs and simples. Even Lady Cecilia would be absent and Brother John could guarantee nothing but the care of her soul. Not really, despite his protestations. Thus as she surveyed the kitchens, I truly believed she was torn by her predicament.

'But, my lady, what would you do without me?'

I laughed. Hollow, mirthless.

Lead, woman. Lead by example!

'I would manage,' I said. 'I have already started, have I not? Albeit without the salt. And we have a day or so for you to teach me as much as you can. Peter cannot travel until he can move, after all.'

But they cannot leave much later, Ysabel. Less than a sennight…

'But what about Master William? What if…'

'If they come, Biddy, I shall run with him. Far away where none can find us.'

Her face crumpled further – how she loved William.

'And you know, Biddy,' I continued, standing to fill bowls for Berto and Walter whom I could hear mounting the stair. 'I am very good at running and I am also excellent with a knife.'

I placed the bowls and bread on the table as the two men walked in, Berto's size a thing of wonder. If his fellow wrestlers were built similarly, we would need to roast an ox daily to feed them.

I took three small bowls and filled them, placing them on a tray, slicing bread into pieces and piling cheese and olives alongside. 'Tis all we have until Saul sends our provisions, but take this for Gwen, Peter and yourself.'

She picked up the salver, cast another look around the kitchens, and heaved a sigh, her eyes settling on me as if she were waiting for an apocalyptic vision to shatter our lives.

'S'cuse, *Madama*.' Berto held out his bowl in a bear's paw. 'More please?' He smiled, revealing a few broken teeth, his misshapen nose sliding even further to the side of his face as he did so.

Berto, it would seem, would be our trebuchet. I hoped that anyone beyond our walls would not be able to withstand even a finger-flick from these wrestlers, let alone a grip around the body. I fed three more of them and despaired of any food being left for Mehmet, Toby and William. I did not care for myself. When Biddy had spoken earlier, my appetite had vanished like water down a drain.

But what about Guillaume, Ysabel? He cannot starve.

No. Of course…

He came late, apologising, saying he had been fletching.

'You are accomplished at many things, *Monsieur* Guillaume.'

'I am a fletcher by trade, my lady. I make…'

'Yes?'

Did I care?

'I make weapons.'

'Ah.' It all became clear. To a king, a duke, a knight – a weapon maker was as good as a cache of coin. In Outremer, Guillaume would have been worth a king's ransom to his liege. Not just as a master archer, but a fletcher as well. But he invited no further conversation and I had a dirty kitchen. I stacked bowls and spoons and placed them in a pan of warmed water.

'May I speak, my lady?'

I turned back to him, wishing he would not.

'You do not like me.' A matter of fact, spoken quietly and with no rancour.

How ironic that I, the runner, had nowhere to run at that moment. I could not answer.

'May one ask why?'

'*May one ask why?*' The way he asked was so genteel, far from the vernacular of an armourer or weapon maker and the confusion must have flashed across my face.

'My lord Gisborne asked me to stay, my lady. I did not seek this.'

No. But you needn't have accepted.

He took his knife – a long bone hafted killing blade – and cut a chunk of bread.

'Indeed,' I answered. 'Then I trust my husband's judgement.'

He pushed the bowl away, took some cheese and moved to the door.

'Thank you for the excellent bread,' he said, his eyes not meeting mine.

And then he was gone.

Every time we collided, Guillaume of Anjou made me feel *more* uneasy rather than less. I felt vulnerable near him, as if he were the snake in our grass. This time was no different and I scraped the last of the pottage into three more bowls, adding left-over bread scraps to the table as Mehmet and Toby walked in with William.

'Toby,' I pounced on him before he had time to breathe. 'Teach me to use a sword.'

William's eyes lit up. 'Me too, pleathe?' He grabbed my hand and pumped it.

'My lady, I don't doubt your ability to learn,' Toby began and I could see prevarication writ large. 'But I doubt you could lift a sword. Have you ever held Sir Guy's?'

In fact I had, when moving it out of the way in our chamber and it was indeed heavy but I would admit to nothing so I shook my head.

Tobias continued, 'Then imagine lifting it and trying to swing. The weight of it would cause you to drop your shoulder and throw your body completely off-balance. No, it is far too dangerous.'

Mehmet had maintained a diplomatic silence, busying himself with his pottage and breaking his bread.

'Mehmet?' He would agree with me, surely. If nothing else he might consider it would keep me amused in a time of tension.

'I must agree with Tobias, my lady. And besides, there is no need for you to learn…'

'If I must, Mehmet, I shall over-rule you…' William's eager gaze swung between us. 'I shall use *your* sword, Toby. It shall fit perfectly. If it is suitable, I shall have one made the same size. I intend to learn and none shall gainsay me.'

I swept out of the kitchen, William on my heels. 'And me, Mama. Can I uthe Toby'th thord.'

'No William, you may not. You may watch Toby teach me and perhaps you can fight me with your wooden sword and I shall use a stave. We will be partners. Now go and sit down next to Toby and eat or I will become very angry.'

He obliged, shouting to Toby that he was 'to be Mama'th partner'. I doubt he understood what was meant.

As I stepped off the bottom of the stair to get some air, Guillaume pushed himself away from the wall. He brushed crumbs from his tunic and wiped his mouth carefully.

'I heard your request, Madame. You wish to learn the sword? I will teach you.'

'I thank you, but no. Toby…'

'Toby is a minstrel, if I may be so bold. He wears a sword for decoration. His weapon of choice is a knife. I, on the other hand, can handle a war sword with the best of them.'

He pulled his sword from its scabbard, the blade sighing quietly as it left the leather and bronze sleeve. He tossed it from hand to hand, threw the remains of his bread in the air and in a swift uppercut, sliced it in half before it had reached eye level. He passed me the weapon. 'Your turn, my lady.' And threw one of the bigger crusts up in front of me.

Whilst my intent was to lift and cut as he had done, I found I could barely move the sword from its downward angle, my hand would hardly encircle the grip and with sweaty embarrassment, slid to the quillons. The bread fell to the ground, mocking me.

''Tis as Toby said. You need a light blade. We shall use his.' He strode away swiftly, calling over his shoulder. 'Tomorrow at cockcrow.'

It was decided – with the speed of a fast-moving river and before I had time to refuse him. He left me feeling weather-beaten and exhausted.

I did not see Biddy again as I tidied the kitchen, making up more loaves for the morrow and there was no more flour, no more anything except for roots and leaves.

Saul, do not delay…

I walked to the guardhouse where Johannes sat sharpening his blades, the sound of the whetstone sending shivers across my shoulders. Everything about our villa was changed. The sounds now were of weapons and men, the place itself with gates slammed shut and in a state of siege.

'Johannes,' I called and he looked up and as quickly stood, bowing in the familiarly formal way.

'My lady…' his hair fell across his forehead and he twitched it back behind his ear.

'Johannes, we have no food but for some bread. I need you to explain to the men that I believe we will have our villa re-provisioned by tomorrow eve. In the meantime…'

'My lady, in the meantime those of us who are off-duty can fish outside the gates. Do not forget we are men who are used to foraging on campaign. We will not starve.'

'But is it safe to do so? I would not wish any further danger upon us.'

'We would not go out if such an action threatened us or the household. It is quiet currently.' His Lübeck accent, heavy and cool like the man, was the perfect thing to colour his words, such a strength to me at this time. 'But I will ask Mehmet for approval.'

A good man, loyal and thorough.

I purloined Toby's sword before bed, weighing it in my hands. ''Tis a thing of beauty, Toby, as well as practicality. I shall try not to damage it.'

'I thank you, my lady…' His face had the look of a man who has loaned his favourite gelding for a race, knowing its leg might be broken. Was it not bad manners to ask to borrow a man's own sword? I smiled and bid him goodnight.

In Gisborne's and my chamber, I laid it carefully by my bed, wrapped in my old grey cloak. If I could learn to adequately wield a sword, I would feel more adept – knife, bow, sword – nothing would stop the she-cat from protecting its kit.

I woke before Matins. Biddy had crept in during the night and lay snoring deeply.

'Peter?' I had asked as she pulled off her clothes.

'Better. Tomorrow will be a good day.'

'Gwen?'

'Maudlin. But relieved nevertheless. Goodnight to you, my lady. Sleep well and … thank you.'

I smiled in the dark. 'I do love you, Bridget,' I whispered.

'Yer a good girl,' she mumbled.

And now she snored and I liked it. It showed me that she slept deeply and the rhythm of it and the darkness of the room was like to keep William asleep for that much longer.

I crept down the stair, dressed in the familiar, tired tunic, hose and boots of yesteryear, with the grey cloak over the top. Stopping by the well, I freshened my face with cold water, plaiting un-combed hair with damp hands as the dirty oyster sky became streaked with umber and the rooster of prior days began crowing. I caught a glimpse of our men on the walls, armed and vigilant at each corner, and one of our wrestlers, perhaps Berto, standing watch at the gates.

There was a sense of expectation in the air. The more so for me because I hoped Gisborne would return this day. I passed the garden and on to the butt with no sign of Guillaume, but his bow and a clutch of arrows lay on a trestle, cushioned by a dark cloak. Birds began to sing as I idly picked up the weapon. It had the up-curved nock of the traditional Saracen bow but the ebony wood was one I did not recognise. Worn brown leather wound tightly round the grip and the nocking points at each end of the bow were tooled cleverly to represent a wild cat's jaws. It was a piece of art.

I held the bow and idly sighted the target, then with an unconscious action, reached for an arrow, nocked it and let it fly. It hit the butt almost dead centre and I nodded, grabbed another arrow, straining the string back to my cheek, elbow lined up with my ear. Loose! But it went wide of the centre and I frowned.

'Not as good as the first shot, but you are not new to this, I think.' Guillaume took the bow from my hands as my cheeks flamed.

'I apologise,' I said. 'I should not have used your bow.'

'No matter,' he replied with his usual paucity of words. 'You have Toby's sword? Remove the belt and scabbard, if you please, and withdraw the sword … good…'

He began – teaching me the grip, the stance, having me stand over slightly flexed knees. He directed me to swing and step, following his own action and I felt as if we traced the Greek alphabet in the air. But with every sweep I swear I could see the unknown Templar before me and I scythed him through the middle again and again, until the sweat rolled down my face and blood spatters obscured my vision.

'You work with hate and fury in your veins, my lady. Do not. You will make mistakes.'

Guillaume swung slowly and let it be said gracefully and for just this moment, I put my distrust aside and learned. We worked until I felt sweat beneath my arms and on my back and until the villa had woken. I could hear William in the kitchens and guessed Biddy had begun to cook yesternight's loaves.

'Remember, my lady, a swordsman who defends rather than attacks will lose. And you must anticipate. Read your opponent. Now put the sword down and we shall fight with staves as make-do swords.'

He passed me a stave the length of a sword, stood back and weighed his own as if he held the actual weapon and then suddenly whirled in a circle, his stave sweeping toward my middle. As he had begun to whirl, some instinct caused me to step back and then two-handed, I brought my stave up to knock his sweep aside. Immediately I stepped in, releasing one hand, pulling the stave back and thrusting it upward again. He met me so that if we had swords, they would have clashed, jarring rattling my arm to its sockets. The wooden staves slid down their lengths to what would have been the quillons of our swords. Locked as we were, I could think of only two things – to knee him in the groin or stamp hard on his foot. The latter would mean nothing to a man of his height from a small-framed person like myself. Our eyes had not often met at any time but so close up I had no option but to look directly at my opponent. His were deep brown, normally hooded and guarded – now they glinted and the dour mouth split into a cynical grin.

'Come on my lady, attack!'

And so I hefted my knee hard into his groin, his grip on the weapon loosening as he sagged with a gasp. I knocked his stave away as he bent, then lifted my own to come sweeping down toward the back of his head.

'You are dead,' I said, my stave lying on his neck.

'You are clever,' he panted. ''Tis well done. An opponent unmanned is an opponent disarmed.'

I didn't apologise. I walked to the trestle, laid down the stave, sheathed

Toby's sword and turned to thank Guillaume. His face was grey and I guessed he wanted to clutch at his manhood and groan. But pride is important to men.

'I thank you, Guillaume. You have taught me much and swiftly. However, I am needed in the kitchens. Cockcrow tomorrow?'

Pained, he nodded and I hurried away.

See now, Guillaume of Anjou. The mistress of the house learns quickly.

As I passed under the fig's branches, a wide-shouldered figure limped toward me, stick in one hand, wife holding onto the other.

'Peter! Mary Mother but I am glad to see you about.' I reached to touch his arm.

'Don't do to lie abed, my lady.'

'Indeed. If Mehmet says so.' I turned my attention to Gwen and smiled tentatively. 'What think you, Gwen?'

Her expression did not soften but she shifted her feet as if she were uncomfortable. 'I think he must do what he wants, my lady. Besides, is it not all men to the gates?' She was as diffident as I had been and I wanted to reach out, to hug…

'Of course. Peter, you must do exactly what is right for you. Does your leg pain you?'

'Not so badly and it does not bleed.' He spoke with his attention elsewhere, perhaps anywhere but me. His hand gripped the crutch with an intensity that might have belied his words, but what right had I to disagree?

'Your head?' I persisted.

'Better.' A man of few words.

'Then, Gwenny, look after him well. Where do you go?'

Gwen tucked her hand tighter through Peter's arm, 'To the guardhouse to discuss how Peter can take up his duty.'

'I see. You know we are augmented with three more men and that Sir Guy and Adam will have returned by this evening.'

Peter's attention snapped back to me, his mouth downturned, eyebrows drawn together. 'Sir Guy returns this night? So soon?'

'Do not concern yourself, Peter. He will not expect you to take on any more than you are able.'

He nodded and began to move toward the guardhouse, Gwenny's arm slipping free.

'My lady, I'm so very sorry. I was so caught up in my concerns…'

'Tis of no account, Gwen. Surely you knew that I would understand. Look at what I have done in the name of love for my own husband. And besides, I know you are with ch…'

'Hush! I have not yet told him.'

'Then you must and soonest. Tis only fair. Has Biddy told you both what I wish for you?'

'Yes, and I thank you.'

My eyes smarted as I realised she did intend to leave us. I had hoped… 'When?'

She clasped her hands around herself, almost as if a ghost sat at her graveside. 'Before the sennight is done.'

Oh Gwen.

I nodded. 'Go to Peter, my dear. He may need you.' I smiled then and walked on toward the house from where the ubiquitous sound of William floated.

He and Toby sat playing tablemen, and he jumped up. 'Mama, I winned again.' He ran around the dining hall, our grandly-named everything chamber. 'I winned, I winned.'

'Tis as well he wins, my lady,' said Toby as he began to pack the game away. 'It keeps him in a good frame of mind.'

'But he needs to learn about losing as well, Toby. Do not forget.'

'Perhaps after this trouble is over, yes?'

'Perhaps.' I sighed as I laid his sword on the table. 'I thank you for its use. As you can see, it is undamaged. We only used it for shadow swords and we fought with cut-off staves.'

'It went well?'

'It did. Oddly.'

'You sound surprised.'

'I am,' but I didn't enlarge. 'You know, it seems so very quiet around the villa at the moment. As if we worry for nothing.'

'It does not pay to drop one's guard, Lady Ysabel. It is like this before a battle engages. A period of furious activity as the sides prepare and then profound quiet which serves to unsettle one even more before the charge is sounded.'

'Will he come today do you think?' Plaintive again. Sometimes I wasn't sure if I wanted Gisborne back to admonish him roundly or to have him hold me and say everything would be well. And of course, Toby knew I meant my husband and not the enemy.

'It's in God's hands. My lady, when I left him near Udene he asked me to tell you something. He was unable to say what, thinking I suspect, that I would know. And I believe I do. He wanted me to remind you of why you and he married. That is all.'

My hands came together and tears welled, but I willed them not to run. I, Lady Gisborne, must be stronger than that. Yes, I did remember why we had married – it was not a marriage of convenience. But that said, I was still filled with ire that he could leave us at this time.

William sidled in between us. 'Mama, can I see Peter?'

'Oh, yes, yes, of course. Toby, Peter is up and walking. He has gone to the guardhouse.'

'You say? That is such good news.' He began to follow William who had dashed down the stair.

'Is Mehmet within, Toby?' I called after him.

'He was gone early. I heard him leave but I do not wake easily…' He waved and disappeared from sight.

The aroma from the kitchens met me before I had even entered. The bread smelled wholesome and reminded one of things simple and good in our world. Biddy looked up from knocking a cooked loaf.

'Good bread, Lady Ysabel. Listen…' She tapped it again.

I shrugged. 'It is all we have left, Biddy. That and some wine.'

'Ah well – flesh and blood of Christ, huh? I'd even say Christ Hisself was providing for us.'

'What say you?'

'John has been fishing, my lady.' She slapped two silver-scaled mackerel on the table. 'And they were caught in a heartbeat. He says he'll catch more…'

'They have opened the gates?' My voice pitched slightly higher.

'Mehmet said only if Berto and one of the other big fellers stood at the gates and that guards remained on the walls.'

'Oh Biddy, I just worry. They are good men, of course…'

'Oh by God's Holy Toenails, my lady! Go to the gates and see for yourself.

Maybe you'll be happier then.'

Happier? Not till Gisborne is back and until we have food and a plan.

Walter passed me on the stair. 'Three more fish, my lady. Peter's catching them as fast as he can, but a river mist is creeping in.'

'Peter?' I asked, surprised.

'John had to go to his duty,' Walter replied as he hurried to the kitchens.

Berto stood at one side of the gate, his equally well-muscled friend, Aldo, at the other. On the parapet – Johannes, John, Toby and Guillaume.

Four corners.

The distance from the gate to the water was negligible depending on the tide, and the banks were lined with small trees, reeds and grasses. In amongst the reeds, I thought I detected movement but it was hard to discern as delicate ribbons of fog curled in and out of the foliage, shifted by a breeze. The cool damp pierced my clothing and what water I could see was the colour of a sword blade.

'Peter?' I called.

No reply.

'Peter!' I shouted.

Johannes yelled from the parapet. 'Madame?'

'I cannot see him and he does not reply,' I responded.

I pushed through the reeds and they added their whispering silvered tones to the air as I searched up and down in front of the gate, Johannes puffing up to me.

'Madame, he was here. He, Gwen and Master Gisborne.'

No! No!

CHAPTER SEVEN

We began to beat the reeds and call loudly, sending up flocks of wild fowl in a cacophony of angry squawking.

Nothing, no sign at all. William…

I held my breath, faintness creeping upon me, but pushing forward through more reeds. There! A shape! Lying in a bower of broken and bent river foliage.

'Gwenny, Gwen. Johannes,' I cried. 'Here.' I flung myself down by my maidservant. She lay with blood seeping from her gown folds and from a knock to her head.

'Mehmet! Get him, quickly.' I scanned the area. 'William, answer me!' The fear and anxiety in my voice would have been obvious it were not smothered by the mist that grew as if possessed, to surround us and shield the villa from view. I knew there would be no reply.

That what I had feared had come upon us.

William had been taken.

'Madame, none of us have seen Mehmet since last eve when he gave me this morning's orders.'

'Did Mehmet agree to the gates opening when you spoke?'

'No, my lady. He counselled against it.' Johannes knelt by Gwen's side, his hands pulling at her folds, trying to cover her more completely.

'Then why did you open them? Who said Mehmet had changed his mind?' I could feel a cold hard core thickening inside me. I remembered this once before, when I had been married to Baron de Courcey.

'Peter. He said he had seen Mehmet when he dressed his wounds this morning.'

'And you did not think to check?'

Johannes picked Gwen up and carried her with gentle delicacy toward the gate. 'It was Peter, my lady. Why would we not trust him?'

Indeed, Ysabel. Why not? Now if it were Guillaume...

As we hurried back, Berto and Aldo began to close the gates. 'No! Do not. Do not shut the gates. If William returns... Berto, Aldo – stand to arms and guard us with your lives.

I raced after Johannes who had reached the stair and was hurrying to the kitchens.

'Biddy,' I called. 'Biddy...'

She spun round, dropping a knife, saw Gwen and I thought I should have to run to her and catch her, so pale did her face become.

'Oh, Jesu. Not my precious girl...'

Johannes pushed stools away from the table with his legs and I grabbed bread and fish and thrust them in a cloth to place on the floor. The rest I just swiped off with my hands. Johannes laid Gwen down gently and backed away.

'Madame...' he said.

'Go. Do what you must. Find them, please...' I said, unable to take my eyes from Gwen's bloody gown.

Biddy had grabbed cloths and steeped them in vinegar, wiping her daughter's head. 'It's bad,' she said. 'Needs stitching.'

Although she moved methodically, she was reined in so tight I thought she would split with the effort. And such guilt flooded every part of me because I longed to leave her, to leave Gwen, to search for my son...

'She is in a faint. Her head... Where is Mehmet?' she asked without looking up.

'We cannot find him, Biddy. He is missing. The baby?'

'She begins to lose it. Please go, Lady Ysabel. I will deal with this. Find Mehmet and be with your son.'

I turned toward the door. 'William has gone, Biddy. He and Peter have gone...' I flung this over my shoulder and my last sight was of her lifting Gwen's folds away and placing cloths to staunch the flow of blood.

Johannes met me. 'Madame, we have found Mehmet. He was knocked senseless and left in the furthest corner of the stables.'

'Is he…'

'He lives but with an almighty headache. Madame, someone has been wielding a club with great force I think.'

I shook my head as if I did not want to know. 'William?'

'There is no sign. We have searched round the villa walls and all we can discern are two sets of hoof-prints near the bridge leading away into Venezia.'

I tried to think clearly, to push my fears away. 'Peter has been kidnapped with William. Get the horses…'

But my words were drowned by the welter of hoof beats cantering over the bridge and toward us.

'Oh my God,' I whispered. 'Please let it be William and Peter.'

Two staunch rounceys emerged through the fog and I ran toward them. 'Peter!'

But no…

'Guy! Oh Jesu!'

He flung from his horse and grabbed my arm, my distress no doubt emblazoned across my face. 'What goes, Ysabel?'

His face had set into hard lines. I recall someone saying that one could cut silk with his expression once. Was it Cecilia?

'Ysabel, answer me!'

I realised that I stood speechless and that tears were running down my face as I pushed at his tight grip.

'The young master and Peter,' Johannes broke in. 'They have vanished and Gwen and Mehmet have been attacked. Mehmet is not so bad but little Gwen…'

'God's bones,' muttered Adam as he threw his horse's reins at Berto, running to the guardhouse yelling 'To me, to me!'

Gisborne stood statue still. Anger flickered through his eyes and as quickly vanished. This removal of emotion from his face was the thing I feared most because it meant distancing, dislocation. 'Explain,' he said with such venomous quiet that I diminished in a moment in front of him. All at once, it felt as if his blade sat on *my* neck rather as my own stave had been on Guillaume's.

'They went to fish … the guards were watching.'

'Jesus Christ,' he exploded. 'Fishing!' He pounded his gauntleted fist against the gate frame. 'And Mehmet *allowed* this?'

'Mehmet was nowhere in evidence…' I began to pull myself up, to answer him.

Defend yourself, Ysabel.

'… and Peter told the men that Mehmet agreed with the plan when he tended to him this morning.'

'*Tended* to Peter?'

'He was wounded in an attack.'

'Wounded? *Another* attack? God in heaven,' Gisborne growled. 'I see you do an excellent job of managing our home, Ysabel. Leaving customary chaos in your wake.'

It was tinder to the fire and I burned as if I were a conflagration. 'You dare, you swine!' I shouted at him, beginning to pace. 'You left us knowing this could happen. I begged you not to. I begged you to remove us from here. But in your arrogance you assumed to know best. *My lord,*' I sneered, 'you are as much and more to blame.'

I pushed past him, banging into his side hard with deliberate intent, storming to the stable and grabbing Thea, throwing a saddle on, then a bridle. Dragging her outside to a large stone block and climbing aboard. 'John!' I yelled so loud my voice broke and Thea arched her head and danced sideways across the yard. 'Toby! To horse! We go!'

Gisborne grabbed Thea's reins, a tall black-cloaked streak standing in front of me, almost snarling, 'Dismount, you go nowhere. I shall take the men and we shall search without an hysterical and unbalanced woman in our midst.'

'*That,*' I jabbed my finger in the air toward the opened gates. '… is my son.'

'And mine,' he hissed back. 'Now dismount…'

Adam and the men emerged from the guardhouse, grabbing horses and mounting as Mehmet walked from the house, his robes smeared with what I knew was Gwen's blood.

'My lord,' he said. 'You chastise your lady wife unfairly. We have been gulled and our defences broken and it is not her fault. You must all go immediately and I will stay with Berto and his men and keep watch here. Get yourself a fresh mount.'

Gisborne tried to stare him down but Mehmet said, 'My lord, time passes.'

His hands fell from Thea and he strode to the stable, not looking at me once.

'Mehmet,' I said taking up the reins and grasping them firmly. 'How is Gwenny?'

'She has lost the child and is unconscious.'

'Please help her and help Biddy.' I turned my horse to the men. 'Adam, I am coming with you.'

Gisborne had emerged with his favourite horse – the leggy grey. Mounting, he warned, 'Ysabel…'

'I will come,' I repeated, she-wolf incarnate as I pushed in between Johannes and Toby, leaving my loved and loving husband to take up the rear.

We rode at speed over the bridge, the horses drumming a war cry on the timber. I left some of my soul with Biddy and Gwen but in war, needs must, and I had to forget the pain and emotion. As Guillaume had said, *'You work with hate and fury in your veins, my lady. Do not. You will make mistakes.'*

As we approached the centre of Venezia, Gisborne hauled us to a stop, our horses prancing and snorting, bits and shod hooves clinking and ringing.

'We search in pairs,' he said, dividing us up. I suspect he deliberately paired me with Guillaume rather than himself and it suited me because right now I didn't want to be in the same place as my husband, let alone riding at his side.

Think clearly, you child. Mistakes will lose your son…

We were sent to the docks, Guillaume and I, and as we rode to a hitching post, from where we could walk and ask questions, I realised that apart from my *misericorde,* I was unarmed. I rubbed at my side in agitation. As Guillaume asked if a man and little boy had been seen, I took a breath and steadied myself, willing that dark seam to flood through every part of me. I could feel the cold speeding along my veins, filling me with a type of battle fervour. I walked toward youths leaning against a wall of a waterside inn and asked them the same question Guillaume had already asked a dozen other folk along the docks.

'Looking for a tall man, rope-coloured hair, and a little black-haired boy. The tall man limps.'

'What fer? He yer lover? Has a fancy for boys like you, does 'e?'

Face flaming, the youths chuckling at my distress, I realised that I was still in my men's clothes. 'No. He's my brother and he's not right in the head.' I tapped my temple. 'Taken his master's child for a jaunt and there'll be hell to pay.' I kept myself calm and lying well – it seemed to come naturally and I thanked the Virgin for stiffening my spine.

'As it 'appens, so we 'ave. They got horses from the livery there. Left a while back.'

'A ducat if you can tell me the colours of the horses and how many men?'

The youths' eyes widened as I felt in my purse, coins jingling under my fingers and I saw greedy hands settling upon knives at belts.

A voice said at my shoulder, 'Four men and a boy, I was told at the inn…' Guillaume stood easily, bow over shoulder and hand resting on the pommel of his sword. The youths looked up at him and backed away, all except one.

'A ducat for colours of the horses?' he asked.

'Aye,' I answered.

'Two browns, a black and a chestnut,' he said and held out his hand.

I dropped the ducat into it and said, 'Another if you know where they are headed.'

He laughed. 'Probably Hell with winter comin' but I 'eard one say the roads are still open to Genova.'

Genova!

I threw the ducat into his grubby cracked palm and we left to retrieve our mounts as I heard the laughter behind us. Were we gulled again? Just as we had been within our own walls?

'Do they tell the truth?' I asked as I mounted Thea.

'They do. The men at the inn heard the same thing.'

I was too overwrought to speak again to Guillaume as we rode back to meet the others near the half-finished church in the square, nursing my distress, allowing it to grow and prosper.

'Madame, I must speak with you.'

'And I would not talk with you, Guillaume. Now is not the time.'

Churlish, Ysabel. You learn nothing!

'But…'

'No. We must get my husband and speed onward to Genova. Recovering Peter and William is all I care about.'

'This *is* about Peter, my lady,' he replied as we wove in and out of the crowds filling the dockside markets.

I dragged on Thea's reins and turned her broadside to him. Behind us, a velvet-clad merchant on a black stallion almost walked into Thea's hindquarters and I earned a curse and a glaring look as the fellow rode on. Be damned to *him*, I thought. *He* probably lives openly in some large, wealth-bestowed villa close to the Doge and has not lost his son. I gestured rudely after him. Gisborne had trained me well as I swear I heard ice cracking in my veins, just as it does in winter in a river, shifting, re-freezing. My manner, formerly angry and frenetic had cooled in an instant.

'And…' I said, the word dancing before us both. Icicles to further chill the moment.

He took Thea's reins and led her, guiding his own horse off the thoroughfare where he could speak to me quietly and without bother. His thin frame had filled out a little under Biddy's care and his dark hair glittered in the winter light. His eyes however remained empty, unreadable.

'On that first eve within your house when I shared Peter's quarters, I did not sleep. It is a habit formed from my time in Outremer. Peter however, slept all night. Restlessly. Tossing and turning, dreaming, talking in his sleep.'

Guillaume stopped and scanned my face, gauging whether I believed him.

'Go on.' I gestured with my hand.

'Word for word, madame, this is what he said.' He took a breath and began. ' *"I cannot. Do not make me"*. But then Madame, he tossed from side to side and was silent for a moment, and then, *"A godless mother, neglectful…"*

I ran the reins through my fingers. Was it me Peter meant? Did he really believe I was so uncaring of my son?

'He said, *"God's child. A little lamb"*, and then the bells rang for Vigils and he stirred, beginning to pray as if he were a monk, I swear.'

Peter – aware of monks' prayers at Vigils?

I doubted it. Guillaume noticed my expression.

'I thought the same, my lady. No offence to Peter, but he is a mere blacksmith. When would he have learned monks' responses?'

In Toulon. At the Commanderie. They could have taught my blacksmith much.

My heart began to jump and I wondered if I wanted to hear what else Guillaume might say.

' *"Not Gwen"*, Peter said. *"Please don't harm my Gwenny. I will get him. I promise"*. It was then that I realised something was badly amiss and I took a great risk. I spoke to him very quietly. *"Tell me again, Peter"*, I said. *"Why must you get him"?"* Guillaume looked out over the crowd, giving me time to digest this latest.

I felt such loss and disenchantment in respect of Peter. Another one I trusted.

I knew whatever would come next it would hurt, raising memories of such magnitude.

'He drifted for a little, not answering, and I thought I would have no response. But then he turned over and muttered *"To save his soul. To save mine. To save Gwenny's. You won't hurt him, will you"*?

The ice inside me cracked so loudly I thought I should shriek with fear. Instead, I answered Guillaume with sarcasm.

'And why should I believe you? You could be merely seeking Gisborne's approval. You would have much to gain.'

He blinked and his mouth settled into a harsh line. It reminded me so much of my husband that I sat back in the saddle.

'I could,' he said. 'But there is little point. I stand to gain nothing from telling you this beyond assurance that a little boy might be rescued. To be frank, Lady Ysabel, you can't afford not to trust me or you might never see William again.'

This time, his stave settled on *my* neck and I felt the pressure.

He noticed and his grim expression softened. 'Madame, I asked him one more question.'

'Yes?' I whispered my reply, conscious for a chilly moment of my manner, my rudeness and my total lack, concentrating on my fingers, winding the reins round and round till the blood stopped flowing to the tips.

'*"What have the others said they will do, Peter?"* I asked. He moaned in his sleep. *"Don't know. William's soul…"* I left well alone then, my lady. He was becoming restless and I was afraid I would cause him to wake.'

'What did you say to him the next day, Guillaume,' I asked. 'Because for sure, he changed vastly from that day.'

'The bells were ringing for Matins, when he arrived outside the stable. I was already sitting there, re-stringing my bow. He commented that I did it with ease and I told him I was a fletcher and made arrows and bows in Outremer. He asked who for and it was then that I took another risk. I said Templar knights. That they wanted to give the *musselmen* some of their own back and so I had taught myself how to make the lightweight Saracen bows the knights might use in the same manner as the Saracen archers. I idly asked Peter if he knew any Templar knights and his face paled to moon colour and he said, *"No. 'Course I don't. How could I?"* Which I thought was extremely odd coming from a man I had found out was immured in a Templar Commanderie for some time.'

'*Peter*,' I whispered, anguish in the word. Then louder, '*He* is a traitor to us. *He* has taken my son. *He* is the breach in our walls…' I turned Thea and tapped her sides hard, putting her into a canter and scattering men, poultry, women, dogs and children as I headed toward my husband and his men.

They waited for us, faces set, standing with their horses. Toby was still mounted and standing together with a mounted stranger whose back was to me. He raised his eyebrows as we rode up.

'Well?' barked my husband.

'Tell him,' I ordered Guillaume.

The men clustered around as the events of that night were recounted.

'Why did you not tell us?' Gisborne's mood had darkened even further. This was the Gisborne who had caused me such confusion when he had been my escort so long ago.

'My lord, I was familiar with none of you. For all you knew I could, as your lady wife so kindly pointed out, have been ingratiating myself. In respect of Peter, every one of you knew him and trusted him.'

Gisborne said nothing but I could see him assessing Guillaume once more. *Good or bad, husband?*

I thrust Thea between them. 'You know now, husband. Peter is a traitor. And he travels overland as far as Genoa with our son. We ascertained this from some youths near the livery. We must go…'

My gaze slid passed the stranger who had turned, and then slid back.

'Ariella!' I gasped and she nodded in response.

'We heard about four men with a child mounted in front…' Toby broke in.

'But we did not hear they travelled to Genova,' Adam added. 'My lord?'

'It is our only lead. Walter, you are one of my best couriers. Make pace. Contact any of our men along the road between here and Genova. Go via Bologna. I have a feeling and I need information. Go!'

Walter threw himself on his horse and raced away in a scattering of stones and Gisborne continued, 'Johannes, you and John escort Ariella back to her home and then take Lady Ysabel to the villa, and I would that you take command again until we either return or you have word from me.

Understood?'

'No,' I broke in. 'I am coming with you.'

'I would come too,' Ariella added quietly.

'Ariella, I admire your loyalty and your kindness in seeking us out at this moment, but *my* loyalty to your father is greater. You will go home. Lady Ysabel,' Gisborne's eyes bored through me. 'It is a wife's role to obey.'

The men's heads all turned toward me, waiting for a response.

'Sir Guy,' I replied, my voice as hard as steel. 'It is a mother's role to protect her child, as it is the father's. And it seems to me, sir, we have both failed. Do not deny me this, my lord.'

Toby's eyebrows reached for the sky and he waited, as did all the men. Like me, I suspect they held their breath.

I knew how hard such a thing would be for my husband to face – not just my public disobedience but also the knowledge that we *had* both failed William and were being held accountable. There were times when I wondered if this was God's way of punishing us for all the lives we had taken or ruined. Guy mounted his horse with a creak of leather, the big grey standing steady as his rider's weight settled in the saddle.

To add even more insult to him, Ariella said, 'My lord, when Walter passed by our booth and told us what had happened, I asked my father if I could attend Lady Gisborne. He sanctioned my idea and I changed immediately into men's clothing,' she indicated her hose, tunic and cloak. 'I am known to pass for a youth and I am adept with a weapon.'

'But I cannot guarantee your safety, Ariella. Your father is my friend and I cannot do this.' Gisborne's tightly contained anger fed down the reins to his horse which backed away from us all, ears flat, tail swishing.

'Sir, with the greatest respect, I think I proved myself in the Arsenale. If you remember.' Ariella once again became that cool woman of my first acquaintance, a force to be reckoned with.

Gisborne's teeth gritted. 'Then come, both of you. But be sure I do not want you to stand in the way of anyone's safety, especially my son's. We do not have time to tend to weak-willed women.'

'So be it,' I replied tartly.

But what about yours and my safety, Guy? Do you not care? A child without father or mother is lost. You and I must surely remember this from our own experience.

I pressed my heels into Thea's sides, pushing her away from the square and toward the outskirts. Gisborne and Adam led the way, Ariella and I followed and Toby and our master marksman, Guillaume, brought up the rear as the name Genova beat like a drum in my head – Genova, Genoa – the town where William and I had lived and where I had jumped from a wall to chase a dream of a knight's loyalty and affection.

We turned south almost immediately after leaving the Venetian lagoon, heading for Ferrara at a steady canter when we could, galloping when space and the roads allowed us. The roads were rutted, in some places muddy, but the rain that had fallen in these early days of winter had been gentle and we had no flood to worry us. In fact the softness of the going was kind to our horses and I privately thanked the Lord it should be so. For Thea's sake.

'Ariella,' I managed at one point. 'I am indebted…'

Her expression didn't change as she guided her horse over rocks that edged a stream. 'I love William too, Ysabel.'

Water dogged our path. No sooner had we left the lagoons of Venezia than we happened upon the river delta they call Bodincus or Eridanus and which we splashed through at pace. Mud, river stones, wet clothes, it was all the discomfort of travel I remembered – but we closed the distance by riding through the night.

We halted outside the walls of Ferrara when a single bell clanged mournfully for Vigils. How we did not break our horses' legs riding after dusk was a miracle as it was moonless and the night dark and dense. Perhaps God could see how we struggled, Guy and I, with the loss of our son. He had after all lost His own and must know our pain.

Looking up, we could see the flicker of braziers and torches along the parapets and an occasional call and answering shout from guards.

'It is best we remain concealed,' said Gisborne, dismounting. 'Adam, on the morrow when the gates are opened I want you to enter, find out what you can, see if Walter has left a message.'

'Get some food as well,' chimed in Toby. 'My stomach will call the Dead the way it is whining.' He slid down from his horse and rubbed his thighs. Sometimes, I had to remind myself that Toby was actually a minstrel, so often did he attend Guy at these intense moments. So much lately he had acted as an entertainer to William that one could forget this small man had dealt with kings, knights and prelates in Outremer.

What think you now, Toby? Does your heart break like mine?

We settled for what remained of that night. No fire, cold, horses hobbled and grazing what grass they could find. Ariella and I nestled close to each other to keep warm and I said, 'I cannot dissolve my fears, Ariella. I am at a loss…' The tears pricked as I thought of William without Gwenny, without Biddy, without me.

'Talk to your husband,' she advised. 'You need to work together with strength, not division.'

I sighed as I watched my husband stand solitary near his horse but I stayed wrapped in my own misery and did not approach him. The hours drifted slowly and eventually I had to pace about to work off my fearful thoughts – back and forth until a finally supine Gisborne muttered, 'Desist, Ysabel. We would sleep,' from the depths of his cloak.

How could he, I wondered? William might be within the walls and it seems so misguided that we wait.

The birds broke ranks before the sun had even woken next day, joined by the bells for Matins. Dew covered us, our clothes clinging and cold, the horses' coats spangled with diamond drops of moisture, their breath huffing in foggy clouds. As the winter-pale sun rose, we and our mounts began to steam and the smell of wool and horse wrapped round us as we pulled up close by the town. Adam rode on alone through the open gates and we waited beneath the walls. I lay my head on Thea's neck, the softness of her thick winter coat soothing me.

'Do not tax yourself with worry, Ysabel, you *must* believe in the best outcome,' Ariella said as she ran a hand through her horse's mane. 'If you succumb to the worst thoughts, it will deplete your reserves and you will be a weighty nuisance on the journey. Methinks it would take very little for Sir Guy to send you back to Venezia. Besides, when all is said and done, we do know Peter loves little William as if he were his own son. It must surely count for something.'

'What you say is true,' I agreed, noticing Guy moving a little closer to us as we talked. Guillaume and Toby stood apart, silent, looking around. Most would assume they were just idly watching the crowd, but I knew they scanned every face that came and went. 'Peter's affection for William is the one God-given thing through this. That he will care for him. But I wonder what story he has spun to our son so that he is not afraid.' My voice trembled as I said this last and I cursed my frailty.

'Ysabel,' said Gisborne, 'How do you fare?'

Ariella clicked her tongue, moving her horse to where the others stood, tactfully leaving me with my husband.

'As well as one can expect a mother to be, my lord,' I replied, bitterness in my words. 'I worry for our son – that we may have missed him. Why do we not enter Ferrara and search immediately, alert the authorities?'

Guy leaned against a wooden hitching post and spoke evenly. I wished we could touch each other, but he was removed by the width of a person from me and I could see he would not reach across. It was if he had lifted an imaginary drawbridge and exposed a vast moat between us.

'It is best no one knows we are here. Better for William's safety. We *will* find him, Ysabel. I stake my life upon it. But it must be done my way.'

'Your way smacks of time lost and secrets, my lord,' I replied angrily.

He did reach across then, grabbing my arm and holding it tight. 'You think I don't hurt as much as you? That I don't feel crucified with the pain of William's loss?'

I almost stepped back with the force of his anguish. 'No. I… Of course. I am sorry.'

Perhaps he believed my humble words.

'I think they travel slowly, Ysabel.' He watched the passing population, as alert as his men. 'They can't gallop for fear that William will take a tumble and he is too valuable a commodity…'

He stopped and I saw the pain then. It flashed briefly into his eyes and was gone and I had a fleeting recall of Guillaume doing exactly that thing.

'Finish what you would say, Guy,' I said softly. I wanted him to come back to me, to remember his wife who had married him because she loved him, and not for convenience's or propriety's sake.

He gave a faint shake of his head, almost as if he had forgotten I was there. 'Too valuable,' he continued. 'He is bait to draw me in and they will not risk his death. That at least I am confident of. It is the only thing in our favour.'

'But they can *pretend* he is alive, Guy. They can say anything to draw you in now he is gone from us.'

'Indeed,' he replied. 'But I don't think they will.'

'I wish I had such profound confidence, but sadly, after Halsham and de Courcey, I do not. Men forget about children in the circle of war. Besides,' I argued. 'What if they apprehend you in the meantime? Before we can retrieve William. If they exact their revenge…'

We both knew I meant *"if they kill you"* but I could not bring myself to enunciate those words so baldly. Not to my husband who was already dying a thousand deaths that he was likely the cause of our son's disappearance.

'Then,' I continued. 'What of William?'

Gisborne leaned back against the walls of Ferrara and closed his eyes. His dark-clad shape was almost a warning, so marked the contrast between his cloak and hose and the stony walls. His face, fresh-shaven before chasing after his liege, was now stubbled, almost bearded, and his hair lay messily on his nape. He looked more like a felon or lowborn *routier* than a noble and yet I wanted him to take hold of me and soothe my pain. But of course he had his own and would never allow me to ameliorate by return.

Ah, nothing changed.

'What of William?' he said, his eyes opening again. Our gaze locked with such intensity it rivalled an Occitàn summer sun – powerful, searing. 'If I am killed they will not care what happens to him. My guess is they would sell him to the slave markets. He is an attractive child with a melodic singing voice. A Byzantine merchant would pay a high price for him…'

'Jesu!'

Are you really surprised, Ysabel? Whoever said there is a code of honour amongst felons?

'It is why we must find him and remove him. If they must have me, they shall not have my son.'

My hand reached for my husband but Adam pushed through the crowds at that moment, dragging his horse behind. He was flushed, his red hair flopping in wild curls over his forehead.

'You made the right choice, my lord, to head south. But they have bypassed Ferrara and are headed to Bologna. A priest we use wrote this from Walter…'

he handed Gisborne a rolled message and Gisborne quickly read it.

'And now they are further away. Jesu!' I cursed.

'We must leave! Walter will be close behind them and will keep us informed…'

'What if he is unable to get a message to us…'

Cease this whining, Ysabel. This fractiousness is just the weak link Ariella referred to…

'He will. We have many friends,' Gisborne replied shortly as he tightened his horse's girth.

Of course. The faceless men – priests and prelates, merchants and nobles, *routiers* and gatekeepers who sourced information and passed it to Gisborne who then sold it again for an even greater price. It was a dangerous game to play – like wielding a two-edged sword in the dark. We took up our formation again, after Adam had passed us stale grapes, cheese and some wrinkled figs.

'Christ,' muttered Toby. 'This is not food, it's leavings. I'd kill for a capon or a loaf of bread!'

'Then you will have to wait for your murderous meal, Toby,' Gisborne said. 'We eat on the run and must be glad of it.' He kicked his horse into a canter with Guillaume by his side, Ariella and I next and Toby and Adam riding the rearguard.

All concentration was on the roads and eking what we could from mounts that were tired and hungry. As they began to flag, it was obvious we must slow if we were to reach Bologna with able horses beneath us. Gisborne chafed. I could hear his expletives from behind as Ariella eyed me ruefully. We eased to a walk and then halted when the orange roof-tiles of Bologna were in the distance.

'We will reach the town gates before they are closed,' said Gisborne. 'Should you be asked, we are…' he stopped, no doubt wondering what provenance to give us.

'Students, of course,' said Toby, preening. Always ready to act a role, he had excelled a hundredfold working for Gisborne. 'Philosophy perhaps. We are from Venezia, Padua, Genova. Maybe Paris.'

'Aye,' agreed Gisborne. ''Tis good enough. And we must change horses. These are done in. Adam, remember in Aquileia there was merchant who was returning to Bologna. He won a purse-full at dice and you saved him from a cutpurse. Find him and remind him of his debt. He can have our horses to sweeten the pain of giving us new ones.'

When I dismounted, as my feet hit the ground a sizzling pain rushed up to my knees like a lightning flash. I could not help groaning, rubbing the insides of my thighs to push the blood through.

'Me too,' grumped Toby, the unhappy minstrel-knight.

'And I,' admitted Ariella.

'A good enough chance to rest I think,' said Toby. 'And please excuse me if I seek comfort behind a tree.'

None of us watched him go, wrapped up in our discomforts and holding horses who snorted and shook themselves as if trying to rid their backs of all burden. Gisborne and Adam moved from one animal to another, running hands down legs and lifting hooves, feeling for heat and bruising. Guillaume stood with his back to the trees, drinking deep from his costrel. The surrounding scrub and woods were quiet and there was no sign of travellers behind or in front.

I held Thea loosely, rubbing away the sweat beneath her browband when of a sudden she threw up her head, her ears erect, her legs no longer tired as she danced to the end of the reins, pulling me with her, my arms stretched tight.

'Whoa, whoa,' I called. 'What ails you, silly girl?'

'Ysabel,' hissed Ariella. Her tone raised hairs on my neck and I pulled at my *misericorde* with one hand, trying to soothe Thea with the other and knowing when I turned that something untoward would face me.

Toby stood under the twisted and sparsely leafed trees surrounded by five men wrapped in the *brunete* cloaks of the Templar lay brothers. That alone delivered burning acid onto my tongue, fear trying to break through the ice of my veins. A knife lay across the minstrel's throat. His eyes stared valiantly through me and his bravado was as strong as any knight of the realm as he stood there, fists clenched, standing tall, defiance in every pore of his body.

A quick glance showed no sign of either Gisborne or Guillaume, although Adam held the horses and barely acknowledged my desperation.

What should I do?

'Seems you are missing one or two of your party,' said the man who held Toby, in Occitàn. 'If you want this little toy to live, you'd best call 'em out.'

The words were directed to me and raised even more hairs; these men knew us, they had been waiting. Would they kill us or were they just there to slow us down? Toby's head moved very slightly. *"Do nothing"*, he was saying.

But Toby, you are the light of our lives, the flame toward which my son flits each day.

My knife almost slid out of a sweaty palm and I tightened my grasp. We were outnumbered without Guy and Guillaume.

Where are they?

My heart pumped, breath coming too fast.

Be calm and clearheaded…

'We're not patient men,' said the man who would be leader. 'Bring out the others, or the dwarf…'

An arrow whined through the air, over the top of Toby's head and straight into his captor's neck, front to back. He fell backward, blood fountaining from his mouth and neck, his legs twitching. Toby dashed away, bent double, the other *brunetes* stirring, swinging back to back, swords lifting. Adam drew his sword and Ariella and I let our horses go, crouching with daggers drawn. In that brief heartbeat moment, a second arrow loosed from behind the trees, hitting another of the men between the shoulder blades with an audible thunk. He fell, the haft sticking up, the feathers Guillaume's own. I dared not take my eyes from the remaining men. With one yell that I remembered – *"Beau Sante!"* – one that could fell me in a moment with the ugliest memories, they charged us.

Adam, Toby, Ariella and I split apart as though God's hand had reach down and divided us. Adam and I swiftly jumped to the left, Ariella and Toby to the right flank, weapons at the ready, forcing the oncomers to make choices, for in choice lies confusion, error and death.

One ran at Ariella, an ugly brute moving with speed. His face was stubbled and his few teeth bared in a snarl like a wolf about to leap for the throat. One hand was tattooed with the Templar cross and it surprised me, so strict was the code amongst laymen and knight alike. Toby had drawn his sword and pulled it back ready to strike but Guillaume leaped from the trees, the high-pitched ululation I had heard from Mehmet's throat knifing through the surroundings. And then he roared *"Allah Akbar!"* his sword lifting, sweeping, the felon wide-eyed at the madman running at him with echoes of Acre. Guillaume's sword flew in a perfect arc, its midpoint taking the man in the neck, blood spurting as he fell headless at Ariella's feet, the head bumping away, eyes staring. I spun away, vomit in my mouth, to see Gisborne engage another assailant in a swift sweep and parry, sparks flying as strike upon strike rang back and forth across the road. Guillaume thrust Ariella next to me, ripping his bow from his shoulder, dragging one of the arrows that hung from his belt, nocking, aiming.

'Guillaume, no! You will hit Guy…'

Gisborne stepped back and forth, striking at an arm and drawing blood, pushing the attacker back. He seemed effortless, even graceful.

'I'll not hit him, my lady, I had faster targets in the desert.'

'There is no need, he wins…'

But the arrow was loosed anyway, striking the man in the shoulder so deeply the haft almost buried itself. In a moment, Toby had pitched a knife into the man's chest and he was done, pricked like a bloated sheep's carcass, the wind gushing out of him.

I tried to count – five men, four down…

One left, Ysabel. On your guard!

I ripped round to see a large man approach Adam from behind and screamed, 'Adam!' The assailant had no sword and bought up his fist, backhanding Adam across the face so hard that our captain fell backward. I flew at the *brunete,* my *misericorde* hidden in my cloak, yelling at the top of my lungs and the brute grinned at me, standing like some immovable rock in the road.

'Come on then, little boy. Do your worst.'

I had no time to see that Guillaume had nocked again, no time to see that Gisborne ran up the road shrieking my name, no time as I ran into the man's bear-clasp, his arms going round me and squeezing the air from my body as he lifted me from the ground. He kept squeezing and in desperation I tried to raise my hand, enough to scratch him with the *misericorde* and he laughed some more and wrung me harder. I struggled to breathe, the odour of his body and breath, of his woollen cloak filling my nostrils and blackness beginning to cloud my vision. My body sagged, the *misericorde* sliding from my fingers, his arms wedged tight round my middle, every life-giving bit of air going, going…

And then I was loosed, falling to the ground in a heap as the felon was wrenched off me.

I lay coughing, sucking in as much of the dusty air of the road as I could, hearing Gisborne shout, 'No, Guillaume, hold. Do as I say!'

The assailant fell to his knees in front of me, but my sight was blurred. *Why does he kneel?*

Guillaume pulled me to my feet with little ceremony and I stared at the man who wanted to squash me like a beetle. He grinned at me, an arrow sunk to its feathers in his chest, a stain on his chemise under the *brunete* cloak. Red froth issued from his mouth as he breathed in and out and Gisborne's sword sat at his neck.

'Who sent you?'

'The Devil and Saint Peter,' panted the man between spitting out clots of blood.

'Say and you shall live?'

'You say?' laughed the brute. His hands scrabbled at his belt and he drew a knife and in one quick movement, had buried it in his gut, dragging it upward as he cried out, '*Beau sante!*' and I covered my ears, the words burrowing into my mind.

We all stood looking at the field of blood, the only sound our rough breathing, Adam rubbing at the side of his jaw where a mass of blue and yellow had begun to coalesce. Swords and knives were scraped through grass to clean them and then slid with a sighs into scabbards.

And it will get worse. Remember the Arsenale, Ysabel? The dogfight? Remember Gwen's bloody form? No quarter given.

Toby walked into the woods, shaking his head and calling for his horse. Gisborne and Adam rolled over the bodies, shaking out purses and cloaks for something apart from the *brunete* that could identify the mastermind behind this but of course there was nothing and Guillaume walked around wrenching arrows from the bodies and wiping them. I hated that I shivered and walked swiftly after Toby, calling Thea, hearing her whicker and when catching at her reins, burying my head in her mane and sobbing as if I had been told my son was dead. Ariella came up behind me.

'Ysabel, you must cease. Gisborne looks for you. You must show him you care little for these men, that you are still as strong as ever.'

I wiped my eyes, sniffing hard. 'How do you do this, Ariella? How do you accept a man's beheading, or that you could have been struck through the middle with a war-sword?'

'You forget I was in the tower in York, Ysabel, when my mother died. My father was in the town and I never thought to see him again as Jew after Jew poisoned their families and then killed themselves to avoid those on the outside of the tower. I left the tower the next day with those who lived and managed to run from the mob that then killed them. It was bloody mayhem and it hardened my heart and taught me that one must cope to live and live to cope. One learns, Ysabel, as you must. You have done it in the past. You can and will, do it again.'

We walked back to the men, pulling the horses with us.

'Would they have killed us all?' asked Toby of Gisborne. The men seemed remarkably sanguine of the encounter, a normal part of travelling the road. Attacks on travellers were common and this no different perhaps. Except it was. Further proof that what we waged was war and this an attack on our flank and it seemed to me that the event had honed our purpose like the proverbial whetstone and I was glad.

'All except my lady wife and I,' my husband answered.

'Truly?' Toby shuffled off to digest this as we all tightened girths and prepared to mount. For one brief moment I wondered if any of today's experiences would reach one of his ballads. It would be a sad verse, for sure. But he called out to Guillaume, 'And my friend from Anjou, what was the purpose behind *"Allah Akbar"*? I thought I was back in Outremer and expecting to see the Saracen archers bearing down upon me and to be filled full of barbs in an instant.'

'It was nothing but scaremongering, Monsieur Tobias. They wore the *brunete* of the lay Templars and I thought they would find the call unsettling if they had returned from the desert recently. Many Christians find it so.'

'Scaremongering?' Toby muttered. 'God's legs but if I hadn't emptied my bowels behind the trees beforehand, I would have filled my *braies* on hearing that.' He bowed toward Ariella and I. 'Begging your pardons, of course, dear ladies.'

The gates of Bologna were near shutting when we rode in, Toby singing a lusty ditty in Latin and Guillaume and Adam hanging their voices on the odd chorus.

'We went hunting,' said Gisborne, an inane and inebriated smile on his face, 'and got lost…'

The guards gave us a half-hearted warning, but bored with a surfeit of students who were often loud and bothersome, they barely looked at us as we rode past. We began to follow a ribbon of students of various ages and quality who had places to go and a purpose to be there.

Gisborne turned his horse down a narrow cobbled way and through an arch into a paved yard.

'It seems quiet and out of the way. It will suffice. Adam, find our friend, and the rest of you, take the horses to the stalls and feed and water them whilst I seek shelter and food from the innkeeper. Guillaume – I would that you go to the inn they call *Acta Urbana*. It is where many of the *teachers* of philosophy will be.' The look he gave Tobias as he emphasised the word was rather crushing. 'Find Folco. He is the innkeeper and will have word from Walter.'

You hope.

He strode away through the door to our inn and Guillaume and Adam left on foot. We who remained led the horses to the trough to drink their fill and then into the stalls one by one. As we unsaddled them, Ariella said, 'By the folds of the Virgin's robes, I am so stiff I doubt I shall be able to sit on a stool ever again.'

My heart was too heavy to smile and I wondered if levity would ever be a part of our lives again as I carted armloads of sweet hay to the animals. Presently the only sound was the horses chewing.

'Lucky nags,' Toby muttered. 'At least they have food…'

'Cease complaining, Toby,' said Gisborne, returning quietly. 'And go inside. The innkeeper has a simple meal for us. We must all share the one room unfortunately. It seems I have chosen the inn to which devotees of William of Tyre come to extol his virtue and it is full this night.'

'Well, well,' said Toby. 'William of Tyre. I wonder if our excellent liege lord, Richard of England, read William's treatise on Jerusalem before he sailed for Outremer.'

'Toby, he is quite an educated man, you know,' I responded and then wondered why on earth I would seek to defend a man like Richard, who wrought trouble wherever he went. It served to remind me that Gisborne had ridden on to Udene not long since and I resolved to ask what had emerged from that delay. Because for sure, if he had ridden back with Toby and the wrestlers, I felt sure William would still be with us.

I turned back to seek him out as Ariella and Toby entered the inn and he stood once again solitary, arms crossed and looking down at his boots. The torches around the yard lit his face and the sharp angles were more pronounced than ever. This man had killed to protect me and had turned traitor to his king in order to support his family. And now his back was against a wall and the only way he could survive was to come out fighting as he had never fought before. Ariella had told me to go to him but in truth, when he was like this one would only find objection, introversion and even obfuscation in their path. My husband folded in on himself and sometimes … sometimes…

'Guy,' I chanced.

He looked up.

'Please…' I went to him, close by, reaching a hand into his crossed arms to seek his fingers, pressing my cheek against them. 'Please…' A tear slid down and I could not stop it. I dared not move as I felt the tension in his arms ease slightly. His hand cushioned my neck and I tilted my head. His lips crushed mine, so hard I thought they might bleed with pressure against my teeth. But then softer and I knew the drawbridge had been lowered as I kissed him back, my tears flowing.

'We will find him, Ysabel. We will. On my life.'

But how many lives must we offer in this war, Guy. That is what worries me…

Adam returned with two men and six fresh horses on leading ropes. The men took our own away and I gave Thea the bread from our meal as a farewell. I tried not to care that she went, but it was another absence to bear on top of so many others. And then Guillaume arrived and my heart hurt as I waited to hear the news.

'It is not good, my lord,' he said. 'Walter left no note but told Folco what you needed to know. He followed them as far as the gates and then lost them in the crowds after they had left their horses at livery. The horses are still there and we must assume that they have fresh mounts…'

'They have gone…' I said definitively.

'Walter asked the livery if the four men had given any indication of their plans. He passed much money over my lord.'

'To what end?'

'I would say none,' Guillaume replied frankly. 'He had no result for the outlay. But he claims to have picked up news at the gates of a party of four men and a child leaving just before the gates closed yesternight.'

'Oh Jesu! We passed them…' I cried.

'And that is all?' Gisborne barely acknowledged my distress.

'Aye, my lord. He is tracking east to Canossa concealed amongst a group of merchants and their wives, in the hope he will catch sight of them.'

'What think you, Guillaume?'

'I think they still head for Genoa, my lord. We would do well to follow. I trust the information we sourced in Venezia.'

'Adam?' Gisborne turned to his captain.

''Tis as Guillaume says. They choose Genoa for a reason.'

The next morning, ears ringing with student chatter and argument, I was dismayed at the time-wasting that went on with academic titter-tatter. I wondered if any of these men had seen real life – had seen a man pierced with an arrow, knifed in the back with a dagger or disembowelled at a sword stroke. They were thin, ascetic men, almost starved one would say as they hustled between one teacher in one inn to another in a tiny room somewhere else. Like a flock of marauding birds they flew in loud, argumentative throngs around the town, exhausting the tree of knowledge in every garden.

They tried my patience as we saddled the new horses. '*Effete* fools,' I muttered.

'But my lady, if we did not have learning, there would be no music, no poetry, no philosophy of love and loss and what then would a poor troubadour like me do?'

'You would still make music that would turn a court's heart, Toby,' Ariella replied.

'Imagine what ballad you will be able to pedal around the courts of Europe after this, Tobias,' I said in my most cutting manner. 'The story of a little boy who was lost to his family.' I mounted the small horse that was my ride and headed toward the arch.

'That was uncalled for, Ysabel,' Ariella said in her cool way.

It was and I apologised to Toby. But I added, 'I suspect you write the story in your head as it unfolds, Toby. Tell me I am not wrong.'

'Aye, Lady Ysabel. You know me too well. But I tell you this – I have an ending and it is a sweet one. It will arouse cheers and tears of goodwill in any hall across the land.'

He winked and a little of my ice melted. 'You are incorrigible.'

'My lady, I can jest with the best of them if it will bring a smile to sore hearts.'

'I do love you, Toby. Never doubt it. As much as William does,' I responded.

He reached over, his thick, short fingers lying across mine as I held my reins. He patted me like a man pats his dog as Gisborne signalled for us to move on.

After Bologna, we moved as fast as our terrain dictated, defined by the width between my horse's ears. When we rode at speed the plucky little ride laid its ears back, its mane and tail streaming. When we slowed to a trot or walk, the ears became upright. When we passed other horses – sumpters, rounceys, palfreys, even destriers and mules, then the ears would flick with interest. We would nod to fellow travellers, occasionally speaking because apart from Ariella and myself, our group were all information gatherers.

It was always reassuring news – four men with an endearing child. When we asked about a group of merchants behind them, we were told 'Yes, with wives chattering like a flock of chaffinches.' Thus we knew Walter was positioned where he needed to be – close enough but not too close.

Once we came across a group of lepers on the road. Their clappers resounded with dire warning as we approached and Gisborne signalled for us to halt and then rode close by them, speaking – French I thought – for quite some time. Then he threw some money into the begging bowl held by their spokesman and we trotted on. But I looked back and the leader of the poor unfortunates waved. I signalled back then urged my horse up by Gisborne's side.

'And?' I asked.

'They are from Aquitaine. They intend to walk to Rome where there is a hospice. To them it is a pilgrimage, even though they know they shall probably never return.'

'You paid them for that?'

'Not at all. I paid them because when I asked had they seen many travellers and, they told me in detail.'

Why would they be so loquacious, Gisborne? They are outcasts to whom our kind are an anathema. Perhaps you told them about your own father…

'There is more?' I prompted.

'Not specifically. But it does seem we follow the right path.'

But you are not convinced. There is something in your voice…

'God bless the lepers,' I said, my confidence still weak. 'And Walter?'

'Right behind them in his group of merchants and their ladies. He will bide his time, because our quarry travels slowly.'

My heart swelled with pain as I envisaged my little boy exhausted from tears of woe, tired of riding, even if it was in Peter's arms. Wanting his mother.

'And William?' I whispered.

Gisborne kept his eyes on the road ahead. 'He sits in front of Peter and seems well, if quiet.'

Mary Mother! Of course he would be quiet. He would be confused, afraid…

I added another prayer to the five hundred supplications a day I sent to any saint who would listen.

Canossa's bulky walls reared above us as we rode by in a heavy rainstorm. With our hoods pulled up we barely noticed its ramparts and the hissing of the rain made any sort of call impossible. Besides, the Devil sat at our tails. We needed to make pace to Genoa and enter close behind our target.

After what seemed a lifetime in the saddle, when my rear throbbed beyond numb to red-hot, when my cold fingers could barely unfurl from the reins, when my backbone ached from neck to tail and when the inside of my knees burned with spurious chafing, we halted. Water sparkled within sight, struck by the winter sun.

'Tis Genova,' breathed Ariella. 'Thank the stars. I am melded to my horse and doubt I shall ever walk on my own two legs again.

Genoa.

I could scarce believe it. Days and nights had passed in the rough surroundings of the traveller's way. Living off our wits and whatever we could buy from inns, monasteries, or villeins in the field who would share bread and olives for a coin. And none of it to Biddy's standard.

Oh, Biddy, how do you fare? And what of my little Gwen?

Mehmet would do everything to protect them both – to ensure their health and safety, but what of Gwen's mind? She had lost her child before she even had a chance to hold it. And what would she think of her mistress who had a child but lost it anyway?

The Genoa seawall curved around the harbour like a whore's legs around her lover. Even from this distance the Light could be seen standing sentinel proud on its rocky platform.

'Ariella, he is there. William is there.' The anxious mother's heartbeats resonated *fortis*.

'We will have him back with us any moment, Ysabel.' She turned to me, her expression less intense. 'I wish Tanti was with us – for William, Tanti is an angel in disguise.'

'God needth dogth like Tanti to be here. They are like angelth,' my son had said only days ago.

As we had ridden, so Ariella had become a mother-sister to me. I would not reveal my weaknesses to Gisborne but Ariella let me cry, allowing me to enunciate my doubts and uncertainties. She understood that a mother would struggle to survive the loss of an infant son. It was said that a mother should never have to bury her child, so surely she should never ever have to see her child used as a pawn in a heartless, vengeful game. Do they say what happens to the mother if she loses her child? Does she lose her mind? Does she lose the will to live and love?

Ariella would walk with me during our halts, speaking in measured tones. 'In my heart, I know Peter will have cared for him, seeing him safe. He will be found, Ysabel, and returned safe. I guarantee it.'

At the commencement of this chase I thought she humoured me, drawing me back from a piteous abyss, but as league upon league flew under the iron of our horses' hooves, her confidence seeded itself in my tortured soul and began to grow. The face I turned upon her as we gazed at the water must have looked less lined and weighted with sorrow, because for the first time since we left Venezia, she smiled.

'We shall enter Genoa not long after noon,' Gisborne called over his shoulder. 'Toby, get you to our usual haunts and seek our friends. Tell them what you must. Adam, you shall come with me, and Guillaume, I would that you escort our ladies to the Via Dolorosa. My wife knows the way well.'

'No, Guy!'

Guy's face tightened. 'Wife…' he said, that single word filled with annoyance and frustration.

Let him be, Ysabel. Do you not think he chafes with your kind of pain, with your anger?

'…'tis best you remain concealed until we locate them. I would not have you captured and ransomed as well.'

'Better that I am with William than not,' I argued.

'No,' he replied. And I wondered how I could even dare to argue further as whatever fury he felt toward the men who had stolen our son, it currently vibrated between myself and my husband, a veritable thunderstorm. 'You will go with Guillaume,' he said.

'But Gisborne, the Dolorosa. Aaron…' I stopped as images of Aaron of Antioch with his throat cut and lying by our son's bed filled my mind. Then, 'I have come this far. Please. I need to be there…'

'Ysabel,' whispered Ariella, taking my reins. 'Come. Do not upset yourself or Sir Guy any further. He thinks only of your safety…'

I dragged my reins back from her grasp. 'I will *not* go to the Dolorosa. Gisborne, I implore you. I need to be there when you find them. I want justice!'

Some might call it revenge but whatever name it is known by, I wanted it. I wanted to take it by the grip and bury it up to the quillons in someone's miserable guts. Is that not what one does to secure justice?

Gisborne weighed my words. I dare say he assessed my turbulent mood as well and my heart sank. But then suddenly he gave in, shrugging, although his shoulders were rigid and it was done with ill grace.

My heart rose with tired and unexpected euphoria anyway.

Our entry into the city was unremarkable, surrounded as we were by tradesmen carrying tools, by vendors carrying baskets of wintergreens and the last of the fruits from harvest, by carts loaded with barrels and bales. Horses and men moved steadily from the gate to the wharves or to the inner town.

Monks walked by – five rows of two. Their cassocks swung, hoods hanging down their backs, hands concealed within wide sleeves, their monkish tonsures ragged and thin, crowns shining in the early afternoon light revealing freckles, scabby sores, dry skin. Perhaps they walked from a monastery outside the town walls, I knew not, but as they filed past us, they chanted:

163

'Ave Mundi spes Maria, ave mitis, ave pia, ave lena gratia.
Ave virgo singularis, quc per rubrum designaris non passus incendia.
Ave rosa speciosa, ave Jesse vurgula: Cujus fructus nostri luctus relaxavit vincula…'

It warmed my heart, it could have been a sign, because if ever I believed that anyone could help me find my son, it was She who had lost Her own.

'Hail hope of the world, Mary, hail, meek one, hail, loving one, hail full of grace.
Hail o singular virgin who wast chosen to not suffer flames through brambles.
Hail, beautiful rose, hail staff of Jesse: whose fruit loosened the chain
of our weeping…'

Was it an omen? Or mere irony on God's part? One of the city guards looked up as we rode through the gates and his eyes widened but Gisborne gave a tiny shake of his head and the recognition faded, sliding over other more worthy people.

Without a word, Adam and Toby moved away from us, heading to destinations unknown to me. Guillaume edged his horse by Ariella's side and I heard a faint murmur of man and woman conversing but within the resonance of Genoa I could not decipher detail. As I nudged my horse up by Gisborne, it occurred to me that my friend and Gisborne's *protégée* were two of a kind – singular, contained and capable. I knew little of Guillaume's nature beyond being a master archer and weapon-maker but I grudgingly assumed there to be some learning within him. Ariella I knew to be highly educated by her father and accomplished in many things, not the least of which was music and knife-wielding.

These things passed through my mind in the time it takes to nock an arrow and as I rode without speaking, I wished I had a sword strapped to my side. We left the horses at a livery familiar to Gisborne. It sat near the horse-market where I had my first fateful encounter with Halsham's accursed Templars and I knew if I walked past the church and then turned along the waterfront and followed that line of taverns and booths, I would find the bottom of the street called Via Dolorosa – the Way of Grief. Revisiting all of these memories was like flagellation – every part of me stung, my chest tight with breathlessness.

'My lord Gisborne,' the livery owner said with quiet deference. 'It is good to see you returned to Genova. You were not expected. Do you wish for your mounts to be tended and then taken to the Via Dolorosa?' he spoke as though he shared secrets and I knew at once that he was one of the faceless men. His chin was coated in blue-black stubble, as if he were painted in woad, and thick coarse hair poked from the top of his chemise. He had a woven caplet sitting like a dark thundercloud over wild black hair.

'Tis good to be amongst friends, Dario, but we come unannounced for a reason and discretion would be appreciated.'

Dario nodded. 'Of course, my lord…'

'As to the horses, check their feet if you would and if they require work, I would be grateful if you could arrange it. I would that you kept the mounts here until they are needed.' He reached into his saddlebag and withdrew a small leather pouch that clinked as he passed it over. 'This should suffice.'

The Genovese bowed his head. 'Indeed, sir.' He ordered two grooms to lead the horses away after anything of use to us was removed. Ariella and I, of course, had nothing. But then neither did Guillaume beyond his weapons. Gisborne merely pulled out two more chattering drawstring bags, passing one to Guillaume who secreted it in his purse. The other, my husband placed in his own purse.

'Now we must wait until Toby and Adam return and best if we do it concealed within a tavern close by,' Gisborne led the way and I trod hastily after him.

'Wait? Why wait? Surely we can begin to seek now!' I chafed to tear Genoa apart in the search for William and waiting was bound to chafe me like a badly buckled girth.

'Yes, wait,' said Gisborne. He kept his voice low.

I trotted alongside like some faithful hound, looking up at him. 'For how long, Guy?'

'Until we have the information we need to proceed.'

Down the cobbled street we moved, Ariella and Guillaume behind, past booths with food for our fancy. I hadn't thought I was hungry until the smell of roasted bird caused my belly to seethe, but I pushed it away. No time. No interest.

It was pointless to engage with Gisborne further whilst we moved up and down alleys to a tavern that crouched liked a weathered old woman on a corner.

With a mug of wine each to hand, we sat with our companions, feeding from a platter of the ubiquitous bread, oil, salt and olives. Just as I was about to renew my questions, Guy stood, informing us he would return forthwith. The mood trailing behind him was tightly coiled, like a serpent about to strike, and for one brief moment I wondered if William's captors had any idea at all what would launch at them when we found them.

As Guillaume pulled his bread apart, Gisborne reappeared.

No change in the mood…

'I have taken a room for us and ordered bowls of heated water and cloths. I have also asked the innkeeper, who knows us, if he could fetch clothing. We need to refresh and regird. This may be the last time we can do so…'

Was he saying the battle would commence the moment we sighted William's captors? Or was he saying further travel was likely? As we all climbed the stair, I held him back.

'What news do we wait for, Guy? We waste time…'

He nodded for Ariella and Guillaume to continue on and we halted, me on the step above, meeting him face to face.

He had aged. The wrinkles at his eyes, so much of his charm when he smiled, were deeply incised and between his brows, two marks presaged anger. Long lines of tiredness slashed between nose and mouth, indicating loss of weight, and grey threaded further through his hair. He reached for my hand, a movement that shocked me as we had barely touched since that profound moment between us in Bologna.

'Ysabel, it will be less time than you think. By the time you are washed and changed, Toby and Adam will have returned.' His thumb rubbed at my knuckle. 'The information I seek is where Peter might be with William. There is no doubt to me that they intend to sail somewhere and I suspect they wait for a boat to leave. They are somewhere hidden out of the way. If Walter has done his job well enough, he will have this information for me. We will know what is planned.'

'What do you *think* is planned?' I asked, watching his thumb rubbing back and forth. Tense beyond belief, for one brief moment I could feel his touch, my anxieties dropping away to allow the sensation of husband touching wife to lighten my ever-darkening soul.

'I believe they plan to journey to Toulon. It is logical. It is where the poison was originally blended. Peter is tainted with it and is a vessel for their purpose. He netted the bait, and now the bait must sit within the Commanderie of Saint Christoph, waiting for this fish,' he tapped his chest, 'to be hooked.' His lips stretched into a grim smile. 'Ironic, do you not agree? The home of Halsham's Templars.'

'Ironic? Sick 'tis what it seems.'

'Part of this is torture of the mind. Whoever plans this revenge does so with cunning but also with sick amusement. Do you not feel he takes you to the edge of the abyss?'

I nodded. 'Do you?'

'Oh yes. But I can't afford to fall, can I? Our son's security depends upon it.' His arm ran along my shoulder and he drew me down toward him. Our foreheads touched. 'I would this had never happened, Ysabel. I will give my life for our son.'

I closed my eyes. Said nothing. Just moved so that my lips grazed his cheek with more love than I thought possible. 'Gisborne, we shall fight together. Make no mistake, William will lose neither of us.'

You think, Ysabel? That is not the way games are played. Someone always loses.

But to use a child?

The hairs on my neck stood up at the implication we dealt with an insane mind bent on a *game* of revenge and it was *that* which fed my own desire for revenge. How dare someone use my child, my son.

Ah well, insanity breeds insanity…

Chapter Eight

The mood was one of desperate impatience. We washed, the men standing outside whilst we discarded torn and dirty men's wear in favour of clean but no less old tunics and hose. Our boots and cloaks must suffice, and I folded my ancient grey garment and laid it at the door. We then took our turn outside whilst the men divested themselves of old smells for new. At any other time I might have laughed at a wife turning her head from her husband's nakedness but levity was a thing left behind and like never to be experienced again.

Ariella and I retired to the one large bed, Gisborne and Guillaume standing at the shutters, watching the alley outside. The similarity between the two men was quite marked as beards manifested and hair lay untidy. They talked quietly with their backs to us and again I wondered what it was about Guillaume that so induced a level of trust from Gisborne. Perhaps it was that we were *in extremis* and Guillaume knew the soldierly way to behave. But I was too tired to think on it any more. I had room only for William's dilemma and it exhausted me, eyes shuttering down as the light at the window turned from pale grey to blood-infused woad and then unsullied black, the bells chiming the hours and voices drifting from the drinkers beneath our chamber.

My dearest son…

'Ysabel, wake you. 'Tis the men…'

Ariella shook my shoulder and I growled as I vaguely noticed dawn lighting the edges of the shutters.

'Do I care?' I mumbled, a grey fog slowing my response.

'A message has come with Toby,' she continued. 'Ysabel, wake up!'

But the word "message" had pierced the fug and it was as if iced water had been poured over me.

'What?' I jumped off the bed. 'What does it say?'

'Be still, Ysabel and I shall see.' Gisborne flicked the leather thong away and the small note unrolled. 'It's in Fra Angelo's hand…'

Fra Angelo?

'A priest who helps us when he can. Besides, Walter cannot read nor write.' Gisborne scanned the note. 'It seems our quarry are at a hospice near the church of Saint Sebastien and are preparing to meet a ship. Toby, we know that hospice – do you remember? Take Adam and watch. When you can, get word to me. Guillaume, you and I will investigate any ships at the dock likely to leave in the next day. There will be precious few, it being winter. And then we will wait…'

'And Ariella and myself, Gisborne? We too shall be at the docks, shall we not?'

'I could hardly stop you,' he uttered as he threw on his cloak and walked to the door.

I grabbed my own, swathing it round, rushing after Gisborne, all of us hurrying down the stair.

'This is the moment,' Toby puffed beside me. 'William is close, madame. You must be happy now.'

'Happy, Toby? Not yet. When my son is in my arms. *That* will be happiness.'

We parted at the corner of the alley, Toby and Adam disappearing amongst the trail of men and women who frequented the tawdry establishments. We turned toward the waterfront – a cold wind grasping at us, cloaks flapping like ill-reefed sails of ghost ships. We lowered our heads against the chill and stepped right and left to avoid the crowds. Large and small vessels rose and fell in the bad-tempered swell and wavelets slapped fractiously against the stonewalls. Seabirds wheeled and cried, a sure sign of bad weather as they hovered above the port.

'My lord?' Guillaume asked.

'We ask at every boat – if any are leaving in the immediate future.' Guy scanned the harbour, eyes closed to slits against the weather, the creases at the sides deeply incised. Round the arc of the port, boats strained at their moorings, bumping against the walls.

'But Guy, there are so many,' I said.

'Not so many,' he replied. 'Remember our quarry is heading west toward Toulon. The vessel will be one that could cope with a longer voyage, a small galley perhaps. We'll go in pairs. Guillaume and Ariella take that side. Ysabel, you attend me.'

The wind buffeted our words as we shouted to crewmen manning the larger vessels, usually one man on deck looking mutinous at being given the watch in such weather, whilst fellow crewmen sat warm and inebriated within the arms of inns and whores.

'To sea?' they shouted. 'You jest. Madness in this!' A thumb would jerk over the shoulder to where the sea sprayed in fierce arcs over the rocks at the Light.

The answer was always the same, vessel after vessel, and a sharp fall of rain made our task more desperate still. Ariella and Guillaume signalled from further away with shrugged shoulders and out-turned palms.

Bells rang for Sext and I knew then that '*happy*' was not to be the day's outcome. We had turned up nothing and such an emptiness echoed inside me. I knew if I acknowledged the loss of my child with anything less than hope, grief would overwhelm me and, as I had been warned to keep my head and heart clear if I was to function as any sort of helpmeet to my husband, I pushed it away, no recognition…

Harden yourself. You have done it before and can do it again.

But then I heard a voice roaring 'Christ!' and knew it was me as I looked up to the heavens, the rain drenching my face.

'Hush,' Gisborne ordered, grabbing my arm and dragging me along to shelter. 'Let's get out of the rain.'

The four of us huddled under the awning of a booth with a dozen others, the trader growling at us all to move on and give him selling room, fellow Genovese ribbing him and asking who'd want to buy his tawdry goods anyway? When I managed to catch of glimpse of his table under a raised arm, I saw carved children's toys – sheep, donkeys, goats, pigs, and horses like William's rounceys.

Githborne, Ounthee!

Such a pressure built inside me that I wanted to scream, but Guy's hand crept around mine, fingers squeezing, drawing me back from the abyss.

'Look Ysabel, look,' he said. He nudged the others. 'See?'

Toby and Adam walked past the booth without noticing us, intent on a larger group of cloaks and hoods ahead. The rain had eased to a wind-teased drizzle as we slipped in behind them, walking along with deliberate purpose.

Carefully, Ysabel. Carefully.

Toby and Adam acknowledged us with a mere glance and moved to the left as four men peeled away from the larger group, heading toward a larger galley. My heart fluttered like a trapped moth.

Is William under one of those cloaks? Held against Peter's chest?

Gisborne and Guillaume skirted to the right leaving Ariella and myself at the head of a circle that could be drawn to strangulation point. We all moved swiftly, drawing knives and holding them firmly beneath our folds. The four men stood at the seawall, one calling to any crew standing on deck but no one answered. He called again, the wind whipping his words away, fragmenting them and tossing them into the air unheard.

Our circle closed rapidly, arms encircling throats, knives pressing through wet cloak folds, enough to warn but not wound and it was all I could do not to thrust mine as deep as it would go.

'Hey!' yelled one of the men. 'Hel...' but a hand clamped over his mouth, a knife resting in an unfriendly line across his throat.

'Where's the child?' snarled Gisborne.

'Gone!' cried the man whose throat was close to being garrotted.

'*Where?*' Gisborne's voice grated so deeply, I doubt there was flesh left on the man's back.

'To my mother's house,' the stripling man replied. He would have had as much strength in his whole body as I had in my little finger but he was tall, almost as tall as Gisborne, maybe even as tall as Peter...

'What say you?' The words fell from my lips and I was unaware my knife had dug deeper against the body of the man in front of me until he yelled, 'Please!'

'My son,' said the man Gisborne held. 'Not that it's any business of yours.' His face had paled to a cadaverous shade.

'Go on,' prompted Guy in that same threatening tone.

'My son has been motherless since my wife died. I brought him to live with my own mother here in Genova whilst I teach in Bologna. As if it's your affair!'

I moaned and Ariella's arm crept to my shoulder.

'Sir,' said the man on the end of my *misericorde*. 'Have pity. We are teachers and come to collect one of our own from this vessel and to take him back to Bologna. It was a chance for our colleague to deliver his son safely. Please let us go.'

Oh God above! How could this have happened? Who is doing this to us?

Gisborne took a step back, bowing to the men. 'I owe you a most humble and heartfelt apology. Sirs, I ask your forgiveness, but my own son has been stolen and I was told he was attended by four men from Bologna. We will trouble you no more. Again,' he sheathed his dagger. 'I beg your forgiveness.'

He turned without waiting for a reply, his expression mirroring my own I was sure – disbelief and horror that this had been for nought.

No sign of our son.

He began to walk away and I hurried after him, the others following, pressing close. At first I didn't bother to observe our direction but then one thing and another began to appear familiar. A turn here, a turn there and then a long street beyond which one could see the vast elongated shape of the new cathedral.

Oh Guy, no, no!

I had hoped never to return here, home of my ill-thought schemes and plans and where a dear Jewish man had died trying to protect William.

Via Dolorosa. Way of Grief.

Our feet clipped on the cobbles, the crowds having thinned. None of the companions said a word nor tried to draw us back, deferring to their superior, allowing him to lead them where he would. We moved up the slope, my breath becoming a little ragged.

Why, Gisborne?

I grasped his arm, pulling hard.

'Stop Guy! Please…' Perhaps my tone of voice pierced his concentration, perhaps the drag on his arm was enough, but he halted and I said, 'Why this way? Surely we find Walter at the hospice and discover what has gone wrong?'

'We go to find Walter at the villa.' His voice was iron-shod. 'I know what went wrong and the Via Dolorosa will confirm it.'

'Guy, please. You speak in ambiguities. Tell me…'

He shook his head and took a small step back from us all. 'We've … no, that is wrong. *I've* been played. Pure and simple. All that,' he gestured back to the waterfront, 'was a lucky coincidence which our enemies happened upon and manipulated to their advantage. Once they discovered another man and child leaving Bologna, they removed Peter and William from the board. They sent us in one direction and changed direction themselves.'

'Then *where* are they?' I asked in desperation.

'Far from Genoa, by now, I think.'

'But still heading west, my lord?' asked Toby.

'I believe so. We will confirm that at the villa.'

'And Walter?' Guillaume asked.

'At the villa,' Gisborne replied and began to walk on.

The gate predictably was unlocked and ajar. No noise as we sidled in – no squeaking and scraping.

'Such a sound was a deliberate thing; no one could ever enter our Via Dolorosa house without any of us being aware.'

Equally, no Tobias or Tommaso sitting up the steps with bow and arrow trained through the slit in the wall. For Toby and myself it was a journey into an ugly past. Ariella, Adam and Guillaume however, looked around with interest. And Gisborne? Unreadable, a return to past times and manners.

Nothing had changed – the little fountain still spouted from its mossy tap against the wall, the water casting a tranquil ambience in the silence of the place. The yard was swept and clean except for one dove feather that rolled damply back and forth in the wind that whistled through the loggia. I almost expected William to come hurtling from beneath the arches to throw himself at his father's legs.

Toby would know how I felt as we stood there and I cast an anguished glance at him. Perhaps Ariella saw, because she slipped beside me and in the faintest whisper, said, 'Courage, Ysabel. You asked to *be* his partner in this ill-made game, remember.'

As if I can forget…

I looked up at the shutters of my old chamber and shuddered and then Gisborne broke the quiet of the yard as he gave orders. As he spoke, a dove, soft pewter and rose and presumably the owner of the damp feather, flew up in alarm from the loggia, its wings flapping loudly in the oppressive atmosphere.

'Adam, lock the gate. Toby, please stay here with Lady Gisborne and Ariella. Ysabel,' his eyes burned into mine, 'Just for once I need you to stay here. On your oath.'

The intensity of his request burned like a hot iron and it shocked me enough to nod, compliance a given.

'Adam, Guillaume, arm yourselves and follow me.'

The quiet sigh of their swords as they slid them from scabbards filled the yard. Such a disparity – quiet and yet roaring. What did he expect to find? Not William, to be sure. Our enemies? I doubt they would bother to confront us here. They had played their piece on the board and now had us on the run, our minds chasing them in a game in which their tactics had no boundaries. No matter what we did, as long as they possessed William, they had the Queen piece – the piece that could put us into checkmate with one thrust of sword to the hilt.

Of a sudden, I *knew* what Gisborne would find in the villa and I ran forward but Toby was there in front of me, trying to drag the door shut in my face. But I saw just enough. Just enough before any remaining Christian kindness left inside me was strangled, breath halted, my soul now blacker than Hades.

'Remember the Arsenale, Ysabel? The dogfight? Remember Gwen's bloody form? No quarter given...'

Walter lay on the floor in the shadows – an odd shape floating in a vast pool of dark, dark blood...

'Enough, my lady! It will be dealt with.'

'Jesu, Toby...' Any hysterics, any fear, had disappeared with that quick glance through the door, fury taking its place. 'He was from my home...'

Home, Ysabel? You have no home!

'He was a Moncrieff man.'

Guillaume reappeared. 'They have dismembered him.' He said it quite dispassionately, but then he *had* seen Richard's slaughter at Acre. 'We will do what we can for him but my lord asks you to return to the inn and we will be with you as soon as we are able.'

Ariella's hands had flown to her mouth at his first words and my arm crept round her shoulder by return. 'Ariella, I am so sorry. Here, sit for a moment.

Toby, some water.'

Toby dashed to the faucet and wet a linen square, offering it to her and she dampened her wrists and hands. 'I am alright,' she said looking directly at Guillaume. 'It reminds me of York. I have seen it before, Man's inhumanity. It stays with you, does it not, Monsieur Guillaume?'

He said nothing, merely bowed his head and stepped back the way he had come, shutting the door quietly and with respect. I could almost like him at that moment.

'Between us,' I said to Ariella, 'we have seen many wrongs and will no doubt see many more. But I think we shall manage, you and I, because we have the strength of an army and shall not be cowed.'

'Indeed. Not while William's breath sweetens this world.' She stood, tucking the damp square in her tunic sleeve. 'Toby, let us leave this place and may your God have mercy on poor Walter's soul.'

I crossed myself as she spoke, more from habit than fervour and we followed Toby as he unlocked the gate. It creaked open and then he locked it behind and tossed the key over the wall. 'They will see him right, Madame. Fra Angelo will give him the sacraments and they will bury him within the church grounds. He will not be a forgotten soul, I assure you.'

'Of course, Toby. But it is just one more innocent from Moncrieff who has suffered for me and mine and I suspect God or one of his Saints is keeping a running tally and will hold Gisborne or I to account one day.'

Meanwhile, I thought, I just want to leave Genoa and move on. Vengeance is such a powerful thing.

The room at the inn was as if we had never left. The bed still had my form pressed upon it and a half drunk mug of watered wine sat on the window ledge. Ariella's old caplet, the one she had discarded, lay on the floor.

'Oh,' she said, bending down. 'I hadn't realised,' and she folded it beneath the belt at her waist.

As we took up positions around the room and before we became lost in grim thoughts, I spoke to them both.

'I confess, I'm at a complete loss. Gisborne was so sure that we would find William here. Instead we find Walter…' I could not finish the sentence, images of the poor man floating in a sea of blood.

'Indeed,' my minstrel replied, seeing my distress. 'Whomever is the master behind this charade, he's playing us like the strings of my *vielle*.'

'It must be so galling for Sir Guy,' said Ariella. 'He is an intelligent man, thinks rationally and yet this unknown enemy has him at every move.'

'But don't you see?' I tried to sooth my passions, to speak calmly. I could not afford to lose control – so much yet still to do. 'That is their purpose. Using William as bait is perfect because they know my husband will trek to the ends of the earth searching for his son. As long as he is away from the centre of his intelligence web so it weakens, until finally it snaps. As long as they have his son, they have him, destroying his credence in the eyes of kings, dukes and emperors. Already Eleanor will charge him with treason for not continuing the search for Richard.' I shifted on the bed, my hands clasped tightly. 'It's as if we are mere puppets to be moved this way and that until the master gamer becomes bored. *That* is when I shall truly fear for William's and indeed Gisborne's lives. We have exactly as long as this stranger's patience lasts to find my son and seek revenge.'

Silence crept round the room dragging bloody images of Walter behind it.

Finally Ariella spoke. 'I worry that they are treating William badly.'

'You say what I have not stopped thinking,' I replied. 'If they play games with our minds, what do they do with his?'

'But you forget Peter, Madam,' Toby said. 'As long as he has our little man in his care, I think William will be treated well. In a strange way, I think Peter sees William just as a father sees his son.'

'William's father would *never* do what Peter has done, Toby. Never! And whilst what you say is true, I hate him. Jesu, how I hate him!'

I hurried out of the chamber and down the stair, into a room filled with wine-soaked strangers who cared not one bit as I fled through, knocking the occasional arm. I tugged the door open and plunged into the sea-fresh air, pacing back and forth until I finally leaned against the wall to suck in vast breaths.

The words I had spoken to my companions were God's truth. I *was* at a loss. How could such a good man like Walter warrant a terrible death because he worked for Gisborne? We had tried to discover who dealt us these blows and the men ranged against us were so loyal they killed themselves rather than reveal anything. And thus, my hardened self saw no reason why we shouldn't toss our own values to the side as well. Such a vengeful act as stealing a child smelled of Halsham's ilk. He had done it once before and been prepared to keep me prisoner and prolong my memory loss to suit his needs, losing his life because of it. That his brother Templars would follow steadfastly in his footsteps and seek to avenge him was a given and whilst I couldn't begin to understand the violence implicit in this, perhaps we *did* need to investigate the Commanderie in Toulon.

Mary Mother, in the name of Your Son, forgive me my loss of kindness and charity, but I have lost my son and suffer because of it…

Every moment that William was absent from my care felt like a blade sawing through a hemp rope. With each moment, another fibre snapped and another and another, and Gisborne and I more than ineffectual. I had thought Gisborne's intelligence web across foreign lands would have served us well and perhaps in time, it could, but we had no time.

After all, a little boy can only cope for a small amount of time before his mind is turned and he forgets who and what he is.

A disloyal thought squirmed through my worrying – that my husband, a man I had thought so infallible, was being bested time and again and diminishing more by the moment. It was like watching him at the *quintain*. With every pass, it swung round and hit him, winding him, weakening him until I must turn away from the image of a fallen man. Harsh? Probably. But when one is hurt and desperate, one's behaviour is never remarkable. Mine particularly.

Drizzle began to fall and I burrowed under my hood, shivering and thinking of my blessed Brother John, begging him to pray for William's safe return. Thinking of Beatrice of Locksley and Cecilia and wanting them to intercede for me and for William. And lastly I thought of Thea at Saint Eadgyth's, as my fingers found a knot on the hem of the cowl.

Dearest Thea, as you slip your fingers over the knots in your girdle in chapel, please will you pray for my son?

I whispered 'Amen' and crossed myself, jumping as a voice beside me said with insidious softness,

'Lady Gisborne, you seem distressed.'

I moved sideways, closer to the tavern door, one hand reaching behind to touch the wall, the other sliding under my cloak for the *misericorde*. He wasn't tall, this stranger, and the voice had emerged from a deep hood. In the weathered daylight, nothing much could be seen but a dark shadow swathed in quality cloth falling from broad shoulders.

'You are mistaken, sir,' I said in a low-pitched voice, 'if you think I am a woman. You insult me. Excuse me…' I moved a couple of steps closer to the door as a trio of bickering seamen swaggered out.

But the voice followed me, keeping close. 'But I *do* think, my lady. That is rather the point and one you and the knight your husband need to remember. Patently, thinking is not a great strength for either of you.'

God! This apparition peeled away my skin with his words. He knew us, knew we were scrambling to find a position of strength.

This is the game-player! This is the one we seek!

I could barely breathe, my heart once again in my throat, bowels loosening. It was as if I faced Halsham all over again. I had called it a battlefield so often and now I was faced directly with their strongest knight and I felt inept, powerless.

'And I repeat, sir, I am no lady. You are mistaken.'

Talk to him, Ysabel, delay him. Guy will come…

A deep chuckle emerged from the confines of the hood – he moved closer again, so that the smell of sandalwood filled my nostrils, reminding me of Mehmet – Mehmet and Toby playing chess…

'No lady, you say? Ah, I will grant you that. You played your first husband false and you killed a man who loved you I have heard.' He clucked, an acid tone that felt like pricks from a dagger. 'But I think you play a game with me, do you not? Playing for time perhaps? How wonderfully courageous of you. Where is your husband? Not here to protect his wife from danger? He's rather adept at that, is he not? They tell me he was absent when your son was abducted.' Another prick, this one deeper, drawing blood. 'Tell me, my lady, do you *miss* your son?'

I flew at him like a madwoman, a rising cry, not even checking if anyone was close by. I would kill him, slaughter him, cut him into pieces. My *misericorde* swept up but he countered it, grabbing my arm in a gauntleted fist and twisting hard, almost snapping the bone so that the weapon fell harmlessly to our toes. He trod on the dagger and let my arm go where it hung – useless, numb, fingers unable to clench.

Leaning close to my ear, he whispered, 'Spirit. Good. Better than that failed knight they call Guy of Gisborne. I look forward to more of the same – Ysabel.'

I couldn't bear to believe this dreadful conversation occurred as people moved around us, the daily life of Genoa continuing unaware. The misty drizzle thickened, rain spattering the ground, drinkers rushing to the inn, the door opening and closing, not one soul casting a glance at the two hooded figures in intense conversation next to the wall. I wanted to scream for help but my voice had vanished.

The inn door flung open again and voices burbled out in a confused stream, Toby adding his to the rest. He glanced the other way and then turning, saw me.

'There you are!' Falsely jovial. 'It's raining, you half-wit. Let's finish the game…'

'Oh yes, let's…' whispered the voice beside me so that Toby couldn't hear.

'I found the dice under the table,' Toby said – always the actor.

'Play your little game, Ysabel, and we shall meet again in Toulon.' The stranger leaned so close his clove-scented breath touched my cheek and I shrank back.

He bent to pick up my *misericorde* and handed it over, brushing past me. 'Your pardon,' he said and then continued away, lost in a wet mass of grey and black cloaks until he was just another amongst many.

'Come on,' said Toby. 'I'm getting wet!'

I closed my eyes, taking a huge breath as I replaced the dagger in its sheath and then pushed past our minstrel, back into the fug between trestles of men leering down the open chemises of street sluts, hands up gowns. Lewd laughter nipped at my heels as I took to the stairs as if the Devil whipped me. Throwing open the chamber door, I dashed in, Toby rushing behind and holding his hand to his chest as I threw off my wet cloak.

'Holy Hell, my lady…' the words puffed out. 'What goes?'

'Ysabel?' Ariella stood, expectant.

'It was him…'

'Who?' they both said.

'The nobleman who took William. He spoke to me.' They both looked at me as if I had finally fallen into the abyss. 'No, please listen. I speak the truth. Jesu, Toby, how much longer will Gisborne be? We must make haste…'

Ariella took me by the hand to a coffer and gently pushed me down. Toby crossed his arms, saying 'Sir Guy will take long enough to give a good man a decent burial. Calm yourself and tell us. A nobleman you say?'

'Yes. He spoke in a superior, flawless way, as if he has kept the company of kings and barons. I know the type, as do you. He made my flesh crawl. It was his voice … there was something…'

'Was he English, French?' Toby asked, his interest sharpened.

'You believe me?'

'Of course I do,' he said. 'My lady, nothing about this is normal nor predictable. We can expect the unexpected constantly. Did you see his face?'

'Mary Mother, no. He had pulled the cowl far forward and it was gloomy beneath the eaves of the inn but his cloak and boots were of excellent quality and he was armed with a war-sword in a tooled leather scabbard. He *reeked* of nobility, I tell you. And he wasn't tall – not much more than a head above myself, but broad and muscular.'

'Is he a Templar, think you?' asked Toby.

'I don't know. If he is, he wears his colours very lightly. There was nothing of a Templar's robes upon him.'

'A plethora of detail, Ysabel,' Ariella said.

'But not what matters! He could be anyone until we see his face.' I stood and walked to the shutters, looking out. Hoods, cloaks and hats passed beneath, and any or none could have been the stranger. Taking hold of the lintel, my fingers struggled to spread and I slipped up the sleeve of the tunic to examine a tapestry of blue and yellow bruising.

Ariella had followed me to the window and took my arm in gentle fingers. 'Did *he* do this?'

I nodded. 'I tried to stab him when he asked if I missed William. It was like battle fever, a red mist sliding through my head and over my eyes. In that moment, I could have wantonly disembowelled him.' I stared out through the shutters, trying to think. 'His voice – Jesu, it's as if he flays one and then rubs salt into the bloody flesh. There was a tone … something… Oh God!'

'What?' asked Toby, springing up, hand on dagger. 'What is it? What do you see?'

'Nothing out there, it is what he said. As he left me, he said *"We shall meet again in Toulon"*. He means the Commanderie and it is proof positive, surely. Christ God! He has watched everything we have done. He plans his moves and knows exactly how we will respond. Since we left Venezia, he has played Walter like a chess-piece, destroying him when he was no longer of use in his game. Toby, surely they will have buried Walter by now. I do not wish you to think I don't care, but if we don't follow this man immediately to Toulon, Walter will have given his life for nothing.'

'Softly, my lady. If this so-called nobleman is the fellow we seek, it doesn't matter if we leave now or in a sennight for Toulon. He will wait. He wants Sir Guy in the end-play.'

'But what of William?'

'He needs our little boy alive and well in order to draw Sir Guy in. So *I* believe anyway.'

But I caught the disturbed glance Ariella gave the minstrel and knew he only tried his best to keep me calm.

'I think you are wrong,' I said, beginning to pace. 'If he tires of waiting, if he needs to vent his frustration at Guy not confronting him, then he will begin a process of retribution. First he will threaten William's life and we will hear about it. And then if we are still tardy, make no mistake, this man has no heart and will kill my son and wantonly display the wreckage.' The words flowed from my mouth so dispassionately I could barely believe that the woman whose insides were palsied and whose heart jumped and jibed hundreds of times in a day, could also be the woman who could think so coldly.

I was two separate women, and I realised then how most noblewomen coped when their son, product of their loins and focus of their heart, rode away to begin training in a foreign household as a boy-squire. He would be consigned to memories and any contact would be rigorously formal. Any pain a mother might feel would be held in tightly, arms wrapped around the middle, and any likely tears would be brushed aside as dust in the eyes. No doubt some mothers saw their sons as merely rungs on the noble ladder. But that was most assuredly not myself. My son was my *causa est* and I cursed that I had not run with him when the thought first occurred to me after the dogfight.

None of this would have happened if I hadn't been so slow-witted.

'We must hurry to Toulon. Horseback, boat – I don't care. We must go!'

'Go where, Ysabel?' Gisborne pushed the door ajar. His hair hung in bedraggled ringlets and dripped on his cloak – a cloak stained heavily with blood. He pulled off his gauntlets and unbuckled his sword, loosening the cloak and throwing everything in a damp heap on the floor.

'It is done then, Sir Guy?' Toby asked, going to the cloak, hanging it on a peg on the door, laying the sword with the gauntlets neatly on the floor.

'Yes,' Gisborne replied wearily. 'It is done. Ysabel, I repeat. Go where?' He sank onto the coffer near the bed as Ariella handed him a mug of unwatered wine. It was a task that should have been mine and so I took a cloth and wrung it out in a bowl, passing it to him to wipe his face and hands.

'Toulon, Guy. I have…'

'She has been confronted by the man you seek, my lord,' interrupted Toby. 'He called her by name and said he would see her in Toulon.'

'Tell me more,' Gisborne ordered, his eyes darkening to night and glittering. I recounted the moments of earlier, leaving nothing out, showing him the bruising to prove I did not imagine it.

'He knew who I was, Guy. Even dressed like this and staying in this tavern where we are not known, he found me. He has men as good as yours I think, for him to know our every move.'

Gisborne's lip curled. 'Good men? They may be proficient, but they aren't good. *Walter* was a good man. See this?' He threw a scrap of parchment on the bed. It was bloody and the ink could barely be read but the word *Toulon* was scantily decipherable. 'It was crushed in one of Walter's hands deliberately for us to find, hands that had been cut from the arms that this *knight* had dismembered.' Gisborne tossed back the wine, leaning to grab the jug and pour another. 'So yes, Ysabel. We go to Toulon. Adam and Guillaume are finding a galley and we will leave as soon as we are able.'

'You believe it *was* him,' I asked. 'The man we seek?'

'I do. Christ but he's monstrous game.'

He raked fingers through his hair and twisted it away onto his nape. His face had never been more starkly revealed. Where once I had seen tiredness and pain, now I saw nothing but cold, grey-as-steel fury honed to hair-splitting sharpness. It took my breath away.

Guy was ready.

He would meet this nobleman and fight him, no quarter would be given, none expected. It would be bloody and it would be to the death.

A vision of Halsham's half-hewn body appeared before me.

Gisborne, I will be at your back as I have been so often.

He looked at me. 'I cannot stop you from coming, can I?'

I shook my head.

'Tobias? Ariella?'

'Not at all,' said Ariella.

'I need the experience for my next ballad, my lord.' Toby said. 'What is a song without such veracity?' The words were spoken lightly but there was nothing but fierce loyalty in his upright stance and the fingers resting on his strapped sword.

'There is just one thing, husband,' I said.

'Yes?' He sat back, looking up at me. Did he see the fierce need in me to see our son's captor dismantled piece by piece as had happened to Walter? Or did he just see a woman, a mother, parading as a youth and speaking wild words in a fit of agony? He did something then, that I had not seen for a long time. His head tipped quizzically sideways as he waited and for one brief moment, I was young Ysabel of years ago, being escorted to Moncrieff by a steward whom I grew to love. 'I want my own sword,' I said.

'Done,' he replied.

He and I left our companions to wait for Adam and Guillaume and we walked swiftly to an armourer's, finding weapons of all shapes and sizes. At the back of the booth, lying in a box were three or four swords that could almost have been forged for children but for their ugly sharpness. Gisborne looked on as I tested each blade, gripping it as Guillaume had taught me, weighing and then swinging – undercut, uppercut. I had little other knowledge and must hope for the best. One lightweight but well-made blade stood out. I remained balanced as I swung, and it did not hurt my shoulder. It had a strip of damascening down the gutter and its hilt was leather bound, the quillons plain bars with pointed ends.

'This one,' I said.

'You seem sure.' Gisborne felt for his purse.

'As much as it is possible to be when I only have one lesson beneath my belt.'

Gisborne asked the armourer if he had scabbards to fit and the fellow, a large man with a bald head and fat, loose lips, showed us plain leather scabbards fit for a squire and nothing like the Toulon nobleman had been wearing. Money clinked from one hand to another and we walked away after I had strapped the sword to my waist. I felt odd, almost as if I had a third leg by my side and I realised that its movement, echoing my stride, was something with which I would have to become familiar.

'A lesson, you say? Who? Johannes?'

'Not at all. It was your close friend, Guillaume.'

'You let Guillaume teach you?' he said unbelievingly.

'Yes. He gave me no option.'

'Indeed.' At any other time he may have grinned, but now? 'Then I am glad. This is not a fair we go to and I would see you armed with more than a dagger.'

'Bows and arrows are my weapons of choice, Guy.'

'I remember…'

Nothing more was said as we wove our way past food booths back to the tavern. If I had been dressed as a woman, I would have slipped my arm through his. As it was, I trotted along as if I was indeed his squire. The rain had disappeared and the pewter-coloured sky was beginning to break, the odd streak of blue appearing and as quickly vanishing as the strong sea winds continued to buffet Genoa.

The woman who was weak and who hid behind an armour of ice and fire longed to be held, to have hair and sensibilities smoothed. She longed to be kissed and to kiss back, for in that kiss would be assurance that a child would be safe and enemies vanquished. But the ice and fire woman touched her sword and allowed her fingers to slide over the grip and curl and she took pleasure in the solid feel under her hand, imagining the blade sweeping through the air, no parries to throw off her direction, just a clean cut – right where it mattered.

'Gisborne…'

'Yes?'

We turned into the alley and walked toward the tavern door.

'Is this man one of Halsham's Templars, think you?'

He stopped and we leaned against the wall in a beam of weak afternoon sun that slipped between the eaves in the alley. It warmed where we were cold but could not seem to cut through the ice that had set inside both of us.

Probably for the best…

'Truth? No. I don't believe he is a Templar. But a friend of Halsham's? He would have to be a *very* good friend to go this extreme. Perhaps even a lover. If sodomy is good enough for prelates and kings, it is good enough for knights and God knows Halsham was more lapsed than any.'

'Does it concern you that we do not know who he is?'

'No. An enemy is still an enemy, no matter what name he goes by. He could be Saint Peter and I would still meet him with a blade in my hand. No, Ysabel, I care not *who* he is anymore. It is enough that he has taken our son and killed Walter. The fact that he parades so readily in front of us is to our advantage. Remember how Robert was filled with arrogance and ego? In the end it was his undoing. So it is with this man. He will strut before us, forgetting that backs are as vulnerable as fronts. I will kill him, Ysabel. As God is my witness, this man will die for what he has done. And if he has harmed William, he will die twice and on the third time he will be begging to be turned from his misery.'

This was a Gisborne I had never heard before. As the weak woman it terrified me. But as the ice and fire woman, I merely nodded, accepting his words as words of war.

It was like that in the field.

So they say.

Chapter NINE

The small galley pitched in the swell – a lumpy sea that seemed to bounce off the coast to hit the larboard side with a smack. Each time a wave struck, the sail would empty, flap and then fill again with an ear-splitting crack that sent the prow slewing across the ocean and which would swill the contents of one's guts from one side to the other.

An inoffensive little vessel, it had a triangular sail, a bank of six shipped oars each side, a side-hung helm. The Saracen crew's faces looked like badly tanned ox-hide. They claimed to be Byzantine but the questionable nature of their vessel and the adaptable serviceability of it reminded me of the sneaky *nef* that had been my home through the Middle Sea. However, they had done us a favour agreeing to sail in winter weather and we would make it worth their while. Privately I hoped our journey would get no rougher as I doubted the ship's facility to sail without being swamped; its seaboard was far lower than Davey's and I wondered if this was what had faced my royal god-brother as he ran between Acre and Aquileia.

Adam had left us in Genova. Sent back to Venezia by Gisborne, he was to assume charge of the guards and protect our household from any further onslaught. Although the opinion of all was that with Gisborne and myself gone, and William in the enemy's hands, they would centre their attention on us. As they had on the road to Bologna.

Adam took messages to Mehmet and Saul from Gisborne and Ariella, and I sent to Bridget and Gwen through him. Like Gisborne, I wrote nothing down. Trusting Adam to his boot-soles, I asked him to relay my affection to them both, telling them that we would meet again in spring and that William was in our sights. To convey to Gwen how much I despised Peter for her injuries and for the loss of her child must remain unsaid. I trusted to God and Mehmet that she would know. But then perhaps she hated me with the strength of a woman wronged. To be sure, blame might be something I would discover in due course and it sent small cracks snaking round the ice-maid I had become.

Toby hung over the starboard side. He had long since emptied his last Genovese meal into the waves and was as empty as a whore's womb. Ariella slumped against the side and although her face had paled, she did not puke the way Biddy had when we sailed from Marseille to Genoa. Gisborne sat with Guillaume more often than not – intense discussion writ in furrowed brows and grim mouths. I remained on my own, examining my soul and watching my husband planning this attack. And waiting. Waiting, for him to include me, waiting for the watch to call *Toulon off the starboard bow!*

I shuffled over to Ariella who had wrapped her cloak around tightly, her mouth and nose hidden beneath.

'You are cold?' I said.

'A little – and you?'

'I have been cold and getting colder,' I rubbed my arms briskly, 'since we left Venezia, Ariella. It is the way of it. It helps me focus on what we must accomplish. If I am warm, I fear I shall become lazy, incompetent. Do you see?'

She nodded, swallowing.

'Do you feel nauseous?'

'My stomach slops here and there, but when we left England a seaman told us to always keep dry food in the belly so I chew on our stale bread.'

Guillaume had grabbed two loaves before we embarked and Gisborne and I had both been keeping a lining in our own gut although I had never been seasick in my life and had no intention of succumbing now. After all, this was not a storm and I had been in far worse.

'It helps to stay away from Toby too,' added Ariella wryly. 'Vomit grows more vomit.'

I patted her hand. 'He usually settles in a day and a night. We must wait it out.'

I glanced to the stern and noticed Gisborne now stood alone. With his dark cloak flapping in the wind and his hair streaming from his forehead, he could almost have been a figure from Norse legend, perhaps Beowulf. But no – I would not see my husband end his life like that hero, meeting his Maker in the battle to come. Please God.

Guillaume wove his way via rigging, shoulders and spars to our side. He acknowledged us with a dip of his head and said, 'My lord Gisborne thinks we are not far from the marshlands to the east of Toulon. Perhaps by dusk, Toulon harbour will be in sight.'

'Shall the master take the boat in or anchor along the coast until dawn?' I asked.

'We suspect the latter. He will no doubt prefer to negotiate between moored vessels in good light. But we may leave the vessel before that.'

'Truly? Does my lord Gisborne think we are ready?' I stood, grabbing at Guillaume's arm to steady myself. My antipathy toward him had evened out a little as I watched he and Ariella engaging with each other. Always serious, the two seemed to have a mutual respect which surprised me. At any other time, I would have quizzed Ariella, but at this moment I did not want to disturb the equilibrium of our group, not with so much at stake. Often when we sat eating, or merely passing time, I noticed an equality of station amongst us; after all, the five of us were on this journey for the same reason – to rescue a little boy and confront whatever hellhounds stood in our way, so who was I to dispute such equality? No doubt noble courts of my experience would decry such behaviour, but to Hell in a hand basket with them. It was why I wanted to live far from such society.

'He does and would speak with you.' Guillaume had not used my title since we boarded as the longer we could avoid interest the better. It seemed we were a troupe of jongleurs, travelling to Aquitaine to perform for Otto of Brunswick during the Feast of Saint Stephen and the fiction had been accepted.

I reached Gisborne who leaned his elbows on the starboard rail, lost in thought. Over the last month I had watched him change – reverting to a well-remembered type and one that sat heavily with me. Quiet, not sharing ideas or events with me and if pushed, turning to anger with such rapidity it reminded me of wild fire.

I touched him and he started as if he had been far away from the moment. He looked around with a frown, the expression remaining even though he looked at his wife.

'Have you decided what you will do when we reach Toulon?' I asked. There was little point in skirting round the question. Despite his expression and his preoccupation, this was my battle as well and he had accepted that before we left Genova.

'I have.'

'And? Mary Mother, Guy, why do I have pull things from you as if they were rotten teeth? Tell me what you expect of me!'

His eyes closed to momentary slits and then, 'I expect you to obey me, Ysabel. That is what I expect. When I ask you to do something, I must ask for full obedience. I have asked for you cooperation so often and repeatedly you have denied me. With adverse outcomes.'

Unfair, Guy. Unfair.

'Do you talk of my disobedience in Cyprus, Guy? If I had stayed in the boat with Davey and Eli and within that cave, you may not be alive to berate me now.'

'No. I speak of your behaviour in Venezia. Walking about without a guard so that William was abducted outside Saul's. It showed to our enemies that you are our weakness, that you are often wilfully misguided. This man, our nemesis, has relied on that ever since.'

'And of course your absences had no part to play, did they? How dare you blame me for everything…' I spoke in strangulated tones, not wishing the crew to hear our exchange.

'God and the Saints, Ysabel, stop puffing out your chest. This is neither the time nor the place. You know as well as I that you are capable of ignoring an instruction in favour of your own intuition. These last few years have been filled with such undeniable behaviour. You must also understand that things have changed. Previously we played with our own lives, it was our choice. But in this instance, if we ignore orders we are risking William's life. Do you understand?'

It would be churlish and ignorant of me to deny his reasoning. Perhaps I was indeed growing. So I replied, 'yes' quite meekly as I dismounted from my high horse.

'Good,' he sighed, sliding down to the deck to sit with his knees pulled up, hands resting loosely over them. To anyone watching he seemed relaxed, but I saw the muscle working in the cheek and the shadows pouched beneath his eyes. I folded next to him. Still dressed as a youth, I could not touch him for fear anyone might see and pocket the information for sale to those in Toulon who might buy. Although as it was, I imagine we would be as obvious as knights in a nunnery to those who waited for us.

'Is the Commanderie close by Toulon, Gisborne? Do you know of it?'

'I do know.' He closed his eyes and leaned his head back against the planking. *How? Tell me.*

But of course he would not and I could not ask.

'You are tired,' I said.

'I am many things, Ysabel, but tiredness is not one of them. Fury prevents sleep from visiting me these days.'

'Nevertheless, *I* see tiredness. Tell me of your strategy.'

He opened his eyes and laid his plan before me in simple terms. It had no twists and turns in it because we had little room to manoeuvre around our enemy. There was really only desperation with which to arm ourselves and when he had finished, I asked,

'Do you wish me to inform Ariella?'

'Guillaume is doing that right now, and I shall inform Tobias. If he ever stops puking.'

For a little time we sat watching the sail belly and flap, hearing the boat groan as a roll of swell hit amidships. Gisborne and I had often talked about the dreadful events that had befallen us in Cyprus prior to our marriage, but something unspoken always pulled us back from picking apart his previous life in England, or mine in Aquitaine. Perhaps it was that we were different people then. And yet…

'Gisborne, why did you truthfully become my father's steward?'

He sat back, eyebrows raised, wondering no doubt why such a question had any validity at this time. But I was so tired of sitting encased in the black cloak of grief and inaction, that conversing on anything was balm – even previous lives.

'I told you why when we met.' He took up a small fragment of rope lying on the deck and which had unravelled, and he began to plait.

'To make your way in the world? And you think I still believe that?'

He finished the plait, knotted it off and tossed it to me, grabbing his untidy hair as it blew in the wind. 'No. Of course you don't. Or you would not have asked the question.'

I passed the plait back – our fingers touching. 'Perhaps you should tie your hair back with this and tell me the truth.'

He laid the fragment on the deck, pulled a thin leather strip from his purse and tied his hair roughly at his nape. It was done with gritty impatience and I waited. I had learned over the years that he would speak best when he was ready. Not that such observations had curbed my own impatience or loquaciousness.

'You assume incorrectly. It was the truth when I said I wanted to make my way in the world. You know I had lost everything. I started information gathering as soon as my mother died. It began innocently enough when I learned of a certain bishop with a taste for very young boys. I sold it secretly; no one knew that I was the finder or the purveyor. I was but a nobleman's son fallen on hard times and began to perfect the art of anonymity.'

My head swung to Guillaume.

'Yes,' said Gisborne. 'He manages it well. So does Toby. One learns to recognise the artform quickly in others if one values one's life.'

He settled to the telling of this unmentioned part of his life. We had skirted around it for an age and I knew enough to make me worry for him but the detail was something else, something new and forbidding.

'The information one learns is usually exploitive by its very nature,' he continued. 'And it is easy to make oneself a target. In respect of de Courcey, William the Marshall had suggested he might be a risk to England and to Henry. De Courcey was a *routier* baron and wealthy because of it and the Crown has never felt comfortable when their knights have more funds than they. Henry was privately concerned about de Courcey's force of men at a time when his relationship with his own sons was breaking down dramatically. Thus it suited me to spy on de Courcey and make money from it and when he began circling your father, it was a simple matter for me to become your father's squire.' A strand of hair escaped from the leather and blew across Gisborne's face and he wound it behind his ear. 'It was an uneasy shock though, when my cousin, the man with whom I had been reared and who managed to remove my inheritance from my hands, turned up in France on our journey back from Aquitaine to your father. For sure he wanted to inveigle me into his Free Lance guard but it would only have been to belittle and ruin me.'

Such verbosity from Guy was so unexpected. We had been like this with each other in the early days in Venezia but it had rapidly and perhaps justifiably reverted as tension climbed.

'Once Henry died, Eleanor quickly saw the need to shore up Richard's claim to the throne. I was part of that and… What?'

'My *godmother* commissioned you? *She* knew who you were all along? And you never saw fit to tell me?'

'Yes, she did know who I was. Some of the Court did – for example, your men de Turnham and de Camville. But they were trusted and trusting men. My anonymity was in their hands and before you ask, yes – they knew me in Cyprus but preserved the fiction. In respect of me not telling *you* such detail, you have to remember that part of the success of anonymity lies in protecting those one loves by saying nothing. At any rate, it is immaterial because Eleanor will see my defection from the hunt for Richard as nothing but treason and from the moment I turned my back on her messenger, I effectively became an outlaw. I remember being cast as one after de Courcey's death but that was purely a fabrication so that I was free to spy for Richard.'

That much I know, husband.

'But Guy, do you not think that your history of spying for and against this and that person could be the cause of William's abduction?'

'I am sure it is. I am under no illusions. But until I know the identity of the nobleman, I will never know why – although it is of no account because he is a dead man. He could be French and guarding Phillip's interests, or German and acting for the Hohenstaufen. He might even be a legate acting for the Pope, I care not.'

'You have spied on the Pope?' I squeaked.

'Popes, princes and paupers, Ysabel. It hardly matters. Secrets and lies are the very foundation of our world – it's a fact and I make money from it and that's an end to it.'

My hands lay in my lap as he spoke and they clenched with this last. 'But William, Guy…'

He stood, leaving me, his "squire", to lever myself up.

'Yes,' he said. His face was as bleak as the northern English moors in winter. 'William. *That* is enough to make me curse the day I was born.'

His eyes were like the entrance to Hell and I could say nothing that would ameliorate the pain.

'Might I ask you one last question?'

An eyebrow lifted.

'Does being a spymaster reinforce trust in others, or weaken it?'

'Trust?' He grimaced. 'Trust has no bearing.'

'Do you trust me?'

'I'd like to,' he said, referring back to earlier in our conversation and giving me the ghost of a smile.

'Ariella? Toby?'

'Of course.'

'Guillaume?'

Silence. Bird cries, the creak of stays and ropes, the continued crack of the sail, voices calling orders, ribald joking.

He swung round to watch the coast passing. 'I keep my friends close to me, Ysabel, as I have told you before, and my enemies even closer. So close I can see their nose hairs.'

Meaningless, husband!

'But is he a friend or…'

'Look,' he pointed. 'The marshes. And beyond that promontory – Toulon. We are nearly there. By dawn tomorrow, we will be on land. By tomorrow night, we will have William returned and corrupt souls despatched to the Devil.'

With boots removed and our cloaks rolled over our shoulders, we jumped from the prow of the small boat that had conveyed us ashore in two trips. Mean wavelets snapped at our heels and the onshore breeze froze the droplets to our skin and clothes. They called the wind the *Ostro* and it blew from the coast of Al-Mahgreb carrying messages of sand dunes lying one after another to infinity, pale like a northerner's knuckles. They say the sand creates dreams and nightmares and that people are confronted with their God there. That water is unknown for leagues and leagues and yet men and animals survive. And that the heat crispens one's brains like the skin of a roasted pig.

And yet… and yet this angry seawind was cold against our faces.

Behind the little dunes on which we had landed were salty marshes and I was so chilled I imagined the crystalline sparkle of a frost would reveal itself at first light. But then frost is always shy of settling beneath the bitter veil that is salt air. No – it would wait for us further inland no doubt, my freezing wet toes curled in protest.

Gisborne had rewarded the ship's master with a substantial bag of silver dinars – the man had flashed white teeth in his dark face, touching his forehead and his chest in the Saracen way.

'May Allah protect you, sir. And if you should remember Ahmed's name in the future, then Allah will bless you with many sons and all of them in your image. Ahmed has been honoured to be of service, sir.'

Gisborne took the man by the shoulder and walked along the deck with him, talking quietly and the man nodded and bowed.

Another one of your faceless men?

Gisborne had said that if we walked for all the daylight hours at our disposal, that we might reach the Commanderie not long beyond dusk – it was near thirteen leagues from the coast. If we could find carts moving in that direction, even donkeys or horses, our time would be even less. But we had agreed with his strategy of landing before Toulon rather than in the town itself. We had few advantages but surely surprise must be the greatest and thus we would move as swiftly across country as we could, heading for the old Roman Aurelian Way and thence into the demesnes of the Saint Christoph Commanderie.

We plunged around the edges of the salty marshes, crunching the crust beneath feet that we could barely see. But as the first light appeared from the east, a pearl light tinged with the gold that is surely Byzantine, we could see birds – many of them, long legged and heron-like, they seemed as if they had been dipped in the warmth of sunrise and sunset. Ariella and I stared for a moment, never having seen such creatures, but the men kept walking, urging us to hurry. We splashed through shallows and spiky grasses, gaining higher ground. And then we put our heads down and walked, pushing through sparse coastal shrubbery, and over ground that seemed unforgiving and harsh and which glowed ever more ruby-like as the sun rose higher.

The shipboard cold that had stayed with us through the marshes began to dissipate in the warmth of the southern sun and we stopped briefly to drink from costrels that Ahmed had filled with watered wine before we left the galley, rolling our cloaks as a further burden to be carried. A coastal range reared above and I despaired having to climb it – even though I could see a track carved into its side. But as we sat resting and chewing on shrivelled dates that threatened to meld our upper teeth to our lowers, a cart could be heard rumbling toward us from the west, the driver singing lustily. A song which was obviously familiar to Tobias and which he immediately began to hum.

I sucked a deep breath through my nose, hoping the cart was empty and that Gisborne would be able to secure a ride for us. The sharp essence of *rosmarinus* and wild thyme freshened the air the higher we moved above the shore and the wind dropped away, the clouds of earlier burning off as the wintersun climbed higher.

A donkey appeared around a stumpy clump of resinous pine trees, dragging a cart behind, and my heart sank thinking it to be loaded, the donkey walking with such a resigned and penitential air. But it was empty as was the one that followed behind, the rear donkey stepping pedantically in the footprints of the lead beast. Each of the drivers stiffened when they noticed us, hands moving swiftly under cloaks but Guillaume held up both hands, greeting the drivers with a smile. They halted the donkeys uncertainly, their grizzled faces aware that we were strangers on the road, noticing the swords, staring at Tobias who had begun to hum their little ditty.

I presume Guillaume asked for a passage for us, and when they looked at each other as if we were lepers, he dipped into his purse, pulling out a small bag of dinars which he let slide in a silver trail across his hands. In moments we were aboard the two carts, the valiant donkeys pulling us ever upward. We had nothing to share with the men but our money, and for that we received some fresh bread from Toulon. The drivers were peasants from close by Lucus and had been to the markets in Toulon to sell olive oil for their *seigneur*. They had been fleeced they said; no one in the towns understood how hard it was to survive … the lack of money, the effort, the greediness of *Le Seigneur*.

I had heard such things many times before…

But Toby began to sing and within a short moment, they joined in quite happily. We stopped to eat, bells ringing for None from all the churches across the Holy Roman Empire, across France, Anjou, Aquitaine and Normandy, and even across England, to let the world know that our time passes into God's hands and that we should pray for His love and guidance.

I ate of their bread and cheese sparingly because my stomach was filled with fire and it would suffice until William was in my arms. We told them we headed for Brignolo to sing at the Saint Stephen feast and they said we would be there by dark. We left them as good friends do, with much back-slapping and good intentions. But I was glad the donkeys had conveyed us so far and glad too that my energy had remained untouched because it would be needed in a very short time. We trod the Aurelian Way now and I thanked God that this road had weathered the generations well enough for our feet and ankles not to be strained.

'Not far to go, I think, my lord,' said Guillaume.

'We are all ready?' Gisborne asked.

My fingers slid to my sword and Toby grinned at me and winked. It was as if he said *'Nearly over…'*

Gisborne and I exchanged a glance, so much at stake here, so much… No words were spoken and I expected none.

And thus, as the sun sank toward Aquitaine in the west and the shadows changed to indigo, we moved quietly around the edge of Brignolo using evening and the thickets of dried bamboo as cover. The stems crackled and in the late dusk breeze, the leaves shivered and whispered as we passed by.

A narrow stream chuckled far too happily over pebbles, the sound almost mocking us as we jumped across the rippling surface to stand under a belt of dense trees – pines, oaks and hornbeams – the needles and leaves lay in a thick cushion beneath our feet, the dampness of the fallen detritus deadening the sound of our footsteps. Rich leaf mould and rot filled the air along with the sharp smell of pine and I sucked it in as greedily as if I thought I might never breathe again. Once I had stood in front of the Venetian villa by the water and let my breath go, farewelling so much tawdry memory with it, thinking that I would never have to hold my breath again.

How naïve!

The rich smell of turned earth hung in the dewy night air as we moved closer to the edge of a field that sloped up toward heavy shadows. A horse neighed and I blinked, Ariella gasping beside me.

I remembered a long time ago, talking about an army waiting to charge – about loose bowels and twisted innards, dry mouths and twitching hands and knees. About fear. But this time was so different. Now I was filled with iron – I was calm and every noise sounded as clear as drops of water falling on pewter plate. My hand closed on the grip of the sword as if it was a lover, sliding around, squeezing gently – my feet were steady, each step confident, my faith in my commander as complete as it could be, my belief that we would find our son this night, firm and unyielding.

We could *not* be beaten.

Gisborne split us up at the foot of the field, sending Guillaume, Ariella and Toby to the other side to make the stealthy ascent whilst he and I tackled the right side. We watched them disappear into the dark shade and then Gisborne turned to me, laying his hands on my shoulders.

'I would that you were not here, Ysabel. Whomever our tormentor is, he respects neither child, woman nor man and you and Ariella are as much a game to him as William.'

'We have discussed this, Guy...'

'I know,' his grip tightened. 'Then let it be said that I have no doubts about your courage. It is part of your lifeblood, has always been. Ariella as well. You are forces to be reckoned with. All I can say is be careful, God protect you and...'

He bent forward and kissed me gently, a shadow kiss, but more intimate, more filled with love and care than any we had ever shared.

'And?' I asked as my hand rubbed against the stubble on his cheek. 'What else would you say?'

'Be obedient...' He patted my shoulder as he brushed past and began to climb the slope.

The Commanderie sat like a threat at the top of the hill. The moon tried to shine, but heavy cloud drifted back and forth, plunging us into a protective gloom. Unable to see across the field, we had no knowledge of our companions' whereabouts – in truth we may as well have been blind.

Nightbirds, perhaps owls or nightjars, gave sporadic and haunting cries and once a baying sound filled the air. A hunting dog? Perhaps a wolf? But nowhere the suggestions of men...

'Odd,' whispered Guy, 'but not unexpected because he thinks to play the unexpected game and we must try and anticipate. I suspect he might rather wield the final cut as a solitary hunter rather than as part of a hunting party.

He reminds me of Robert...'

Then he must *be Halsham's man...*

We crept on – a stone structure, perhaps a well, almost at the top of the field. Dirt clung to our boots but it was a welcome padding against noise. Night sounds beat on the air again and I would swear I heard a cry filled with agony.

'Listen!' I grabbed Guy's arm.

''Tis nothing,' Gisborne's voice hardened and I knew it was not merely *nothing*. We pushed through another belt of trees, crossed a pale track and climbed onward to a wedge of tree shadow that enabled us to look back down upon the two buildings making up the settlement.

'It feels wrong, Guy,' I whispered, trying not to pant and breathing hard through my nose. 'There must be someone...'

He whipped his sword hand over my mouth, his other holding a glinting knife and immediately my heart began to pump with much more than exertion. Sweat prickled in my armpits and my stomach cramped with ugly pain.

William. William. William...

I repeated it over and over to try and keep the ice frozen and the head clear of rampaging thoughts as we gazed down upon the Commanderie. The moon slid from behind a cloud and the shape of a chapel stood out quite clearly, the rounded apse giving a benign edge to the building. Inside, lights flickered, indicating life of some sort and my stomach turned again.

William...

This had been Robert Halsham's nest from where he had begun to hatch a plot against the Throne of England and from where he planned the demise of his hated cousin, Guy of Gisborne. From where too, he had convinced a misbegotten cadre of holy warriors to form a fiercely loyal sect – one that had inevitably brought the Templar name into disrepute. There was much hatred to be found within the walls of these buildings, but was it all theirs? Or was some of it ours?

Gisborne moved on, walking so carefully, touching nothing. We could be glad of the damp leaf-litter as it silenced every step. Pressing hard against the chiselled stone of the walls, we moved around the curve of the chapel, Gisborne sucking in a breath and reaching swiftly to clamp a hand over my own mouth as we stumbled against the body of a guard. Then another.

Fallen into the folds of their *brunete* cloaks, a slit across their necks and their eyes wide with surprise, we stepped over them and into the company of those we knew – friends who had murdered enemies.

Guillaume signed to Guy. No one around. Anywhere.

Relief? Anger?

All of that.

A door faced us – the entrance to the chapel. It stood ajar and a beam of golden light filtered through the narrow space. Except that my fanciful mind wondered if a door left open was an invitation. Guy levered it with his toe and it swung wide, no announcing squeak.

Nothing like the Dolorosa.

I swallowed on a lump in my throat.

Calm, Ysabel. Now is the time.

We crept in like thieves.

A perfect vaulted ceiling arched above us. Two narrow glazed windows were positioned either side of the semi-circular structure and I imagined that at sunrise, light would fall on the altar from one side, and at sunset, a similar gleam from the other side would illuminate the gold cross that stood on the altar. Two plain gold candlesticks stood either side of the altar, their flames dancing in the slight breeze that wound around us through the open door. No heavy tallow smell hung in the air, the candles of the best quality. Even the oak table in front of the altar was exceptionally carved.

Except that parts of it were hidden by the body of a man stretched across it.

'Peter!' I cried out and Ariella and I ran to him as Gisborne, Guillaume and Toby drew swords and surrounded us with backs toward the altar.

He had been stripped to his *braies* and he was scarred with crusted wounds across his chest. I had no doubt they would be on his back as well.

Lash wounds…

And even though he had stolen my son and attacked his own wife, causing them to lose a child, and even though he had beaten Mehmet about the head, my pity knew no bounds.

'Peter, dear Peter,' I whispered, rubbing my hand over his head which was bruised and bloody. His eyes opened, and vaguely I think he may have recognised me, but he was far gone. Much of his blood had pooled on the floor of the chapel and I suspected he had been left like this for a day, maybe more.

William. Where is William?

Ariella grabbed a jug of water from the altar and pulled at a cloth that lay beneath a gold bowl, wetting it, wiping it over his face. His eyes fluttered.

'Peter,' I said. 'Peter, where is William?'

He looked at me, recognition filling his eyes and tried to open his mouth which was coated in blood, lips swollen and cracked. The agony in his expression split my soul to pieces. Was he telling me William was dead?

No!

'Where is he?' His hand grabbed and he pulled me toward him, groaning, a strangled sound emerging. 'What do you say?' I squeezed his hand, my voice rising in panic. 'Where is he?'

I had never ever seen such fear on someone's face, such pain as he tried to respond. A tear slid from his swollen eyes and he sucked in a breath that had the rattle of death in it.

'Peter, tell me!' I shook him. 'Please!'

'Don't, Ysabel. He can't. His tongue has been cut out,' said Ariella as she tried to wipe his face clean.

'Yes,' a cultured voice said from the shadows at the back of the chapel. 'His tongue was removed because he refused to tell where he had hidden the child. And after we had looked after him and trained him so well to be one of us. Ungrateful, I say.'

Peter had lapsed into a deep faint, perhaps so deeply gone I knew I would never wake him again.

As Gisborne yelled, 'Show yourself!' I pulled my cloak from my shoulders, unrolled it and lay it over our blacksmith, turning then and drawing my own sword.

A tinder sparked in the gloom at the far end of the chapel and a flame flared from a cresset. But still we could see very little beyond the altar – a shadow-like man, his head and face concealed by a dark *keffiyeh* wrapped cleverly to conceal much.

He took a step forward, unsheathing his sword and inspecting it, then leaning against the wall. 'God in Heaven but you've taken an age to get here, Gisborne. Two days ago, your milksop son's snivelling rankled me so much I could have ended his days then and there…'

No!

'…but I realised I would be losing an investment.'

He pushed away from the wall and took another step. He was just as I remembered – not overly tall, but muscular and broad-shouldered as befits a swordsman. His eyes glittered in the light of the cresset, any other feature well concealed. Even his voice, that voice that raised more than hairs on my neck, was slightly muffled, adding a distance to it.

'Have you any idea,' he continued blithely, 'how much such charming innocence could realise for me at the slave markets? My coffers would overflow thanks to his beauty and he *is* a beauty – you should be congratulated. Many a man would welcome him in their beds.'

Gisborne stood rock-still, Guillaume's arm holding him tight, but fury radiated like burning heat. 'Not yet, my lord,' he said so very softly. 'He plays you, that is all.'

'Find William,' Gisborne responded urgently, 'Go!'

But none of us moved. Were we directly disobeying him? No. Simply, the man in front of us held us in the palm of his hand with his charisma, the kind of poise that had brought men to Gisborne's side through the years. I could bare believe my husband might have met his match and I suspected we all thought the same. But it was a Devil-wrought thing, the words that sprang from the knight's throat. We wanted to hear what he said and yet we wished to stop our ears.

'At any rate,' the fellow continued. 'You're here now and I can finally conclude what I started so long ago. It's been an expensive game you know, having you watched, hearing reports of your activities, sizing you up and attacking your flank when your guard was down. But it served its purpose. It weakened you, I think, maybe even confused you.'

I thought of Gisborne's words – *he will strut before us, forgetting that backs are as vulnerable as fronts.*

'It was enough to abduct the little son', he continued. 'Having Peter under my care for so long whilst you followed our liege was perfect. The simple blacksmith – so easy to mould – a little fear and worry sown into his mind and he was mine. I knew that in his own good time, Peter would deliver your son to me far healthier and fresher than if I had sought him out myself.'

Gisborne shook Guillaume off, and in pretence of pulling at his boot, he whispered, 'Find him!' He took steps forward, closing the distance by more than half, his sword held low, the grace and power of his walk a thing of great beauty, no obvious sign of tension. But I saw that his knuckles were white and his face cut from stone. He towered over the knight in front of him – anyone less bold would have folded in an instant as he advanced.

'Except, *Simon,*' Gisborne growled in the way we all knew presaged danger. 'You don't have my son. Do you? Peter betrayed you at the last.'

The fellow's eyebrows creased momentarily. Was he wary? But then the expression was gone.

'You think I do not know who you are?' queried Gisborne. 'A point to me, I think.'

And in barely a heartbeat the knight came back, cocksure, 'And I claim your point back by saying no matter what happens now – *you* have *lost* your *son.*'

'No!' My cry was wrenched from deep in the bowels of my body and I lifted my sword and went to run forward, Guillaume grabbing me and Gisborne yelling, '*Obedience,* Ysabel. Go!'

Guillaume pulled me out the door as the knight's laughter chased us. 'My God but she's a liability, isn't she? I have heard it said often…'

Toby and Ariella pushed from behind and I could see and hear nothing now – I had left my husband in the lion's den.

'We must do as he says and find William,' said Toby. 'He is here somewhere, alive, I am sure of it. I suspect Peter had a moment of clarity, realising that William's life was at stake. I am sure he hid him somewhere beyond the reach of the knight.'

I could hear nothing from the chapel and felt as if I were being split into two hopeless halves – one without a son and one without a husband. Once Guy said *I will give my life for our son* and such fear filled me that all the ice and fire I had nurtured melted in a heartbeat. An almighty crash filled the night as something fell inside the chapel and the ringing of blade upon blade began.

'Guillaume,' Toby said breathlessly. 'I have an idea of how to find William but you must go back to Sir Guy. We saw another door, do you remember? It will lead into the building and you can get back into the chapel. Make your way up to the sleeping quarters by the stairs.'

He was asking Guillaume to go back and defend Guy from above, to aim an arrow and loose to kill.

'Please Guillaume...' I begged.

The man from Anjou needed no second urging. He ran off into the night along the length of the building, his bow on his shoulder, sheathing his sword as he departed.

I closed my eyes. 'Toby...'

'All will be well. Come, ladies, quickly...' and strangely, he began to sing. Verse after verse of *"Somer is y comen in"* as we moved along walls, into corners, and finally through the door left open by Guillaume.

Too close to the chapel...

Toby's voice dying as we heard swords clash...

We turned away and I knew I was nothing but a traitor to my husband. It felt as if I dragged chains behind me.

'Ysabel, come *on!*' Ariella chivvied me. Into the dining hall, along a passage, past chambers with thick doors lying open, Toby's voice rising in song again Back to the door and outside, into the stables and out – the song beginning again.

'Toby,' I choked, 'What if he is muffled or drugged? We could have passed him a dozen times...'

'My lady, I will not stop till I have found him.'

But he was not anywhere in the yard of the Commanderie, not the barn, nor the buttery nor cookhouse and I despaired, looking through tears to the field. It was an obsidian river flowing down, down, down but guarded by the strange beehive shape we had passed as the moon had struggled to shine.

'Toby, there is another structure we have missed!'

Ariella followed my gaze. 'The well,' she uttered. 'Surely not...'

We ran then, all three of us down the slope lit by the moon and Toby began singing as we climbed through a ragged line of trees.

'Somer is y-comen in,
loudë sing, cuckóu!'

Glory to God, as we reached the side of the well with its wooden door, a faint childish voice began to sing in canon, my heart breaking.

'Cuckóu, cuckóu,
Wél singést thou, cuckóu, ne swik thou never nou!

Sing cuckóu nou!

Sing cuckóu! Sing cuckóu nou!'

We flung open the door and William sat on a ledge in the pitch black, weeping.

'I wath quiet, Mama. Peter thaid I mutht be quiet. But it wath dark…'

I pulled him out and crushed him to me. 'Your are a *such* a good boy, William.' Toby took a deep breath and Ariella slammed the door shut behind him.

'Toby, Gisborne must know…' I said over the top of William's head. 'He must know his son is safe, that we have won the game. He must…'

He must because he said he would give his life for his son…

'Go then,' said Ariella. 'Fly!'

'William,' I said, holding him away from me. 'I must run and tell your Papa that you are safe. I shall be back in a moment. Don't fret now. You have Ariella and Toby…' I kissed him and hugged him and ran back up that hill as if my legs were wings.

Sped to the back door into the building, drew my sword, found the stair and leaped two at a time, my throat burning with effort, legs aching, almost folding at the knee. And all the while, hearing grunts, swords striking stone, clashing.

'Guillaume!' I called.

And then I saw him, laid out flat, his bow lying in open fingers, one arrow by his side, the other still in his belt. A cold realisation that I had been shadowed as I entered the gallery hit me like a blacksmith's hammer and I swung in a swift circle, sword lifting, hitting the man behind me, the blade entering his side, his own sword crashing to the floor, driving mine on through his flesh. No thought, no fear…

He subsided as I withdrew my blade, no hope, and fell forward onto his face.

Please God, let there be no others. Protect William and my friends…

'Guillaume,' I reached across the dead man and shook our archer, *'Guillaume!'*

He groaned and I knew he would live but he was of no use to Guy and as I leaned over the balustrade, I knew I was reliving every moment of Cyprus. With one exception, I thought, as I pulled Guillaume's bow from his fingers, lifting the arrow and nocking it.

The man I would kill was not Robert Halsham, nor was it Ulric.

As the man's voice lifted to the vaulted roof, mocking my husband,

I knew immediately who our enemy was…

The two men were bloodied versions of those we had left behind barely a cockcrow before. Gisborne's arm shone in the light of the one remaining candle on the altar, blood running freely down his sleeve and onto his hand. He repeatedly wiped his palms on his hose, grasping the sword double-handed, moving swiftly on feet that seemed as fresh as if he'd just begun. The other knight's leg was badly gashed and every now and then, he would grunt as weight was transferred. He had slowed in his action, but his words, albeit breathless, still fell like Greek fire upon my husband.

'They say you have become a traitor to the throne, Gisborne, that there is a price on your head. No church to flee to now. No king's protection. Just my pity. And what of your wife? They say she spreads herself for any who take her fancy…'

But Gisborne was immune. Or so it seemed. The candle at the altar fell as the pair swung at each other and then they split, one on one side of the altar, one on the other and poor dead Peter lying like a sacrificial offering between them. An ill-judged swipe from the knight's blade and then momentary darkness, feet clipping away, breath sucking in and blowing out. I sighted the arrow in the faint light from the cresset. But who was I aiming at?

Hold Ysabel, hold!

And then they were directly below me, a wild sweep from the knight met full-on by Gisborne's weapon, sparks flying, the blades slipping down to the quillons, the two men snarling in each other's faces like wolves in a fight.

Swing him round, Guy, swing him round!

'He is safe!' I called out.

The knight looked up and I loosed the arrow. It missed his face, missed his neck which was a shame as knowing who he was, it would have been the most perfect irony. It entered his right shoulder from behind. A pointless wounding except that his arm drooped and his sword clattered to the floor. Both men stared at each other and then the knight ducked around Gisborne and ran back down the nave so swiftly I could bare believe it, pulling a pew over with his left hand, through the door to outside, slamming it shut. Gisborne flung around and followed, his hand wrenching at the door.

'Guy!' I yelled. 'Stop! We have William. Please stop!'

I shook Guillaume and he groaned again and then I leaped down the stair to Gisborne. 'Toby found him in the well. He is scared and weeping but he is alive. He needs you. Let the knight go…'

'Christ!' he roared, striking his sword against a pew, wedging it in the timber and then having to tug it out, pushing his foot against the wood, swearing at God and the Virgin all the while. He shook his head. 'For now, Ysabel.' His chest rose and fell. 'But it isn't done. Jesu, it is not!'

'I know but William's needs are paramount,' I said. 'Besides, I know who the man is…'

'As do I,' still his breath came in exhausting gasps.

'You say?'

'He talked, God how he talked! I suspect he would be a worthy opponent if he would just desist. In any case, I placed the voice. He sounds much like his brother – rasping, forthright, perhaps a little more cultured, but I think we are not wrong.'

'De Courcey,' I said, my memory still too fresh.

Gisborne sheathed his sword and wiped his face with the altar cloth. 'Yes, Simon de Courcey. Baron de Courcey, your deceased husband's brother.'

CHAPTER TEN

We could not be beaten.

It resounded in my head like a war cry and we had not been beaten. To give in was to give up on William's life and thus the thought of my dearest son's hand curling into mine was the goad.

'Find me, Mama. Find me.'

As I sat in the Commanderie's yard with William on my knee, my chin resting on his head, I thought I could be given the wealth of kings and nothing would match the warmth that spread through my soul. That ice-maiden, the dark woman who would kill, had thawed like a stream in spring. All at once I felt like a flower opening its petals one by one. And all because of this little boy who had been courageous and stalwart.

''Ella?' he asked. 'Ith Tanti waiting for me in Venethia?'

'Oh he is, William, of course he is,' she replied. 'But do you know something very special?'

William looked up at her as she sat in her tawdry men's clothing. 'Ith it a thecret?'

Secrets. Already perfecting his father's way.

'Perhaps,' she bent toward him, turning to left and to right as if to check for eavesdroppers. 'Tanti has a lady friend.'

William digested this. 'Are they married like Gwen and Peter?'

Ariella's expression didn't change as she nodded, 'They were married secretly one day when I was at the booth with Papa.'

I smiled, thinking of that bright little dog fronting a priest...

'Whatth her name?' interrupted William.

'Oh, did I not say? She is called Mea. And she is brown and white and very pretty.'

'Mea,' mouthed William, tasting the word. 'Is she big?'

Was he recalling those huge hounds from the dogfight?

'No bigger than Tanti.'

'Will they have babieth?'

Ariella nodded and caught my eye and I knew instantly what would emerge next.

'They will have puppieth?' he squeaked, turning round to face me. 'Mama, Tanti will have puppieth. Pleathe can I have one?'

Show me a mother anywhere who would deny her son anything if he had travelled such a journey as William. Thus I nodded. 'Of course, and perhaps, Papa and I will have one too.'

'Brother and thithter.' He lay back against me, sucking his thumb, then mumbled, 'I with I had a brother or thithter.'

Ariella laughed. 'Always something, Ysabel, always something.'

But I did not mind.

I had been so close to losing him forever and there was a great risk of that thought and the image of his hiding place and of Peter's death repeating over and over in my mind. I had no intention of allowing that to happen. Not now – there was too much else to think on and plan.

Besides, Ysabel, do not forget, your tormentor still lives.

'Mama, where'th Toby?' said William stirring. 'Can I play with him?'

'Not just now, sweetheart. He and Papa have business to attend to with Guillaume.'

He squirmed to get off my lap. 'Where'th Peter? I would play with him inthtead.'

The pain began to sharpen, twisting like a deep splinter in the palm of one's hand.

'My little man,' I took William and turned him toward me. 'Peter has gone back to Venezia to Gwen. Papa sent him back because Gwen needs him. Do you understand?'

His face creased as he thought about this. 'Gwenny loveth Peter like

Tanti loveth Mea.'

'Yes,' I agreed.

He bent to the ground, sorting through pebbles and then pitching them over arm, child-fashion, at the door of the Commanderie's barn. Softly at first, then with increasing strength, even agitation.

'Peter took me to Papa. He thaid I would only be thafe where Papa wath.'

So that's how it was done…

'He thaid you already left but Gwenny came and he left me on hith horthe near the bridge and took her back. He thaid she mutht thtay with Biddy and the guardth.'

The stone throwing stopped and Ariella and I sat as if carved from marble.

Say more, William.

'He told lotth of thtories and it wath very warm under hith cloak. We ate lotth of food and I drinked wine without water. Thometimeth he gave me a drink I didn't like. It made me very thleepy.'

A stone was thrown again, then they were all gone and he turned back to Ariella and myself, walking into my arms.

'But he doethn't thing like Toby. He thoundth like a cow.'

Quiet. And Ariella and I did not move.

'But I love him becauthe he brought me to Papa.'

Nothing more, just hens clucking and pecking the soil, a pig whose snort sounded like an old man coughing, and a kite shrieking from high up. We all looked toward the bird in the clouds.

'Indeed, William. He did. Safely so,' I replied and heaved him onto my lap again, leaning back against the winterwarm wall, closing my eyes and allowing the sun to bleach everything to white. I asked for God's forgiveness for lying to William. By the time we reached Venezia again, if that was the plan, we would be able to find something kind and gentle to say that might explain Peter's absence. The good things about Peter would be preserved for William's sake. And perhaps even for Gwen's – a lock of Peter's hair lay in my purse. I would give it to her if she wanted it.

It was well past None when Toby and Gisborne returned to us – dirty, dishevelled but with none of Peter's or the guards' blood on them. Ariella and I had played chasings with William, had ventured to the stream and allowed him to dangle his toes and had thrown sticks in further upstream, so that he had to run to see whose twigs reached the hornbeams first. Now he lay asleep, cocooned in Ariella's cloak as we rested our own eyes. Footsteps sounded and I sat up as the men joined us.

'Done?'

'Yes,' said Gisborne. 'There is a small cemetery not far from the chapel and perhaps it might help Peter's soul to be interred with God-fearing Templars. As for the guards – their souls are in another's hands.' He touched his son's hair. 'And William?'

'Remarkable. He told us a little. I have no doubt he will have challenging moments to come, but he was given to believe you would be here and in fact that is what eventuated so he has no reason to doubt Peter.'

'Then,' said my husband. 'That is how it shall remain. Do you think he can be moved?'

The sun had drifted behind wintercloud and I shivered, the shadow of the chapel and quarters stretching apocalyptic fingers toward us.

'Yes. I have no wish to stay here and I wish for him to be gone from a place of terror. I have no doubt that de Courcey would have frightened him. Why else would Peter hide him? Let us be gone, please!'

Guillaume emerged from the stables leading three saddled horses and I asked, 'Where do we go?'

'Brignolo. To gather ourselves…' was all my husband said. No detail, no further explanation.

Brignolo was becoming shadowed by night – eaves leaning heavily over cobbled and dirt-paved alleys, half-timbered buildings pressing against each other. We found an inn with beds for us and a stable for the horses on the outskirts of the town and whilst Guillaume saw to the mounts, we walked toward water, food and sleep. The men would share one room whilst Ariella, William and I shared another and I could be forgiven for wondering if I would ever sleep in connubial bliss again. I wondered if Gisborne had concealed his wound from the innkeeper when he asked for board, because we wanted no attention, no trouble – I imagined that the wound was as secret as anything else.

William shuffled along toward the inn, dragging his feet, pulling on my hand until Gisborne picked him up, the action evincing no grimace as the sword cut gaped.

'So young and vital, William, and yet you are slower than your Aunt Ariella.'

'I am tired, Papa,' he whined. 'And hungry.' The lip jutted. 'I want Ounthee and Githborne.' The tears began to flow. 'Peter had them in his purthe and he'th gone,' he wailed.

'But no, little Sir William,' said Toby, walking backward in front of Gisborne. He reached into his own purse. 'Look!' He held up the battered toys. 'Now dry your tears.'

William pushed at his father's arm, desperate to be put down, and a grateful glance passed between Guy and the minstrel.

'See,' said Toby lightly. 'Not just a pretty face.' He cut a fancy caper, his legs describing a dainty *rondelet*. *'Puceles carolent at dancent, trestuit de joie feire tancent'* he sang in a melody of which Monsieur de Troyes would have approved.

Gisborne's mouth curved. 'If ever you imagined I thought you to be just a pretty face, Tobias, then your brains are in your *braies*.'

We washed, Ariella dressing Guillaume's head and Gisborne's arm.

'You need stitches, Sir Guy. It is very deep.'

'Then stitch it. I will get a needle and thread from the innkeeper's wife.' He was gone a mere moment and again, one wondered what story he told, Ariella stitching it as if she embroidered some of Saul's silks. In and out, the skin pulling a little, Gisborne betraying no discomfort as William watched from my lap.

'Papa, doeth it hurt?'

'No. Ariella is a very fine stitcher.'

'When Thaul did it to 'Ella, *the* thaid it hurt.'

'But I am a knight, William. And knights feel no pain at all.'

No pain, Gisborne? Knights know no pain?

We ate quickly, only interested in putting William to bed. He could barely stand, his energies running out like water through a hole in a bucket. He slept the moment I lay him on the bed and his father and I stood together as if to make sure we had succeeded in retrieving him.

'How can he escape from this last unscathed?' I asked. 'Please God, spare him. He is exhausted, Gisborne, and really needs to rest for a little before we move on.'

213

'I don't plan to move from Brignolo immediately, Ysabel. I agree he needs time. But I suspect he needs to be home ultimately, where life is familiar and where he is once again the centre of all our lives.'

Do you plan for us to take up our Venetian life again, husband?

It sounded as if that was indeed what he meant. But equally, I could not forget that he had sworn to hunt Simon de Courcey down, if de Courcey did not get to him first.

'Guy,' I took him by the hand and led him away from the bed to stand by the door. The burble of voices, of feet passing over the stone floor and up and down the stair was hardly the stuff of peace that we needed. A priory hostel would have been better and if, as Guy had indicated, we were to stay longer than a night then I would seek one out.

'Do you plan for us to continue our lives in Venezia?' I asked.

He leaned resignedly against the door, holding it shut. 'By which you mean you would prefer to live elsewhere.'

'We were attacked…'

'Because of de Courcey.'

'He might continue to hunt us.'

'Yes.'

'Then surely we would be safe elsewhere.'

'Where would you have us go, Ysabel?'

So resigned, Guy. Am I such a trial?

'To the north, the Low Countries, or even further north? Maybe the east – Constantinople perhaps? There are mercantile opportunities, a challenge for you. Saul…'

'Indeed.'

'Shall you think on it?'

His eyebrow lifted as he unbuckled his sword, holding it with one hand whilst his other reached to twitch the doorlatch.

'I think on many things, Ysabel.'

He kissed me on the lips, a full kiss – one of intent and I was left breathless as he walked from the room.

But you do not share those things with me, Guy of Gisborne.

If he felt exhausted after his duel he did not share it. If he suffered from the wound or from bruising, he still walked with grace and strength. As to his mind, who would know? Perhaps to others he seemed no different, but I knew something was awry. I swear to God sometimes I wondered if my husband needed protection from himself.

Ariella pushed open the door. 'He sleeps?'

'Soundly.'

'He is such a courageous child, Ysabel.'

'Like his father, I think,' I muttered as I pulled off my tunic.

'Not unlike his mother, I would say.'

'Poor child...' I dragged off my filthy hose. 'We need clean clothes. William too. These are rank.' I uncoiled my hair, ran my fingers through it, plaited it roughly and still in my unclean chemise, slid into the bed.

As Ariella took off her own clothing and uncoiled her thick hair, I asked, 'How is Guillaume?'

There was a momentary silence and then, 'Do you care?'

Well aimed.

'Of course...'

'But it was not always so.' She climbed into the bed, her chemise no better than my own, careful not to disturb William as she pulled up the covers.

'Indeed. But I was wrong, I think.'

'He is a good man, Ysabel, fallen on difficult times. Gisborne could do worse than have him protecting his back.'

We both lay with our thoughts for a while and William breathed gently between us.

'I think you are interested in him, Ariella.'

'Perhaps,' she said slowly. 'We think the same about many things.'

'Then I wish you well,' I replied.

'Thank you.'

Silence filled the room. Even the inn had quieted and it was possible to feel for once that we might find peace.

Somewhere a bell rang once, halfheartedly, and I guessed the wind knocked it as dreams were chased across the roofs of Brignolo. I closed my eyes and waited for sleep to come.

'Ysabel,' whispered Ariella. 'Do you sleep?'

'No...'

'Then may I speak with you?'

'Go on…'

'Has Sir Guy said we are to leave for Venezia immediately?'

Oh Ariella, do you pine for your father?

'He has said nothing. Although he felt William must return to his home and to things familiar.'

'Then it is a *fait accompli*,' she responded. 'I had thought he might continue the hunt for William's abductor.'

'As did I. But for the moment, he is concerned for William – that his son must see that he has a papa who lives and one who loves him deeply. And like me, he believes William needs to rest a little before setting out.'

'Of course. He must be handled lightly, I think,' my friend said, yawning.

The son, you think? Or perhaps you mean the father.

The next morning dawned drear and with a damp fog hanging down from the eaves and everywhere was noise and faces in a town that filled for the Christmas feast. We heard tell of an *abbaye* with a priory attached and I longed to escape scrutiny and hide behind safe walls.

Sanctuary? I long for sanctuary.

I had forgotten that the celebration of Christmas began – when? On the morrow? We were far from our home amongst strangers. Thus the priory seemed even more suited to our needs. I sought out the companions and Ariella and William were playing clapping rhymes with Toby. 'Where is Guillaume?' I asked.

'Still abed,' said Ariella. 'His head aches and he is unwell.'

Toby grabbed a giggling William as he said, 'I suspect whomever bashed him, did so with the intent to send him to Heaven. He was lucky…'

'Watch him, Ariella,' I said. 'Make sure he is sensible. Toby, where is Sir Guy?'

He shrugged. 'I have no idea. You know I am tardy of a morning and with Guillaume concussed, he was gone before either of us had stirred.'

Gone.

I tried not to worry. Gisborne had always lived his own day and I hoped this was no different. I asked Ariella and Toby if they wished to accompany William and I to the priory to see if we could find beds and they agreed, sensing my unease.

The walls of the Abbaye de la Celle represented all I wanted – security and sanctuary. Large blocks of stone enfolded the *abbeye* as it stood on one side of a square and on the other, a small and unassuming priory – the Priorie de Saint Perpetué. Monks and nuns worked or walked to and fro and it was to a monk that I called through the opened wooden gates, asking if there was space for travellers within their *dorter*. He looked me over with some disregard, for I was still dressed in filthy men's garb.

'All men to the *abbaye's* hostel and women to the hostel of Saint Perpetué. Children,' he surveyed William from the top of a very hooked nose, 'go with the women.' Having dealt this information, he walked away, his Benedictine robes swinging, his tonsure in need of a trim.

'He smellth,' said William.

'Well, my lady,' Toby put a hand over William's mouth by way of admonishment. 'Shall you sleep in the men's quarters?'

'I think not, Toby, because whatever else, I intend to have William by my side. Sister,' I called to a passing nun. 'Sister!'

A woman of indeterminate age, unprepossessing and dumpy but with cheeks the size of church plates and dimples that promised humour, walked to the gates.

'Sister, we are in need of beds for two women and a child and we are accompanied by three men. Do you think the *abbaye* can accommodate us?'

'Of course. But you are the last, as our *dorters* are crammed with pilgrims just now.' Her eyes drifted to our clothes and she raised her eyebrows then knelt in front of William, taking his hand. 'Good day, little man, and what is your name?'

'William,' he grinned.

'Ah, Guillaume, eh…'

Guillaume? No…

'Well little Guillaume, when you return, if you seek out Soeur Marie, I will take you to see our new baby goats. Would you like that?' She stood to address me. 'I suspect you are this child's mother? Hm, how interesting.' She eyed my clothes again. 'I am in charge of the priory's hostel and will welcome you on your return. As to you, sir,' she spoke to Toby, 'take your friends to the *abbaye's* hostel and tell them Soeur Marie has sent you.'

'Our thanks to you, Sister. I am grateful,' I replied.

She nodded, tapping William on the shoulder. 'Soeur Marie, remember? And then the baby goats.'

'Thank you, thithter,' he replied.

At the inn, we found Guy sitting with Guillaume, having purchased vervain and mullein for headaches. The archer sipped from a mug and shuddered at the taste.

'Where did you buy it?' I asked my husband.

'From the *abbaye*. They have a fine herbarium and an excellent herbalist monk who knew what might help.'

'But we were just there. I have arranged for us to move to the *dorter* for the rest of our stay.'

'Have you indeed, wife?'

'It is too crowded here and becoming more so and I would feel safer within the *abbaye* grounds.'

'You do not have to convince me, Ysabel – security and peace for us all, I believe.'

'And we need clean clothing, Guy, William especially. He reeks of mould from the inside of that well...'

'Which is why I have purchased some, even for you, Tobias, although I apologise that it is not to your elegant standard. It is mediocre to be sure but more suitable for us because of that.'

Appropriately clean and clothed, as we walked back to the *abbaye* I said to Guy, 'There is a nun, Sister Marie, who took to William straight away. She wishes to introduce him to the priory's newborn goats and to have such normality, such calm, will be a boon to him. He can forget for a moment.'

'Good,' replied Gisborne, looking down at his son and smiling.

Can you *forget, Gisborne?*

We settled ourselves easily within the priory's confines and as with the worlds of Locksley, of Saint Eadgyth's and even of the Priory of Linn, I felt protected by a world apart. Once again, shallow breaths became deeper and muscles unlocked.

We met in a communal *frater* for the evening meal, two rows of large trestle tables for the travellers and the rest of the stone chamber taken up by rows of nuns on one side and equivalent rows of monks on the other. The meal proceeded in peace, a monk reading passages to us as we chewed and swallowed and it suited our tumbled nerves to be so soothed. Lines smoothed, colour returned, William remaining mercifully quiet. Thank God.

And Gisborne?

With the others he was the same as he had always been – thoughtful, succinct, even charming, perhaps leading everyone to believe that problems were far from his mind. But some part of me did not believe the evidence before my eyes. In the past, he would sometimes mock my intuition but in truth I needed to be aware.

For his own sake.

That night, William slept on his own cot on one side of me and Ariella on the other, the rhythm of the church pulsing around us. The *dorter* was filled with travellers, mostly pilgrims on the road between Compostella, Rome and Jerusalem and we exchanged friendly platitudes, discussing the road, the weather and other things. The following day, Christmas Day, the bells rang loudly and nuns woke us by giving us God's blessing and directing us to Mass.

We went, as one does, and bent knees, crossed ourselves, and gave thanks for the birth of the Christ Child. Listened to the nuns sing a glorious carol, *Guadete, Christus est Natus,* and sighed with the sheer beauty of it. Tobias's eyes lit up and his foot tapped to a subtle beat. William predictably was bored – standing at one point and clapping to the music until I grabbed him, Soeur Marie smiling behind her hand.

Outside in the wider world, a fair drew crowds like women to a wedding and the town cavorted and feasted, almost pagan-like in its celebration of Christmas. There were booths that sold wine, food, fabrics and toys, ribbons, leather goods and spices. There was an archery butt as well, a competition taking place and it was to this that Gisborne and Guillaume drifted, Toby seeking minstrels, actors and storytellers. I wished I did not feel so odd and insecure amongst crowds but it was a penalty earned from our experiences of the last few months, even years perhaps, and so Ariella and I followed in Gisborne's wake, dragged by William.

'Come *on,* Mama. You too, 'Ella. Look!'

Men of all persuasions loosed arrows far and wide to much laughter and good-tempered booing. Occasionally, someone would step up and loose an arrow to the mark with accompanying cheers, but it seemed Brignolo was not the home of accomplished archers. Neither Gisborne nor Guillaume made any move to enter, for which I was glad. Safety and anonymity were two halves of the same but William, trial that he was, shouted to his father.

'Papa, can I thow you how I have learned? Pleathe?'

'Not today, William. It is for men, not children.' He took William's hand. 'Come, let's have a look at the toys.'

But William jerked back. 'No! I want to be an archer.' He dropped to his knees, wailing. 'Now!'

So, his experiences begin to rub.

I had never seen William throw temper our way but it seemed this was to be the day and no amount of Gisborne's talking would divert him. One way or another, people were beginning to stare.

One of the officials accepting entries said, 'Come then, let him compete. He can't do any worse than those who have gone before.'

All eyes swivelled between father and son. I expected Guy to be furious with William. Instead, he laughed. 'I'm persuaded then. But surely a three year old needs an advantage.'

'He's got three year old eyes,' said one wag in the crowd. 'That's better n' anyone who's loosed an arrow so far!'

'Give 'im a little bow!' yelled a woman.

'Let 'im closer to the butts,' called a youth.

No one bore William any ill-favour and it smacked of festive fun. Toby pushed in next to us and asked 'What goes?'

'William has inveigled himself into an archery competition,' Ariella said.

'So much for secrecy,' Toby snorted earning a sharp glance from Gisborne.

'Take your son closer to the butts, sir. Here is a smaller bow for him.' The official passed over what seemed to my uninformed eye to have the appearance of a small Saxon bow. 'Best of three after you pay a fee.'

The crowd booed. 'Let 'im do it for nothin'. It's Christmas.'

Gisborne shrugged but placed coins on the table anyway and man and boy walked toward the heaped earth target. Halfway down, they stopped and Gisborne knelt, speaking quietly to William. William nodded and then Gisborne helped him nock the arrow, standing back to watch the little arms strain to draw the string back. The first arrow went wildly wide, the crowd letting out a collective moan and he turned an agonized face to his father. Gisborne knelt – more soft words. Nocked again.

The arrow swooped away and lodged at the very edge of the target before teetering and then falling to the ground. The crowd cheered for him anyway, but William's lip jutted and he swung to Gisborne, his child's eyes dark with a fury I had never seen. Gisborne squatted, put his arm across William's shoulder and they conversed, William listening intently.

The crowd quieted, the only sound faint music from other parts of the fair and the crack of pennants and bannerols flapping in the winterbreeze. The sun moved from behind a cloud and everything was illuminated with bright clarity.

My son stood in the middle of the sward, his plain tunic and hose indicating nothing of wealth, his fine black hair lifting in the breeze. His father towered over him, his own dark hair blowing, his face shadowed by a beard that had been clipped neatly for Mass. No one would know that underneath his sleeve lay a bone-deep wound or that two nights ago he had almost killed a man and had buried three.

William drew back the bow further than before, channeling his anger through the wood and string, his face red with effort, his tongue between his teeth.

Is this anger at life, William? At your captors? Or merely the desire to win above the odds?

Part of me wanted him to hit the mark, but the greater part of me wanted to hide him away and I was sure Gisborne must feel the same dilemma.

The arrow flew straight and sure and lodged just above the centre of the butt. The crowd roared and William threw up his arms.

Gisborne's eyes widened with innocent surprise, his mouth opened with feigned shock, his shoulders shrugged, palms lifting as if it was beyond his fatherly understanding. William just grinned, trotting back to the official, handing over the bow.

'Well done, little boy. Where are you from?'

Gisborne reached William's side. 'From Avinhon,' he said with an Occitàn accent. 'We are travelling to Tolon.'

'Well, m'sieur, he has won the prize. Here is his purse.' The official held out a chamois bag.

William looked around for me then and I beckoned him over. Surprisingly and thank God, he came and I heard Gisborne say, 'He's but a child. I'm sure there are others to claim the prize. For my son, being an archer for just a moment was reward enough. Thank you.'

With that, he backed away, his position usurped by a crowd eager to see who would be named the winner.

He scooped William up, his face benign. 'Come, little archer. The sun begins to sink and I think it is time for you to see Soeur Marie.' We followed behind like a loyal entourage as he strode away to the *abbaye's* precincts, passing William over when we reached the gates. 'The men and I would go to the livery to check the horses, Ysabel.'

Ariella said she would go with the men if I did not mind and I suspected she wanted time with Guillaume so I waved her away, smiling.

Sister Marie sat in the setting sun beneath a leafless oak, ostensibly waiting for William. 'Time to put the goats to their beds, little Guillaume. Are you ready?'

'I winned the archery, Soeur Marie,' he said guilelessly as he walked with the nun and when I looked back, it was to see all the others talking seriously with my husband outside the gates.

What do you talk of, my husband? What do you say to our friends?

William opened the withy gate to let the goat and her kids into the pen and then he collapsed on the straw to be nibbled upon and crawled over. There existed a comfortable silence in the barn – animals chewing, the sound of a hoof scraping, the soft bleat of the goat as she sniffed one of the kid's rumps. And for no reason that had any earthly meaning, I asked a question of the nun.

'Sister, do you know of the Commanderie of Saint Christophe?'

'But of course. In the past, we supplied the Templars with herbs, unguents, wines, even bread and vegetables on occasion. They were good Soldiers of God.'

'Most recently?'

'No. Why do you ask?'

'As we travelled we passed the buildings and one of our companions told us it was a Templar Commanderie. My mother's brother was a Sergeant-Brother in the First Crusade…'

Mary Mother, forgive my untruths…

'Then he is to be blessed, my child. Commendable. No, most recently the Commanderie has been empty as there was a scandal. The less said, I think.

Suffice to say the Grand Master thought to sell the building. Those close by think it is haunted. Guillaume, do not let them jump on you. They must learn to be handled properly.' Persisting in calling William, Guillaume, the nun clapped her hands lightly at the kids. 'I remember once, the Templars sent us an Englishwoman. Said she had been rescued from an attack upon travellers on the road and was quite addled from her experience. She was a nice woman, I thought, a good worker, and rather brilliant in the herbarium, but disrespectful of us and our horarium. Her name was Bridget and eventually she was collected by someone she knew and taken I know not where. Huh. She told the most outrageous stories…'

My eyes pricked as I listened. Even here in Saint Perpetué our tragedies and joys stayed with us. Soeur Marie climbed into the pen with William, looping up her robes in an unholy way, and together they made the goats comfortable and thus there was an end to our conversation. No one knew of Simon de Courcey or cared for the empty building, it seemed. Which led me to wonder why the man had acquired the building at all. Was he so obsessed with vengeance that he would spend a fortune to perpetuate an idea that it was Halsham's men who hunted Gisborne and not someone else entirely?

Would Gisborne set a false trail in the same way?

The sun sank, the priory's barn reduced to a comforting darkness lit only by a horn lamp on a ledge and the bells began to chime for Vespers.

'We must return for the services. Shall you come?'

'Sister, I think I will take William to the *dorter*. He has overeaten and been thoroughly overexcited. I think it is time to rest.'

She smiled, 'Then walk with me as far as the hostel.' She picked up the lamp, let William through the gate and we made our way in the evening shadows, the echo of the bells fading on the breeze. She left us at the cloister, walking toward the *abbaye* along with the monks and her fellow Sisters.

'I wonder if one could adapt to this life,' mused Toby, walking to my side.

'I know I could not. I am a sore trial within the Church. As for you…' I frowned. 'Never.'

He grinned. 'Sit with me for a moment.'

I hauled a silent William onto my lap as we subsided onto a stone bench in the cloister, his thumb jamming into his mouth, eyelids closing.

Toby tapped his foot against the stone.

On edge, my friend…

'My lord says we leave with a party of pilgrims on the morrow.'

'You say? But he has said nothing. Pilgrims to where, in God's name?'

Goddamn you, Gisborne. Why did you not share this with me? This is what makes me so angry, what makes me doubt you…

'The pilgrims go to Rome and think to find some vessel to sail them to Genoa. In winter! Good luck I say. At any rate, my lord thinks we shall be tucked up safe and secure in a crowd of many. Not that I want to sail again so soon, I can tell you.'

His little asides did nothing to smooth me over and I commented, 'Then he *is* still concerned with de Courcey. Surely this is why he does what he does.'

Toby's face crinkled.

'Has he said anything at all about de Courcey?' I persisted.

'No…'

'Unconvincing, Tobias.' All my intuitions started ringing bells and shouting and I squirmed, trying hard not to wake my son.

'Only because he *has* said nothing. He acts as if the whole terrible business hasn't happened.'

'Perhaps he does it for William.'

'Well, if you believe *that*, you will believe in dragons,' Toby snorted.

'Then what are you hinting at? Be clear.'

'I have known Sir Guy for a long time, my lady, and I have *never* seen him behave so blithely. Ariella and Guillaume would not notice I am sure, as they haven't known him long. It is why I have said nothing to them. But something is awry…'

'What think you?'

Toby scratched his head with fervour. 'Truth? I think he plans to hunt de Courcey down. But the how's and the when's are beyond me.'

Ah Toby. You and I think the same, it would seem…

'You confirm what I believe, Toby. My concern is how he plans to carry this out. We have no idea where de Courcey went and if it means that he must leave William and I yet again…' I sighed, holding my son close. 'We can only be wary, Toby. There is little else to be done. We can hardly bind him in chains.'

My minstrel friend huffed. 'Sometimes I think that's exactly what we should do. Sometimes I think he is his own worst enemy. But arguing with Sir Guy is exactly like arguing with King Richard and I have watched many men try that to no avail.' He sighed. 'I am not saying his sense of righteousness is as kingdom-high as the King's, nor that his ego demands he do what he wants. But I do think he is obsessed with revenge of a sort and that it is geared to some chivalrous notion that he protects his family in the process. But enough,' he shrugged and then stood and bowed. 'I will see you on the morrow. The pilgrims leave at midday – a short journey to Toulon where they will spend the night as they try to find a plucky sea captain. I am sure my lord will explain all this when he sees you.'

'Oh I am sure he will, Toby, and in the most pleasant way perhaps. Enough to beguile me even. Ah, I feel I must be more alert than ever. I have been through this in the past and to have to deal with it again – the fear of loss, of maiming…'

Toby patted my hand, said nothing at all and left me with my black thoughts.

I put William in his bed as Ariella informed me Sir Guy waited in the cloister. My stomach churned over and my neck tightened as he turned when I walked down the stair. He took my hand, kissed it and tucked it in the crook of his elbow.

'We will walk,' he said.

Lights flared in the cressets along the cloisters and somewhere doves burbled sweet goodnights to each other. The warmth of Guy's arm heated my fingers – it was always the same. His proximity was like lying next to a roaring fire – one never knew if it would comfort or burn.

'We shall leave tomorrow at midday, Ysabel.'

A fait accompli.

'I see…'

'There is a group of pilgrims leaving for Toulon and it seems sensible to join them. If we are lucky and the weather stands in our favour, if Ahmed is in dock and willing to sail, we will be in Genoa and then back to Venezia in no time. I think it is vital for William.'

That it was in fact an order was obvious, and prevarications were pointless.

'You seem to have thought this through.'

He took me by the shoulders beneath a cresset and I lifted my eyes to his. Serious. Believable. Determined. He was all of those.

'I have, Ysabel – long and hard. We could stay in Toulon and be at ease, perhaps. But it is just one more home to which William must adjust. If we take him back to Venezia, he has his beloved Gwenny and Biddy to care for him, Mehmet to doctor him, Saul, Ariella, Tanti and the puppies, the guards who idolize him. Toby, Tomas, Guill…'

How could I demur? He was right. So much to ease my son from terror and back to a normal life.

'Alright. You convince me.'

So persuasive, as I had told Tobias you would be.

'But in the short term only, husband. I do not believe our home is in Venezia. It has always felt temporary, as if we trod water. Security – nay, that is the wrong word. *Normality* is what I crave, more than anything else you could give me.'

He kissed me.

I pushed at him. 'Guy, stop it. I feel like a wanderer, a pilgrim unable to find that soul place. The villa does not feel like our home; it has been shaped by other hands and eyes and I want so much more than that.

'Then I shall build a new villa.'

'That is not at all what I implied.'

'Then it *will* be for the short term, Ysabel. After that, we will seek our final haven.'

'Do you promise, Gisborne?'

'Ysabel…'

'Do it. I almost lost my son and I could have lost you. Somewhere in this world is a place where we will be unknown and safe and blessedly normal. So swear to me…'

He gave that slight sideways quirk – that expression that could mean anything. 'Then I swear in the name of God the Father, in the name of the Virgin Mother, the Son and all the Saints, we shall seek our peace.'

Footsteps clipped close and Sister Marie's voice reached us from the sparsely lit cloister. 'Sir, such a pledge! And in a place of God. Be careful not to break it or you will do this lady here an almighty injustice.'

'Soeur Marie,' I said, indicating Guy. 'This is my husband, Sir Guy of Gisborne.'

He placed his hand on his heart and bowed.

'Well!' she said, looking up to his face. '*Sir* Guy, eh? My dear, what a story you could tell. But you hide it away and best so, I think. Sir Guy, many knights make promises before God. As if it absolves them from desertion, from killing, adultery. Many things. So do not treat your wife with disrespect. Do not give the promise lightly.'

Gisborne acknowledged her admonishment with a dipped head. 'There is very little in life I take lightly, *ma soeur* – a fact to which my lady wife can attest. I have only the safe and secure interests of my son and his mother at heart.'

Sister Marie tucked her hands into her voluminous cuffs. 'Good. I am sure God is watching. Goodnight, Sir Guy. Goodnight *Lady* Ysabel.'

She walked on, her sandaled footsteps fading, the cloister finally our own. The cressets flared as the breeze flicked by and my husband reached for me, saying, 'Always remember that what I do, I do for you and for William.' He kissed me then, so softly and so long that I drowned in contentment, forgetting that he had said those words to me years ago and that my intuition had been blinded…

It was so long since Gisborne and I had shared any tender moments and I basked in the warmth of my husband's clasp, his touch and not least his words. In the back of my mind, a voice called *'Ysabel, Ysabel, beware!'* but I pushed it away.

As I slipped into my bed within the *dorter*, Ariella had whispered, 'Is all well?'

'Yes. We begin the return journey tomorrow.'

'I am glad,' she said. 'I miss my father.'

'Ariella, I am ever grateful to you for accompanying me, and William finds so much joy in your presence.'

She laughed softly. 'He talks nothing but puppies and we have been through hundreds of names. I love him dearly, he is a very sweet child and we rub along quite well together.'

'You do. I have seen it. It is good for him to have people he loves and trusts around him.'

She sank into quietness then and presently her breath sighed with placid regularity and I felt glad for her that we left tomorrow, and for myself and William as well. However as I took a deep breath and rolled on my side, that voice spoke again.

But what about Gisborne, Ysabel? Remember what Toby said?

I rolled onto my other side, facing William. Around me the *dorter* snored, grunted, groaned, passed wind. I had thought I would sleep so well. Instead, Toby's words and my thoughts went round and round. Anxiety crept upon me, a nameless fear that nothing would be the way it should be and eventually I just longed for the bells to wake the *dorter* on the morrow.

If only to get us on the road and Gisborne firmly by my side.

The pilgrims in the women's *dorter* woke like chattering blackbirds, louder than the bells so that the Sisters had to clap their hands to be heard. They ordered us to the priory chapel for Matins, after which we could break our fast and then attend the *abbaye* for a blessing for our departure. One does not argue with those women who had cared for us so generously during our stay and so we dressed swiftly and followed the nuns to the priory service.

'*So I have looked upon you in the sanctuary, beholding your power and glory,*' I prayed, believing that there *had* been sanctuary – for two days.

Ariella, poor Jewish daughter that she was, attended with us as she had since we entered Saint Perpetué. Polite, attentive, she watched and listened as I went through my mechanical responses. My faith was gratuitous and Brother John would be so disappointed with me, I knew. I turned to God frequently when I wanted something but for the rest I took it or left it. I wondered if Ariella detected my desultory behaviour and hoped that she didn't as I welcomed her respect.

In the *abbaye*, she nursed William and he was blessedly quiet, playing with Ounthee and Githborne and a little wooden dog, a fair gift from his papa that he had named Jaffa. I had asked why he called the dog such a name and he said that he heard Adam and Guillaume use the word and he liked the feel of it in his mouth.

'Do you know that it is a port in Outremer, William? Where your father has been?'

'No,' he had replied and run off, not the least interested.

The church was full and Ariella, William and I were relegated to a crushed pew in the middle of the crowd. I searched for Guy's head, even Guillaume's, and turning round craned my neck to search behind. Unknown eyes met mine – some blank, some curious, some hard, some lascivious and I swiftly swung back to face the altar. The smell of incense dampened down the unholy fragrance of sweat and urine – stale odours of a most unpleasurable kind.

I lost interest in the service and wondered where the men were. Such things would be bound to occupy me until we were mounted and away to Toulon.

'Et Benedictio Dei Omnipotentis: Patris, et Filii et Spiritus Sancti, descendat super vos et maneat semper.'

Thank God!

At the end of the blessing, I sought Sister Marie and thanked her for her kindness to William.

'God's pleasure, my child,' she replied. 'A blessing to you all. Stay safe, my dear, and may that husband of yours honour his promise.'

I smiled, and hurried away, hearing Ariella calling me. She stood outside the gates, one hand holding a bundle, the other holding William who jumped on the spot as pilgrims mingled. Chatting, finding their mounts, seeking out carts purloined for the more frail and for the truly stoic – foot travel. Part of the crowd would journey the other way to Paris and further but we would attach ourselves to the remaining twenty or so men and women for the journey to Toulon. The sun shone warmly in the middle of the winterday and it was perfectly right to think God was on our side. Some of the women we knew already from the *dorter* and they introduced us to their husbands.

'I have negotiated a ride in a cart for William and I thought we could take a turn each to sit with him,' Ariella said. 'And this bundle is our men's clothes. I had them washed. You never know if we might need them,' she added.

No. You never do.

'A good idea, Ariella. Do you want to ride in the cart first?'

'I…' she spied Toby speedily weaving through the crowd. 'Tobias, here!' she waved.

He puffed up to us. 'Have you seen Sir Guy?'

'No,' I answered, heartbeat jumping. 'Is he not with you?'

'He … he…' he stopped as Guillaume trotted toward us mounted on a black rouncey I had not seen before and leading the two plain browns we had taken from the Commanderie. His mouth curved down and Toby swore, stamping his foot.

'We all went to the *dorter* together yesternight,' he growled. 'We went to sleep. Christ, he was there in the cot next to mine! When the monks woke us at Matins, he was there. We went to the abbaye together, broke our fast together and even joined the crowd walking back to the *abbaye* for the blessing…'

'Tobias?' I grabbed his arm.

'Gone. Damn it to God, he's gone!'

'What? What say you?'

But it was a question of no account at all.

My husband had done exactly what I knew in my soul he would do.

Gone…

CHAPTER ELEVEN

'Always remember that what I do, I do for you and for William.'

If I'd a rock to throw, I would have thrown it far.

God damn you to Hell, Gisborne. You do not! You do it as much for yourself and your misplaced idea of revenge. So full are you of anger and hate that you can barely see straight ahead...

'Ysabel!' Ariella jerked me back to the moment at hand. 'The pilgrims are beginning to leave. What would you have us do?'

What? What indeed?

I looked to Toby for help and I think he recognized the panic on my face and that I was visiting another time when the man whose child I bore had used those same glib words and had then slipped out of my life and set me on such a convoluted path.

Somewhere in the far reaches of the world and back in history, men had been tortured most cruelly by legs and arms being tied to two horses and then the horses whipped and sent off in different directions so that limbs were torn away.

And so it felt.

Because in my mind, half of me chased after Gisborne and the other half took William home to apparent safety.

'My lady, it is like we said,' Toby held my hand. 'He needs to be saved from himself.'

'But how...'

'Guillaume and I could find him but you cannot return to Venezia unescorted.

It is unseemly and dangerous and he would flay me if I allowed it.'

And of a sudden my blood froze again and the ice-maid was reborn. Perhaps it was a saving grace – the only way that I could prevent myself from splitting in half.

William turned round and grinned at me, oblivious to the vicious turmoil his father had created. If I let it, my heart would have filled my throat as I realised I had only one course open to me. My hand crept to William's head and the silky hair slid beneath my fingers.

William, I love you more than life itself. I do. But I want your father to be here, to love you too…

'Toby, I have decided and it pains me, God how it pains me! You and Ariella are to take William home. He adores you both and he would miss me less if you both parent him…'

'Ysabel!' Ariella's mouth opened but Toby grasped her hand and shushed her as I continued.

'Guillaume and I will ride after Gisborne.'

William was singing '*Somer is y-comin in*', his precious voice lifting and entertaining those close by, smiles raining down upon him. His head dipped from side to side in rhythm and cold tears trickled down my cheeks; but when one is made of ice it is easier to ignore them.

'Toby?' I asked of him.

'Are you set upon this, my lady?' The pilgrims were now ready to leave and looked to us who held up their departure. 'Please,' he said to the assembly. 'My lady's plans have had to change. Forgive us, we shall we be with you in a moment. My lady?'

'I am sure. Listen to me, you must only sail with Ahmed and if he will not, take heed and wait. He understands the sea. And in Genoa, you must go to Dario and ask for guards and good horses to see you to Venezia and Toby, you must send message after message with the couriers. They will find us on our way…'

'What way?' Toby pinpointed our problem immediately.

'Northerly,' broke in Guillaume. 'To Calais. He goes to England.'

'England!' I gasped.

Treason…

'How do you know?'

'Sir Guy knows de Courcey is a supporter of Prince John. It is obvious.'

'Then we go west to Avignon,' I said, 'and then follow the Rhône to Lyons. Then overland to Anjou and then Calais…'

'Ysabel,' Ariella hugged me and thrust the bundle into my hands. 'Take these.'

I could say nothing to her. I was rejecting my son, surely. Did she think I had made a false choice? 'Ariella, do you despise me?'

'I understand, I do, and I will care for William as my own. You will come back safe and you will bring his father. It is a given.'

Her glance passed quickly to Guillaume and I said, 'He too will come home. Go to him.'

She hurried to his side and I bent and pulled William to me.

'My dearest boy, Mama must go to meet Papa. He is settling some business and needs my help. No, listen to me, little one – Toby and Ariella are going to take you back to Gwen and Biddy and to the puppies and you must choose one for yourself and one for Papa and Mama. Can you do that? And you must be the knight in charge of our house and be very good and make us proud.'

'Can I have a man puppy and you have a lady puppy?'

'Of course. In fact you can name her…'

'I have thinked, Mama, already. And itht hard to find a lady'th name.' Then his eyes lit up. 'Oh, what about Itheult? And I can call mine, Trithtan. Toby told a thtory one day…'

'Iseult? I like it. Darling, you must hop on the cart, that's it.' I lifted him up, hugging him tightly, kissing his smooth cheek and he kissed me back, noisily and with laughter. 'Think on it, my sweet and by the time you get home, you will have the best names ever. Ariella?'

She pulled herself onto the cart with William, and Guillaume dismounted to give Toby a leg-up onto one of the rounceys. He looked down at me and I took his hand in mine.

'Toby, I am trusting you with half my heart.'

He bent down and thrust a small piece of parchment into my hands. 'And I am trusting you with this. It might just save the other half of your heart.'

I crushed the fragment into my hand as the cart began to roll away, William waving excitedly.

'Thee you thoon, Mama, thee you thoon! I will look after Itheult for you!'

Ariella placed her arm around him and waved to us but her eyes were on Guillaume.

'Until later, then,' said Toby. 'Be safe.' He clicked his horse on and in a bare moment, the group had rounded the bend in the road and were out of sight and Guillaume and I stood staring at a frantic future.

I unrolled the scrap of parchment. It was a list of names, with a town by each. *The faceless men.*

But none until Lyons. Until then, Guillaume and I were on our own.

I hiked the folds of my gown into the rolled girdle at my hips, choosing the rouncey on which Guillaume had strapped the sword Gisborne had bought at my demand. The sight of its plain scabbard and of its fundamental nature further thickened the ice that was my friend and I quickly mounted, turning the rouncey away from the direction William had taken. As I swung the horse around, I glimpsed Soeur Marie watching from the gates of the *abbaye*. By her rigid face, I assumed she guessed what had happened and as Guillaume mounted his own horse, she lifted her hand in a blessing and I took it, clasped it to my frozen heart and nodded to her. Then pressing our heels to the horses' sides we sprang to a gallop, stones skittering, dogs, hens and goats crying in surprise, people shouting at us, waving fists and jumping out of the way.

We caught up with the Paris-bound pilgrims almost immediately, slowing to a trot and moving around them as politely as possible, nodding to those we had met in our respective hospices. Once past, we again sped, heading to the foothills beyond Brignolo and beyond which again the saw-toothed mountains displayed a mantle of snow. We ran the risk of running into steep gorges and opaque green water if we did not keep to the tracks that had been travelled along for centuries and we steered away from any that might lead to mountain tracks. The mountain passes were dangerous and slow, whereas the Rhône river offered smooth and consistent travel as far as Lyons. We had no floodwaters with which to contend this winter and I anticipated no problems beyond time and finding a vessel that would accommodate us between Avignon and Lyons.

We had to slow repeatedly to allow the rounceys to gain their breath and at one point, in a pass high enough and wide enough to halt and from where we could see the river and Avignon in the far distance, we dismounted, loosing girths on puffing horses and letting them shake the sweat from their bodies and hang their heads.

'We might make Avignon by nightfall,' said Guillaume. 'But it will be close-run and if we do not, we may have to sleep roughly.'

'I have slept in the open many times, Master Archer, do not worry.'

'Lady Ysabel, your reputation within the household is one of indomitable mettle and iron will. I am not worried. No, if I am at all concerned, it is that we have finite funds and no real food.'

Costrels could be filled anywhere to ease our thirst, that did not concern me. But without money we would starve and without coin we would be unable to secure passage on boats. I rested my hand on the cantle of the saddle behind which was strapped the bundle of clothing.

'Guillaume, I would change to my men's clothing if you would hold my horse?'

'My lady,' he said, dipping his head and taking the reins.

'And another thing,' I added as I unstrapped the bundle. 'We are to travel a long way together. Please call me Ysabel.'

I walked away to the shelter of stunted pines, putting up a woodpecker that left in a swirl of wingbeats as I untied the *bliaut* and let it fall to the ground, dragging the thick tunic over the top of my chemise, pulling on hose and then the boots that had kept me shod since Genoa. I plaited my hair, knotting it tightly under a cap and then threw my cloak over it all, taking the gown and rolling it over the bundle of remaining clothes. As I scooped up folds, a tiny leather *scrippe* fell out, clinking as it hit the ground. I undid it, the strap unknotting with ease and inside in the cocooned darkness of the leather, lay two coins.

Ariella must surely have forgotten the bag was there, or would she not have removed it before she rolled the clothes? I crushed it in my hands, re-rolled the bundle and hurried back to Guillaume.

'See here,' I waved the *scrippe*. 'Monies! It must be Ariella's!' He opened the bag and slid the coins out – two silver dinars, a king's ransom in our current situation and money that I had thrown around with abandon in Genoa when searching for William. 'I will pay her back, Guillaume. With interest. But can we not use this readily on our journey?'

'Of course. Once we get to Lyons, we can find a moneylender and change the dinars for something else, some French *deniers* or *livres*. This is very pure Byzantine silver and worth a lot I should think, to someone willing to buy.'

I felt for the little scrap of parchment in my own purse. And throwing caution to the wind, I unfolded it. 'Guillaume, if you work for my husband, you know he deals in secrets and that throughout the Empire and France, and in England, even Outremer, he has men he uses to field and courier his information…'

'I am aware, yes,' he said cautiously.

'This is a list of those in Touraine, Anjou, Marche and Normandie. They may be of help to us if we need it.'

'But you do not know if you can trust me with that list, do you?' He was quite phlegmatic in his comment and I took a step back.

'No. I … that is…' the warmth rushing through my cheeks would have been enough to melt snow on mountains.

'Ysabel,' he said, withholding my title with ease. 'I have done all I can to be of use to your house and to show that I am trustworthy and I can do nothing more. I have said this before. It is now a problem for you to solve. Keep the list if you are concerned. I would not have you think I would compromise Sir Guy's business or his safety.'

He handed me my reins, took the bundle of clothes and strapped it behind my saddle and then mounted his own horse. I tucked the list in my purse, and chastened, grasped the stirrup and mounted the rouncey, following behind him and adrift with my thoughts.

'He cannot be so far ahead,' he drew me from my guilt and I looked ahead at his back. Sometimes, only very vaguely, his dark hair, height and broad shoulder could be confused with Gisborne's. But then Gisborne's build had more substance. Guillaume always looked as if his body battled demons, not exactly whip-thin but with the lean length of an athlete. 'He left at some time whilst we were in the *abbaye* for the blessing. A head start to be sure, but not such a start that we can't catch up if we move swiftly to Avignon.'

Indeed.

But you don't know my husband, I thought. Not like I do. If there remained the remotest chance he suspected he was followed, he would ride past towns, change horses – obfuscate at every opportunity.

We entered Avignon at dusk as the town gates began to close. The wind had changed to a miserable whining *mistral* blowing from the northwest and chilling through to the bone. I had heard tell of this wind and prayed to God that it would not affect any passage we might make. Our way to Lyons flowed in a swift band that cut through the country like lifeblood, carrying with it vessels of all shapes and sizes. We would travel upstream on a craft that would most likely be propelled by oar and sometimes pulled by horses and men when the going became tough, for the river had a mind of its own.

'I will try, Ysabel,' Guillaume responded when I asked him if we should seek passage now or wait till the morning. 'But many of the rivermen will be three parts drunk now, if they leave on the morrow.'

'Which will make them easier to manipulate to take two travellers on board. Do you think he is here?' I added.

'A normal traveller would be, but Sir Guy is vastly different.'

'You think he has travelled on?'

'It is hard to say. He is your husband. What say you?'

I looked around. A beautiful bridge, the one they call Bénézet, spanned the river with its symmetrical arches, more than twenty pontoons supporting traders and townspeople as they hurriedly finished their business before curfew.

Guillaume took my silence for an answer and sighed. 'I will seek shelter for the night and in so doing, may find news of him.'

'Guillaume, I am sorry. But I don't know what Gisborne would have done…'

If the archer heard the resignation in my tone he did not admit it, instead handing me the reins of his horse outside an inn with livery. He was gone but a moment and returned, saying, 'I have secured a chamber, a monk's cell would be bigger, and it's as black as Hades, but we cannot afford to be discriminatory. I apologise in advance. You see to the horses whilst I ask around for barge passage.'

One room?

Again, if he recognised anything in my expression he chose to ignore it and instead strode down the street toward the riverbanks and where barge after barge was moored, curlews and sandpipers crying as the last of the dusk fell into night.

I nodded to the youth working on a couple of worn mounts within the livery as I led our horses into stalls out of which a lamb could kick its way. I unsaddled, unbuckling my sword and laying it on the floor where I could grab it quickly and then bunched a haywisp to wipe them down as they once again shook themselves. They dragged their lips across the water I fetched and then drank deeply before pulling half-heartedly and then more hungrily at the oaten hay. I lifted their legs and pulled the limbs forward, stretching them, checking the hooves for stones and bruising, rubbing up and down the legs firmly. We would be parting with these beasts on the morrow and needed them to be quite sound in order to make a good sale. The youth blinked at my industry and then returned to dragging a cloth over some dirty saddlery, saying nothing.

'You know and like horses, I think,' Guillaume's voice startled me as I replaced the last hoof, standing upright and arching the ache from my lower back.

'I do. I have always done,' I replied. My mind held echoes of another time and another man with whom I had travelled and who knew of my love. 'Did you have any success?'

'I secured passage on a barge carrying bales of cloth to Lyons. The merchandise is from Toulon I am told and they finished loading at dusk. It is the last haul for the season until new shipments arrive from the east after winter.'

It sounded as if a winter Middle Sea emptied of vessels like a house emptying of inhabitants with the plague and I wondered if Tobias would find Ahmed and subsequent passage back to Genoa.

So many variables and none positive.

'And Gisborne?'

'Nothing.'

Hardly a surprise, but heartbreaking even so. If one didn't have a heart that had frozen solid.

We ate a meal within – a trencher with pieces of roasted meat, perhaps ox, and herbs and root vegetables. That this tawdry place through which the *mistral* slid its bitter breath between cracks could provide such a meal surprised us. Even more so when we tasted the wine the innkeeper slopped down on the table in an etched and crazed jug. We were two strangers amongst weathered and reddened folk who cared nothing for us and showed no interest. But despite a belly of food and good wine, an ache palpated in my heart and my stomach writhed. The ice was still there but I had to make such an effort for it not to thaw, reminding myself I was a person in the middle of a winterfreeze because I had much to accomplish.

We walked together to the one room and Guillaume said, 'I have secured a deal with the innkeeper,' he rattled a small bag. 'He has bought our rounceys for the cost of the room, the food and a little on the side.'

He held the door ajar allowing me to precede him, but I stopped, the air dense and stale like a cell beneath a castle and no less bright.

'Wait,' said Guillaume. 'I will get a light from the innkeeper.'

He returned in a moment, a tallow candle flickering fit to gut, casting figures of shadow people on the walls and we passed into the tight space the innkeeper called a room. I pressed against the wall as the hessian slung cot mocked me with its singular nature, its straw-filled mattress and thin blankets.

'Do not fear, Ysabel. I *am* to be trusted.' He unbuckled his sword and placed it close by the door, dragging off his cloak and laying it on the dirt floor, taking one of the motley blankets from the cot, lying down and wrapping himself in it.

As I lay down, my own sword as my bed partner, he asked if I wanted the candle snuffed and I said no, if he did not mind. He didn't answer, just turned on his side away from me and we sank into the partial darkness and our thoughts and the high-pitched whine of mosquitoes, loud enough to drive anyone to madness.

'Jesu and Joseph!' I growled, swatting and then grabbing my cloak from atop the bedding and wrapping myself tightly in it with my hood up. We would have slept better in the rough, I was sure of it as the straw stalks poked through hessian, wool and skin and insects tried to bite me. Finally, I could stand it no more and swung my legs to the ground, trying to step over Guillaume who was a mere dark shadow on the floor, the stinking candle having almost worn to a stub.

'Ysabel?' His voice croaked from the depths of sleep.

'I can't settle with the insects, with the straw and with that wind. I would seek a *privé*. And I might just stay outside or find a church. For sure, I would sleep far better.'

'I'm sorry,' he said as he levered himself up. 'It was convenient at short notice.'

'No, no,' I said quickly. 'I am liverish and anxious for my husband and I am a notoriously bad sleeper at the best times. How do *you* manage to sleep?'

'You forget. I have served in Outremer. It teaches one many things, not the least of which is to do with little sleep. One learns to sleep when one can, with distraction all around. Equally, one sleeps for short moments – longer and one invites death. I will escort you.'

'Escort me? But I am supposed to be a youth.'

'Nevertheless.' He took up our swords and we left the inn, the *mistral* hitting us directly so that we grabbed cloak folds and held them close.

'The *privé* is really just a space behind a building or a tree, is it not?'

'Regretfully,' he answered. 'But I will make sure you are undisturbed.'

Later, we walked to the closest church, a squat stone building of no great charm, but its worn timber door was closed and locked and so we retraced our footsteps to the inn, the wind behind us, biting at our heels and whining like a bevy of lost souls. The sky had begun to lighten and people were moving about, a bell further away ringing for Matins.

'I think we should eat at the inn and perhaps fill a bag with some food. I am not convinced the bargemen will have a lot to share with us, even if we do pay.'

Despite the unsavoury lodgings, the innkeeper's bread was fresh and he was content to pass us two loaves and take back the money he had paid us for the horses. As Guillaume placed the loaves in a small sack acquired at cost from the same innkeeper, I commented wryly.

'Our funds trickle through our hands faster that the Rhône flows to the sea.'

Guillaume's mouth curved slightly. 'We will manage. I pilfered some dried fruit from last night's table and with the bread used judiciously, we will survive on campaign pickings. I will not let you starve.' He began to walk confidently toward the riverbank and I followed in his footsteps. The wind had eased a little but our cloaks flapped like the wings of ravens and I jammed my cap hard over my head, shivering a little.

'I suspect this wind does not bode well for our travel,' I said.

'They will continue regardless. With strong oarsmen, the barge can move forward readily.'

Of course I knew this, having travelled on flat-bottomed vessels in Aquitaine, France and in England. But I said nothing as we continued down steep steps cut into the riverbank, water swirling with strength and speed past us. The dawn light had begun to seep through grey and amber cloud, maybe a sign of bad weather, perhaps even snow in the mountains.

There were two barges moored to a dock made of hefty logs, Guillaume stopping at the furthest one. Large hessian covered bales were lashed in neat rows and there were seats starboard and larboard for ten oarsmen, and a long stern oar. There was also a small mast with a furled lateen sail but I doubted its use in a swift downstream journey. A canopy was stretched amidships and I imagined all our living would occur beneath this canvas.

Guillaume and the boatsman greeted each other in French, a twisted version thereof, made worse by the remains of very few teeth in the fellow's mouth and a tongue that slid repeatedly out to wet his lips and then flicked back in like the Cypriot lizards that had scampered over villa walls a lifetime ago. The fellow glanced at me, Guillaume gesturing my way and I assumed I had been designated as a servant, at best an apprentice of some sort. We were directed to sit beneath the canopy and Guillaume explained that when the barge was in motion, we must stay clear of the oarsmen.

By now, the sun had risen and then retreated behind leaden clouds and the river colour had changed to a sombre iron hue. Ropes were cast off and the oars broke water, feathering and beginning to take up the slack as we drifted slightly downstream away from the dock. The oarsmen were massive beasts with shoulders as wide as pike handles and arm muscles like ox haunches. To make way initially, they stood, pulling hard and in rhythm, the boatsman calling to them, the barge moving forward with a jerk so that I had to grab at the nearest bale of cloth. Avignon slid away from us as we began to proceed upstream with such ease that one could be forgiven for thinking no effort was expended at all.

The men chanted a song of the river, the chorus with heavy downward beats as the oars broke the water, then dragged through to breathe again on the other side of the stroke. I found a place against a bale, half under the canopy and out of the way of everyone, gazing at the riverbanks without seeing, wondering at what point in his journey my husband was.

'Guillaume,' I said. 'Do you know if any barges left yesterday for Lyons?'

He rattled off my question to the boatsman and the fellow nodded, holding up two fingers whilst watching his crew.

'Then he is aboard one or the other,' I said. 'Ask if one of the barges took a passenger.'

He gave me a look that indicated he had already done so but I truly didn't want to hear the answer in case it was an empty one.

'Has it occurred to you he may have taken another route altogether?'

The archer sat next to me and I was grateful for the way his body shielded me from the breeze.

'Would it be any more swift than by river?'

'No.'

'Then he is on one of those barges, Guillaume, I know it.' I huddled against one of the bales longing for a warm bath and a soft bed.

And my husband.

The river swirled and twirled past us, some stretches showing roughcut shallows and over which the boatsman and his oarsmen manoeuvred. I became used to their dexterity and would move here and there on the boat with growing confidence but always looking for somewhere beyond the chill wind that stayed with us as we progressed upstream. I cared little about the river surrounds or even the river itself as I tried to second-guess Gisborne, willing the barge to make haste. Once, I was standing when the boatsman called to the oarsmen to beware the shallows. The first scrape nearly threw me onto my face. Oars were shipped rapidly, coils of ropes grabbed and the oarsmen jumped over the wales, waist-deep in freezing water, pulling the craft before she slid back into the downstream current. The brute strength of these men hauled the rumbling and moaning barge over the stones and rippling shallows into deeper water.

It was the first of many such passes in the journey and when we reached the first gorge, ropes draped along the white walls below stunted green growth thriving on the cliff face. The oarsmen pulled us hand over hand upstream and for one very brief moment as I watched the muscles in their arms bunch tight, the veins standing proud with effort, I imagined that nothing had changed since the Romans and Gauls had used the river – a timeless moment and I *had* no time. The oarsmen reminded me of Berto the wrestler and his friends in Venezia, but it was a path down which I did not want to roam and once again, as I began to shiver, I closed my cloak tight around me.

I must have dozed because Guillaume shook me and hissed, 'Ysabel, wake you. We are moored.'

My head and eyes ached with a cruel ferocity as I looked around in the dusk. 'Lyons?'

'Of course not,' he said. 'Do you need to go ashore?'

I was so cold and the thought of moving brought on a shudder. 'I must

I suppose,' I answered and stood as a heaven-load of stars burst across my eyes and I staggered.

'Is aught wrong?' Guillaume grabbed my elbow.

'Not at all,' I said, willing my voice to strengthen.

'I will come with you and keep watch.'

Which he did with appropriate etiquette and we walked back to the riverside where the men had lit a fire. I sank by its heat gratefully as Guillaume passed me chunks of bread, some dates and a costrel. I chewed mindlessly of the bread, passed the dates back but drank heavily from the costrel of wine and then leaned back against a log that had been washed ashore during a flood, closing my eyes and drifting away.

During the night I thought I had slid too close to the fire because I became hot and shrugged off my cloak. As Guillaume tried to pull it back over me, I broke into a sweat and then lay back, sleep and something painfully heavy claiming me.

I knew little from then on, except for limbs that ached beyond measure and a bout of such heat I thought I was dead and in Hell. And then such a chill I thought the ice-maid had completely consumed me. With the fever, I became soaked in sweat, speaking to Gisborne and William who answered me and bore me away on a horse. And then I would freeze again – the pain akin to someone shoving a sword through my innards front to back.

Once I jerked from fevers as the barge scraped, the noise like a pig being slaughtered. It listed, the bales shifting, the ropes belaying them beginning to creak but then there was a splash as it slapped back, flat onto its hull and I fell into a frenzied dream of drowning, Brother John saying *'Did you enjoy that, my child?'*

Later, Guillaume told me we had hit a shoal, one that had formed since the last time the barge had travelled upstream. We'd pulled into shore and one of the men had waded into the water to check the hull but apart from sharp grazes, there was no structural damage and unbeknown to me we'd continued on.

I woke in the evening to find I had been carried ashore and laid by the fire. I was swaddled in cloaks and my hair let loose and brushed away from my face.

'Jesu,' my hand grabbed my lank locks to hide them.

'Tis too late, Ysabel,' Guillaume said.

'No…'

'I have told them we are lovers and that your father threatened to send you to Saint Perpetué in Brignolo if you did not marry the man of his choice. It seems they are fond of the romantic ballad and have coddled you since you became ill. How do you fare?'

'Better. No pain. But as dry as your Outremer sands. A little hungry as well.'

'Then eat.'

He gave me bread soaked in warm goat's milk and he sliced a pear into wafers through which I could see my fingers and I sucked the pieces until they melted in my mouth.

'You have the tertian fever,' he added.

'God no! That surely means I shall succumb again and soon…'

Not now. So far to travel… Mary Mother!

Ah yes, Mary Mother. I wondered if She bothered to watch over me at all.

'Damn it to God!' I pounded my fist on the ground. 'How did I get such a fever?'

'I've watched it consume men from Aquitaine to Outremer, Ysabel. Anywhere there are rivers and marshes.'

'But they say men die…'

'Yes, it is true. But you will not.'

'How can you be sure? Listen,' I grabbed his sleeve. 'Don't let anyone bleed me, please. You must get some feverfew, some yarrow. Jesu…' I tried to remember how Bridget treated fevers. 'Yarrow! You must infuse it and soak cloths in it and then wrap them around my ankles, round my wrists, place a cloth on my forehead. And the feverfew…'

'Calm yourself, Ysabel. We know. These men,' he said with a sweep of his hand, 'live with tertian fever along the length of this river. They would no more bleed for it than fly. They have herbs and have treated you exactly as you say.'

'Truly?' I sat up and turned to look at the river giants who had nurtured me and they grinned, nodding their heads. '*Merci,*' I offered gratefully and they nodded again.

Guillaume took my hand and I jumped, trying to pull it back but he held it firmly in his cool grasp. 'Remember we are lovers and try to show some apparent affection. Now – we are not too far from Lyon; perhaps another two or three days if we don't run aground again. It happened quite frequently while you were ill.' He passed me a mug of watered wine, an opportunity for our hands to unclasp. 'That said, in two days the fever will renew itself and after it is done, you will barely be able to stand. But I think you know this, do you not? As for riding across Touraine, Maine and Normandie to Calais…'

'But I must, Guillaume, weakness or no…'

'I know what you *want* to do,' he said. 'But my lord Gisborne would challenge me to the death if harm should befall you.'

He shifted, the fire throwing shadows over his thin face and I swear I could have been forgiven for thinking I sat with my husband but then he moved and sadly I was left with the archer from Anjou and not the muscular knight most recently from Venice.

'I intend to find him,' I said. 'Succumbing to this fever is unavoidable and yes, I will be weak but perhaps it's God's will that I am sick on a river journey where I can sleep it away than on a road journey where a day's illness is a day's loss.'

He passed me some more pear and I sucked it for a moment and then lay back. Exhausted with eating, with speech and with thought.

'Just look after me until Lyons, Guillaume, and then strap me to a horse and point me in the direction of Calais. I think we will have word of him in Lyons…' My mind began to slow as sleep dulled the edges. 'Surely…'

Two days and nights passed with me able to engage with the barge crew, even laughing at their questionable songs. And I talked with Guillaume about what we should do in Calais. But in truth, I slept frequently, unable to keep my wits as much about me as I wanted. I waited in some trepidation, and then like a bad memory a shiver ran through me and I shifted against a bale, my back beginning to ache. I closed my eyes, cursing the God I was supposed to worship and wishing He and all his Saints and every other God-rotten inhabitant of Heaven to perdition as I wiped a hand across my burning face.

'Ysabel?' Guillaume asked.

'Tis come,' I replied. 'Pass me a costrel with the feverfew, if you please? It may be the last cogent request I make for a time.'

And so it was.

The Rhône drifted past me, taking my sweat and tears with it as I entertained all with my delirium, and during the chatteringly cold bouts, suffered their thick woollen cloaks to be draped over me. In brief periods of respite, I despaired. Leagues yet to travel at a gallop on land and I knew I would barely even stand to mount the animal. But in between wakefully intense moments, I began to sleep without dreaming, having no idea of time or place.

Once I thought I heard a woman's voice, 'Gently. There…'

And then a man's voice, 'Perhaps half a day? Not more, to be sure…'

But they were voices of little consequence and I shifted down the bed to find feathers and handsome velvet coverings. Eventually, perhaps a sennight for all that it felt like it but perhaps only moments, sunlight levered my eyes open. A golden bar widened to reveal a window frame and beyond it the lacy winterbare branches of an oak tree.

I turned my head and found I was in a bright, whitewashed room hung with a tapestry of a unicorn in an orchard. It would have been tempting to drift away to that orchard but I knew it was essential I wake now. The time had come and I could waste none of it.

Beside me, a well-dressed woman sat stitching. Her chemise shone like light on snow and her rich velvet *bliaut* was as red as a wild hawthorn berry. On her fingers sat two rings a-blush with garnets and her ample hips were girded with a silk and silver girdle. Her needle and stitching silk slipped in and out with a mesmeric shushing sound, but I would not let it lull me. I moved my body and she looked up from her work.

'*Ma douce…*' she said. She was older than Ariella by only a few delicate wrinkles at the corners of her eyes. Her hands were unspotted and her eyes now surveyed me with nutbrown good humour. 'I thought I would have to shake you awake. But see, patience is all and you have emerged from wherever you have been. Welcome.'

Oh, she had such a sweet, engaging face. Plump with rose-tinted cheeks and an ample chin constrained into behaviour by a piercingly white wimple and veil. Any abbess would have been proud of her headwear. But this lady was far from being a nun. Wealth radiated from her and comfort was something she enjoyed and bestowed in great measure, I thought.

'Of course, tertian fever is not to be sneezed at. Here…' She passed me a goblet. 'Warmed wine with honey and cinnamon. I am Amé de Clochart and my husband is Jehan the cloth merchant.'

Jehan de Clochart. Jehan. Cloth… Jesu! One of the faceless men…

I struggled up, throwing off the bedclothes. 'My husband…'

'My dear, your husband is not here; you were carried from the barge through the *traboules* by your manservant. A nice honest man, I think.'

Honest? He stole the list from my purse. How else would be I be here?

'Fortunately he knew of us from Sir Guy. But how serendipitous that you travelled upon the barge that carried the last of our cloth for the winter. Sometimes things are just God sent, are they not?'

God sent? Ha!

A hand rapped at the door and the latch rattled, a paunchy man walking in, trailing the smell of rich fabric and monies behind him, but his face was no less generous or cheerful than his wife's as he bowed and said, 'My lady…' Behind him stood tall, thin, serious Guillaume of Anjou.

'Monsieur de Clochart, thank you for your hospitality…'

'Pfft.' He waved his fingers through the mellow air of the room. 'I am always of assistance to my lord Gisborne. We are good friends. And you have just missed him! What a pest it was that the barge grounded so often or you would have caught him easily. My friend Guillaume here says you have urgent news and that you will ride after him. My lady, I must caution…'

'By how much have I missed him?'

My heart was pounding. To be this close…

'A half a day, no more. He rides for Tours.'

And of a sudden I recalled another such ride, where Gisborne and I had sent aged and heartsore Marais back to Cazenay. Where in Le Mans, I had farewelled my beloved mare, Khazia, and met Gisborne's wretched cousin and where in Calais, Gisborne and I had sprinted to a worn boat called the *Marolingian* and sailed away from Baron de Courcey, later to become my much hated husband, a man I tried to murder and whom Gisborne in fact killed. An eye for an eye, I thought – history seemed to be repeating itself and I decided it was a perverse joke laid upon me for all the pain I had caused so many. But no more…

'Then I have no time to delay. I must leave immediately. Please, Madame, can you fetch clothes – men's clothes, not women's? And Monsieur, I need a horse for Guillaume and myself. And money. It will be recompensed.'

'My lady, Guillaume has arranged everything. But it is against my better judgement…'

'Then I shall be sure to tell my husband of your assistance and that you warned me but that despite my frailty I chose to ride on. Do not fret.'

'My lady, I care not for myself,' de Clochart said with a worried expression carving his round face into pie slices. 'I care for you.'

'And sir, I am grateful. But if you give Guillaume and myself a good meal, I shall be more than able. I feel much revived just by the very news that I have nearly caught up with my husband. Guillaume,' I turned inquisitory eyes upon him. 'I trust you have my purse. Or at the very least, its contents.'

'Madame, everything is in your purse. As it should be.' His response was guileless and guilt-free.

We shall see, then, Guillaume. Shall we not?

The men left us and Amé hurried after them, telling me she would return swiftly. I clambered from the bed whilst she was gone, willing my legs to have strength, begging God to ignore my behaviour of the past and to please help me now. I would make a pilgrimage, I would endow an abbey, I would do anything if He could just help…

Brother John, please pray for me. And you too, Thea. Beatrice of Locksley, Soeur Marie – all of you know God, you can be my intercessors, I beg of you. Tell Him I am not a bad person.

I locked my knees into place, grasping the edge of the mattress, and then I took a step. God's bones but it was hard, infants must find it easier. But I persevered and took steps to the window.

I can do this. Plenty before me have and I am as strong as any of them.

But the truth was different. I was weak and under no illusions as to what the ride to Calais might do to me. It was why I so desperately prayed to God. Outside, the sunlight showed me it was late morning, and below, the people of Lyons busied themselves, walking along a cobbled street. I could see entrances to small alleys and men and women entered and left these *traboules*, pulling handcarts piled with goods, or carrying baskets of purchases. Lyons had the look of a prosperous town, one like Venice that thrived on merchants' business. And like Venezia, it rang with the sound of chisel, hammer and adze as buildings took shape, a cathedral beginning to soar, the town humming with the kind of excitement I had felt in Venezia. But the thought of the far off villa and all that it represented hastened butterfly beats in my belly and I was glad that rotund Amé burst back into the room with arms piled with clothes.

'Now,' she said. 'I have no intention of allowing you to leave unless you wear a good thick tunic and this quilted gambeson. The hose are the finest wool we have and the cloak, well it is an awful colour – winter grey, dear God in Heaven. But it is woven from the best wool from England. And, my dear, I have a fine silk chemise for beneath all this fabric. You should be quite warm. I noticed your leather boots were very worn and we have found a pair that are almost new that belong to my son. They will fit you. Oh, and a hood. It is not very good quality but it will serve to conceal your hair and keep your head warm and see,' she held the cloak up. 'A very deep hood on this as well. Jehan is fitting Guillaume in the same way because the further north you travel, the colder you will be.'

Once she was in full sail, I could see that turning her from her course would be impossible and so I let her talk on, the flow of words comforting. It had been a very long time since I had been cosseted by a motherly woman – balm to the soul.

'It is so very important that you stay warm and dry, my lady. And you must eat and drink good regular meals as well. You are as spare as a sparrow! Look at you.'

I looked down at my stomach and noticed how flat it was and that my chest was barely there – a scrawny traveller, a beggar. Would Gisborne still love me, I wondered?

Of course he will. Does he not say that what he does, he does for you and for William? Do not return to the insecurities of the past, Ysabel.

Wise words. I had faith in the constancy of my husband and must not lose that, even if I disagreed with his motives.

Amé tugged and pulled and eventually I was dressed, my hair, the sweat-laden filthy headful, had been brushed, plaited and wound into a knot and tucked away as the hood was pulled over my head and allowed to drape down my back. 'Pull it up when you leave, my dear. Now, come. Some food and then Jehan will take you to our stable. He has two excellent horses. If you get as far as Calais without meeting Sir Guy, Jehan will give Guillaume the name of a man who will take the horses and return them to us. We do this oft times when the couriers take messages for my lord Gisborne.'

A whole world I know nothing about…

Amé knew what an invalid might best eat to build strength and she had her cook prepare gentle things – fish in almond sauce with winter greens, a small piece of roasted poultry, some root vegetables roasted lightly and poached apples spiced with nutmeg and cinnamon and sweetened with elderflower and honey. The spices enlivened me and with a lump of clotted cream over the top, I felt nourished and revived.

Jehan and Guillaume settled to a more robust piece of pig and Amé sampled everything on her table, chattering all the time, not minding that I barely answered. I liked she and her polished apple husband and wondered what they had seen in my spouse that had drawn them to his side. What was it about him that made them risk life, limb and liberty to purvey secrets. I looked around at their well-furnished and comfortable house, at their generous table, at their silks and velvets and decided it wasn't the money. Perhaps there was a dark secret that prompted them to seek revenge against the Comte d'Auvergne. But no, in truth, I suspected they enjoyed the excitement of it all.

In any case, there was no time to ask. Gisborne had more than a half day's start on us and we must fly to make up the time, or at the very least hope that his horse went lame. Jehan had our horses led out whilst Amé explained the saddle bags were filled with food, that an extra blanket had been strapped to the saddles for each of us and could we take these leather costrels filled with the best wines?

The rounceys were long of hair but with good clean legs and a depth of chest that made me think they could sustain a goodly pace. Their glossy coats lay flat, manes snaking down their necks, tails lustrous and long. But their colour was inevitable.

'You see,' said Jehan. 'They blend with shadow on the road. All brown and black like a good bruise.' He laughed aloud at his own joke. 'They are good animals, these two. Take heart, they know the way north better than you.'

'Monsieur de Clochart, what colour is the horse my lord Gisborne rides?'

'Black. It suits him,' said the cloth merchant from beneath the saddle as he tightened my girth.

Of course. But as hard to spot as our own.

I gathered the reins and took the stirrup of the brown horse in my hand, mounting quicker and more spritely than I imagined I could. As I settled in the saddle, I looked down at the merchant and his wife and a thought struck me. 'Monsieur, do you know of Saul Ben Simon, a silk merchant in Venezia?'

'Of course, my lady. He buys silks for me in the Byzantine souks. I have never met him, but we correspond. I am lucky that in my business, to read and to write is not just a gift but a condition.'

'He is a very good man, Monsieur. Just like yourself. I am ever grateful and shall be sure to tell my lord Gisborne what you have done for us.'

'God's Blessings, my dear,' said Amé, stepping out of the way of the rounceys. 'And good luck.'

As Lyons' bells rang for Sext, we moved under the arched gateway and into a dark *traboule,* quickly finding our way onto a main thoroughfare. The peninsula separating the Rhône from the Saône lay to our right as we moved northwest heading to a town gate, passing candle makers with baskets of wax cylinders, women with bundles of kindling on their backs, carts piled high with stinking animal skins, dyers in stained aprons, monks in dark robes and stonemasons covered in a layer of fine dust.

'You read the list in my purse, Guillaume,' I said as I pushed my horse up level with his.

'It seemed sensible to get you to a safe house where you could revive.' His reply was laconic as he surveyed the citizens of Lyons.

'I see.'

'And you think that now that I have seen the list and remembered it, I will dismantle my lord Gisborne's web, filament by filament. Am I not right?' he asked.

I shrugged. 'Perhaps. Who knows? In the meantime, I owe you thanks for taking me to Monsieur de Clochart's. I feel better already.'

'That is good to hear because when we leave Lyons we will gallop as often as not and you will tire rapidly.'

It was true. Sitting atop a walking horse was a simple task but even so, I welcomed four strong equine legs replacing my own two weak ones. And once we were at a gallop, my legs would be required to use every bit of strength to cling, my body would be required to balance forward on the horse's wither and I would rapidly use up any energy Amé's food had given me. But I would not let Guillaume see I was worried. I needed to fool him that I was fit and well almost as much as I needed to fool myself.

Thus we passed through the gates, circled around the edge of the crowd heading along our path and when the way was clear, closed our legs hard on the horses and began the chase.

Chapter Twelve

Auvergne and La Marche passed between my horse's ears with no sign of any riders in front of us. Our cloaks flapped behind like the wings of eagles and I wished we could fly overland and reach our destination more quickly. My nerves stretched fit to break as we were forced to settle for the night in a copse of trees, a fire lit because Guillaume was worried I would chill and become sick with a fresh malady. Whilst the horses grazed, watered from a small stream close by, we settled to the handsome foods from our saddlebags and wine from the costrels.

'Do you feel well enough to travel on?' Guillaume said as he passed me a piece of salted meat.

'Of course,' the wine coursed through my taut body, loosening the strained muscles and enabling me to speak plainly. 'We must be gone by dawn. I need to reach Tours as soon as possible, Guillaume, and if I could, if it wasn't risking the horses' legs, I would ride on right now.'

He said nothing, just piled up the fire and passed me a blanket in which to cover myself and I wondered if we would ever reach a happy partnership before we found Gisborne. I was aware I had caused the divide between Guillaume and myself and wasn't really sure I wanted to bridge it, and yet I relied on him to keep me safe until we met up with my husband. It was a thought that plagued me. To trust or not. I had never been good at trusting and once when I did, a friend's life had ended.

As we entered Tours, I said, 'You know who you must seek out from the list,

Guillaume, so lead me to them. Besides, I am sure you know Tours quite well, having spent a large part of your life close by.'

Patronising ignorance, Ysabel...

'In truth, no, my lady. I never left Anjou until I departed for Outremer and even then we moved south through Aquitaine to Marseille.'

He is angry... 'I see. I apologise. My mood gets no better, Guillaume. Can you make allowances?'

'I know you want to find my lord Gisborne, my lady. We can only try.'

But Tours revealed nothing except a memory of some prophetic words that Gisborne had uttered so long ago. His fine face had been hard, his gaze bleak as he'd said, *"Status is power".*

And now we were without status, declared treasonous by Queen Eleanor. And power? We had our own, I suppose – the power to change our lives for the better – although Gisborne saw that quite differently from me.

As we left Tours behind, Guillaume said, 'I heard news, Lady Ysabel.'

'Yes?'

'King Richard has been captured by Leopold of Austria and Henry Hohenstaufen. They are asking a terrifying ransom and it appears he has been incarcerated in some unknown hideaway.'

So Richard, cousin and king, had met his match. All his arrogance reduced to a value. Almost like an outlaw. And I didn't care one bit.

'Serves him right. He should have put country before crusade, Guillaume. I think one could call it *hubris.*'

And we began to gallop to the town of Le Mans where Richard had denied his father and sided with the enemy, an enemy who saw no harm in betraying him to the Christian world.

And now he and his mother are our *enemies. Life changes on the point of a blade.*

Le Mans and the Priory Saint Jean. This time the list revealed an innkeeper across from the Priory and yet I was unable to stay with the nuns because I was effectively a man. The innkeeper was short and ruddy, as if he spent time drinking his own supplies but if one looked closely, there was a glint in the eye, a clarity that wasn't there at first acquaintance. He was a sharp individual and when Guillaume said who we were, he replied, 'You have just missed him. Only two or three hours since. His horse was lame and we had to find another…'

'Guillaume, we must go,' I chafed. 'Now!'

'Our horses are exhausted, Ysabel.'

'Then,' I turned to the innkeeper. 'Can you find us fresh ones?'

'Yes, but it will take time…'

'I want to be gone before the sun sets, we must be well on our way…'

'Ysabel, you cannot ride through the night.'

'I will. We are so close and besides, it is a full moon. Remember how lit up it was last even? If the weather stays fine, we will have few problems.'

'Madame, I counsel you…' he said.

'No, you do not,' I broke in. 'We are this close and I will *not* lose the advantage.'

Rouen. Place of an awakening – where I learned that my family's status had been destroyed and where the only power I possessed lay in my name and what lay between my legs. Ah, how far I had come in short few years. Full circle. No estate. A false title. And in fear of the future.

Our faceless man was a priest, a scribe from the Abbaye de Saint Ouen, and he too said we had just missed my lord Gisborne. So those hours of carefully tending our horses' legs as we travelled through the night had been pointless. We had not lessened the gap.

'No,' said Guillaume. 'We have not. But equally we have not lengthened it.'

The priest hurried off to secure fresh horses and food and whilst he was gone, we stripped our gear from the old mounts, rubbed them down and left them to the *abbaye* in exchange for the new ones.

The bells rang for Sext and we washed our hands at the well and proceeded to the *frater* to eat humble food, for when one is hungry one cares for nothing but substance in one's gut. Afterward and against my urging to do otherwise, Guillaume insisted I sit in the sun whilst we awaited the priest. It was penetratingly cold, a chill wind that moaned through the cloisters, tossing desiccated leaves before it and pressing the monks' robes hard against their ascetic bodies. What hair they had lifted and sat back again, awry and dishevelled. Even the bells of the *abbaye* clanged as the wind hauled at their clappers.

'It does no good to force an unreasonable pace, Ysabel. Even armies take occasional halts to rest,' Guillaume said.

In truth I was grateful. For days I had ached in every secret pocket and part of my body and so I rested my back against a stonewall, lifting my head to the windy sunshine.

'Do you have brothers and sisters?' I asked to fill in the time. Better to converse than think about each league further on that Gisborne rode.

Guillaume was sitting on the ground, long legs propped before him, his arms stretched over his knee, wrists flopping to cover a hole in his hose. He looked into the distance as if he examined his family from afar.

'I had a brother once,' he replied slowly. He seemed to be thinking over what he had just revealed with discomfort and I resolved not to broach the issue again.

'Have your family always been fletchers?'

'Yes. But they are gone now.'

'I am so sorry. I too have no family, Guillaume…'

Our conversation fell apart as the sun moved across the forecourt and I saw moments wasting.

'The friar's time is ludicrously fluid, do you not think?' I asked.

'Indeed.' He hefted himself to his feet. 'I shall seek him out.'

I watched him go, his stride long. He carried his height well, I had never noticed before, and he walked with purpose. In truth, you would imagine him to be confident and outgoing – nothing like the withdrawn, sober man who travelled with me.

I stood and stretched my legs, feeling the old anxiety creeping forth and so I began to walk along the cloister. Anywhere away from the ugly breeze that haunted the *abbaye* like a pauper's soul. The surroundings were quiet apart from the wind and the odd clang from the belltower, and here and there monks worked at their tasks. Some carried sheafs of parchment to the scriptorium, others cut back herbs in the infirmary gardens, another walked along a path of crushed stone with a glass bottle of wine hanging from his hand, oblivious to the fact that a beam of light shone through the golden liquid as if it had been marked as God's own.

I walked until I reached the door to the *abbaye* and then turned and walked back again, passing a chamber where a pair of monks worked with mortar and pestle, grinding the powders for illumination pigments – pots of jewelled colour and some as valuable as a king's ransom.

Richard – worth a bag of lapis lazuli? Or perhaps alum for the dyers' trade…

Coming to the forecourt again, I was surprised to see Guillaume talking readily to someone. The archer spoke and the other man replied, Guillaume laughing and taking a step back as if he could barely believe his luck. That surprised me far more than what he did next – slipping some silver into the messenger's hands. Was this one of Gisborne's couriers? Or someone else entirely? He clapped the man on the shoulder and then walked to the barn.

To see Guillaume so animated was out of character and made me shiver. What could have induced such a response and was I prepared to enquire? I set off in the direction of the barn and he was of course there before me, the priest holding two fresh mounts.

'Ah, I was about to fetch you,' the archer said. 'It is time to leave.'

We saddled up, the priest gathering food for our saddlebags. He was a quiet man and as he passed me a small bag of bread and dried meat and dates, I noticed his hands were stained blue, green and black, the front of his scapular likewise. He saw the direction of my gaze and smiled ruefully.

'My work,' he indicated with a brush of his hand.

'Your skill is God-given. What is a little pigment?' I slipped a hand beneath the girth to check it was tight. 'I thank you for what you do for us. Will you court trouble by doing this?'

'No. It does not happen often and they think I fetch our supplies from the town. See?' He held out a small bag with clinking pots within. 'Powdered turnsole for the blue in our work.'

'I am in awe,' I said smiling.

Guillaume had been buckling our swords onto the saddles and then with a firm pat on the rump of one of our mounts, he said, 'We are done…'

Farewelling the priest after pressing *livres* into his hands, we led the horses beyond the gates and mounted. Trotting away, I kept thinking *Ask him, ask him.* But I reneged until we were beyond the gates of Rouen. Clouds had drifted across the sky and the day had a heavy feel like my mood. In my heart, I knew we would most likely not catch Gisborne before Calais. My slimmest hope lay in the fact that no boat would be mad enough to cross to England immediately.

'Guillaume, to whom were you speaking at the gates of the *abbaye*?'

He gave no indication of having been caught out and replied smoothly.

'I had news of a boat in Calais. It would serve our purpose quite well.'

Really?

'But what if Gisborne finds it first?'

'It is a risk, to be sure, but I suspect God might be on *our* side at last.'

'Do not be oblique, please explain.'

'This boat sails along the coast as we speak and we and they shall probably arrive in Calais together.'

'Truly?'

'It seems so...'

'But that is too perfect. For once I feel I can breathe.' And I turned such a smile upon the archer that he had no choice but to give me a rare smile in return. His thin, elongated face transformed. Lines softened and eyes warmed. Did I believe him? Strangely, I did. Despite the voice that whispered it might be my downfall.

'Ysabel, may I ask you a question?' he said as we negotiated a shallow stream. 'Why do you need to stop him from what he plans to do? Do you not trust him?'

I could not look him in the eye for fear that he would see something I didn't want him to see – the issue of trust. But then trusting whom?

'If he kills de Courcey, surely your family is safe,' he continued.

'Yes, but he could just as easily be killed himself. An enraged man is a blind man. Have you not seen this in Outremer?' Our horses stretched up the bank on the other side of the stream and I reined my mount to a halt. 'Gisborne hates well, Guillaume. That this grudge carries him back to England where he has been named a traitor is too much of a risk just to even a score. I think he is blind...' I stopped speaking, playing with a lock of my horse's mane, flipping it back and forth over the animal's neck. 'I am afraid. He has allowed his fury to compromise his own safety. Simply he is a danger to himself and needs a rational voice to speak reason...'

I waited for him to say, 'And you are that voice?' but he said nothing, so I added 'I am the reason he killed Simon de Courcey's brother. I want to do all I can to protect my husband and repay the debt.'

'Including wielding your own blade?'

Our horses continued on a fast walk as I answered, 'If I must. Try and think on it this way,' I said desperately. 'Gisborne spent a large part of his life without a father and became dark and angry because of it. I once said bitterness is a hard nut to crack and I don't want his son to grow the same way.'

'Then what about abducting him before he has a chance to confront de Courcey?'

My head flew up. It was something that had never crossed my mind.'

'Jesu! Do you think we could?'

He shrugged. 'Anything is possible.'

'Then let us go!' I gathered up my reins and the horse danced with tension.

'But there is just one thing, Ysabel,' Guillaume said.

I cocked my head.

'A man such as Gisborne will bear such a grudge for not being able to finish what has been started. Are you prepared to risk your contentment?'

I thought about a fatherless child.

'Yes.'

We began to gallop.

As we moved closer to Calais the next day, my exhaustion threatened to unravel me. Unable to sleep when we had halted because it was too dark to continue, as soon as I heard the first lone pipe of a bird heralding a sun that still lay buried on the horizon, I woke Guillaume and urged him onto the road. His expression could have curdled milk so I apologised. He shrugged and merely said,

'Watch where you put your horse in the pre-dawn, Ysabel, or you will tumble.'

I wished I had seen the hole in the road. The horse tripped, almost falling to its knees. I tipped from the saddle, landing hard on my shoulder.

I groaned, rubbing at the point of impact. 'Damn it! Damn it to hell! Is the horse still fit?'

'Fortunately. Are you?'

'Yes,' I levered myself up, swallowing on the searing pain in my shoulder, taking the rouncey's reins and hauling myself back into the saddle. 'Yes, I'm fine.' I had no intention of admitting that I could barely turn my head, nor that my left-hand fingers would hardly close on the reins. I pressed my heels into the horse's side and rode forward next to Guillaume.

'How long before dawn and how far to Calais?'

'Dawn approaches rapidly and we will be at the Calais gates by mid morning. But Ysabel, I am uneasy about this path in the dark, listen…'

As I sat with my shoulder throbbing, I heard a rhythmic rumble. 'The sea. It is the sea! We are on the cliff road that leads to Calais…'

'Until it is light we must take our time and feel our way,' said Guillaume. 'One wrong step and we drop to the water.'

More time wasted.

Guillaume must have heard me sigh. 'I am asking for a short delay only,' he said. 'Have patience. You are of no use to your husband or your son smashed on the rocks.'

'Always remember that what I do, I do for you and for William,' I heard Gisborne say as the waves crashed below and a seamist drifted over us, wafting between tangled trees. I pulled up my hood, pains shooting through my shoulder, twitching the reins as Guillaume turned his horse along the curve of the road and through a dense copse, the naked branches twisted thickly like briars. The light had brightened and birds chirruped around us. High up, the shriek of a hawk streaked across the gold sky. And then there was nothing but the horses snorting and the hooves shifting the damp detritus.

I closed my eyes against the throbbing ache and allowed my mount to follow Guillaume – somnolent, my mind and emotions for once becalmed.

Without warning, a roar, reins grabbed by unknown hands, Guillaume shouting, ripping his sword from its scabbard.

I drew the *misericorde,* pain forgotten. Slashed at the ill-covered arm reaching to pull me from the saddle, drawing blood.

A shriek.

I kicked the rouncey hard. 'H'yar!' and it leaped forward, dragging reins free. I dropped the knife, drawing my own sword, turning to see the fellow I had cut running toward me with murder in his eyes, mouth open, rotten teeth bared like a rabid wolf. Guillaume's horse circled on the far side of the copse as he raised his sword and with a swift slash, almost beheaded his assailant. Before the stroke had ceased, he was dragging his blade free and spurring back to me but I swung my own sword as I turned the rouncey to face the man I had wounded. Sending the horse forward I continued the swing, catching the man's raised arm on the blade, slicing through and riding on as the blood spurted.

'Come on!' Guillaume shouted and I dragged the horse round again and at a full gallop, fled past the brigands, joining the archer, flying out of the copse to a clear stretch where we could see Calais not far distant.

We galloped with bloody swords hanging, one hand on the reins until I yelled to the archer to halt, pulling hard on my horse's mouth. The animal jerked to a stop, its breath heaving, eyes rolling, skittering in nervous circles.

And of a sudden, I leaned over and vomited, coughing and choking. Guillaume pulled his horse up next to me.

'I'm sorry,' I said. 'I've seen it all before but it gets no easier.'

'There is nothing to apologise for,' he said. 'The most seasoned warrior does it. Tell me when you wish to ride on.'

I wiped my mouth, slaking the foul taste with the costrel, then spitting the wine out. We sheathed swords, bloody as they were and Calais' walls and gate loomed before us.

'I need to walk…' I murmured.

We entered the town with a pair of carts and perhaps a dozen folk on foot – one with a brace of fowl over his back. Beyond us the mist had rolled back and the sea glistened in the light of a glaring winter sun and as I surveyed the harbour, for a moment my eyes filled with tears.

Relief? Belief that we would find Gisborne? Pain from my fall? Violence? Memories of another time and a *pers*-tinted gown? Ah, all of that. But I blinked them away and looked to Guillaume, eyebrows raised.

'We must find Jehan de Clochart's friend and if there is news to be had, it will be there. And then we must make pace to the docks. I fear the boat may not wait.'

We trotted through the tight thoroughfares, ever closer to the docks, passing merchants, monks and maidservants. It occurred to me that Guillaume knew Calais and yet he had told me he'd never left Anjou until the crusade.

Turning down a narrow alley with narrow houses and an even narrower view of the sky, he stopped in front of a newly-timbered gate.

'We leave our horses in here,' he said. 'Wait in the yard whilst I see the merchant.'

We passed under a timber and stone arch and filed into the yard of a dwelling of recent construction and the gate slammed shut behind us, Calais receding to leave us in a secure and peaceful setting. We dismounted, my shoulder shouting in dismay at the jolt and Guillaume hurrying toward the house, led by the gate guard. Watching him leave, I ached. God but I ached; I swear I could have slept standing up if there had been no anxiety.

'Quick,' Guillaume came running back with a wool and fur-clad merchant. 'Unbuckle your sword and hurry. *Mon amic* will care for the horses.'

I did as he bid, trying not to groan, and then we were passing back through the gate and turning to run to the docks, down the darker alleys, winding in and out of shadow, twisting ourselves in amongst the folk of Calais.

The quay stretched away in a sweep of splinter-like masts, dark slashes against the virginal blue of the sky. Sails were furled, no pennants fluttered, vessels moored firmly fore and aft, craft rafted next to craft, all abed for the winter. Guillaume led me swiftly toward the larboard end of the quay as I puffed,

'Do you have news? Is he here?'

But he didn't answer as seabirds squawked above us. I seemed to recall the last time I had run through Calais, I had scanned faces, absorbed detail, but not this time. I wanted to find Gisborne and if this ship was sailing, I was positive he would seek it out. He could not possibly have gained time – it *had* to be this ship…

Guillaume drew to a halt. 'I think this is the craft,' he said.

I pushed past him to stand at the edge of the dock wall. The vessel was a tired *nef* on the deck of which stood a man coiling rope between elbow and hand.

'Sir,' called Guillaume.

The man, clothed in wool and leather, turned toward us.

Jesu!

His gaze slid past Guillaume and met mine, his mouth dropping open.

'God's gobbets and guts! Lady Ysabel! What the hell are yer doin' here?' He dropped the rope. 'Ah, but then why am I surprised?'

'Davey! *You* are our boat to England?'

'Am I now? And why do you think I sail to England in the middle of winter?'

'We were told sir, by one of my lord Gisborne's men in Rouen.'

'And who might you be?' Davey's voice could have stripped caulking from planks.

'Guillaume of Anjou, one of Sir Guy's Venetian guards accompanying Lady Ysabel to meet my lord.'

'And my lady, Sir Guy meets yer here?'

But Davey knew my husband did not and he sighed, swearing under his breath. 'Come on board.' He held out his hand as I stepped from the dock, and said quietly in my ear. 'History repeats?'

Guillaume jumped on board, the boat rocking faintly. With presence of mind, he headed for'ard, leaving Davey and I to speak.

'What now, Lady Ysabel?'

'Gisborne seeks revenge, Davey, for a wrong done to his son by an English nobleman…'

'You want to stop him?'

'If I could. I want William to have the benefit of a father. Gisborne's mind is *thick* with murder and mayhem and Guillaume has come with me to try…'

'And what?' asked Davey, pulling at his pearl-hung ear. 'Convince him to walk away like a coward? Abduct him like they have the King?'

I swear my face did not move a muscle, but Davey knew.

'Oh perish the Pillars of Hercules! You did!' He burst out laughing. 'Well here's your chance…' He bent over, slapping his knees and crowing as I spun round.

'Ysabel. Wife. Well met.' Gisborne stood behind me, mane of hair knotted and threaded with grey, beard straggly, clothes covered in rips and mud. His eyes were the colour of winter ice but I quailed for less than a moment, my own ice re-freezing.

'Gisborne, please do not. I know everything you will say, so do not. William is safe with Ariella and Toby. By now they will be in Venezia or at the very least, journeying with Ahmed.'

'Do be quiet,' my husband ordered. 'If you have precipitated anything happening to William,' he said through gritted teeth, 'God but I will make you pay.'

'Make *me* pay? Need I remind you that if you had stayed with us and been a true father to your son instead of one bound up with ideas of revenge and atonement, then we would have all been safe and leading a quiet life in an anonymous place. Don't even try and argue this with me, Gisborne. It is old ground and you will lose.'

Davey humphed behind me and I heard him stomp off. Guillaume still stood in the bow with Eli, talking quietly.

Gisborne walked away, then turned and walked back again. 'Ah, Ysabel. Nothing changes, does it? Listen,' he took me by the hand and sat me on the wale of the *nef*. 'De Courcey will seek us out. He has the cunning, the wealth and the far-flung contacts. If you thought his brother was powerful, this man is far more so. He is the last of his family, he has no wife, no child, no by-blows even. And he is disliked … nay, hated, by all bar Prince John. He is cruel, indiscriminate and I intend to repay him for nearly killing my son. He wants to fight me and he shall. And after it is over, we, the Gisbornes, shall vanish – swallowed by an anonymous population.'

'But what if *he* is successful?' I squeezed his hands. They were so scarred – I hadn't noticed before.

'He will not be. Do you not have faith in your husband's sword skill? I am as dirty a fighter as he if I want.'

His arm moved across my shoulder, drawing me toward him and I winced, sucking in a breath.

'What ails you?'

'Tis nothing. I fell from my horse and we had a scrape with some felons and when I took one's arm, I think I tore a muscle…'

'Jesus wept. You took him in the arm,' he muttered before a laugh burst forth. 'Ah, my Ysabel. Poor William – what nefarious parents he has.'

'Oh, my poor little boy…'

'He is safe,' Gisborne's voice warmed. 'A message arrived immediately behind you in Calais, the horse steaming and the courier exhausted beyond belief. Ahmed sails them to Genoa and from there, Dario will escort them to Venezia. All will be well. In truth, I knew you were here because of that message and prepared myself.'

'You have good people working for you, Gisborne. Was the courier from Toulon?'

'No. The message was but the couriers change at stops known only to my men. So there are always fresh and adept riders and horses to take the next leg.'

'It must cost a king's ransom.'

'It costs money but then secrets make money as well.'

'Then if you leave this world behind, what will happen?'

'To the men who work for me? I will still employ them because secrets are always valuable. It is just that the throne of England will no longer employ *me*. But there are other duchies and crowns who will. And besides, I have investment in other business.'

'With Saul? In merchandise from the east?'

'You are observant.'

'Yes, I am, and you might remember that occasionally,' I said. 'He's getting two puppies you know. One for himself and one for us. He plans to call them Tristan and Iseult.'

'God in Heaven, poor dogs.' He grabbed at his hair, so unclean and wild. Just like my own.

'Gisborne, where is de Courcey?'

'Where I expect him to be.'

'Yes?'

'Locksley.'

The lost inheritance...

'We go there now?'

'I see I will not be able to convince you to wait here for me...'

'No.'

We both faced our own guilt at leaving our cherished son behind – we knew the risks. But sometimes the only way was to kill or be killed. We lived in a brutal world where insult was only ever ameliorated by the stroke of a sword and guilt and remorse were for the confessional.

Gisborne stood, bending to my shoulder and feeling along it, taking my arm and stretching it gently across my body and back. 'I think it is a torn muscle and with rest, should mend. You will live. Davey's ship heals most things, if I recall.'

A veiled reference to our shock and dismay at Ulric's defection and passing. Gisborne smiled at me and walked for'ard to Guillaume whom he arm-clasped and thumped affectionately on the back. There was not a vestige of tiredness in his manner or his words and I remembered Mehmet telling me how soldiers fed off the energy of the battle to come, often alight from within. Examining Gisborne, he was bright with it and it terrified me. But terror had no place here and instead I waved to Eli as he ordered the crew to push us off. The oars pulled through the water and we glided away on a wintercalm sea, the sun gilding us.

One could almost ... *almost* ... believe God was on the side of righteousness.

'A northerly crossing to Yarmouth,' explained Davey. 'Then yer on yer own overland. But I'll wait in the Yare for yer.'

'Give me a sennight, Davey. Two at most. After that, you leave.'

Dead silence from us all and then,

'If yer say so, my lord,' Davey coughed and walked away.

I resumed my old friendships and my space in the ribs of the *nef*. And once I even sat with Guillaume, just he and I alone.

'Guillaume,' I said, turning to him and his expression took me by surprise. I had thought to see relief on his face at handing me to my husband, but for one infinitesimal moment, the time it takes for the wingbeat of a moth, I swear I saw consternation and then *pouf*, gone in another wingbeat.

'My lady?'

'No more my ladies, please,' I said. 'We have spent too much time together and you are Gisborne's friend. Indeed you are William's friend and you delivered me to Gisborne. I give thanks to you.'

'I am a member of his guard. It is what is required.'

'I know, but … well, thank you anyway.'

He sat back. 'Are you content that you are by his side?'

I frowned. 'Yes…'

'But this de Courcey is the worst kind of enemy,' he replied.

'So my husband says,' I rubbed at my shoulder.

'You are not afraid he will have my lord's measure and will meet him at every turn?'

I thought about this. Gisborne stood in the bow, his hair flying back from his face in the breeze, his cloak billowing around him like a foresail. 'I can only trust in my husband's wisdom and skill, Guillaume. It is all I have. I will not mourn de Courcey's loss and I will stand at my husband's back as he does the deed. I am determined we shall emerge the victors and that we shall then live the life of unencumbered freedom we deserve.'

'Strong words. And where in this life of freedom do your servants fit? Do you cast them off to make their way in an unequal world?'

Guillaume could almost be Brother John, so laden were his comments, reminding me that we had an enormous moral responsibility outside of our own selfish existence.

'Those of our family – the twins, Mehmet, Biddy and Gwen, the guards – they would be welcome to remain with us wherever we go. But it will be their choice to make, not ours. I despise the position of the feudal overlord.'

'Strong words again…'

I shrugged. 'It is the way of it.'

And thus our passage was defined by odd conversations that served to fuel unease rather than quell it. If I laughed at all, it was with the crew who knew about secrets and kept them. We sailed close by the English shore, Davey using every bit of nefarious skill he had. The oaken hogsheads were emptied of fishnets and we fished for herring as we approached Yarmouth, filling the hogsheads and entering the harbour with the stink of a fishing vessel.

As we moored and the crew heaved the scale-filled hogsheads dockside, there was no doubt God had seen us safe to English shores and I crossed myself. It was not often that seas were so calm at the start of January, that cold period to which I had heard Biddy refer gloomily as "*wulfmonath*". With all the wild connotations of such a name ringing in my head, I jumped ashore, Gisborne and Guillaume leading the way with a hogshead each on the shoulder as Davey had already begun to sell the herring at the marketplace. We slipped away unnoticed toward the Benedictine priory where we knew there would be help and horses.

Horses indeed and we left Yarmouth behind us, heading nor'west to Nottingham, our clothes covered by the darkly dirt coloured robes of the monks and with a woollen cowl pulled against the damp, our old cloaks over the top and draped over horse rumps to hide swords in scabbards.

'Do you think he knows we are here?' I asked Gisborne.

'I would like to think he does not, but it is best to assume he does.'

'What do you plan then? To just walk into the lion's den, wielding a sword wildly?'

'At the moment we are Benedictine monks travelling to Locksley Abbey to spend two or three days learning from their eminent infirmarian, whereupon we are destined to return to Yarmouth with a selection of their herbs for our own *hospitium*.'

'Locksley Abbey!'

Gisborne glared at my loud indiscretion. Locksley Abbey, Beatrice of

Locksley, Cecilia of Upton my godmother … I said nothing more. We stopped not far on and the men lit a fire, and we ate the bread and salted herring from Yarmouth, along with drinking the caustic wine the monks had provided.

'You appear to have a particular relationship with churchmen, Gisborne,' I said.

'Do not be misled by their supposed asceticism, Ysabel. They need to pay for any extra comforts within the abbey, even things as simple as a thicker blanket or better sandals or boots. It is not what we expect – that they should have comfort in a place of sanctity and scourge, is it? But that said, the ones that I know are good men, loving of their God and loyal to a fault. They would never betray me.'

'You are so sure.'

'I have only ever been wrong about a man once in my life, Ysabel.'

Ulric.

I had looked across at Guillaume as Gisborne spoke and he met me glance for glance, almost as if he dared me in some way.

'Gisborne,' I said, using conversation to look away from the archer. 'Do you know that Cecilia is at Locksley on a retreat?'

'Yes, but it should not affect us if we are careful and pursue anonymity.'

For three days we rode – sometimes cantering, but mostly trotting at a steady, ground-covering pace. Once torrential rain forced us under a stony overhang within a forest of oaks but we moved on as soon as we could toward smoke curling above the trees, smelly robes and horses steaming.

'Nottingham,' said Gisborne. 'But I would bypass the town and push on through the lower reaches of Sherwood to Locksley.'

'You are afraid you will be recognised?' I asked.

'Yes. We have managed to come this far without incident. It seems an advantage worth noting.'

Guillaume had barely spoken about anything beyond the practical and this time was no different. 'A good plan, my lord. Play the advantage.'

We had only talked briefly about Locksley and the fact that we were men arriving at a nunnery. The lay workers would very smartly spread the word about three strangers in the confines of the place and it would be sure to reach de Courcey's ears. The question I wanted to ask of Gisborne was whether that was what he wanted.

But my question was soon answered when we stopped to rest and Gisborne said, 'Guillaume, it is almost time to play the game again, I think. De Courcey does not know your face from Brignolo, does he? No, I thought not. You were in shadow. Then I would that you ride to the abbey when we are closer, but in your own clothes. Say to the gatekeeper that you are a pilgrim in search of a bed within their *dorter* for the night. Once in, you must ask to see the Mother Superior. Think up a suitable lie – blessings, confessions, stomach ache, anything. Tell her we wait in the copse adjacent to the belltower. She will know. After that, be guided by her. She will make sure you are safe. What think you?'

The archer had been polishing his sword. 'I will do it. The sooner the better for I am tired.'

'Indeed,' said Gisborne, his gaze upon Guillaume sharp and interested. 'You are a worthy man, my friend.'

Guillaume continued rubbing at his blade with a wad of sheep's fleece, no further comment, his angular face reflected in the brilliant metal.

We rode through the oak, fern and moss-filled forest of Sherwood in a light drizzle, sounds muffled and birds quiet and I recalled the tracks as if my life as the housekeeper of Locksley Manor was only yesterday. Our horses picked their way through the lower edge of a deer-leap, parts pale with new timbers from the woodwards and built by boon work. A doe raised her head, stared at us and then leaped away into the forest of shadows.

As the afternoon progressed we heard the bells for Vespers from the abbey and then the beautifully carved gates were beyond the heavy aged branches of the forest, smoke from the little village along the road hanging low in the damp atmosphere. The smells of roasted meats, of excreta and mud clung to the wispy air and I realised how unused to poverty we had been living in a town like Venezia that thrived and grew on the wings of trade All at once I felt sad for England and what Richard had reduced it to. I knew of desperate outlaws scattered throughout the land and I was glad of wintercold and early darkness in which to hide ourselves on our journey.

'This is where we must stop, Guillaume.'

The archer pulled off his robes and shoved them under the roots of a nearby tree.

'Go with God, my son,' Gisborne said in mock reverence, arm-clasping Guillaume who nodded before remounting and riding away without a word.

But I watched my husband examining the archer and I noticed his mouth grimace and his eyes close to slits. He turned and caught my eye and as quickly removed the expression.

'So,' he said.

'Are you concerned you may not see him again?' I asked as my stomach rumbled. We had finished our meagre supplies a day since and I longed for roast fowl or a grain-thickened pottage.

'More than I can say. He is a good man as you have discovered. Have you not?'

'He has been loyal and kind…'

'But?'

I frowned. 'There is no *but*, Guy…'

'Of course there is, Ysabel.' Guy's voice rumbled with warning. 'It's just that you won't tell me.'

I let his comment hang until the perpetual mist washed it away and as the afternoon grey turned to evening shadow, I said,

'There are outlaws in England now, Guy. In abundance. Richard's absurd crusade has bled this place dry and now Eleanor will seek to bleed it more for her son's ransom. It is such an unworthy endeavour against a country that had potential.'

'I would say don't dismiss it so swiftly. But I think you compare it with Venezia.'

'Yes. If you are successful, shall we stay there?'

'You have made it quite clear to me that you would not like that.'

'But distance is teaching me much, Guy, and we have such good friends there in Saul and Ariella.'

By now it was fully night and I hunkered into my damp cloak, trying to think on a new life where my husband played the role of a merchant and we enjoyed the largesse with our extended family. Gisborne pressed against me for warmth and my hand crept to his under our cloaks.

An owl hooted and the branches around us creaked with the process of life and somewhere a boar snorted and I jumped. The owl hooted closer and Gisborne stood, hand to sword. Curiously he made a call back and there was a distinct echo.

A cloaked figure hurried from the forest subfusc. A nun…

'Mother Abbess,' I cried, pushing to my feet.

'Quiet, Ysabel! No, Sir Guy,' she pulled her hand from his as he bent to kiss her ring. 'We have no time for formalities. Quickly, follow me.'

We hurried after her as she bent in and out of the trees to a copse of thick ferns with a bank of fallen branches and moss-covered logs. Looking up, it was possible to discern a stone bulwark and the Mother Superior pulled at fern fronds and low hanging branches to reveal an iron door. Unlocking it, she pushed it inward and we stepped from the shadow of night to the blinding dark of a tunnel in the side of the *motte* of Locksley Abbey.

Our feet crunched on stone and the walls slid moistly beneath the palms as we touched them. Not a word was spoken but I looked beyond Guy's frame to see the abbess's head haloed in light as we approached a flaming cresset and then another. She began to climb stairs and then unlocked another door and we stepped quietly into a plain nun's cell – the bed bare, blankets folded at its foot.

'It was the first abbess's cell but we don't use it. I confess to prefer a little more comfort, God forgive me.' Beatrice opened a door on the other side, holding back a huge cloth as we filed into a larger chamber that I recognised from a lifetime ago. I remembered the wall hung cloth as well, an altar cloth of glorious *Opus Anglicanum* and I was sure Ariella would adore it. Beatrice's horn window had been filled with thick glass and large beeswax candles burned comfortingly.

She turned, asking us sit on stools and coffers. 'Your manservant is in the *frater*. I shall make sure he finds his way to the tunnel from outside our walls before the night is done. I think it best he is gone from the community before the abbey wakes as we have only a short while with which to protect your anonymity. As for you, Sir Guy, I must counsel you against this foolish idea…'

'Thank you for sheltering Guillaume and seeing him safe. He is a valued member of our family. As to your counsel, I thank you, but I shall do what I must.'

The thin, tall nun sucked in a petulant sigh and I could almost see her wielding God's sword. 'Then I can only tell you that Sir Simon is in residence at your former manor. He is feared by all and has a peculiar relationship with

Nottingham's sheriff and has no relationship with his God, whatsoever.'

Guy grimaced and gave the faintest *I told you so* twist to his head whereupon Beatrice continued,

'Which doesn't mean I believe his life is forfeit.'

'In the temporal world, Reverend Mother,' Guy's response was as crisp as a chip of ice. 'His life is very forfeit but that matter is between myself, Sir Simon and God. I ask only that you shelter my lady wife and Guillaume until my task is done.'

'Guy...' I stuttered.

'I can do naught but agree to give sanctuary to Ysabel and your man,' Beatrice said, her face troubled. 'Locksley remembers you as a stern but fair overlord and there are those who owe their lives to you. I stand to repay that debt. Beyond that, I can only pray for your soul.'

'Then I am grateful if you do that, thank you.'

'You are both tired. Rest now and I will make sure your man finds the tunnel. After that, I shall keep a vigil in the chapel until Matins. I shall be the very picture of innocence, should I be questioned at any time by our less than honourable Sheriff.' She held out her hand and Guy knelt and kissed her ring. 'God go with you,' she said and left, her robes swishing through the door and silence enclosing us.

I had no wish to speak, no wish to shatter the message that she had delivered. Gisborne walked to the tray, passing me bread and cold meat. He poured thick wine for us and I leaned against the wall, eating.

'Jesu, it's as cold as a...' I began.

'Nun's cell?' asked Gisborne.

I huffed in reply. As he offered me a piece of apple, the door latch twisted and he grabbed me, thrusting me behind him and concealing us both behind the opening door.

'Ysabel,' a voice whispered. 'Guy...'

'Ceci!' I pushed Guy out of the way and he quickly shut the door, locking it as I flung myself into my godmother's clasp.

She pushed me to arms' length. 'Oh God, my dearest child, look at you. Even dirty and dishevelled, you are more beautiful than I remembered. And look,' her knobbly fingers with their clashing garnet rings traced my temple. 'Your scar! It's almost gone.' She turned to Gisborne, 'And Guy, I am so relieved to see you… and yet not so, if I understand rightly.'

'Cecilia, how did you…' he began.

'Beatrice told me.'

'She should not.' Peremptory words from Guy as he walked Cecilia to a stool and bade her sit.

'Perhaps not.' Ceci was as thin as a rake in her heavy grey gown, as if she had begun to fade. Her skin was transparent and age sat heavily upon her. And yet she seemed illuminated. 'But she knows how much I have missed you all, how Ysabel is as good as my own and I think she felt we all deserved a moment together as a gift from God. Frankly I agree with her. And with God. I just wish I could persuade you to leave now before they find you…'

'I would do this for the future of my family, Lady Cecilia. It is the way of it, else we would be running for the rest of our lives. I must go…'

'Guy, no! You cannot go alone, not yet. Wait for Guillaume, please, or let me come in his stead.' I grabbed at his arm, holding tight.

'Ysabel, no. It is as it must be. Just know that having you as my wife and having William as my son and my heir is like being crowned king of the richest country in the world. As such I will defend such bounty to my last breath.' He kissed me on each cheek and then kissed my hand and in a familiar gesture, closed my palm on the kiss. He then kissed Cecilia, lifted the cloth on the wall and left, leaving an aching anxiety in his wake.

'Nothing changes,' commented Cecilia.

'And still a de Courcey,' I replied with rank bitterness.

With brevity and a tight voice, I explained what purgatory de Courcey had subjected us to and that Guy had become blinder with wrath by the moment.

'But why are you here, Ysabel? Did you think to rationalise his hate? Prevent him from defending what means most to him? For I think you have failed.' She hugged her cloak around her like a heavy shroud and it seemed I looked at a woman diminished in health. I wanted to sit and ask questions but had no time.

'Nothing changes, Ceci. You said so. I have pleaded, begged and rationalised until the sun set, to no avail. He sees the issue of revenge as part of being a father to his son. And so I have no choice but to stand by my husband.'

'And what if de Courcey wins?'

'Then I race to William and we would hide somewhere far beyond his machinations.'

'Methinks you should have done that months since,' Ceci replied irritably. 'Tuh, life is so short. A pity you both don't realise it. And you will fight with him?'

'If I must,' I said feeling for the hilt of my sword. 'There is part of me that wants to strike the death blow, Ceci. I am a loss to God, to be sure.'

'No better than Gisborne. Then you had better say your prayers and join him.'

When did you become so tart, Cecilia?

'He is simply, my dear, a man of our time. There is nothing you can do. Richard, Henry, Guy, even my own loved husband. All the same.' She rubbed at her head as if she had an ache, pushing at the wimple. 'It is so cold in Beatrice's chamber. Methinks she tries too hard to be saintly. Thank the Blessed Virgin I have a fire in my chamber else I would have forgone my retreat long since and made haste back to Upton with my tail between my legs.'

'My dearest Cecilia, I have missed you beyond belief. When this is done, would you return to Venezia with us?'

She looked at the carving of the crucifixion hanging on the wall as if she expected an answer to emblazon itself beneath, then she smiled slowly. 'Yes,' she replied. 'Yes and then yes again. I am tired of England and its problems, tired of loneliness, and to be with you again and my little William... I think it would be an eminent thing to do. Perhaps I can even make a pilgrimage to Rome.' Her smile widened and the lines on her face drifted and faded. 'Oh, dear child, such food for thought. Now listen,' she became serious immediately. 'You must go. Find Gisborne and his man.'

'He wants me to remain here...'

'So do I, but when have you ever seen sense or obeyed an order? You will be no use on your penitential knees, look at you. You can barely keep still.'

No urging was needed and I kissed her fleetly and in a moment was following in Gisborne's footsteps. All the while I wondered what I would do if Gisborne lost this battle – I would lose half of me that mattered. The other half of me was William and how does a body and mind manage with only half its being?

In the dank dark space, thoughts became overlarge. He had gone. Was he alone? I began to run along the tunnel, out into the forest – the dark.

But I knew this place well. I had walked the tracks of Locksley, picking roadside herbs, visiting the abbey, and so I kept running through the night shadow, keeping to walls, to tree trunks until I saw the manor ahead, cressets flaming, guards standing around.

Odd.

This was not the place of a duel. There was the desultory rumble of men on very relaxed duty, passing costrels to each other. Slack. No one in charge.

Back away, Ysabel. Carefully…

Simon de Courcey was not in residence. My husband was not there.

Nor Guillaume.

Where? Think?

Whilst there was no doubt that de Courcey would meet Gisborne in single combat, I also had no doubt he would have a second somewhere, one who could loose the dishonest stroke at a moment of weakness, making it easier for the death blow.

But then Gisborne had Guillaume.

Didn't he?

I could think of one place only where two men filled with hate would meet to duel, one perfectly constructed amphitheatre.

The deer-leap.

Chapter Thirteen

I began to run, ankles turning, feet tripping over roots and fallen branches. Stopping, turning breathless circles.

Which way, which way?

Dawn was hours hence and would only light the bloody fields of the dead. By the time the sun had risen, the deed would be done.

How had either of these stupid men known the other would await him at the deer-leap? Is it like minds? Was my Gisborne merely a reflection of a darker man?

Darker, darker…

Stars exploded across my vision as something hit me from behind. I fell across a log, landing on knees and hands, head spinning, and for a moment I crouched, winded, vomit rising, steps crashing away from me through the undergrowth.

Who was it? Who hit me?

Lifting a hand to the back of my head, I felt blood and a large bump as I tried to stand, but the ground fell away and I fell with it.

It seemed an age that I lay or perhaps only the flick of a star across the heavens, but a low groan sounded behind me and my eyes flew open, events crowding in on me, my heart galloping. I crawled away from the sound, throat choked with fear. In the distance I heard a noise, a metallic clash and…

Again a groan – a voice I recognised…

'Guillaume!' I scuttled across the damp ground to the prone form. Could barely see until the moon slid out from heavy bands of wintercloud and there lay my husband's man at arms. No use at all.

Wounded.

'Guillaume, where are you hurt?'

His eyes fluttered open and he tried to focus. 'Ysabel...'

I saw the blood pooling behind his ear and rolled his head gently to the side to see he had been too, had been hit from behind. I grabbed the bottom of my tunic, ripping it and wadding it with urgent fingers as a clash rang through the night. I felt the archer's head very gently, not stoved in, God be praised.

'Guillaume, wake. Listen. I shall come back...'

His hand grabbed me.

'Ysabel...' he dragged my hand to his thigh.

Jesu!

An arrow was embedded halfway down the shaft.

'It must stay there until I return. You know this.'

'I know,' he whispered. 'I would have protected him...'

And then, with the blinding light of reason, I knew how wrong I had been.

'I know. I will return, I swear.'

'You have no sword...'

My hand flew to where the hilt should have rested.

No...

'My bow,' Guillaume uttered. 'Take my bow...'

He lapsed into unconsciousness then and I slid the bow from underneath him, pulling two arrows from his belt. I touched him softly and ran toward the sounds, my head aching and blood trickling down the back of my neck.

The deer-leap had been meticulously prepared, lit by flaming *torchères,* but there was more shadow than light and two dark silhouettes moved back and forth, their swords crashing and screeching off each other. They had stripped to chemise and hose, and already there were patches of red on the white. And somewhere, somewhere out there would be a second man, Gisborne in his sights for that moment when he might falter.

De Courcey came at my husband, sword raised in two hands, but Gisborne met him with an upward cut and the clash resounded across moss and fern. The blades slid down toward the quillons with a screech, drawing the men close and de Courcey's hand moved, a knife drawn and jerking toward Gisborne's side. But his knee came up into de Courcey's groin, jamming into his manhood. The man groaned loudly, doubling over, almost dropping his sword, the knife falling in the light of the flame, Gisborne scooping it up and pitching it far into the dark.

Why didn't you use it, you fool?

I shook my head, eyes blurred, gritting my teeth, about to move.

'Bastard. Son of a bitch!' hissed de Courcey and I knew it was the signal, scanning the leap for movement.

Blink, Ysabel. Clear your sight.

There! A lighter shade amongst the dark, an archer drawing back – my assailant.

I grabbed the shaft of one of Guillaume's arrows and nocked it, the feathers bristling against my fingers, drawing back the taut string with every bit of my strength, my shoulder crying out just as my arm had once before. The shadow moved to the side to aim more easily.

I loosed and staggered a little.

So odd, I feel odd…

The archer shrieked and slumped forward into the flame-lit space, his own arrow flying wide and falling against the wood of the palisade.

'No one to assist you now, Simon,' Gisborne goaded. 'How unfortunate, and how demeaning to think you needed help. Were you afraid you would be undone without assistance?'

'But then you used your own man, did you not?' De Courcey pouched his manhood with care and grimaced. 'It seems we are like minds, Gisborne.'

'I think not…' said my husband as de Courcey hefted his blade and swung wide, Gisborne ducking the blow, jumping over a log, the Englishman following, swinging again, Gisborne running behind a tree, the enemy blade hitting the trunk with a dull thud.

'Cease running, coward,' the wretched nobleman yelled hoarsely. 'Fight me, damn you. Have you come all this distance to meet me and run?'

But Gisborne had made use of the cover of trees and branches to come from behind, lifting his sword high to bring it down square in de Courcey's back. I sucked in my breath, holding it…

Guy, wait…

Too late. De Courcey had seen what I had seen – the moving shadow of his attacker and he'd spun round, lifting his sword to parry. It was clash of sparks – and a huge roar from both. Gisborne backed away but his enemy advanced swiftly, lifting his sword.

It was as if my hated former husband had been resurrected. The swagger, the hair tint when the flame caught its warmth in the light; even the voice, and if they hadn't slashed and parried with such ferocity, holding no stance for longer than a heartbeat, I would have aimed and killed him. I hated him so much that I could feel the blood pounding in my temples.

Think clearly, husband. Wait…

The men's pace had steadied, tiredness beginning to pull at them, wet chemises clinging to the body and illuminating muscle and tendon, hair dripping with sweat. They spoke little. Each knew it was a fight now, where an ounce of energy expended wastefully was a step closer to death.

Guy began to strike two-handed, a sure sign of tiredness and once he tripped and de Courcey leaped in laughing, his blade tip scoring a perfect ruby line across Gisborne's right arm. My hand crept to my mouth and then to the second arrow in my belt, nocking it, beginning to draw…

De Courcey had taken fresh heart now and was attacking like a madman, Gisborne barely ducking and spinning, but his length of stride and reach saved him again and again and he returned a slash downward on de Courcey's sword arm. Grunts filled the night when before it had been nothing but the crash of metal.

Gisborne used another tree as a shield and de Courcey's sword thudded into the bark, lodging firmly, as he swore on a rising crescendo, the green timber closing on his blade. Gisborne stalked swiftly round the tree and away, putting space between he and his assailant, giving himself time to breathe and to wipe his bloody hands. He loosed his grip briefly and flexed his fingers and it was at that moment that de Courcey wrenched his blade free and sped into the twisted shadows, disappearing.

Gisborne realised, grasping his sword double-handed, crouching, circling to face every corner, listening. But there was no sound but for his breath rasping in and out, my own in time with his and my heart banging like a tabor. I grabbed the tree trunk close by as the scene before me began to waver.

Through a shifting veil, I saw de Courcey appear from behind, launching at William's father, my own scream echoing across the leap. He swung the sword in a perfect arc, shouting 'This for my brother!'

It hit my husband in the side, a dreadful wound and I screamed again, my world turning bright white and then black as the blood receded from my head, my yell growing fainter and fainter...

There were bells but I hated them and turned my head to the wall. I didn't want to wake because in waking there were truths and truths hurt beyond measure. Tears crept onto the fine pillowsheet beneath my face.

'Open your eyes, my dearest child,' Beatrice smoothed my forehead, my hand held in chunkily be-ringed fingers whose shape I knew well.

'Yes, my Ysabel, open your eyes,' said Cecilia, squeezing my hand softly. *Leave me to my grief. Go...*

I wanted to scream at them in my pain, rant, tear at my hair and so pulled my hand from Cecilia's grasp.

'Your head is merely bruised and sore, Ysabel, but *he* is alive,' said Ceci. 'Terribly ill, but alive.'

I rolled away from the wall.

'Yes... You see? That makes all the difference, doesn't it? But he needs care and time and God to protect him.'

'Jesu. Help me,' I flung back the covers and stood, the walls receding and then moving forward again. 'Clothes, I need clothes.'

'Slowly, take it carefully,' said Beatrice. 'Wash and dress and have a little to eat and I will take you to him.'

She left as the bells rang for Sext and I sobbed in time to the clanging. Alive, Ceci had said, but grievously wounded. I prayed as if my heart would crack apart:

I fly to thee, O Virgin of virgins, my Mother to thee I do come, before thee I stand, sinful and sorrowful. O Mother of the Word Incarnate, despise not my petitions, but in thy mercy hear and answer me. Care for him...

'Guillaume too is alive,' added Ceci, oblivious to my inner turmoil. 'Terrible leg wound. Both he and Gisborne will need much nursing before they can travel. I tell you, Ysabel, I feel old and young with all this excitement...'

I muttered from beneath the folds of a worn *bliaut*, 'I can't believe he lives. De Courcey struck his side so hard.' I pulled the *bliaut* down and began lacing. 'Is de Courcey dead?'

'Oh yes. And buried far into the forest. No one will find him. Or his man.'

'How did he die? There was no one else and Guy was…'

'Gisborne will tell you.'

'How bad is he?'

'It has required much stitching but holds together well and the infirmarian thinks she has infection under control, but time will tell. Time and prayer and much hard work and more to come.'

Of a sudden, the world faded again and my frail godmother was pushing me into a seat against the wall, saying,

'Jesu, child. Have faith! He was inordinately lucky. Take a breath. Here…' She pressed a mug of wine into my hands as Beatrice of Locksley re-entered the chamber, Ceci's chamber to be sure as there were comforts and a fire. The cool stone against my back and the wine coursing down to my toes fortified me and I sat straight, willing my heart to slow.

'The sword entered his side,' Beatrice said, 'and he was badly gashed, but before the blade could be pushed further to where it would do terminal damage, de Courcey was pierced in the head by an arrow – a truly stunning shot and me a religious woman saying that.' She crossed herself.

'An arrow? Who…'

'You will meet him in due course but I think you need to see your husband, my dear.'

Please…

We walked along a hall, our footsteps echoing, no sign of any of the religious or lay community. 'The hospice is kept very quiet and we have the sisters doing other things just now. The infirmarian and myself can nurse the men and of course, you will help us. It will be a sennight at least, maybe two before he can travel.'

'Then I need to get a message to Yarmouth, Reverend Mother, to our ship's captain. He waits for us and has been told to leave if we have not arrived in a sennight.'

'Write it and it will be sent, do not worry. I have ways and means.'

'I would prefer it to be spoken, for our safety, if that is possible.'

'Whatever you prefer. The messenger is to be trusted.'

We stopped outside a door and she said, 'This is his room. Guillaume is in the one next door. They are close to the *hospitium* and are chambers we no longer use. Our abbey is shrinking…' She said it sadly and it occurred to me that she loved all her community and would move Heaven to care for them.

I smoothed down my folds, and pushed at stray hair curled from the hasty plait I had made, touching my marriage ring with damp fingers, mouth dry. From the door, I could see that the shutters had been drawn back and sunbeams streamed across the floor and out into the corridor. The light caught on the faded gold of my ring and it was almost as if there was a Divine message. *'This will last,'* it said. *'It will last as long as you both shall live and beyond. Be at Peace.'*

Calm filled me, creeping up from my toes where the sunlight touched them as I glimpsed Guy lying still, draped with sheets and woollen blankets and a cloak folded at his feet. Pale, eyes shadowed, he seemed asleep, but as I moved to enter, his eyes opened.

Gisborne…

His glance held mine, those stormblue eyes steady, the strength of his gaze surprising in one so wounded. But then perhaps not, perhaps he drew from me as I had drawn from him so much in the past.

He smiled. Nothing big for when was it ever? But my God, when his mouth tipped up and the lines fanned from the corners of his eyes, I was done for. I ran then, throwing myself onto my knees by his cot and taking his hand to my cheek.

'Don't chastise,' he said, voice gravelly with pain and something else.

'Never. I thought … I saw…'

'Yes. But I live to fight another day.'

'Fight? You jest…'

He smiled a loose smile and his eyelids closed again and so I sat quietly, giving thanks. Cecilia crept in and sat.

'He sleeps heavily because they have given him potions for the pain. But he will mend while sleeping. He was most concerned about Guillaume, you know.'

'As he is about all his men.'

'Perhaps. But this was deeper. I take it you don't know?'

'Know what?'

She shifted back against the leather of the chair. 'Gisborne and Guillaume are brothers, my dear.'

'What? Don't be silly, Cecilia. I would know!'

'Well patently you don't. Guillaume is Gisborne's milk-brother. Same father of course, because Gisborne's father saw to Guillaume's mother a number of times. But she nursed the young babe when Ghislaine's milk dried and when the elder Gisborne's eye began wandering again when Guy was five, Ghislaine sent Guillaume and his mother to her family in Anjou. He grew up well-trained as a fletcher and in fact was much sought after.'

'I am at a complete loss, Ceci. Did Guillaume seek Guy out?'

'Yes. They met in the battlefields of the Holy Land and when Phillip departed to leave Richard to fight on, Guillaume left, taking ship for Cyprus and eventually…'

'Found him in Venezia and thank God…' I said, breathless with the shock of Ceci's news.

'My dear, while Guy sleeps, do go and see Guillaume.'

He lay under an identical window embrasure to Guy, the light through the horn covering it, diffuse and mellow. The shadows under his eyes were more pronounced and he seemed even more gaunt than ever.

'Guillaume…'

'I cannot stand,' he said, indicating his copiously bandaged leg.

'No matter,' I waved the lack away. 'I am glad you are alive and will mend. Guillaume, why did you not tell me?'

He knew straight away to what I referred. 'It was Gisborne's idea. He felt it could damage the mood of the guard at a time when solidarity and strength were vital.'

'But me, why not tell me?'

'He felt ignorance was the best protection. Besides, you seemed set against me from that first moment in the Arsenale.'

My cheeks flushed as I recalled my manner. 'Ah, my brother, so much to apologise for. I have read things so badly.'

'You know now, tis all that matters. And I am glad for it has been a tiring weight to carry. How does he?'

'Sleeping, but sharp-witted when he wakes. Guillaume, mend well, I will visit often and I am so sorry…'

'Please let us move onward to happier times, Ysabel. The enemy is vanquished and we have freedom for the first time in a long while. Let us enjoy it with William.'

I bent to kiss him and he offered me his cheek and a burgeoning joy began to spread toward my heart.

I returned to Guy's chamber and it was in shadow, Ceci gone. I knelt and took Guy's loose hand.

'Oh Gisborne, a master of secrets. I have just met your brother…'

He stirred and opened his eyes, licking his lips and squirming against the pain of his wound. 'You met my brother you say?'

'Yes. I still do not understand why you could not inform me.'

'Anonymity is all, Ysabel.'

'So you say often enough.'

A cough sounded from the back of the chamber and I quickly pulled folds from under my knees to stand. A man emerged from where he had been sitting at a table in the darkened corner. Perhaps Guy's age, he was shorter but broad and strong in the shoulder with a neatly trimmed beard and hair the colour of burnished oak. His eyes were guileless as he bowed.

'The man who saved me, Ysabel,' Guy's voice was thick as the poppy took hold again and dragged him to sleep.

I studied the fellow more fully. He had moved with a determined tread, his clothes dark and worn. Not a man of substance perhaps?

'You are to be thanked aplenty, sir.'

He shrugged off my words. 'I welcomed the chance to rid the world of a bastard of de Courcey's ilk. Locksley lives to breathe again until the next time.'

'Whatever the case, sir, you saved my husband from certain death and I shall ever be indebted to you.'

He grinned. 'To be indebted to me, my lady, many may find laughable and if not that, then most definitely treasonable. It seems your husband and I share the bond of being declared traitors. In the meantime,' he took my hand and bent over it in the most noble fashion. 'I am your immediate servant. They say you need a message taken to Yarmouth.'

Guy coughed and moved and for a moment I watched him until his chest rose and fell with the even cadence of sleep. I turned back to the man before me.

'I do. We have a friend there who holds his boat for us for a sennight but we will not make the appointment and he needs to know and to sail for his own safety.'

'Give me the detail and it shall be done.'

I frowned. 'This is so very kind but you have me at a disadvantage, sir. You know my husband and you know me. Who am I to be friends with?'

That smile came back as swiftly as the flight of a well-aimed arrow. Mary Mother but this fellow had presence. I would match him with Gisborne at any time.

'They call me Robin, my lady,' he said. 'I am Robert of Locksley. But some call me Robin Hood…'

THE END

AUTHOR'S NOTE

The inspiration for this final book in *The Gisborne Saga* has come from the book *Blondel's Song*, by David Boyle – a book I found stimulating and refreshing for the equal exposition of legend and common view, as well as academic fact. It led me to consider that a little boy could be the hero of a story – a little boy who had a friend who was a troubadour and who loved singing.

This led me once again, back to the book *Medieval English Lyrics 1200-1400, Thomas G Duncan (editor) Penguin Classics London 1995*, and to a song *'Somer is y-comen in'*.

As I mentioned in the Author's note in *Gisborne: Book of Knights,* Duncan lists the song as thirteenth century and this trilogy is set in the last decade of the twelfth century, but I decided to use it because it fits the plot of the book so perfectly. The song is sung in round form and it takes very little to imagine it being sung by a child and a troubadour. I hope readers will allow this liberty.

Sir Guy of Gisborne is in essence a legendary character, possibly first mentioned in *Child Ballad #118* but potentially in an even older story. Traditionally he is associated with the legend of Robin Hood but I have chosen to move far from the familiar canon and imagine what might have happened to him in completely altered circumstances.

Because Gisborne is familiarly linked to the reign of Richard Lionheart, the story takes place at the cusp of the twelfth and thirteenth centuries and I have tried where possible to be faithful to the times. But as in any medieval research, there is variation and disagreement over much historical fact. I have taken those facts that suit my fictional narrative and in some occasional instances have taken words from a later medieval/ Renaissance timeframe because they too suited the narrative when there were no other words to suffice. Thus I also ask the reader to allow *this* liberty in the hope it will not lessen their enjoyment of the story.

And finally, I am an Australian who was educated in the Queen's English, which I write and speak and the novels are edited by an Englishman so American readers may find there is an occasional discrepancy.

Acknowledgements

As always, to my editor John Hudspith, without whom
my books would never have had the requisite nip and tuck.

To my daughter Clare, for consistent and creative artistry,
a remarkable series of covers and for print formatting.

To Brian and Yveline Cobb for their fine, detailed research and
investigation on my behalf. They have spent much time in parts
of Toulon, the Rhône surrounds, Saint Christoph's Commanderie
and much else that is from what we now call Southern France.
This novel would be so much less without their involvement.

To Tim Carrington who delivered a blow by blow account
of his voyage *upstream* on the Rhône.

To my beta readers, Jane and Pat. Thank you for every bit of
discussion, common sense and effort you have put into these books.
I value your objectivity and your friendship.

To my JRTs – my little muses.

But mostly to my husband who has stood by whilst I had this
affaire with a legendary knight in the knowledge that it would end
*'And all shall be well, and all shall be well, and all manner of thing
shall be well.' (Julian of Norwich)*

Lightning Source UK Ltd.
Milton Keynes UK
UKHW020655040822
406842UK00009B/670